Critical acclaim for James Lee Burke and his classic Dave Robicheaux novels

HEAVEN'S PRISONERS

"Burke _____ DATE DUE _____; deeply about his characters. . . . *Heaven's Prisoners* is a powerful, compelling book."

—*The Denver Post*

"Vivid and distinctive characters and a great deal of hard action. . . . Burke's dialogue sounds true as a tape-recording; his writing about action is strong and economical. . . . Burke is a prose stylist to be reckoned with."

—*The Los Angeles Times Book Review*

"Heartstopping suspense."

—*Publishers Weekly*

"*Heaven's Prisoners* never loses tension. . . . Strongly recommended."

—*The New York Times Book Review*

THE NEON RAIN

"Dialogue that's so right, so real, so true to the personality you'd swear the guys were right there in the room with you; and a setting . . . that's so vivid you can feel the heaviness in the air, see the heat lightning, and taste the *sauce piquante*. I love this book!"

—*The Washington Post Book World*

Dave Robicheaux returns in James Lee Burke's riveting <u>New York Times</u> bestseller
JOLIE BLON'S BOUNCE

Be sure to read James Lee Burke's acclaimed bestseller featuring former Texas Ranger Billy Bob Holland
BITTERROOT

By the Same Author

Purple Cane Road
Heartwood
Lay Down My Sword and Shield
Sunset Limited
Half of Paradise
Cimarron Rose
Cadillac Jukebox
Bitterroot
Burning Angel
The Lost Get-Back Boogie
The Convict
Dixie City Jam
In the Electric Mist with Confederate Dead
A Stained White Radiance
The Neon Rain
A Morning for Flamingos
Black Cherry Blues
Two for Texas
To the Bright and Shining Sun

JAMES LEE BURKE

HEAVEN'S PRISONERS

POCKET BOOKS

New York London Toronto Sydney

POCKET BOOKS, a division of Simon & Schuster, Inc.
1230 Avenue of the Americas, New York, NY 10020

Copyright © 1988 by James Lee Burke

Published by arrangement with Henry Holt and Company, Inc.

ISBN: 0-7434-4919-3

First Pocket Books trade paperback printing November 2002

10 9 8 7 6

POCKET and colophon are registered trademarks of
Simon & Schuster, Inc.

For information regarding special discounts for bulk purchases,
please contact Simon & Schuster Special Sales at 1-800-456-6798 or
business@simonandschuster.com

Printed in the U.S.A.

For my agent, Philip Spitzer, a prizefighter
who hung in there for the full fifteen, and
those wonderful friends down in Louisiana
to whom I owe an enormous debt of gratitude:
John Easterly, Martha Lacy Hall, and
Michael Pinkston

HEAVEN'S PRISONERS

chapter
ONE

I WAS JUST OFF SOUTHWEST PASS, BETWEEN PECAN AND Marsh islands, with the green, whitecapping water of the Gulf Stream to the south and the long, flat expanse of the Louisiana coastline behind me—which is really not a coastline at all but instead a huge wetlands area of sawgrass, dead cypress strung with wisps of moss, and a maze of canals and bayous that are choked with Japanese water lilies whose purple flowers audibly pop in the morning and whose root systems can wind around your propeller shaft like cable wire. It was May and the breeze was warm and smelled of salt spray and schools of feeding white trout, and high above me pelicans floated on the warm air currents, their extended wings gilded in the sunlight, until suddenly one would drop from the sky like a bomb from its rack, its wings cocked back against its sides, and explode against the water's surface and then rise dripping with a menhaden or a mullet flapping from its pouched beak.

But the sky had been streaked with red at dawn, and I knew that by afternoon thunderheads would roll out of the south, the temperature would suddenly drop twenty degrees, as though all the air had suddenly been sucked out from under an enormous dark bowl, and the blackened sky would tremble with trees of lightning.

I had always loved the Gulf, no matter if it was torn with storms or if the surf was actually frozen with green ridges of ice. Even when I was a police officer in New Orleans, I had lived in a houseboat on Lake Pontchartrain and spent my off days fishing down in Lafourche Parish and Barataria Bay, and even though I was in homicide I sometimes worked deals through the boys in vice so I could go along on the Coast Guard cutter when they went after the dope runners out on the salt.

Now I owned a bait and boat-rental business on the bayou south of New Iberia, and twice a week my wife, Annie, and I headed out Southwest Pass in my converted jug boat and trawled for shrimp. It was called a "jug boat" because years ago it had been designed by an oil company for retrieving the long, thick, rubber-coated cables and seismic instruments used in marine oil exploration; it was long, narrow, and flat, with a big Chrysler engine, two screws, and the pilot's cab flush against the stern. Annie and I had outfitted it with ice bins, a bait well, winches for the nets, a small galley, fishing and scuba gear boxes welded to the gunnels, and even a big, canvas Cinzano umbrella that I could open up over a bridge table and folding chairs.

On mornings like this we'd trawl in a big circle through the Pass, the bow almost out of the water with the bursting weight of the net, then we'd load the ice bins full with pink-blue shrimp, set out the rods for gafftop catfish, and fix lunch in the galley while the boat drifted against the anchor rope in the warm wind. On this morning Annie had boiled a pot of shrimp and bluepoint crabs and was cleaning the shrimp in a bowl to mix with a pan of dirty rice we had brought from home. I had to smile as I watched her; she was my Mennonite-Kansas girl, with curly gold hair that lifted on the nape of her neck in the breeze, and eyes that were the most electric blue I had ever seen.

She wore a man's faded denim shirt with the tails hanging over her white ducks, and canvas shoes with no socks; she had learned to clean fish and shrimp and handle a boat in a gale as well as if she had been born in the bayou country, but she would always remain my Kansas girl, sewn together from blue-bonnets and sunflowers, tilting awkwardly on high heels, always awed by cultural difference and what she called "weirdness" in other people, although she came from a background of wheat-farmer pacifists that was so pervasively eccentric that she couldn't recognize normality when she saw it.

She had a tan even in winter, and the smoothest skin I had ever touched. Small lights played in her eyes when you looked into them. She saw me smiling at her, set down the bowl of shrimp, and walked past me as though she were going to check the rods, then I felt her behind me, felt her breasts touch the back of my head, then her hands collapsed my hair like a tangle of black snakes in my eyes, and her fingers traced my face, my brush mustache, my shoulders, the *pungi*-stick scar on my stomach that looked like a flattened, gray worm, until her innocent love made me feel that all my years, my love handles, my damaged liver were not important at all. Maybe I had grown foolish, or perhaps fond is a better word, in the way that an aging animal doesn't question its seduction by youth. But her love wasn't a seduction; it was unrelenting and always there, even after a year of marriage, and she gave it eagerly and without condition. She had a strawberry birthmark high up on her right breast, and when she made love her heart filled it with blood until it became a dark red. She moved around the chair, sat on my lap, rubbed her hand across the thin film of sweat on my chest, and touched her curly hair against my cheek. She shifted her weight in my lap, felt me under her, looked knowingly into my eyes, and whispered as though we could be heard, "Let's get the air mattress out of the locker."

"What are you going to do if the Coast Guard plane goes over?"

"Wave."

"What if one of the reels goes out?"

"I'll try to keep your mind on something else."

I looked away from her toward the southern horizon.

"Dave?"

"It's a plane."

"How often do you get propositioned by your own wife? Don't let opportunity pass, skipper." Her blue eyes were merry and full of light.

"No, look. He's in trouble."

It was a bright yellow, two-engine job, and a long trail of thick black smoke blew from behind the cabin all the way across the sky to the horizon. The pilot was trying hard to gain altitude, gunning both engines, but the wingtips wobbled from side to side and wouldn't stabilize and the water was coming up fast. He went past us and I could see faces in the glass windows. The smoke twisted out of a ragged hole just in front of the tail.

"Oh, Dave, I thought I saw a child," Annie said.

The pilot must have been trying to make Pecan Island so he could pancake into the salt grass, but suddenly pieces of the rudder shredded away like strips of wet cardboard and the plane dipped violently to port and turned in a half-circle, both engines stalling now, the smoke curling as thick and black as smoke from an oil fire, and went down hard on one wing against the water's surface, flipped over in the air like a stick toy, and landed upside-down in a huge spray of green and white water and floating seaweed.

The water boiled and danced on the overheated engine housings, and the hole in back actually seemed to create and suck a river deep inside the plane. In seconds the bright yellow underside of the plane was dimming in the low waves that slid across it. I couldn't see the doors, but I kept waiting for somebody in a life preserver to break through the surface. Instead, big balloons of air rose from the cabin, and a dirty slick of oil and gasoline was already obscuring the sun's winking refraction off the wings.

Annie was on the shortwave to the Coast Guard. I pulled the anchor free of the mud, threw it rattling into the bow, turned the big Chrysler engine over, heard the exhausts cough below the waterline, and hit it full throttle for the wreck. The wind and spray were like a cool slap in my face. But all I could see of the plane now were small gold lights in the floating blue-green stain of oil and gas leaking from broken fuel lines.

"Take the wheel," I said.

I saw her thoughts gathering in her face.

"We didn't refill the air tanks last time," she said.

"There's still some in there. It's not more than twenty-five feet here, anyway. If they haven't settled into the silt, I can get the doors open."

"Dave, it's deeper than twenty-five feet. You know it is. There's a trench right through the Pass."

I got the two air tanks out of the gear box and looked at the gauges. They both showed almost empty. I stripped down to my skivvies, hooked on a weight belt, put on one air tank and a mask, and slipped the canvas straps of the other tank over my arm. I picked up a crowbar out of the gear box.

"Anchor outside so one of them doesn't come up under the boat," I said.

"Leave the other tank. I'm going down, too." She had cut back the throttle, and the boat was pitching in its own wake. The side of her tanned face was wet with spray, and her hair was stuck to it.

"We need you up here, babe," I said, and went over the side.

"Damn you, Dave," I heard her say just as I plummeted with a clank of metal tanks through the water's surface.

The bottom of the Gulf was a museum of nautical history. Snorkel and scuba diving over the years, I had found clusters of Spanish cannonballs welded together with coral, U.S. Navy practice torpedoes, and the flattened hull of a Nazi submarine that had been depth-charged in 1942, a cigarette boat that dope runners had opened the cocks on before the Coast Guard had nailed them, and even the collapsed and twisted wreckage of the offshore oil rig on which my father drowned over twenty years ago. It lay on its side in the murk in eighty feet of water, and the day I swam down to it the steel cables whipped and sang against the stanchions like hammers ringing against an enormous saw blade.

The plane had settled upside down on the edge of the trench, its propellers dug deep in the gray sand. Strings of bubbles rose from the wings and windows. I felt the water grow colder as I went deeper, and now I could see crabs and jewfish moving quickly across the bottom and puffs of sand from the wings of stingrays that undulated and glided like shadows down the sides of the trench.

I got down to the pilot's door, slipped the spare tank off my arm, and looked through the window. He stared back at me upside down, his blond hair waving in the current, his sightless green eyes like hard, watery marbles. A short, thick-bodied woman with long black hair was strapped into the seat next to him, and her arms floated back and forth in front of her face as though she were still trying to push away that terrible recognition that her life was about to end. I had seen drowning victims before, and their faces had had the same startled, poached expression as the faces of people I had seen killed by shell bursts in Vietnam. I just hoped that these two had not suffered long.

I was kicking up clouds of sand from the bottom, and in the murky green-yellow light I could barely see through the window of the back door. I held myself out flat, holding on to the door handle for balance, and pressed my mask to the window again. I could make out a big, dark man in a pink shirt with pockets and cloth loops all over it, and a woman next to him who had floated free from her seatbelt. She was squat, with a square, leathery face, like the woman in front, and her flowered dress floated up around her head. Then, just as my air went, I realized with a terrible quickening of my heart that somebody was alive in the cabin.

I could see her small, bare legs kicking like scissors, her head and mouth turned upward like a guppy's into an air pocket at the rear of the cabin. I dumped the empty tank off my back and jerked on the door handle, but the door's edge was wedged into the silt. I pulled again, enough to separate the door a half-inch from the jamb, got a crowbar inside, and pried the metal back until I felt a hinge go and the door scrape back over the sand. But my lungs were bursting now, my teeth gritted against my own exhalation of breath, my ribs like knives inside my chest.

I dropped the crowbar, picked up the other tank, slapped the valve open, and got the hose in my mouth. The air went down inside me with the coolness of wind blowing across melting snow. Then I took a half-dozen deep hits, shut the valve again, blew my mask clear, and went in after her.

But the dead man in the pink shirt was in my way. I popped loose his seatbelt buckle and tried to pull him free from the seat by his shirt. His neck must have been broken because his head revolved on his shoulders as though it were attached to a flower stem. Then his shirt tore loose in my hands, and I saw a green and red snake tattooed above his right nipple and something in my mind, like the flick of a camera shutter, went back to Vietnam. I grabbed his belt, pushed under his arm, and shoved him forward toward the cockpit. He rolled in a slow arc and settled between the pilot and the front passenger seat, with his mouth open and his head resting on the pilot's knee, like a supplicant jester.

I had to get her out and up fast. I could see the wobbling balloon of air she was breathing out of, and there wasn't room for me to come up inside of it and explain what we were going to do. Also, she could not have been more than five years old, and I doubted that she spoke English. I held her small waist lightly between my hands and paused, praying that she would sense what I had to do, then dragged her kicking down through the water and out the door.

For just an instant I saw her face. She was drowning. Her mouth was open and swallowing water; her eyes were hysterical with terror. Her close-cropped black hair floated from her head like duck down, and there were pale, bloodless spots in her tan cheeks. I thought about trying to get the air hose in her mouth, but I knew I wouldn't be able to clear the blockage in her throat and she would strangle before I could get her to the top. I unhooked my weight belt, felt it sink into the swirling cloud of sand under me, locked my arms under her chest, and shoved us both hard toward the surface.

I could see the black, shimmering outline of the jug boat overhead. Annie had cut the engine, and the boat was swinging in the current against the anchor rope. I had gone without air for almost two minutes, and my lungs felt as though they had been filled with acid. I kept my feet out straight, kicking hard, the bubbles leaking through my teeth, the closure in my throat about to break and suck in a torrent of water that would fill my chest like concrete. Then I could see the sunlight become brighter on the surface, like a yellow flame dancing on the chop and glazing the flat slicks, feel the layers of current suddenly become tepid, touch the red-brown wreaths of sea-weed that turned under the waves, then we burst into the air, into the hot wind, into a dome of blue skies and white clouds and brown pelicans sailing over us like welcoming sentinels.

I grabbed the bottom of the deck rail with one hand and held the little girl up to Annie's arms. She felt as though she had the hollow bones of a bird. Annie pulled her up on deck and stroked her head and face while the little girl sobbed and vomited into Annie's lap. I was too weak to climb out of the water right away. Instead, I simply stared at the red hand-prints on the child's trembling thighs where the mother had held her up into the pocket of air while she herself lost her life, and I wished that those who handed out medals for heroism in war had a more encompassing vision about the nature of valor.

I knew that people who took water into their lungs some-times developed pneumonia later, so Annie and I drove the lit-tle girl to the Catholic hospital in New Iberia, the small sugar town on Bayou Teche where I had grown up. The hospital was a gray stone building set back in Spanish oaks on the bayou, and purple wisteria grew on the trellises above the walkways and the lawn was filled with yellow and red hibiscus and flam-ing azalea. We went inside, and Annie carried the little girl back to the emergency room while I sat across the reception desk from a heavyset nun in a white habit who filled out the girl's admission form.

The nun's face was as big and round as a pie plate, and her wimple was crimped as tightly across her forehead as a medieval knight's visor.

"What is her name?" she said.

I looked back at her.

"Do you know her name?" she said.

"Alafair."

"What is her last name?"

"Robicheaux."

"Is she your daughter?"

"Sure."

"She's your daughter?"

"Of course."

"Hmmm," she said, and continued to write on the form. Then, "I'll look in on her for you. In the meantime, why don't you look over this information and make sure I wrote it down accurately."

"I trust you, Sister."

"Oh, I wouldn't say that too quickly."

She walked heavily down the hall with her black beads swinging from her waist. She had the physique of an over-the-hill prizefighter. A few minutes later she was back and I was growing more uncomfortable.

"My, what an interesting family you have," she said. "Did you know that your daughter speaks nothing but Spanish?"

"We're heavy into Berlitz."

"And you're so clever, too," she said.

"How is she, Sister?"

"She's fine. A little scared, but it looks like she's with the right family." She smiled at me with her lumpy, round face.

Afternoon rain clouds had started to build in the south when we crossed the drawbridge over the bayou and drove out East Main toward the edge of town. Huge oak trees grew on each side of the street; their thick roots cracked through the sidewalks, their spreading branches arched in a sun-spangled canopy overhead. The homes along East Main were antebellum and Victorian in design, with widow's walks, second-story verandas, marble porches, Greek columns, scrolled iron fences, and sometimes gleaming white gazebos covered with Confederate jasmine and purple bugle vine. The little girl, whom I had offhandedly named Alafair, my mother's name, sat between us in the pickup. The nuns had kept her damp clothes and had dressed her in a pair of faded child's jeans and an oversized softball shirt that read *New Iberia Pelicans*. Her face was exhausted, her eyes dull and unseeing. We rumbled over another drawbridge and stopped at a fruit stand run by a black man under a cypress tree on the edge of the bayou. I bought us three big links of hot *boudin* wrapped in wax paper, snowcones, and a lug of strawberries to fix later with ice cream. Annie put the ice in Alafair's mouth with the small wooden spoon.

"Little bites for little people," she said.

Alafair opened her mouth like a bird, her eyelashes blinking sleepily.

"Why did you lie back there?" Annie said.

"I'm not sure."

"Dave . . ."

"She's probably an illegal. Why make problems for the nuns?"

"So what if she's an illegal?"

"Because I don't trust government pencil pushers and paper shufflers, that's why."

"I think I hear the voice of the New Orleans police department."

"Annie, Immigration sends them back."

"They wouldn't do that to a child, would they?"

I didn't have an answer for her. But my father, who had been a fisherman, trapper, and derrickman all his life, and who couldn't read or write and spoke Cajun French and a form of

English that was hardly a language, had an axiom for almost every situation. One of these would translate as "When in doubt, do nothing." In actuality he would say something like (in this case to a wealthy sugar planter who owned property next to us), "You didn't told me about your hog in my cane, no, so I didn't mean to hurt it when I pass the tractor on its head and had to eat it, me."

I drove along the dirt road that led to my boat-and-bait business on the bayou. The rain began to fall lightly through the oak trees, dimpling the bayou, clicking on the lily pads that grew out from the bank. I could see the bream starting to feed along the edge of the lilies and the flooded canebrake. Up ahead, fishermen were bringing their boats back into my dock, and the two black men who worked for me were pulling the canvas awning out over the side porch of the bait house and clearing the beer bottles and paper barbecue plates off the wooden telephone spools that I used as tables.

My house was a hundred yards back from the bayou, in a grove of pecan trees. It was built of unpainted oak and cypress, with a tin-roofed gallery in front, a dirt yard, rabbit hutches, and a dilapidated barn in back, and a watermelon garden just beyond the edge of the pecan trees. Sometimes in a strong wind the pecans would ring like grapeshot on the gallery's tin roof.

Alafair had fallen asleep across Annie's lap. When I carried her into the house she looked up at me once as though she were waking briefly from a dream, then she closed her eyes again. I put her to bed in the side room, turned on the window fan, and closed the door softly. I sat on the gallery and watched the rain fall on the bayou. The air smelled of trees, wet moss, flowers, and damp earth.

"You want something to eat?" Annie said behind me.

"Not now, thanks."

"What are you doing out here?"

"Nothing."

"I guess that's why you keep looking down the road," she said.

"The people in that plane don't fit."

I felt her fingers on my shoulders.

"I've got this problem, officer," she said. "My husband can't stop being a homicide detective. When I try to hit on him, his attention is always somewhere else. What's a girl to do?"

"Take up with a guy like myself. I'm always willing to help out."

"I don't know. You look so busy watching the rain."

"It's one of the few things I do well."

"You sure you have time, officer?" she said, and slipped her arms down my chest and pressed her breasts and stomach against me.

I never had much luck at resisting her. She was truly beautiful to look at. We went into our bedroom, where the window fan hummed with a wet light, and she smiled at me while she undressed, then began singing, "Baby love, my baby love, oh how I need you, my baby love . . ."

She sat on top of me, with her heavy breasts close to my face, put her fingers in my hair, and looked into my eyes with her gentle and loving face. Each time I pressed the back of her shoulders with my palms she kissed my mouth and tightened her thighs, and I saw the strawberry birthmark on her breast darken to a deep scarlet and I felt my heart begin to twist, my loins harden and ache, saw her face soften and grow small above me, then suddenly I felt something tear loose and melt inside me, like a large boulder breaking loose in a streambed and rolling away in the current.

Then she lay close to me and closed my eyes with her fingers, and I felt the fan pulling the cool air across the sheets like the wind out on the Gulf in the smoky light of sunrise.

It was late afternoon and still raining when I woke to the sound of the child's crying. It was as though my sleep were disturbed by the tip of an angel's wing. I walked barefoot into the bedroom, where Annie sat on the edge of the bed and held Alafair against her breast.

"She's all right now," Annie said. "It was just a bad dream, wasn't it? And dreams can't hurt you. We just brush them away and wash our face and then eat some ice cream and strawberries with Dave and Annie."

The little girl held Annie's chest tightly and looked at me with her round, frightened eyes. Annie squeezed her and kissed the top of her head.

"Dave, we just have to keep her," she said.

Again I didn't answer her. I sat out on the gallery through the evening and watched the light turn purple on the bayou and listened to the cicadas and the rain dripping in the trees. At one time in my life, rain had always been the color of wet neon or Jim Beam whiskey. Now it just looked like rain. It smelled of sugarcane, of the cypress trees along the bayou, of the gold and scarlet four-o'clocks that opened in the cooling shadows. But as I watched the fireflies lighting in the pecan orchard, I could not deny that a thin tremolo was starting to vibrate inside me, the kind that used to leave me in after-hours bars with the rain streaking down the neon-lit window.

I kept watching the dirt road, but it was empty. Around nine o'clock I saw some kids in a pirogue out on the bayou, gigging frogs. The headlamps of the children danced through the reeds and cattails, and I could hear their paddles chunking loudly in the water. An hour later I latched the screen, turned out the lights, and got in bed next to Annie. The little girl slept on the other side of her. In the moon's glow through the window I saw Annie smile without opening her eyes, then she laid her arm across my chest.

He came early the next morning, when the sun was still misty and soft in the trees, even before the pools of rain had dried in the road, so that his government car splashed mud on a family of Negroes walking with cane poles toward my fishing dock. I walked into the kitchen where Annie and Alafair were just finishing their breakfast.

"Why don't you take her down to the pond to feed the ducks?" I said.

"I thought we'd go into town and buy her some clothes."

"We can do that later. Here's some old bread. Go out the back door and walk through the trees."

"What is it, Dave?"

"Nothing. Just some minor bullshit. I'll tell you about it later. Come on, off you go."

"I'd like to know when you first thought you could start talking to me like this."

"Annie, I'm serious," I said.

Her eyes flicked past me to the sound of the car driving across the pecan leaves in front. She picked up the cellophane bag of stale bread, took Alafair by the hand, and went out the back screen door through the trees toward the pond at the end of our property. She looked back once, and I could see the alarm in her face.

The man got out of his gray U.S. government motor-pool car, with his seersucker coat over his shoulder. He was middle-aged, thick across the waist, and wore a bow tie. His black hair was combed across his partially bald head.

I met him on the gallery. He said his name was Monroe, from the Immigration and Naturalization Service in New Orleans. While he talked, his eyes went past me into the gloom of the house.

"I'd ask you in, but I'm on my way down to the dock," I said.

"That's all right. I just need to ask you one or two things," he said. "Why didn't you all wait for the Coast Guard after you called in on the emergency channel?"

"What for?"

"Most people would want to hang around. For curiosity, if nothing else. How often do you see a plane go down?"

"My wife gave them the position. They could see the oil and gas on the water. They didn't need us."

"Huh," he said, and took a cigarette out of his shirt pocket. He rolled it back and forth between his fingers without lighting it and looked away at the pecan trees. The tobacco grains crackled dryly inside the paper. "I got a problem, though. A diver found a suitcase in there with a bunch of child's clothes in it. A little girl's, in fact. But there wasn't a kid in that plane. What's that suggest to you?"

"I'm late for work, Mr. Monroe. Would you like to walk down to the dock with me?"

"You don't like federal people too much, do you?"

"I haven't known that many. Some of them are good guys, some of them aren't. I guess you tapped into my file."

He shrugged.

"Why do you think illegals would carry a child's clothing with them when they had no child? I'm talking about people that left the banana farm one step ahead of the National Guard shredding them into dog food. Or at least that's what they tell the press."

"I don't know."

"Your wife told the Coast Guard you were going to dive that wreck. Are you going to tell me you only saw three people down there?"

I looked back at him.

"What do you mean, three?" I said.

"The pilot was a priest named Melancon, from Lafayette. We've been watching him for a while. We think the two women were from El Salvador. At least that's where the priest had been flying them out from before."

"What about the guy in the pink shirt?"

His face became perplexed, his eyes muddy with confusion.

"What are you talking about?" he said.

"I damn near tore the shirt off him. He was in the back. His neck was broken and he had a tattoo over one nipple."

He was shaking his head. He lit his cigarette and blew smoke out into the dappled sunlight.

"You're either a good storyteller or you see things nobody else knows about," he said.

"Are you calling me a liar?" I asked quietly.

"I won't play word games with you, Mr. Robicheaux."

"It seems to me that's just what you're doing."

"You're right, I did get feedback on your file before I came down here. You have an amazing record."

"How's that?"

"You blew away three or four people, one of whom was a government witness. That's real hardball, all right. You want me to come back out with a warrant?"

"I don't think I'm going to see you for a while. You dumped the wheelbarrow on its side, podna. Your people are into something they haven't let you in on yet."

I saw his eyes darken.

"I'd tend to my own business if I was you," he said.

"There's something I didn't tell you. The UPI in New

Orleans called me last night. I told them there were four dead people in that plane. I hope you guys aren't going to tell people I can't count."

"You don't need to worry about what we do. Just keep your own act clean, and we'll get along fine."

"I think you've been talking to wetbacks too long. I think you should give some thought to your words before you say things to people."

He dropped his cigarette on the ground, pressed it out with his shoe, and smiled to himself as he got in his car. He started his engine. A shaft of sunlight cut across his face.

"Well, you've made my day," he said. "I always like to be reassured that I'm on the right side of the fence."

"One other thing. When you drove in here, you splashed mud on some people. Try to be more careful when you leave."

"Anything you say," he said, and smiled up at me, then accelerated slowly down my lane.

Very cool, Robicheaux, I thought. There's nothing like rattling the screens on the baboon cage. But what should you do in a situation like that? Most government employees aren't bad guys; they're just unimaginative, they feel comfortable in a world of predictable rules, and they rarely question authority. But if you run up against the nasty ones and they sense fear in you, they'll try to dismantle you one piece at a time.

I went down to the dock, put fresh ice in the beer and pop coolers, seined out the dead shiners from the bait tanks, started the fire in the split oil drum that I used for a barbecue pit on the side porch, oiled and seasoned the twenty-five pounds of chickens and pork chops that I would grill and sell at lunchtime, and then fixed myself a big glass of Dr Pepper filled with shaved ice, mint leaves, and cherries, and sat at a table under the porch awning and watched some Negroes fishing under a cypress on the opposite bank of the bayou. They wore straw hats and sat on wood stools close together with their cane poles motionless over the lily pads. I had never understood why black people always fished together in close groups, or why they refused to move from one spot to another, even when the fish weren't biting; but I also knew that if they didn't catch anything, no one else would, either. One of the cork bobbers started to tremble on the surface, then slide along the edge of the lily pads, then draw away toward the bottom; a little boy jerked his cane up, and a big sunfish exploded through the water, its gills and stomach painted with fire. The boy held it with one hand, worked the hook out of its mouth, then dipped his other hand into the water and lifted out a shaved willow branch dripping with bluegill and goggle-eye perch. I watched him thread the sharpened tip of the branch through the sunfish's gill and out his mouth, then replace it in the water.

But watching that scene out of my own youth, living that moment with yesterday's people, wouldn't take my mind off that ugly scar of smoke across the sky at Southwest Pass or a woman who would hold a child up into a pocket of air while her own lungs filled with water and gasoline.

That afternoon I drove into New Iberia and bought a copy of the *Times-Picayune*. The wire service story said that the bodies of three people, including that of a Catholic priest, had been removed from the plane. The source of the story was the St. Mary Parish sheriff's office. Which meant the sheriff's office had been told that three bodies were recovered, or that only three had been brought into the parish coroner's office.

It was hot and bright the next morning when I cut the engine off Southwest Pass and splashed the anchor overboard. The waves slapped under the bow as I put on my flippers and air tank, which I had refilled earlier in the morning. I hitched on a weight belt, went over the side, and swam down in a stream of bubbles to the wreck, which still lay upside down on the sloping edge of the trench. The water was a cloudy green from the rains, but I could see detail within a foot of my face mask. I came down on the tail section and worked my way forward toward the cabin. The hole that had gushed black smoke across the sky was jagged and sharp under my hands. The metal was twisted outward, in the same way that an artillery round would exit from iron plate.

All the doors were open forward, and the cabin was picked clean. At least almost. The torn pink shirt of the tattooed man undulated gently against the floor in the groundswell. One of the cloth loops was caught in the floor fastening for the safety strap harness. I jerked the shirt loose, wadded it into a tight ball, and swam back up to the yellow-green light on the surface.

I had long ago learned to be thankful for small favors. I had also learned not to be impetuous or careless with their use. I laid the shirt out on the deck and weighted the sleeves and collar and tails with fishing sinkers. It didn't take long for the shirt to dry in the wind and against the hot boards of the deck; the cloth was stiff and salty to the touch.

I found a plastic minnow bag in my tackle box, took the shirt back to the pilothouse out of the wind, and began cutting away the pockets with my single-blade Puma knife, which had the edge of a barber's razor. I picked out a pencil stub, tobacco grains, sodden kitchen matches, a small comb, strings of lint, and finally a swizzle stick.

A wooden swizzle stick in a tiny sanitary wrapper. A swizzle stick that I knew had letters printed on it because the purple ink had run into the paper wrapper like a smeared kiss.

chapter
TWO

IT WAS MIDAFTERNOON THE NEXT DAY WHEN I PARKED MY
pickup truck on Decatur Street by Jackson Square in New
Orleans. I had coffee and beignets in the Café du Monde, then
walked on into the square and sat on an iron bench under the
banana trees not far from St. Louis Cathedral. It was still a little early to find the girl who I hoped would be in Smiling
Jack's, so I sat in the warm shade and watched the Negro
street musicians playing their bottleneck guitars in the lee of
the church, and the sidewalk artists sketching portraits of
tourists in Pirates Alley. I had always loved the French Quarter. Many people in New Orleans complained that it was filled
with winos, burnt-out dopers, hookers, black street hustlers,
and sexual degenerates. What they said was true, but I didn't
care. The Quarter had always been like that. Jean Lafitte and
his gang of cutthroats had operated out of old New Orleans
and so had James Bowie, who was an illegal slave trader when
he wasn't slicing people apart with his murderous knife. Actually, I thought the hookers and drunks, the thieves and pimps
probably had more precedent and claim to the Quarter than
the rest of us did.

The old Creole buildings and narrow streets never changed.
Palm fronds and banana trees hung over the stone walls and

iron gates of the courtyards; it was always shady under the scrolled colonnades that extended over the sidewalks, and the small grocery stores with their wood-bladed fans always smelled of cheese, sausage, ground coffee, and crates of peaches and plums. The brick of the buildings was worn and cool and smooth to the touch, the flagstones in the alleys troughed and etched from the rainwater that sluiced off the roofs and balconies overhead. Sometimes you looked through the scrolled iron door of a brick walkway and saw a courtyard in the interior of a building ablaze with sunlight and purple wisteria and climbing yellow roses, and when the wind was right you could smell the river, the damp brick walls, a fountain dripping into a stagnant well, the sour odor of spilled wine, the ivy that rooted in the mortar like the claws of a lizard, the four-o'clocks blooming in the shade, and a green garden of spearmint erupting against a sunlit stucco wall.

The shadows were growing longer in Jackson Square. I looked again at the swizzle stick I had found in the dead man's shirt pocket. The smears of purple dye on it did not look like much now, but that morning a friend of mine at the university in Lafayette had put it under an infrared microscope that was a technological miracle. It could lighten and darken both the wood and the dye, and as my friend shifted the grain in and out of focus we could identify eight of twelve letters printed on the stick: SM LI G J KS.

Why would people who went to the trouble of removing a body from a submerged plane and lying about it to the press (successfully, too) be so careless as to leave behind the dead man's shirt for a bait salesman to find? Easy answer. People who lie, run games, manipulate, and steal usually do so because they don't have the brains and forethought to pull it off otherwise. The Watergate burglars were not nickel-and-dime second-story creeps. These were guys who had worked for the CIA and FBI. They got nailed because they taped back the spring lock on an office door by wrapping the tape horizontally around the lock rather than vertically. A minimum-wage security guard saw the tape and removed it but didn't report it. One of the burglars came back and taped the door open a second time. The security guard made his rounds again and saw the fresh tape and called the D.C. police. The burglars were still in the building when the police arrived.

I walked through the cooling streets to Bourbon, which was now starting to fill with tourists. Families from Grand Rapids looked through the half-opened doors of the strip joints and the bars that advertised female wrestling and French orgies, their faces scrubbed and smiling and iridescent in the late-afternoon light. They were as innocent in their oblique fascination with the lascivious as the crowds of college boys with their paper beer cups who laughed at the burlesque spielers and street crazies and knew that they themselves would never be subject to time and death; or maybe they were even as innocent as the businessman from Meridian, who walked with grinning detachment and ease past the flashes of thighs and breasts through those opened doors, but who would wake trembling and sick tomorrow in a motel off the old Airline Highway, his empty wallet floating in the toilet, his nocturnal memories a tangle of vipers that made sweat pop out on his forehead.

Smiling Jack's was on the corner of Bourbon and Toulouse. If Robin Gaddis was still stripping there, and still feeding all the dragons that had lived inside her since she was a little girl, she'd be at the bar for her first vodka collins by six o'clock, do some whites on the half-shell at six-thirty, and an hour later get serious with some black speed and shift up the full-tilt boogie. I had taken her to a couple of AA meetings with me, but she'd said it wasn't for her. I guessed she was one of those who had no bottom. In the years I had known her she had been jailed dozens of times by vice, stabbed through the thigh by a john, and had her jaw broken with an ice mallet by one of her husbands. One time when I was over at the social welfare agency I pulled her family file, a three-generation case history that was a study in institutional failure and human inadequacy. She had grown up in the public housing project by St. Louis Cemetery, the daughter of a half-wit mother and an alcoholic father who used to wrap the urine-soaked sheets around her head when she wet the bed. Now, in her adulthood, she had managed to move a half-mile away from the place of her birth.

But she wasn't at the bar. In fact, Smiling Jack's was almost empty. The mirrored runway behind the bar was darkened; the musical instruments of the three-piece band sat unattended in the small pit at the end of the runway; and in the empty gloom a turning strobe overhead light made a revolving shotgun pattern of darkness and light that could be equaled only by seasickness. I asked the bartender if she would be in. He was perhaps thirty and wore hillbilly sideburns, a black fedora, and a black T-shirt with the faces of the Three Stooges embossed whitely on the front.

"You bet," he said, and smiled. "The first show is at eight. She'll be in by six-thirty for the glug-glug hour. You a friend of hers?"

"Yes."

"What are you drinking?"

"Do you have a Dr Pepper?"

"Are you kidding me?"

"Give me a 7-Up."

"It's two bucks. You sure you want to drink soda pop?"

I put the two dollars on the bar.

"I know you, right?" he said, and smiled again.

"Maybe."

"You're a cop, right?"

"Nope."

"Hey, come on, man, I got two big talents—one as a mixologist and the other for faces. But you're not vice, right?"

"I'm not a cop."

"Wait a minute, I got it. Homicide. You used to work out of the First District on Basin."

"Not anymore."

"You get moved or something?"

"I'm out of the business."

"Early change of life, huh?" he said. His eyes were green and they stayed sufficiently narrowed so you couldn't read them. "You remember me?"

"It's Jerry something-or-other. Five years ago you went up the road for bashing an old man with a pipe. How'd you like it up there at Angola?"

His green eyes widened a moment, looked boldly at me from under the brim of the black fedora, then narrowed and crinkled again. He began drying glasses with a towel, his face turned at an oblique angle.

"It wasn't bad. I was outdoors a lot, lots of fresh air, gave me a chance to get in shape. I like farm work. I grew up on one," he said. "Hey, have another 7-Up. You're impressive, man. A sharp guy like you should have a 7-Up on the house."

"You drink it for me," I said, and picked up my glass and walked to the back of the bar. I watched him light a cigarette, smoke only a few puffs off it, then flip it angrily through the front door onto the tourist-filled sidewalk.

She came in a half hour later, dressed in sandals, blue jeans low on her hips, and a tank top that exposed her flat, tanned stomach. Unlike most of the strippers, she wore her black hair cut short, like a 1940 schoolgirl's. And in spite of all the booze, coke, and speed that went into her body, she was still good to look at.

"Wow, they put the first team back on the street," she said, and smiled. "How you doing, Streak? I'd heard you were remarried and back on the bayou, selling worms and all that jazz."

"That's right. I'm just a tourist now."

"You really hung it up for good, huh? That must take guts, I mean just to boogie on out of it one day and do something weird like sell worms to people. What'd you say, 'Sayonara, crime-stoppers, keep your guns in your pants'?"

"Something like that."

"Hey, Jerry, does it look like we got AIDS down here? It's glug-glug time for mommy."

"I'm trying to find out something about a guy," I said.

"I'm not exactly an information center, Streak. Didn't you ever want to touch up that white spot in your hair? You've got the blackest hair I've ever seen in a man, except for that white patch." She touched the side of my head with her fingers.

"This guy had a green and red snake tattooed on his chest. I think he probably came in here."

"They pay to see me take off my clothes. It's not the other way around. Unless you mean something else."

"I'm talking about a big, dark guy with a head the size of a watermelon. The tattoo was just above the nipple. If you saw it, you wouldn't forget it."

"Why's that?" She lit a cigarette and kept her eyes on the vodka collins that Jerry was mixing for her down the bar.

"There was a tattoo artist in Bring-Cash Alley in Saigon who used the same dark green and red ink. His work was famous in the Orient. He was in Hong Kong for years. British sailors all over the world have his work on them."

"Why would I get to see it?"

"Listen, Robin, I was always your friend. I never judged what you did. Cut the bullshit."

"Oh, that's what it is, huh?" She took the collins glass from Jerry's hand and drank from it. Her mouth looked wet and red and cold when she set the glass down. "I don't do the other stuff anymore. I don't have to. I work this place six months, then I have two gigs in Fort Lauderdale for the winter. Ask your pals in vice."

"They're not my pals. They hung me out to dry. When I was suspended I found out what real solitude was all about."

"I wish you had come around. I could have really gone for you, Dave."

"Maybe I wish I had."

"Come on, I can see you hooked up with a broad that whips out her jugs every night for a roomful of middle-aged titty-babies. Hey, Jerry, can you take it out of slow motion?"

He took away her glass and refilled it with vodka and mix, but didn't bother to put fresh ice or an orange slice in it.

"You're always a class guy," she said to him.

"What can I say, it's a gift," he said, and went back down the bar and began loading beer bottles in the cooler. He turned his face from side to side each time he placed a bottle in the cooler in case one of them should explode.

"I gotta get out of this place. It gets crazier all the time," she said. "If you think his burner's turned off, you ought to meet his mom. She owns this dump and the souvenir shop next door. She's got hair like a Roto-Rooter brush, you know, the kind they run through sewer pipes. Except she thinks she's an opera star. She wears muumuu dresses and glass jewelry hanging all over her, and in the morning she puts a boombox on the bar and she and him scrub out the toilets and sing opera together like somebody stuck them in the butt with a hayfork."

"Robin, I know this tattooed man was in here. I really need you to help me."

She flicked her cigarette ashes into the ashtray and didn't answer.

"Look, you're not dropping the dime on him. He's dead," I said. "He was in a plane wreck with a priest and some illegals."

She exhaled smoke into the spinning circles of light and brushed a strand of hair out of her eye.

"You mean like with wetbacks or something?" she said.

"You could call them that."

"I don't know what Johnny Dartez would be doing with a priest and wetbacks."

"Who is he?"

"He's been around here for years, except when he was in the marines. He used to be a stall for a couple of street dips."

"He was a pickpocket?"

"He tried to be one. He was so clumsy he'd usually knock the mark down before he could boost their wallet. He's a loser. I don't think this is your guy."

"What's he been doing lately?"

She hesitated.

"I think maybe he was buying room keys and credit cards," she said.

"I thought you were out of that, kiddo."

"It was a while back."

"I'm talking about now. What's the guy doing now, Robin?"

"I heard he was a mule for Bubba Rocque," she said, and her voice fell to almost a whisper.

"Bubba Rocque?" I said.

"Yeah. Take it easy, will you?"

"I gotta go in back. You want another collins?" Jerry said.

"Yeah. Wash your hands when you go to the bathroom, too."

"You know, Robin, when you come in here I hear this funny sound," he said. "I got to listen real close, but I hear it. It sounds like mice eating on something. I think it's your brain rotting."

"Who's your PO, podna?" I said.

"I don't have one. I went out free and clear, max time, all sins forgiven. Does that mess up your day?" He grinned at me from under his black fedora.

"No, I was just wondering about some of those rum bottles behind the bar," I said. "I can't see an ATF Bureau seal on them. You were probably shopping in the duty-free store over in the Islands, and then you got your own bottles mixed up with your bar stock."

He put his hands on his hips and looked at the bottles on the shelf and shook his head profoundly.

"Boy, I think you called it," he said. "Am I glad you brought that to my attention. Robin, you ought to hold on to this guy."

"You better lay off it, Jerry," she said.

"He knows I don't mean any harm. Right, chief? I don't get in people's face, I don't mess in their space. I ain't no swinging dick. You know what that is, don't you, chief?"

"Show time's over," I said.

"You telling me? I get minimum wage and tips in this place, and I don't need the hassle. Believe me, I don't need the hassle."

I watched him walk into the storage room at the back of the bar. He walked like a mainline con and full-time wiseguy, from the hips down, with no motion in the chest or arms, a guy who would break into jails or be in a case file of some kind the rest of his life. What produced them? Defective genes, growing up in a shithole, bad toilet training? Even after fourteen years with the New Orleans police department, I never had an adequate answer.

"About that Bubba Rocque stuff, that's just what I heard. I mean, it didn't come from me, okay?" she said. "Bubba's crazy, Dave. I know a girl, she tried to go independent. His guys soaked her in gasoline and set her on fire."

"You didn't tell me anything I didn't already know about Bubba. You understand that? You're not a source."

But I could still see the bright sheen of fear in her eyes.

"Listen, I've known him all my life," I said. "He still owns a home outside of Lafayette. There's nothing you could tell me about him that's new."

She let out her breath and took a drink from her glass.

"I know you were a good cop and all that bullshit," she said, "but there's a lot of stuff you guys never see. You can't. You don't live in it, Streak. You're a visitor."

"I've got to run, kiddo," I said. "We live just south of New Iberia. If you ever want to work in the boat-and-bait business, give me a call."

"Dave . . ."

"Yeah?"

"Come see me again, okay?"

I walked out into the dusky, neon-lit street. The music from the Dixieland and rockabilly bars was thunderous. I looked back at Robin, but her barstool was empty.

That night I rolled along the I-10 causeway over the Atchafalaya flood basin. The willows and the half-submerged dead trunks of the cypress trees were gray and silver in the moonlight. There was no breeze, and the water was still and black and dented with the moon's reflection. A half-dozen oil derricks stood out blackly against the moon, then a wind blew up from the Gulf, ruffling the willows along the far shore, and wrinkled the water's surface like skin all the way out to the causeway.

I turned off at Breaux Bridge and followed the old backroad through St. Martinville toward New Iberia. An electric floodlight shone on the white face of the eighteenth-century Catholic church where Evangeline and her lover were buried under a spreading oak. The trees that arched over the road were thick with Spanish moss, and the wind smelled of plowed earth and the young sugarcane out in the fields. But I could not get Bubba Rocque's name out of my mind.

He was among the few white kids in New Iberia who were tough and desperate enough to set pins at the bowling alley, in the years before air conditioning when the pits were 120 degrees and filled with exploding pins, crashing metal racks, cursing Negroes, and careening bowling balls that could snap a pinsetter's shinbone in half. He was the kid who wore no coat in winter, had scabs in his hair, and cracked his knuckles until they were the size of quarters. He was dirty and he smelled bad and he'd spit down a girl's collar for a nickel. He was also the subject of legends: he got laid by his aunt when he was ten; he hunted the neighborhood cats with a Benjamin pump; he tried to rape a Negro woman who worked in the high school lunch room; his father whipped him with a dog chain; he set fire to his clapboard house, which was located between the scrap yard and the SP tracks.

But what I remember most about him were his wide-set, gray-blue eyes. They never seemed to blink, as though the lids had been surgically removed. I fought him to a draw in district Golden Gloves. You could break your hands on his face and he'd keep coming at you, the pupils of those unrelenting eyes like burnt cinders.

I needed to disengage. I wasn't a cop anymore, and my obligations were elsewhere. If Bubba Rocque's people were involved with the plane crash, a bad moon was on the rise and I didn't want anything more to do with it. Let the feds and the lowlifes jerk each other around. I was out of it.

When I got home the house was dark under the pecan trees, except for the glow of the television set in the front room. I opened the screen door and saw Annie asleep on a pallet in front of the television, the wood-bladed fan overhead blowing the curls on the back of her neck. Two empty ice cream bowls streaked with strawberry juice were beside her. Then in the corner I saw Alafair, wearing my blue-denim shirt like pajamas, her frightened face fixed on the television screen. A documentary about World War II showed a column of GIs marching along a dirt road outside of a bombed-out Italian town. They wore their pots at an angle, cigarettes dangled from their grinning mouths, a BAR man had a puppy buttoned up in his field jacket. But to Alafair these were not the liberators of Western Europe. Her thin body trembled under my hands when I picked her up.

"Vienen los soldados aquí?" she said, her face a terrible question mark.

She had other questions for us, too, ones not easily resolved by Annie's and my poor Spanish, or more importantly our adult unwillingness to force the stark realization of mortality upon a bewildered child. Perhaps in her sleep she still felt her mother's hands on her thighs, raising her up into the wobbling bubble of air inside the plane's cabin; maybe she thought I was more than human, that I could resurrect the dead from water, anoint them with my hand, and make them walk from the dark world of sleep into the waking day. Alafair's eyes searched mine as though she would see in them the reflected image of her mother. But try as we might, neither Annie nor I could use the word *muerto*.

"*Adónde ha ido mi mamá?*" she said again the next morning.

And maybe her question implied the best answer we could give her. She didn't ask what had happened to her mother; she asked instead where she had gone. So we drove her to St. Peter's Church in New Iberia. I suppose one might say that my attempt at resolution was facile. But I believe that ritual and metaphor exist for a reason. Words have no governance over either birth or death, and they never make the latter more acceptable, no matter how many times its inevitability is explained to us. We each held her hand and walked her up the aisle of the empty church to the scrolled metal stand of burning candles that stood before statues of Mary, Joseph, and the infant Jesus.

"*Ta maman est avec Jésus,*" I said to her in French. "*Au ciel.*"

Her face was round, and her eyes blinked at me.

"*Cielo?*" she asked.

"Yes, in the sky. *Au ciel,*" I said.

"*En el cielo,*" Annie said. "In heaven."

Alafair's face was perplexed as she at first looked back and forth between us, then I saw her lips purse and her eyes start to water.

"Hey, hey, little guy," I said, and picked her up on my hip. "Come on, I want you to light a candle. *Pour ta maman.*"

I lit the punk on a burning candle, put it in her hand, and helped her touch it to a dead wick inside a red glass candle container. She watched the teardrop of fire rise off the wax, then I moved her hand and the lighted punk to another wick and then another.

Her moist eyes were bright with the red and blue glow from inside the rows of glass containers on the stand. Her legs were spread on my hip like a frog's, her arms tight around my neck. The top of her head felt hot under my cheek. Annie reached out and stroked her back with the flat of her hand.

The light was pink in the trees along the bayou when I opened the dock for business early the next morning. It was very still, and the water was dark and quiet in the overhang of the cypress trees, and the bream were feeding and making circles like raindrops on the edge of the lily pads. I watched the light climb higher in the blue sky, touching the green of the tree line, burning away the mist that still hung around the cypress roots. It was going to be a balmy, clear day, good for bluegill and bass and sunfish, until the water became warm by midmorning and the pools of shadow under the trees turned into mirrors of brown-yellow light. But just before three o'clock that afternoon the barometric pressure would drop, the sky would suddenly fill with gray clouds that had the metallic sheen of steam, and just as the first raindrops clicked against the water the bluegill would begin feeding again, all at once, their mouths popping against the surface louder than the rain.

I cleaned out the barbecue pit on the side porch next to the bait shop, put the ashes in a paper bag, dropped the bag in a trash barrel, spread new charcoal and green hickory in the bottom of the pit and started my lunch fire, then left Batist, one of the black men who worked for me, in charge of the shop, and went back up to the house and fixed an omelette and *cush-cush* for our breakfast. We ate on the redwood picnic table under the mimosa tree in the backyard while blue jays and mockingbirds flicked in and out of the sunlight.

Then I took Alafair with me in the truck up to the grocery store on the highway to buy ice for the dock and shelled crawfish to make *étoufée* for our supper. I also bought her a big paper kite, and when we got back home she and I walked back to the duck pond at the end of my property, which adjoined a sugarcane field, and let the kite lift up suddenly into the breeze and rise higher and higher into the cloud-flecked blue sky. Her face was a round circle of incredible surprise and delight as the string tugged in her fingers and the kite flapped and danced against the wind.

Then I saw Annie walking toward us out of the dappled shade of the backyard into the sunlight. She wore a pair of Clorox-faded jeans and a dark blue shirt, and the sun made gold lights in her hair. I looked again at her face. She was trying to look unconcerned, but I could see the little wrinkle, like a sculptor's careless nick, between her eyes.

"What's wrong?" I said.

"Nothing, I guess."

"Come on, Annie. Your face doesn't hide things too well." I brushed her suntanned forehead with my fingers.

"There's a car parked off the side of the road in the trees with two men in it," she said. "I saw them a half hour or so ago, but I didn't pay any attention to them."

"What kind of car?"

"I don't know. A white sports car of some kind. I went out on the porch and the driver raised up a newspaper like he was reading it."

"They're probably just some oil guys goofing around on the job. But let's go take a look."

I knotted the kite twine to a willow stick and pushed the stick deep into the soft dirt by the edge of the pond, and the three of us walked back to the house while the kite popped behind us in the wind.

I left them in the kitchen and looked through the front screen without opening it. A short distance down the dirt road from the dock, a white Corvette was parked at an angle in the trees. The man on the passenger side had his seat tilted back and was sleeping with a straw hat over his face. The man behind the wheel smoked a cigarette and blew the smoke out the window. I took my pair of World War II Japanese field glasses from the wall where they hung on their strap, braced them against the doorjamb, and focused the lens through the screen. The front windshield was tinted and there was too much shadow on it to see either of the men well, and the license plate was in back, so I couldn't get the number, but I could clearly make out the tiny metal letters ELK just below the driver's window.

I went into the bedroom, took my army field jacket that I used for duck hunting out of the closet, then opened the dresser drawer and from the bottom of my stack of shirts lifted out the folded towel in which I kept the U.S. Army–issue .45 automatic that I had bought in Saigon. I picked up the heavy clip loaded with hollow-points, inserted it into the handle, pulled back the receiver and slid a round into the chamber, set the safety, and dropped the pistol into the pocket of my field jacket. I turned around and saw Annie watching me from the bedroom doorway, her face taut and her eyes bright.

"Dave, what are you doing?" she said.

"I'm going to stroll down there and check these guys out. They won't see the gun."

"Let it go. Call the sheriff's office if you have to."

"They're on our property, kiddo. They just need to tell us what they're doing here. It's no big deal."

"No, Dave. Maybe they're from Immigration. Don't pro-voke them."

"Government guys use economy rentals when they can't use the motor pool. They're probably land men from the Oil Center in Lafayette."

"Yes, that's why you have to take the pistol with you."

"So I have some bad habits. Leave it alone, Annie."

I saw the hurt in her face. Her eyes flicked away from mine, then came back again.

"Yes, I wouldn't want to tell you anything," she said. "A good Cajun girl stays barefoot and pregnant in the kitchen while her macho man goes out and kicks ass and takes names."

"I had a partner eight years ago who walked up on a guy trying to change a tire two blocks from the French Market. My partner had just gotten off work and he still had his badge clipped to his belt. He was a nice guy. He was always going out of his way to help people. He was going to ask this guy if he needed a bigger jack. The guy shot him right through the mouth with a nine-millimeter."

Her face twitched as though I had slapped her.

"I'll be back in a minute," I said, and went out the screen door with the field jacket over my arm.

The pecan leaves in the yard were loud under my feet. I looked back over my shoulder and saw her watching me through the screen, with Alafair pressed against her thigh. Lord, why did I have to talk to her like that, I thought. She was the best thing that had ever happened to me. She was kind and loving and every morning she made me feel that somehow I was a gift in her life rather than the other way around. And if she ever had any fears, they were for my welfare, never for her own. I wondered if I would ever exorcise the alcoholic succubus that seemed to live within me, its claws hooked into my soul.

I walked on into the trees toward the dirt road and the parked white car. Then I saw the driver flip his cigarette out into the leaves and start the engine. But he didn't drive past me so I could look clearly into the car or see the license plate in the rear. Instead, he backed down the dirt road, the spangled sunlight bouncing off the windshield, then straightened the car abruptly in a wide spot and accelerated around a bend that was thick with scrub oak. I heard the tires thump over the wooden bridge south of my property and the sound of the engine become thin through the trees.

I went back in the house, slipped the clip out of the .45, ejected the shell from the chamber, snicked the shell into the top of the clip again, and folded the towel over the .45 and the clip and replaced them in the dresser drawer. Annie was washing dishes in the kitchen. I stood beside her but didn't touch her.

"I'll say it only once and I'll understand if you don't want to accept it right now," I said. "But you mean a lot to me and I'm sorry I talked to you the way I did. I didn't know who those guys were, but I wasn't going to find out on their terms. Annie, when you love somebody dearly, you don't put limits on your protection of them. That's the way it is."

Her hands were motionless on the sink, and she gazed out the window into the backyard.

"Who were they?" she said.

"I don't know," I said, and went into the front room and tried to concentrate on the newspaper.

A few minutes later she stood behind my chair, her hands on my shoulders. They were still damp and warm from the dishwater. Then I felt her bend down and kiss me in the hair.

After lunch I got a telephone call at the dock from the Drug Enforcement Administration in Lafayette. He said his name was Minos P. Dautrieve. He said he was the resident agent in charge, or "RAC," as he called it. He also said he wanted to talk with me.

"Go ahead," I said.

"No. In my office. Can you come in?"

"I have to work, Mr. Dautrieve."

"Well, we can do it two or three ways," he said. "I can drive over there, which I don't have time for. Also, we don't usually interview people in bait shops. Or you can drive over here at your convenience, since it's a beautiful day for that sort of thing. Or we can have you picked up."

I paused a moment and looked across the bayou at the Negroes fishing in the shallows.

"I'll be there in about an hour," I said.

"Hey, that's great. I'm looking forward to it."

"Were your people out at my place this morning?"

"Nope. Did you see somebody who looked like us?"

"Not unless you guys are driving Corvettes."

"Come in and let's talk about it. Hell, you're quite a guy."

"What is this bullshit, Mr. Dautrieve?"

The receiver went dead in my hand.

I went out on the dock where Batist was cleaning a string of mudcat in a pan of water. Each morning he ran a trotline in his pirogue, then brought his fish back to the dock, gutted them with a double-edged knife he had made from a file, ripped the skin and spiked fins from their flesh with a pair of pliers, and washed the fillets clean in the pan of red water. He was fifty, as hairless as a cannonball, coal black and looked as though he'd been hammered together out of angle iron. When I looked at him with his shirt off and the sweat streaming off his bald head and enormous black shoulders, the flecks of blood and membrane on his arms, his knife slicing through vertebrae and lopping the heads of catfish into the water like wood blocks, I wondered how southern whites had ever been able to keep his kind in bondage. Our only problem with Batist was that Annie often could not understand what he was saying. Once when she had gone with him to feed the livestock in a pasture I rented, he had told her, "*Mais* t'row them t'ree cow over the fence some hay, you."

"I have to go to Lafayette for a couple of hours," I said. "I want you to watch for a couple of men in a Corvette. If they come around here, call the sheriff's department. Then go up to the house and stay with Annie."

"*Qui c'est une Corvette*, Dave?" he said, his eyes squinting at me in the sun.

"It's a sports car, a white one."

"What they do, them?"

"I don't know. Maybe nothing."

"What you want I do to them, me?"

"You do nothing to them. You understand that? You call the sheriff and then you stay with Annie."

"*Qui c'est ti vas faire si le sheriff pas vient pour un neg*, Dave? *Dites Batist fait plus rien?*" He laughed loudly at his own joke: "What are you going to do if the sheriff doesn't come for a Negro, Dave? Tell Batist to do more nothing?"

"I'm serious. Don't mess with them."

He grinned at me again and went back to cleaning his fish.

I told Annie where I was going, and a half hour later I parked in front of the federal building in downtown Lafayette where the DEA kept its office. It was a big, modern building, constructed during the Kennedy-Johnson era, filled with big glass doors and tinted windows and marble floors; but right down the street was the old Lafayette police station and jail, a squat, gray cement building with barred windows on the second floor, an ugly sentinel out of the past, a reminder that yesterday was only a flick of the eye away from the seeming tranquillity of the present. My point is that I remember an execution that took place in the jail in the early 1950s. The electric chair was brought in from Angola; two big generators on a flatbed truck hummed on a side street behind the building; thick, black cables ran from the generators through a barred window on the second story. At nine o'clock on a balmy summer night, people in the restaurant across the street heard a man scream once just before an arc light seemed to jump off the bars of the window. Later, townspeople did not like to talk about it. Eventually that part of the jail was closed off and was used to house a civil defense siren. Finally, few people even remembered that an execution had taken place there.

But on this hazy May afternoon that smelled of flowers and rain, I was looking up at an open window on the second story of the federal building, through which flew a paper airplane. It slid in a long glide across the street and bounced off the windshield of a moving car. I had a strong feeling about where it had come from.

Sure enough, when I walked through the open door of Minos P. Dautrieve's office I saw a tall, crewcut man tilted back in his chair, his knit tie pulled loose, his collar unbuttoned, one foot on the desk, the other in the wastebasket, one huge hand poised in the air, about to sail another paper plane out the window. His blond hair was cut so short that light reflected off his scalp; in fact, lights seemed to reflect all over his lean, close-shaved, scrubbed, smiling face. On his desk blotter was an open manila folder with several telex sheets clipped inside. He dropped the airplane on the desk, clanged his foot out of the wastebasket, and shook hands with such energy that he almost pulled me off balance. I thought I had seen him somewhere before.

"I'm sorry to drag you in here," he said, "but that's the breaks, right? Hey, I've been reading your history. It's fascinating stuff. Sit down. Did you really do all this bullshit?"

"I'm not sure what you mean."

"Come on, anybody with a sheet like this is genuinely into rock 'n' roll. Wounded twice in Vietnam, the second time on a mine. Then fourteen years with the New Orleans police department, where you did some very serious things to a few people. Why's a guy with a teacher's certificate in English go into police work?"

"Is this a shake?"

"Be serious. We don't get to have that kind of fun. Most of the time we just run around and prepare cases for the U.S. attorney. You know that. But your file's intriguing, you've got to admit. It says here you blew away three people, one of whom was the *numero uno* greaseball, drug pusher, and pimp in New Orleans. But he was also on tap as a federal witness, at least until you scrambled his eggs for him." He laughed out loud. "How'd you manage to snuff a government witness? That's hard to pull off. We usually keep them on the game reserve."

"You really want to know?"

"Hell, yes. This is socko stuff."

"His bodyguard pulled a gun on my partner and took a shot at him. It was a routine possession bust, and the pair of them would have been out on bond in an hour. So it was a dumb thing for the bodyguard to do. It was dumb because it was unnecessary and it provoked a bad situation. A professional doesn't do dumb things like that and provoke people unnecessarily. You get my drift?"

"Oh, I get it. We federal agents shouldn't act like dumb guys and provoke you, huh? Let me try this one on you, Mr. Robicheaux. What are the odds of anybody being out on the Gulf of Mexico and witnessing a plane crash? Come on, your file says you've spent lots of time at racetracks. Figure the odds for me."

"What are you saying, podna?"

"We know a guy named Johnny Dartez was on that plane. Johnny Dartez's name means one thing—narcotics. He was a transporter for Bubba Rocque. His specialty was throwing it out in big rubber balloons over water."

"And you figure maybe I was the pickup man."

"You tell me."

"I think you spend too much time folding paper airplanes."

"Oh, I should be out developing some better leads? Is that it? Some of us are hotdog ball handlers, some of us are meant for the bench. I got it."

"I remember now. Forward for LSU, fifteen years or so ago. Dr. Dunkenstein. You were All-American."

"Honorable Mention. Answer my questions, Mr. Robicheaux. What are the odds of a guy like you being out on the salt when a plane goes down right by his boat? A guy who happened to have a scuba tank so he could be the first one down on the wreck?"

"Listen, the pilot was a priest. Use your head a minute."

"Yeah, a priest who did time in Danbury," he said.

"Danbury?"

"Yeah, that's right."

"What for?"

"Breaking and entering."

"I think I'm getting the abridged version here."

"He and some nuns and other priests broke into a General Electric plant and vandalized some missile components."

"And you think he was involved with drug smugglers?"

He wadded up the paper airplane on his desk and dropped it into the wastebasket.

"No, I don't," he said, his eyes focused on the clouds outside the window.

"What does Immigration tell you?"

He shrugged his shoulders and clicked his nails on the desk blotter. His fingers were so long and thin and his nails so pink and clean that his hands looked like those of a surgeon rather than of an ex--basketball player.

"According to them, there was no Johnny Dartez on that plane," I said.

"They have their areas of concern, we have ours."

"They're stonewalling you, aren't they?"

"Look, I'm not interested in Immigration's business. I want Bubba Rocque off the board. Johnny Dartez was a guy we spent a lot of money and time on, him and another dimwit from New Orleans named Victor Romero. Does that name mean anything to you?"

"No."

"They both disappeared from their usual haunts about two months ago, just before we were going to pick them up. Since Johnny has done the big gargle out at Southwest Pass, Victor's value has appreciated immensely."

"You won't get Bubba by squeezing his people."

He pushed his large shoe against the wall so that his chair spun around in a complete circle, like a child playing in the barber's chair.

"How is it that you have this omniscient knowledge?" he said.

"In high school he'd put on different kinds of shows for us. Sometimes he'd eat a lightbulb. Or he might open a bottle of RC Cola on his teeth or push thumbtacks into his kneecaps. It was always a memorable exhibition."

"Yeah, we see a lot of that kind of psychotic charisma these days. I think it's in fashion with the wiseguys. That's why we have a special lockdown section in Atlanta where they can yodel to each other."

"Good luck."

"You don't think we can put him away?"

"Who cares what I think? What's the National Transportation Safety Board say about the crash?"

"A fire in the hold. They're not sure. It was murky when their divers went down. The plane slipped down a trench of some kind and it's half covered in mud now."

"You believe it was just a fire?"

"It happens."

"You better send them down again. I dove that wreck twice. I think an explosion blew out the side."

He looked at me carefully.

"I think maybe I ought to caution you about involving yourself in a federal investigation," he said.

"I'm not one of your problems, Mr. Dautrieve. You've got another federal agency trespassing on your turf, maybe tainting your witnesses, maybe stealing bodies. Anyway, they're jerking you around and for some reason you're not doing anything about it. I'd appreciate it if you didn't try to lay off your situation on me."

I saw the bone flex against the clean line of his jaw. Then he began to play with a rubber band on his long fingers.

"You'll have to make allowances for us government employees who have to labor with bureaucratic manacles on," he said. "We've never been able to use the simple, direct methods you people have been so good at. You remember a few years back when a New Orleans cop got killed and some of his friends squared it on their own? I think they went into the guy's house, it was a black guy, of course, and blew him and his wife away in the bathtub. Then there were those black revolutionaries that stuck up an armored car in Boston and killed a guard and hid out in Louisiana and Mississippi. We worked two years preparing that case, then your people grabbed one of them and tortured a statement out of him and flushed everything we'd done right down the shithole. You guys sure knew how to let everybody know you were in town."

"I guess I'll go now. You want to ask me anything else?"

"Not a thing," he said, and fired a paper clip at a file cabinet across the room.

I stood up to leave. His attention was concentrated on finding another target for his rubber band and paper clip.

"Does a white Corvette with the letters ELK on the door bring any of your clientele to mind?" I said.

"Were these the guys out at your place?" His eyes still avoided me.

"Yes."

"How should I know? We're lucky to keep tabs on two or three of these assholes." He was looking straight at me now, his eyes flat, the skin of his face tight. "Maybe it's somebody you sold some bad fish to."

I walked outside into the sunshine and the wind blowing through the mimosa trees on the lawn. A Negro gardener was sprinkling the flower beds and the freshly cut grass with a hose, and I could smell the damp earth and the green clippings that were raked in piles under the trees. I looked back up at the office window of Minos P. Dautrieve. I opened and closed my hands and took a breath and felt the anger go out of my chest.

Well, you asked for it, I told myself. Why poke a stick at a man who's already in a cage? He probably gets one conviction out of ten arrests, spends half his time with his butt in a bureaucratic paper shredder, and on a good day negotiates a one-to-three possessions plea on a dealer who's probably robbed hundreds of people of their souls.

Just as I was pulling out into the traffic, I saw him come out of the building waving his arm at me. He was almost hit by a car crossing the street.

"Park it a minute. You want a snowcone? It's on me," he said.

"I have to get back to work."

"Park it," he said, and bought two snowcones from a Negro boy who operated a stand under an umbrella on the corner. He got in the passenger side of my truck, almost losing the door on a passing car whose horn reverberated down the street, and handed me one of the snowcones.

"Maybe the Corvette is Eddie Keats's," he said. "He used to run a nickel-and-dime book in Brooklyn. Now he's a Sunbelter, he likes our climate so much. He lives here part of the time, part of the time in New Orleans. He's got a couple of bars, a few whores working for him, and he thinks he's a big button man. Is there any reason for a guy like that to be hanging around your place?"

"You got me. I never heard of him."

"Try this—Eddie Keats likes to do favors for important people. He jobs out for Bubba Rocque sometimes, for free or whatever Bubba wants to give him. He's that kind of swell guy. We heard he set fire to one of Bubba's hookers in New Orleans."

He stopped and looked at me curiously.

"What's the matter? You never got a case like that in homicide?" he said. "You know how their pimps keep them down on the farm."

"I talked to a stripper in New Orleans about Johnny Dartez. She told me he worked for Bubba Rocque. I've got a bad feeling about her."

"That disturbs me."

"What?"

"I'm serious when I warn you about fooling around in a federal investigation."

"Listen, I reported four dead people in that plane. The wire service was told there were only three. That suggests that maybe I was drunk or that I'm a dumb shit or maybe both."

"All right, for right now forget all that. We can pick her up and give her protective custody, if that's what you want."

"That's not her style."

"Getting the shit kicked out of her is?"

"She's an alcoholic and an addict. She'd rather eat a bowl of spiders than disconnect from her source."

"Okay, if you see that car around your place again, you call us. We handle it. You're not a player, you understand?"

"I don't intend to be one."

"Watch your ass, Robicheaux," he said. "If I see your name in the paper again, it had better be in the fishing news."

I crossed the Vermilion River and took the old two-lane road through Broussard to New Iberia. At almost exactly three o'clock it started to rain. I watched it move in a gray, lighted sheet out of the south, the shadows racing ahead of the clouds as the first drops clicked across the new sugarcane and then clattered on the abandoned tin sugar factory outside of Broussard. In the middle of the shower, shafts of sunlight cut through the clouds like the depictions of spiritual grace on a child's holy card. When the sun shone through the rain my father used to say, "That how God tell you it ain't for long, Him."

When I got back home the rain was still dancing on the bayou, and Annie had walked Alafair down to the dock to help Batist take care of the fishermen who were drinking beer and eating *boudin* under the canvas awning. I went up to the house and called New Orleans information for Robin's number, but she had no listing. Then I called Smiling Jack's. The man who answered didn't identify himself, but the voice and the manner were unmistakable.

"She isn't here. She don't come in till six," he said.

"Do you have her home number?"

"Are you kidding? Who is this?"

"What's her number, Jerry?"

"Oh, yeah, I should have known. It's Fearless Fosdick, isn't it?" he said. "Guess what? She don't have a phone. Guess what again? This isn't an answering service."

"When'd you see her last?"

"Throwing up in the toilet at three o'clock this morning. I just got finished cleaning it up. Look, fun guy, you want to talk to that broad, come down and talk to her. Right now I got to wash out my mops. You two make a great couple."

He hung up the phone, and I looked out into the rain on the bayou. Maybe she would be all right, I thought. She had survived all her life in a world in which male use of her body and male violence against it had been as natural to her as the vodka collins and speed on the half-shell that started each of her days. Maybe it was just a vanity that I felt a conversation with me could bring additional harm into her life. Also, I still didn't know for sure that the driver of the Corvette was some Brooklyn character named Eddie Keats.

Saints don't heed warnings because they consider them irrelevant. Fools don't heed them because they think the lightning dancing across the sky, the thunder rolling through the woods, are only there to enhance their lives in some mysterious way. I had been warned by both Robin and Minos P. Dautrieve. I saw a solitary streak of lightning tremble like a piece of heated wire on the southern horizon. But I didn't want to think anymore that day about dope runners and local wiseguys, federal agents and plane crashes. I listened to the rain dripping through the pecan trees, then walked down to the dock in the flicker of distant lightning to help Annie and Batist get ready for the late-afternoon fishermen.

chapter
THREE

IF, AS A CHILD, I HAD BEEN ASKED TO DESCRIBE the world I lived in, I'm sure my response would have been in terms of images that in general left me with a sense of well-being about myself and my family. Because even though my mother died when I was young, and we were poor and my father sometimes brawled in bars and got locked in the parish jail, he and my little brother and I had a home—actually a world—on the bayou that was always safe, warm in the winter from the woodstove, cool in the summer under the shade of the pecan trees, a place that was ours and had belonged to our people and way of life since the Acadians came to Louisiana in 1755. In describing that world I would have told my questioner about my pet three-legged coon, my pirogue tied to a cypress into which was driven a rusty spike with a chain supposedly used by Jean Lafitte, the big, black iron pot in the backyard where my father fried us *sac-a-lait* and bream almost every night in summer, the orange and purple sunsets in the fall when the ducks would cover the sky from horizon to horizon, the red leaves spinning out of the trees onto the water in that peculiar gold October light that was both warm and cold at the same time, and the dark, wet layers of leaves deep in the woods where we dug for nightcrawlers, the smokehouse in back that glistened in the morning frost and always smelled of pork dripping into smoldering ash, and most of all my father—a big, dark, laughing Cajun who could break boards into kindling with his bare hands, throw a washtub full of bricks over a fence, or pull a six-foot 'gator out of water by his tail.

But what images would you find if you unlocked the mind of a six-year-old child who had been flown out of a virtual Stone Age, a Central American village, where the twentieth century intruded itself in the form of the most sophisticated and destructive infantry weapons in the world?

The only Spanish-speaking person I knew in New Iberia was a pari-mutuel window seller named Felix who worked at Evangeline Downs in Lafayette and the Fairgrounds in New Orleans. He had been a casino card dealer in Havana during the Batista era, and his lavender shirts and white French cuffs, crinkling seersucker suits and pomade-scented hair gave him the appearance of a man who still aspired to a jaded opulence in his life. But like most people I knew around the track, his chief defect was that he didn't like regular work or the world of ordinary people.

The skies had cleared almost completely of rain clouds an hour after I had returned from Lafayette and my visit to the DEA, and now the western horizon was aflame with the sunset, cicadas droned in the trees, and fireflies were starting to light in the dusk. We sat in the living room while Felix spoke quietly to Alafair in Spanish about her parents, her village, the small geographic, tropical postage stamp that constituted the only world she had ever known but that sent my own mind back across the seas, back across two decades, to other villages that smelled of fish heads, animal dung, chicken yards, sour mud, stagnant water, human feces, ulcerated children with no pants on who urinated in the road; and then there was that other smell, the reek of soldiers who hadn't bathed for days, who lived enclosed in their own fetid envelope, whose fantasies vacillated from rut to dissolving their enemies and the source of their discomfort into a bloody mist.

But I digress into my own historical myopia. Her story is more important than mine because I chose to be a participant and she did not. I chose to help bring the technology of napalm and the M-16 and AK-47 meat-cutters to people who harvested rice with their hands. Others elected Alafair and her family to be the recipients of our industrial gifts to the Third World.

She spoke as though she were describing the contents of a bad picture show of which she understood only parts, and Annie and I had trouble looking at each other's eyes lest we see reflected there the recognition of the simian creature that was still alive and thriving in the human race. Felix translated:

—The soldiers carry knives and pliers to steal the faces of the people in the village. My uncle ran away into the cane, and the next day we found him where they had left him. My mother tried to hide my eyes but I saw anyway. His thumbs were tied together with wire, and they had taken away his face. It was hot in the cane and we could hear the flies buzzing. Some of the people got sick because of the smell and vomited on themselves.

—That was when my father ran away, too. My mother said he went into the hills with the other men from the village. The helicopters chased them sometimes, I think, because we saw the shadows go across our house and then across the road and the fields, then they would stop in the air and begin shooting. They had tubes on their sides that made puffs of smoke, and the rocks and trees on the hillside would fly in the air. The grass and bushes were dry and caught fire, and at night we could see them burning high up in the darkness and smell the smoke in the wind—

"Ask her what happened to her father," I said to Felix.

"Dónde está tu padre ahora?"

—Maybe he went away with the trucks. The trucks went into the hills, then came back with many men from the village. They took them to a place where the soldiers live, and we did not see them again. My cousin said the soldiers have a prison far away and they keep many people there. Maybe my father is with them. The American priest said he would try to find out but that we had to leave the village. He said they would hurt my mother the way they hurt the other lady because of the clinic—

She went silent on the couch and stared out the screen door at the fireflies' lightning in the dusk. Her tan face was now discolored with the same pale, bloodless spots it had had when I pulled her out of the water. Annie stroked her close-cropped hair with her palm and squeezed her around the shoulders.

"Dave, maybe that's enough," she said.

"No, she's got to tell it all. She's too little a kid to carry that kind of stuff around by herself," I said. Then, to Felix, "What other lady?"

"Quién es la otra señora?" he asked.

—She worked at the clinic with my mother. Her stomach was big and it made her walk like a duck. One day the soldiers came and pulled her out in the road by her arms. She was calling the names of her friends to help her, but the people were afraid and tried to hide. Then the soldiers made us go outside and watch the thing they did to her in the road—

Her eyes were wide and had the empty, dry, glazed expression of someone who might be staring into a furnace.

"Qué hicieron los soldados?" Felix said softly.

—They went to the woodcutter's house and came back with

his machete. They were chopping and the machete was wet and red in the sunlight. A soldier put his hands in her stomach and took out her baby. The people were crying now and covering their faces. The priest ran to us from the church, but they knocked him down and beat him in the road. The fat lady and her baby stayed out there by themselves in the sun. The smell was like the smell in the cane when we found my uncle. It was in all the houses, and when we woke up in the morning it was still there but worse—

The cicadas were loud in the trees. There was nothing we could say. How do you explain evil to a child, particularly when the child's experience with it is perhaps greater than your own? I had seen children in a Saigon burn ward whose eyes rendered you mute before you could even attempt to apologize for the calamity that adults had imposed upon them. My condolence became a box of Hershey bars.

We drove to Mulate's in Breaux Bridge for pecan pie and listened to the Acadian string band, then took a ride down Bayou Teche on the paddle-wheel pleasure boat that operated up and down the bayou for tourists. It was dark now, and the trees on some of the lawns were hung with Japanese lanterns, and you could smell barbecue fires and crabs boiling in the lighted and screened summerhouses beyond the cane that grew along the bayou's banks. The baseball diamond in the park looked as if it were lit by an enormous white flare, and the people were cheering on an American Legion game that had all the innocent and provincial intensity of a scene clipped from the summer of 1941. Alafair sat on a wooden bench between Annie and me and watched the cypress trees and shadowy lawns and the scrolled nineteenth-century homes slip past us. Maybe it wasn't much to offer in recompense, but it was all we had.

*   *   *   *

The air was cool and the eastern sky plum-colored and striped with low-hanging red clouds when I opened up the bait shop the next morning. I worked until about nine o'clock, then left it with Batist and walked back up to the house for breakfast. I was just having my last cup of coffee when he called me on the phone.

"Dave, you 'member that colored man that rent from us this morning?" he said.

"No."

"He talked funny. He not from around here, no."

"I don't remember him, Batist. What is it?"

"He said he run the boat up on the bar and bust off the propeller. He ax if you want to come get it."

"Where is he?"

"Sout' of the four-corners. You want me go after him?"

"That's all right. I'll go in a few minutes. Did you give him an extra shearing pin?"

"*Mais* sure. He say that ain't it."

"Okay, Batist. Don't worry about it."

"Ax him where he's from he don't know how to keep the boat in the bayou, no."

A few minutes later I headed down the bayou in an outboard to pick up the damaged rental. It wasn't unusual for me to go after one of our boats. With some regularity, drunks ran them over sandbars and floating logs, bashed them against cypress stumps, or flipped them over while turning across their own wakes. The sun was bright on the water, and dragonflies hung in the still air over the lily pads along the banks. The V-shaped wake from the Evinrude slapped against the cypress roots and made the lily pads suddenly swell and undulate as though a cushion of air were rippling by underneath them. I passed the old clapboard general store at the four-corners where the black man must have used the phone to call Batist. A rusted Hadacol sign was still nailed to one wall, and a spreading oak shaded the front gallery where some Negro men in overalls were drinking soda pop and eating sandwiches. Then the cypress trees and cane along the banks became thicker, and farther down I could see my rental boat tied to a pine sapling, swinging empty in the brown current.

I cut my engine and drifted into the bank on top of my wake and tied up next to the rental. The small waves slapped against the sides of both aluminum hulls. Back in a clearing a tall black man sat on a sawed oak stump, drinking from a fifth of apricot brandy. By his foot were an opened loaf of bread and a can of Vienna sausages. He wore Adidas running shoes, soiled white cotton trousers, and an orange undershirt, and his chest and shoulders were covered with tiny coils of wiry black hair. He was much blacker than most south Louisiana people of color, and he must have had a half-dozen gold rings on his long fingers. He put two fingers of snuff under his lip and looked at me without speaking. His eyes were red in the sun-spotted shade of the oak trees. I stepped up onto the bank and walked into the clearing.

"What's the trouble, podna?" I said.

He took another sip off the brandy and didn't reply.

"Batist said you ran over the sandbar."

He still didn't answer.

"Do you hear me okay, podna?" I said, and smiled at him.

But he wasn't going to talk to me.

"Well, let's have a look," I said. "If it's just the shearing pin, I'll fix it and you can be on your way. But if you bent the propeller, I'll have to tow you back and I'm afraid I won't be able to give you another boat."

I looked once more at him, then turned around and started back toward the water's edge. I heard him stand up and brush crumbs off his clothes, then I heard the brandy gurgle in the bottle as though it were being held upside down, and just as I turned with that terrible and futile recognition that something was wrong, out of time and place, I saw his narrowed red eyes again and the bottle ripping down murderously in his long, black hand.

He caught me on the edge of the skull cap, I felt the bottle rake down off my shoulder, and I went down on all fours as though my legs had suddenly been kicked out from under me. My mouth hung open, my eyes wouldn't focus, and my ears were roaring with sound. I could feel blood running down the side of my face.

Then, with a casual, almost contemptuous movement of his body, he straddled me from behind, held my chin up with one hand so I could see the open, pearl-handled barber's razor he held before my eyes, then inserted the razor's edge between the back of my ear and my scalp. He smelled of alcohol and snuff. I saw the legs of another man walk out of the trees.

"Don't look up, my friend," the other man said, in what was either a Brooklyn or Irish Channel accent. "That'd change everything for us. Make it real bad for you. Toot's serious about his razor. He'll sculpt your ears off. Make your head look like a mannequin."

He lit a cigarette with a lighter and clicked it shut. The smoke smelled like a Picayune. Out of the corner of my eye I could see his purple suede cowboy boots, gray slacks, and one gold-braceleted white hand.

"Eyes forward, asshole. I won't say it again," he said. "You can get out of this easy or Toot can cut you right across the nipples. He'd love to do it for you: He was a *tonton macoute* down in Haiti. He sleeps in a grave one night a month to stay in touch with the spirits. Tell him what you did to the broad, Toot."

"You talk too much. Get finished. I want to eat," the black man said.

"Toot had a whole bunch of surprises for her," the white man said. "He's an imaginative guy. He's got a bunch of Polaroids from Haiti. You ought to see them. Guess what he did to her."

I watched a drop of my blood run off my eyelash and fall and break like a small red star in the dirt.

"Guess!" he said again, and kicked me hard in the right buttock.

I clenched my teeth and felt the clods of dirt bite into my palms.

"You got dirty ears, huh?" he said, and kicked me in the thigh with the toe of his boot.

"Fuck you, buddy."

"What?"

"You heard me. Whatever you do to me today I'm going to square. If I can't do it, I've got friends who will."

"I've got news for you. You're still talking now because I'm in a good mood. Second, you brought this down on yourself, asshole. When you start talking to somebody else's whores, when you poke your nose into other people's shit, you got to pay the man. That's the rules. An old-time homicide roach ought to know that. Here's the last news flash. The chippy got off easy. Toot wanted to turn her face into one of his Polaroids. But that broad is money on the hoof, got people depending on her, so sometimes you got to let it slide, you know what I mean? So he put her finger in the door and broke it for her.

"Hey," he said in an almost happy fashion, "don't look sad. I'm telling you, she didn't mind. She was glad. She's a smart girl, she knows the rules. It's too bad, though, you don't have a pussy between your legs, 'cause you ain't money on the hoof."

"Get finished," the black man said.

"You ain't in a hurry, are you, Robicheaux? Huh?" he said, and nudged me in the genitals with his boot.

The blood dripped off my eyelash and speckled the dirt.

"Okay, I'll make it quick, since you're starting to remind me of a dog down there," he said. "You got a house, you got a boat business, you got a wife, you got a lot to be thankful for. So don't get in nobody else's shit. Stay home and play with mama and your worms. If you don't know what I'm talking about, think about screwing a wife that don't have a nose.

"Now let the man pay his tab, Toot."

I felt the weight of the razor lift from behind my ear, then the white man's pointed boot ripped between my thighs and exploded in my scrotum. A furnace door opened in my bowels, a piece of angle iron twisted inside me, and a sound unlike my own voice roared from my throat. Then, for good measure, as I shuddered on my knees and elbows, heaving like a gutted animal, the black man stepped back and drop-kicked me across the mouth with the long-legged grace of a ballet dancer.

I lay in an embryonic ball on my side, blood stringing from my mouth, and saw them walk off through the trees like two friends whose sunny day had been only temporarily interrupted by an insignificant task.

I look out the door of the dustoff into the hot, bright morning as we lift clear of the banyan trees, and the elephant grass dents and flattens under us as though it were being bruised by a giant thumb. Then the air suddenly becomes cooler, no longer like steam off an oven, and we're racing over the countryside, our shadow streaking ahead of us across rice paddies and earthen dikes and yellow dirt roads with bicyclists and carts on them. The medic, an Italian kid from New York, hits me with a syrette of morphine and washes my face from his canteen. He's bare-chested and sweaty, and his pot is strung with rubber spiders. Say good-bye to Shitsville, Lieutenant, he says. You're going back alive in '65. I smell the foulness of my wounds, the dried urine in my pants, as I watch the geographic history of my last ten months sweep by under us: the burnt-out ville where the ash rises and powders in the hot wind; a ditch that gapes like a ragged incision in the earth, where we pinned them down and then broiled them alive with Zippo-tracks; the ruptured dike and dried-out and baked rice paddy still pocked with mortar rounds where they locked down on us from both flanks and marched it right through us like a firestorm. Hey, Lieutenant, don't touch yourself there, the medic is saying. I mean it, it's a mess down there. You can't lose no more blood. You want I should tie your hands? They got refrigeration at the aid station. Plasma. Hey, hold his goddamn wrists. He's torn it open.

"That's an ice bag you feel down there," the doctor was saying. He was a gray, thick-bodied man who wore rimless glasses, greens, and a T-shirt. "It'll take the swelling down quite a bit. It looks like you slept well. That shot I gave you is pretty strong stuff. Did you have dreams?"

I could tell from the sunlight on the oak trees outside that it was late afternoon. The wisteria and blooming myrtle on the hospital lawn moved in the breeze. The drawbridge was up over Bayou Teche, and the two-deck pleasure boat was going through, its paddle wheel streaming water and light.

My mouth was dry, and the inside of my lip felt as though it were filled with wire.

"I had to put nine stitches in your scalp and six in your mouth. Don't eat any peanut brittle for a while," he said, and smiled.

"Where's Annie?" I asked thickly.

"I sent her for a cup of coffee. She'll be back in a minute. The colored man's outside, too. He's a big fellow, isn't he? How far did he carry you?"

I had to wet the row of stitches inside my lip before I could talk again.

"About five hundred yards, up to the four-corners. How bad am I down below, Doc?"

"You're not ruptured, if that's what you mean. Keep it in your pajamas a couple of nights and you'll be all right. Where'd you get those scars around your thighs?"

"In the service."

"I thought I recognized the handiwork. It looks like some of it is still there."

"I set off metal detectors at the airport sometimes."

"Well, we're going to keep you with us tonight, but you can go home in the morning. You want to talk with the sheriff now, or later?"

I hadn't seen the other man, who was sitting in a leather chair in the corner. He wore a brown departmental uniform, held his lacquered campaign hat on his knee, and leaned forward deferentially. He used to own a dry-cleaning business in town before someone talked him into running for sheriff. The rural cops had changed a lot in the last twenty years. When I was a boy the sheriff wore a blue suit with a vest and a big railroad watch and chain and carried a heavy revolver in his coat pocket. He was not bothered by the bordellos on Railroad Avenue and the slot machines all over Iberia Parish, nor was he greatly troubled when white kids went nigger-knocking on Saturday nights. He'd tip his John B. Stetson hat to a white

62   James Lee Burke

lady on Main, and talk to an elderly Negro woman as though she were a post. This one was president of the Downtown Merchants Association.

"You know who they were, Dave?" he said. He had the soft, downturned lines in his face of most Acadian men in their late middle age. His cheeks were flecked with tiny blue and red veins.

"A white guy named Eddie Keats. He owns some bars in Lafayette and New Orleans. The other guy is black. His name's Toot." I swallowed from the water glass on the table. "Maybe he's a Haitian. You know anybody like that around here?"

"No."

"You know Eddie Keats?"

"No. But we can cut a warrant for him."

"It won't do any good. I never saw his face. I couldn't make him in a lineup."

"I don't understand. How do you know it was this guy Keats?"

"He was messing around my house yesterday. Call the DEA agent in Lafayette. He's got a sheet on him. The guy works for Bubba Rocque sometimes."

"Oh boy."

"Look, you can pick up Keats on suspicion. He's supposed to be a low-level hit man. Roust him in his automobile, and maybe you'll turn something. Some weed, a concealed weapon, hot credit cards. These fuckers always have spaghetti hanging off the place somewhere." I drank from the water again and laid my head back on the pillow. My scrotum, with the ice bag under it, felt as big as a bowling ball.

"I don't know about that. That's Lafayette Parish. It's a little like going on a fishing trip in somebody else's pond." He looked at me quietly, as though I should understand.

"You want him back here again?" I said. "Because unless you send him a hard telegram, he will be."

He was silent a moment, then he wrote in a pad and put the pad and pencil back in his shirt pocket and buttoned it.

"Well, I'll give the DEA and the Lafayette sheriff's office a call," he said. "We'll see what happens."

Then he asked some more questions, most of which were the formless and irrelevant afterthoughts of a well-meaning amateur who did not want to seem unsympathetic. I didn't reply when he said good-bye.

But what did I expect? I couldn't be sure myself that the white man was Eddie Keats. New Orleans was full of people with the same Italian-Irish background that produced the accent you would normally associate with Brooklyn. I had admitted I couldn't make him in a lineup and I didn't know anything about the black man except that his name was Toot and he slept in a grave. What is an ex—dry cleaner who dresses like a Fritos delivery man supposed to do with that one? I asked myself.

But maybe there was a darker strain at work inside me that I didn't want to recognize. I knew how local cops would have dealt with Eddie Keats and his kind twenty years ago. A couple of truly vicious coonass plainclothes (they usually wore J.C. Higgins suits that looked like clothes on a duck) would have gone to his bar, thrown his framed liquor license in the toilet, broken out all his car windows with a baton, then pointed a revolver between his eyes and snapped the hammer on an empty chamber.

No, I didn't like them then; I didn't like them now. But it was a temptation.

Batist came in smelling of wine and fish, with some flowers I suspected he had taken from a hall vase and put in a Coca-Cola bottle. When I told him that the black man named Toot was possibly a *tonton macoute* from Haiti who practiced black magic, Batist got him confused with the *loup-garou*, the bayou equivalent of the lamia or werewolf, and was convinced that we should see a *traiteur* in order to find this *loup-garou* and fill his mouth and nostrils with dirt from a witch's grave. He saw my eyes light on the pint wine bottle, with the paper bag twisted around its neck, that protruded from the back pocket of his overalls, and he shifted sideways in the chair to block my vision, but the bottle clanked loudly against the chair's arm. His face was transfused with guilt.

"Hey, podna, since when did you have to hide things from me?" I said.

"I shouldn't drink, me, when I got to look after Miss Annie and that little girl."

"I trust you, Batist."

His eyes averted mine and his big hands were awkward in his lap. Even though I had known him since I was a child, he was still uncomfortable when I, a white man, spoke to him in a personal way.

"Where's Alafair now?" I said.

"Wit' my wife and girl. She all right, you ain't got to worry, no. You know she talk French, her? We fixing po'boys, I say *pain*, she know that mean 'bread,' yeah. I say *sauce piquante*, she know that mean 'hot sauce.' How come she know that, Dave?"

"The Spanish language has a lot of words like ours."

"Oh," he said, and was thoughtful a moment. Then, "How come that?"

Annie came through the door and saved me from an impossible discussion. Batist was absolutely obsessive about understanding any information that was foreign to his world, but as a rule he would have to hack and hew it into pieces until it would assimilate into that strange Afro-Creole-Acadian frame of reference that was as natural to him as wearing a dime on a string around his ankle to ward off the *gris-gris*, an evil spell cast by a *traiteur*, or conjuror.

Annie stayed with me through the evening while the light softened on the trees outside and the shadows deepened on the lawn, the western sky turned russet and orange like a chemical flame, and high school kids strolled down the sidewalks to the American Legion baseball game in the park. Through the open window I could smell barbecue fires and water sprinklers, magnolia blossoms and night-blooming jasmine. Then the sky darkened, and the rain clouds in the south pulsated with white streaks of lightning like networks of veins.

Annie lay next to me and rubbed my chest and touched my face with her fingers and kissed me on the eyes.

"Take away the ice bag and push the chair in front of the door," I said.

"No, Dave."

"Yes, it's all right. The doctor said there was no problem."

She kissed me on the ear, then whispered, "Not tonight, baby love."

I felt myself swallow.

"Annie, please," I said.

She raised up on one elbow and looked curiously into my face.

"What is it?" she said.

"I need you. You're my wife."

She frowned and her eyes went back and forth into mine.

"Tell me what it is," she said.

"You want to know?"

"Dave, you're my whole life. How could I not want to know?"

"Those sonsofbitches put me on my hands and knees and worked me over like they would a dog."

I could see the pain in her eyes. Her hand went to my cheek, then to my throat.

"Somebody will catch them. You know that," she said.

"No, they're hunting on the game reserve. They're mainline badasses, and they don't have anybody more serious to deal with than a dry cleaner in a sheriff's suit."

"You gave it up. We have a good life now. This is the place you've always wanted to come back to. Everybody in town likes you and respects you, and the people up and down the bayou are the best friends anyone could have. Now we have Alafair, too. How can you let a couple of criminals hurt all that?"

"It doesn't work that way."

"Yes, it does, if you look at what's right with your life instead of what's wrong with it."

"Are you going to push the chair in front of the door?"

She paused. Her face was quiet and purposeful. She turned off the light on the bedstand and pushed the heavy leather chair until it caught under the doorknob. In the moonlight through the window her curly gold hair looked as if it were flecked with silver. She pulled back the sheet and took away the ice bag, then touched me with her hand. The pain made both my knees jump.

I heard her sigh as she sat back down on the side of the bed.

"Are we going to fight with each other when we have a problem?" she said.

"I'm not fighting with you, kiddo."

"Yes, you are. You can't turn loose of the past, Dave. You get hurt, or you see something that's wrong in the world, and all the old ways come back to you."

"I can't help that."

"Maybe not. But you don't live alone anymore." She took my hand and lay down beside me again. "There's me, and now there's Alafair, too."

"I'll tell you what it feels like, and I won't say any more. You remember when I told you about how those North Vietnamese regulars overran us and the captain surrendered to them? They tied our hands around trees with piano wire, then took turns urinating on us. That's what it feels like."

She was quiet a long time. I could hear her breathing in the dark. Then she took a deep breath and let it out and put her arm across my chest.

"I have a very bad feeling inside me, Dave," she said.

There was nothing more to say. How could there be? Even the most sympathetic friends and relatives of a battery or assault victim could not understand what that individual experiences. Over the years I had questioned people who had been molested by degenerates, mugged by street punks, shanked and shot by psychopaths, gang-banged and sodomized by outlaw bikers. They all had the same numb expression, the same drowning eyes, the same knowledge that they somehow deserved their fate and that they were absolutely alone in the world. And often we made their grief and humiliation even greater by ascribing the responsibility for their suffering to their own incaution, so that we could remain psychologically invulnerable ourselves.

I wasn't being fair to Annie. She had paid her share of dues, but there were times when you are very alone in the world and your own thoughts flay your skin an inch at a time. This was one of them.

I didn't sleep that night. But then insomnia and I were old companions.

Two days later the swelling between my legs had gone down and I could walk without looking like I was straddling a fence. The sheriff came out to see me at the boat dock and told me he had talked to the Lafayette city police and Minos P. Dautrieve at the DEA. Lafayette had sent a couple of detectives to question Eddie Keats at his bar, but he claimed that he had taken two of his dancers sailing on the day I was beaten up, and the two dancers corroborated his story.

"Are they going to accept that?" I said.

"What are they supposed to do?"

"Do some work and find out where those girls were two days ago."

"Do you know how many cases those guys probably have?"

"I'm not sympathetic, Sheriff. People like Keats come into our area because they think they have a free pass. What did Minos P. Dautrieve have to say?"

The sheriff's face colored and the skin at the corner of his mouth tugged slightly in a smile.

"I think he said you'd better get your ass into his office," the sheriff replied.

"Those were his words?"

"I believe so."

"Why's he mad at me?"

"I get the impression he thinks you're messing around in federal business."

"Does he know anything about a Haitian named Toot?"

"No. I went through Baton Rouge and the National Crime Information Center in Washington and couldn't find out anything, either."

"He's probably an illegal. There's no paper on him," I said.

"That's what Dautrieve said."

"He's a smart cop."

I saw a look of faint embarrassment in the sheriff's eyes, and I felt instantly sorry for my remark.

"Well, I promise you I'll give it my best, Dave," he said.

"I appreciate what you've done."

"I'm afraid I haven't done very much."

"Look, these guys are hard to put away," I said. "I worked two years on the case of a syndicate hit man who pushed his wife off a fourth-floor balcony into a dry swimming pool. He even told me he did it. He walked right out of it because we took her diary out of the condo without a warrant. How about that for first-rate detective work? Every time I'd see him in a bar, he'd send a drink over to my table. It really felt good."

He smiled and shook hands.

"One more thing before I go," he said. "A man named Monroe from Immigration was in my office yesterday. He was asking questions about you."

The sunlight was bright on the bayou. The oaks and cypress on the far side made deep shadows on the bank.

"He was out here the day after that plane went down at Southwest Pass," I said.

"He asked if you had a little girl staying with you."

"What'd you tell him?"

"I told him I didn't know. I also told him it wasn't my business. But I got the feeling he wasn't really interested in some little girl. You bother him for some reason."

"I gave him a bad time."

"I don't know those federal people that well, but I don't think they drive up from New Orleans just because a man with a fish dock gives them a bad time. What's that fellow after, Dave?"

"I don't know."

"Look, I don't want to tell you what to do, but if you and Annie are helping out a little girl that doesn't have any parents, why don't you let other folks help out, too? People around here aren't going to let anybody take her away."

"My father used to say that a catfish had whiskers so he'd never go into a hollow log he couldn't turn around in. I don't trust those people at Immigration, Sheriff. Play on their terms and you'll lose."

"I think maybe you got a dark view sometimes, Dave."

"You better believe it," I said.

I watched him drive away on the dirt road under the canopy of oak trees. I clicked my fingers on the warm board rail that edged my dock, then walked up to the house and had lunch with Annie and Alafair.

An hour later I took the .45 automatic and the full clip of hollow-points from the dresser drawer and walked with them inside the folded towel to the pickup truck and put them in the glove box. Annie watched me from the front porch, her arm leaned against a paintless wood post. I could see her breasts rise and fall under her denim shirt.

"I'm going to New Orleans. I'll be back tonight," I said.

She didn't answer.

"It's not going to take care of itself," I said. "The sheriff is a nice guy who should be cleaning stains out of somebody's sports coat. The feds don't have jurisdiction in an assault case. The Lafayette cops don't have time to solve crimes in Iberia Parish. That means we fall through the cracks. Screw that."

"I'm sure that somehow that makes sense. You know, rah, rah for the penis and all that. But I wonder if Dave is giving Dave a shuck so we can march off to the wars again."

Her face was cheerless and empty.

I watched the wind flatten the leaves in the pecan trees, then I opened the door of the pickup.

"I need to take some money out of savings to help some-body," I said. "I'll put it back next month."

"What can I say? Like your first wife told you, 'Keep it high and hard, podjo,' " she said, and went back inside the house.

The sweep of wind in the pecan trees seemed deafening.

*   *   *   *

I gassed up the truck at the dock, then as an afterthought I went inside the bait shop, sat at the wooden counter with a Dr Pepper, and called Minos P. Dautrieve at the DEA in Lafayette. While the phone rang I gazed out the window at the green leaves floating on the bayou.

"I understand you want my ass in your office," I said.

"Yeah, what the fuck's going on over there?"

"Why don't you drive over and find out?"

"You sound funny."

"I have stitches in my mouth."

"They bounced you around pretty good, huh?"

"What's this about you wanting my ass in your office?"

"I'm curious. Why are a bunch of farts who deal dope and whores so interested in you? I think maybe you're on to something we don't know about."

"I'm not."

"I think also you may have the delusion you're still a police officer."

"You've got things turned around a little bit. When a guy gets his *cojones* and his face kicked in, he becomes the victim. The guys who kick in his *cojones* and his face are the criminals. These are the guys you get mad at. The object is to put them in jail."

"The sheriff said you can't identify Keats."

"I didn't see his face."

"And you never saw the Zulu before?"

"Keats, or whoever the white guy was, said he was one of Baby Doc's *tontons macoute*."

"What do you want us to do, then?"

"If I remember our earlier conversation right, y'all were going to handle it."

"It's after the fact now. And I don't have authority in this kind of assault case. You know that."

I looked out the window at the leaves floating on the brown current.

"Do you all ever salt the mine shaft?" I said.

"You mean plant dope on a suspect? Are you serious?"

"Save the Boy Scout stuff. I've got a wife and another person in my home who are in jeopardy. You said you were going to handle things. You're not handling anything. Instead I get this ongoing lecture that somehow I'm the problem in this situation."

"I never said that."

"You don't have to. A collection of moral retards runs millions in drugs through the bayous, and you probably don't nail one of them in fifty. It's frustrating. It looks bad on the monthly report. You wonder if you're going to be transferred to Fargo soon. So you make noise about civilians meddling in your business."

"I don't like the way you're talking to me, Robicheaux."

"Too bad. I'm the guy with the stitches. If you want to do something for me, figure out a way to pick up Keats."

"I'm sorry you got beat up. I'm sorry we can't do more. I understand your anger. But you were a cop and you know our limits. So how about easing off the Purple Heart routine?"

"You told me Keats's bars have hookers in them. Get the local heat to park patrol cars in front of his bars a few nights. You'll bring his own people down on him."

"We don't operate that way."

"I had a feeling you'd say that. See you around, partner. Don't hang on the rim too long. Everybody will forget you're in the game."

"You think that's clever?"

I hung up on him, finished my Dr Pepper, and drove down the dirt road in the warm wind that thrashed the tree limbs overhead. The bayou was covered with leaves now, and back in the shadows on the far bank I could see cottonmouths sleeping on the lower branches of the willow trees, just above the water's languid surface. I rumbled across the drawbridge into town, withdrew three hundred dollars from the bank, then took the back road through the sugarcane fields to St. Martinville and caught the interstate to New Orleans.

The wind was still blowing hard as I drove down the long concrete causeway over the Atchafalaya swamp. The sky was still a soft blue and filled with tumbling white clouds, but a good storm was building out on the Gulf and I knew that by evening the southern horizon would be black and streaked with rain and lightning. I watched the flooded willow trees bend in the wind, and the moss on the dead cypress in the bays straighten and fall, and the way the sunlight danced and shattered on the water when the surface suddenly wrinkled from one shore to the next. The Atchafalaya basin encompasses hundreds of square miles of bayous, willow islands, sand bogs, green levees covered with buttercups, wide bays dotted with dead cypress and oil-well platforms, and flooded woods filled with cottonmouths, alligators, and black clouds of mosquitoes. My father and I had fished and hunted all over the Atchafalaya when I was a boy, and even on a breezy spring day like this we knew how to catch bull bream and goggle-eye perch when nobody else would catch them. In the late afternoon we'd anchor the pirogue on the lee side of a willow island, when the mosquitoes would start to swarm out of the trees, and cast our bobbers back into the quiet water, right against the line of lily pads, and wait for the bream and goggle-eye to start feeding on the insects. In an hour we'd fill our ice chest with fish.

But my reverie about boyhood moments with my father

could not get rid of the words Annie had said to me. She had wanted to raise a red welt across the heart, and she had done a good job of it. But maybe what bothered me worse was the fact that I knew she had hurt me only because she had an unrelieved hurt inside herself. Her reference to a statement made by my first wife was an admission that maybe there was a fundamental difference in me, a deeply ingrained character flaw, that neither Annie nor my ex-wife nor perhaps any sane woman would ever be able to accept. I was not simply a drunk; I was drawn to a violent and aberrant world the way a vampire bat seeks a black recess within the earth.

My first wife's name was Niccole, and she was a dark-haired beautiful girl from Martinique who loved horse racing almost as much as I. But unfortunately she loved money and clubhouse society even more. I could have almost forgiven her infidelities in our marriage, until we both discovered that her love affairs were not motivated by lust for other men but rather contempt for me and loathing for the dark, alcoholic energies that governed my life.

We had been at a lawn party out by Lake Pontchartrain, and I had been drinking all afternoon at Jefferson Downs and now I had reached the point where I didn't even bother to leave the small bar under the mimosa trees at the lawn party and make a pretense of interest in the conversation around me. The wind was balmy and it rattled the dry palm fronds on the lakeshore, and I watched the red sun set on the horizon and reflect on the green, capping surface of the water. In the distance, white sailboats lurched in fountains of spray toward the Southern Yacht Club. I could feel the whiskey in my face, the omniscient sense of control that alcohol always brought me, the bright flame of metaphysical insight burning behind my eyes.

But my seersucker sleeve was damp from the bar, and my

words were thick and apart from me when I asked for another Black Jack and water.

Then Niccole was standing next to me with her current lover, a geologist from Houston. He was a summer mountain climber, and he had a rugged, handsome profile like a Roman's and a chest that looked as hard as a barrel. Like all the other men there, he wore the soft tropical colors of the season—a pastel shirt, a white linen suit, a purple knit tie casually loose at the throat. He ordered Manhattans for both of them, then while he waited for the Negro bartender to fix their drinks he stroked the down on top of Niccole's arm as though I were not there.

Later, I would not be able to describe accurately any series of feelings or events after that moment. I felt something rip like wet newspaper in the back of my head; I saw his startled face look suddenly into mine; I saw it twist and convulse as my fist came across his mouth; I felt his hands try to grab my coat as he went down; I saw the genuine fear in his eyes as I rained my fists down on him and then caught his throat between my hands.

When they pulled me off him, his tongue was stuck in his throat, his skin was the color of ash, and his cheeks were covered with strings of pink spittle. My wife was sobbing uncontrollably on the host's shoulder.

When I awoke on our houseboat the next morning, my eyes shuddering in the hard light refracting off the lake, I found the note she had left me:

Dear Dave,

I don't know what it is you're looking for, but three years of marriage to you have convinced me I don't want to be there when you find it. Sorry about that. As your pitcher-bartender friend says, Keep it high and hard, podjo.

Niccole

I followed the highway through the eastern end of the Atchafalaya basin. White cranes rose above the dead cypress in the sunlight just as the first drops of rain began to dimple the water below the causeway. I could smell the wet sand, the moss, the four-o'clock flowers, the toadstools, the odor of dead fish and sour mud blowing on the wind out of the marsh. A big willow tree by the water's edge looked like a woman's hair in the wind.

chapter
FOUR

THE RAIN WAS FALLING OUT OF THE BLUE-BLACK SKY when I parked the pickup truck in front of the travel agency in New Orleans. I knew the owner, and he let me use his WATS line to call a friend in Key West. Then I bought a one-way ticket there for seventy-nine dollars.

Robin lived in a decrepit Creole-style apartment building off South Rampart. The cracked brick and mortar had been painted purple; the red tiles of the roof were broken; the scrolled iron grillwork on the balconies had burst loose from its fastenings and was tilted at odd angles. The banana and palm trees in the courtyard looked as though they had never been pruned, and the dead leaves and fronds clicked loudly in the rain and wind. Dark-skinned children rode tricycles up and down the second-floor balcony, and all the apartment doors were open and even in the rain you could hear an incredible mixed din of daytime television, Latin music, and people shouting at each other.

I walked up to Robin's apartment, but as I approached her door a middle-aged, overweight man in a rain-spotted gray business suit with an American-flag pin in his lapel came toward me, squinting at a small piece of damp paper in his hand. I wanted to think he was a bill collector, a social worker, a process server, but his eyes were too furtive, his face too nervous, his need too obvious. He realized that the apartment number he was looking for was the one I was standing in front of. His face went blank, the way a man's does when he suddenly knows that he's made a commitment for which he has no preparation. I didn't want to be unkind to him.

"She's out of the business, partner," I said.

"Sir?"

"Robin's not available anymore."

"I don't know what you're talking about." His face had grown rounder and more frightened.

"That's her apartment number on that piece of paper, isn't it? You're not a regular, so I suspect somebody sent you here. Who was it?"

He started to walk past me. I put my hand gently on his arm.

"I'm not a policeman. I'm not her husband. I'm just a friend. Who was it, partner?" I said.

"A bartender."

"At Smiling Jack's, on Bourbon?"

"Yes, I think that was it."

"Did you give him money?"

"Yes."

"Don't go back there for it. He won't give it back to you, anyway. Do you understand that?"

"Yes."

I took my hand away from his arm, and he walked quickly down the stairs and out into the rain-swept courtyard.

I looked through the screen door into the gloom of Robin's apartment. A toilet flushed in back, and she walked into the living room in a pair of white shorts and a green Tulane T-shirt and saw me framed against the wet light. The index finger of her left hand was wrapped in a splint. She smiled sleepily at me, and I stepped inside. The thick, drowsy odor of marijuana struck at my face. Smoke curled from a roach clip in an ashtray on the coffee table.

"What's happening, Streak?" she said lazily.

"I just ran off a client, I'm afraid."

"What d'you mean?"

"Jerry sent a john over. I told him you were out of the business. Permanently, Robin. We're moving you to Key West, kiddo."

"This is all too weird. Look, Dave, I'm down to seeds and stems, if you know what I mean. I'm going out to buy some beer. Mommy has to get a little mellow before she bounces her stuff for the cantaloupe lovers. You want to come along?"

"No beer, no more hooking, no Smiling Jack's tonight. I've got you a ticket on the nine o'clock flight to Key West."

"Stop talking crazy, will you? What am I going to do in Key West? It's full of faggots."

"You're going to work in a restaurant owned by a friend of mine. It's a nice place, out on the pier at the end of Duval Street. Famous people eat in there. Tennessee Williams used to come there."

"You mean that country singer? Wow, what a gig."

"I'm going to square what those guys did to you and me," I said. "When I do, you won't be able to stay in New Orleans."

"That's what's wrong with your mouth?"

"They told me what they did to your finger. I'm sorry. It's my fault."

"Forget it. It comes with my stage career." She sat down on the stuffed couch and picked up the roach clip, which now held only smoldering ash. She toyed with it, studied it, then dropped it on top of the glass ashtray. "Don't make them come back. The white guy, the one with the cowboy boots, he had some Polaroid pictures. God, I don't want to remember them."

"Do you know who these two guys are?"

"No."

"Did you ever see them before?"

"No."

"Are you sure?"

"Yes." She squeezed one hand around the fingers of the other. "In the pictures, some colored people were tied up in a basement or something. They had blood all over them. Dave, some of them were still alive. I can't forget what their faces looked like."

I sat down beside her and picked up her hands. Her eyes were wet, and I could smell the marijuana on her breath.

"If you catch that plane tonight, you can start a new life. I'll check on you and my friend will help you, and you'll put all this stuff behind you. How much money do you have?"

"A couple of hundred dollars maybe."

"I'll give you two hundred more. That'll get you to your first paycheck. But no snorting, no dropping, no shooting. You understand that?"

"Hey, is this guy out there one of your AA pals? Because I told you I don't dig that scene."

"Who's asking you to?"

"I got enough troubles without getting my head shrunk by a bunch of ex-drunks."

"Make your own choices. It's your life, kiddo."

"Yeah, but you're always up to something on the side. You should have been a priest. You still go to Mass?"

"Sure."

"You remember the time you took me to midnight Mass at St. Louis Cathedral? Then we walked across the square and had beignets at the Café du Monde. You know, I thought maybe you were serious about me that night."

"I have to ask you a couple of questions before I go."

"Sure, why not? Most men are interested in my jugs. You come around like a census taker."

"I'm serious, Robin. Do you remember a guy named Victor Romero?"

"Yeah, I guess so. He used to hang around with Johnny Dartez."

"Where's he from?"

"Here."

"What do you know about him?"

"He's a little dark-skinned guy with black curls hanging off his head, and he wears a French beret like he's an artist or something. Except he's bad news. He sold some tainted skag down on Magazine, and I heard a couple of kids were dead before they got the spike out of their arms."

"Was he muling for Bubba Rocque, too?"

"I don't know. I don't care. I haven't seen the guy in months. Why do you care about those dipshits? I thought you were the family man now. Maybe things aren't too good at home."

"Maybe."

"And you're the guy that's going to clean up mommy's act so she can wipe off tables for the tourists. Wow."

"Here's the airline ticket and the two hundred dollars. My friend's name is written on the envelope. Do whatever you want."

I started to get up, but she pressed her hands down on my arms. Her breasts were large and heavy against her T-shirt, and I knew secretly that I had the same weakness as the men who watched her every night at Smiling Jack's.

"Dave?"

"What?"

"Do you think about me a little bit sometimes?"

"Yes."

"Do you like me?"

"You know I do."

"I mean the way you'd like an ordinary woman, somebody who didn't have a pharmacy floating around in her blood-stream."

"I like you a lot, Robin."

"Stay just a minute, then. I'll take the plane tonight. I promise."

Then she put her arm across my chest, tucked her head under my chin like a small girl, and pressed herself against me. Her short-cropped, dark hair was soft and smelled of sham-poo, and I could feel her breasts swell against me as she breathed. Outside it was raining hard on the courtyard. I brushed her cheek with my fingers and held her hand, then a moment later I felt her shudder as though some terrible tension and fear had left her body with sleep. In the silence I looked out at the rain dancing on the iron grillwork.

The neon lights on Bourbon looked like green and purple smoke in the rain. The Negro street dancers, with their heavy metal clip-on taps that clattered like horseshoes on the side-walk, were not out tonight, and the few tourists were mostly family people who walked close against the buildings, from one souvenir shop to the next, and did not stop at the open doors of the strip joints where spielers in straw boaters and candy-striped vests were having a hard time bringing in the trade.

I stood against a building on the opposite corner from Smil-ing Jack's and watched Jerry through the door for a half hour. He wore his fedora and an apron over an open-necked sports shirt that was covered with small whiskey bottles. Against the glow of stage lights on the burlesque stage behind him, the angular profile of his face looked as though it were snipped out of tin.

The weight of the .45 was heavy in my raincoat pocket. I had a permit to carry it, but I never had occasion to, and actually I had fired it only once since leaving the department, and that was at an alligator who attacked a child on the bayou. But I had used it as a police officer when the bodyguard of New Orleans's number-one pimp and drug dealer threw down on my partner and me. It had kicked in my hand like a jackhammer, as though it had a life of its own; when I had stopped shooting into the back window of the Cadillac, my ears were roaring with a sound like the sea, my face was stiff with the smell of the cordite, and later my dreams would be peopled by two men whose bodies danced disjointedly in a red haze.

This district had been my turf for fourteen years, first as a patrolman, then as a sergeant in robbery investigation, and finally as a lieutenant in homicide. In that time I got to see them all: male and female prostitutes, Murphy artists, psychotic snipers, check writers, pete men, car boosters, street dealers, and child molesters. I was punched out, shot at, cut with an ice pick, stuffed unconscious behind the wheel of a car and shoved off the third level of a parking garage. I witnessed an electrocution in Angola penitentiary, helped take the remains of a bookie out of a garbage compactor, drew chalk outlines on an alley floor where a woman had jumped with her child from the roof of a welfare hotel.

I turned the key on hundreds of people. A lot of them did hard time in Angola; four of them went to the electric chair. But I don't think my participation in what politicians call "the war on crime" ever made much difference. New Orleans is no safer a town now than it was then. Why? Narcotics is one answer. Maybe another is the fact that in fourteen years I never turned the key on a slumlord or on a zoning board member who owned interests in pornographic theaters and massage parlors.

I saw Jerry take off his apron and walk toward the back of the bar. I crossed the street in the slanting rain and entered the bar just as Jerry disappeared through a curtained doorway in back. On the lighted stage in front of a full-wall mirror, two topless girls in sequined G-strings with gold chains around their ankles danced barefoot to a 1950s rock 'n' roll record. I had to wait for my eyes to adjust to the turning strobe light that danced across the walls and floor and the bodies of the men staring up at the girls from the bar, then I headed toward the curtained doorway in back.

"Can I help you, sir?" the other bartender said. He was blond and wore a black string tie on a white sports shirt.

"I have an appointment with Jerry."

"Jerry Falgout?"

"The other bartender."

"Yeah. Have a seat. I'll tell him you're here."

"Don't bother."

"Hey, you can't go back there."

"It's a private conversation, podna. Don't mess in it."

I went through the curtain into a storage area that was filled with cases of beer and liquor bottles. The room was lit by a solitary bulb in a tin shade, and a huge ventilator fan set in the far window sucked the air out into a brick alley. The door to a small office was partly ajar, and inside the office Jerry was bent on one knee in front of a desk, almost as if he were genuflecting, while he snorted a line of white powder off a mirror with a rolled five-dollar bill. Then he rose to his feet, closed each nostril with a finger, and sniffed, blinked, and widened his eyes, then licked his finger and wiped the residue off a small square of white paper and rubbed it on his gums.

He didn't see me until he was out the door. I caught both of his arms behind him, put one hand behind his head and ran him straight into the window fan. His fedora clattered in the tin blades, and then I heard them thunk and whang against his scalp and I pulled his head up the way you would a drowning man's and shoved him back inside the small office and shut the door behind us. His face was white with shock, and blood ran out of his hairline like pieces of string. His eyes were wild with fright. I pushed him down in a chair.

"Goddamn, goddamn, man, you're out of your fucking mind," he said, his voice almost hiccupping.

"How much did you get for dropping the dime on Robin?"

"What? I didn't get nothing. What are you talking about?"

"You listen to me, Jerry. It's just you and me. No Miranda, no lawyer, no bondsman, no safe cell to be a tough guy in. It all gets taken care of right here. Do you understand that?"

He pressed his palm against the blood in his hair and then looked at his palm stupidly.

"Say you understand."

"What?"

"Last chance, Jerry."

"I don't understand nothing. What the fuck's with you? You come on like a crazy person."

I took the .45 out of my coat pocket, pulled back the receiver so he could see the loaded magazine, and slid a round into the chamber. I sighted between his eyes.

His face twitched with fear, his mouth trembled, his hair glistened with sweat. His hands were gripped on both his thighs as though there were a terrible pain in his bowels.

"Come on, man, put it away," he said. "I told you I ain't no swinging dick. I'm just a guy getting by. I tend bar, I live off tips, I mop up bathrooms. I'm no heavy dude you got to come down on like King Kong. No shit, man. Put away the piece."

"What did they pay you?"

"A hunnerd bucks. I didn't know they were going to hurt her. That's the truth. I thought they'd just tell her not to be talking to no ex-cops. They don't beat up whores. It costs them money. I don't know why they broke her finger. They didn't have to do it. She don't know anything anyway. Come on, man, put it away."

"Did you call Eddie Keats?"

"Are you kidding? He's a fucking hit man. Is that who they sent?"

"Who did you call?"

His eyes went away from the gun and looked down in his lap. He held his hands between his legs.

"Does my voice sound funny to you?" I said.

"Yeah, I guess so."

"It's because I have stitches in my mouth. I also have some in my head. A black guy named Toot put them there. Do you know who he is?"

"No."

"He broke Robin's finger, then he came to New Iberia."

"I didn't know that, man. Honest to God."

"You're starting to genuinely piss me off, Jerry. Who did you call?"

"Look, everybody does it. You hear something about Bubba Rocque or somebody talking about him or maybe his people getting out of line, you call up his club about it and you get a hunnerd bucks. It don't even have to be important. They say he just likes to know everything that's going on."

"Hey, you all right in there, Jerry?" the voice of the other bartender said outside the door.

"He's fine," I said.

The doorknob started to turn.

"Don't open that door, podna," I said. "If you want to call

the Man, do it, but don't come in here. While you're at it, tell the heat Jerry's been poking things up his nose again."

I looked steadily into Jerry's eyes. His eyelashes were beaded with sweat. He swallowed and wiped the dryness of his lips with his fingers.

"It's all right, Morris," he said. "I'm coming out in a minute."

I heard the bartender's feet walk away from the door. Jerry took a deep breath and looked at the gun again.

"I told you what you want. So cut me some slack, okay?" he said.

"Where's Victor Romero?"

"What the fuck I know about him?"

"You knew Johnny Dartez, didn't you?"

"Sure. He was in all these skin joints. He's dead now, right?"

"So you must have known Victor Romero, too."

"You don't get it. I'm a bartender. I don't know anything that anybody on the street don't know. The guy's a fucking geek. He was peddling some bad Mexican brown around town, it had insecticide in it or something. So he had to get out of town. Then I heard him and Johnny Dartez got busted by Immigration for trying to bring in a couple of big-time greasers from Colombia. But that must be bullshit because Johnny was still flying around when he went down in the drink, right?"

"They were busted by Immigration?"

"I don't know that, man. You stand behind that bar and you'll hear a hunnerd fucking stories a night. It's a soap opera. How about it, man? Do I get some slack?"

I eased the hammer down carefully and let the .45 hang from my arm. He expelled a long breath from his chest, his shoulders sagged, and he wiped his damp palms on his pants.

"There's one other thing," I said. "You're out of Robin's life. You don't even have thoughts about her."

"What am I supposed to do? Pretend I don't see her? She works here, man."

"Not anymore. In fact, if I were you, I'd think about finding a job outside the country."

His face looked confused, then I could see a fearful comprehension start to work in his eyes.

"You got it, Jerry. I'm going to have a talk with Bubba Rocque. When I do, I'll tell him who sent me. You might think about Iran."

I dropped the .45 in the pocket of my raincoat and walked back out of the bar into the rain that had now thinned and was blowing in rivulets off the iron-scrolled balconies along the street. The air was clean and cool and sweet-smelling with the rain, and I walked in the lee of the buildings toward Jackson Square and Decatur, where my truck was parked, and I could see the lighted peaks of St. Louis Cathedral against the black sky. The river was covered with mist as thick as clouds. The waiters had stacked the chairs in the Café du Monde, and the wind blew the mist over the tabletops in a wet sheen. In the distance I could hear a ship's horn blowing across the water.

It was eleven o'clock when I got back home, and the storm had stopped and the house was dark. The pecan trees were wet and black in the yard, and the slight breeze off the bayou rustled their leaves and shook water onto the tin roof of the gallery. I checked on Alafair, then went into our bedroom, where Annie was sleeping on her stomach in her panties and a pajama top. The attic fan was on, and it drew the cool air from outside and moved the curly hair on the back of her neck. I put the .45 back in the drawer, undressed, and lay down beside her. I could feel the fatigue of the day rush through me like a drug. She stirred slightly, then turned her head away from me on the pillow. I placed my hand on her back. She rolled over with her face pointed at the ceiling and her arm over her eyes.

"You got back all right?" she said.

"Sure."

She was quiet a moment, and I could hear the dryness of her mouth when she spoke again: "Who was she, Dave?"

"A dancer in a joint on Bourbon."

"Did you take care of everything?"

"Yes."

"You owed her, I guess."

"Not really. I just had to get her off the hook."

"I don't understand why she's your obligation."

"Because she's a drunk and an addict and she can't do anything for herself. They broke her finger, Annie. If they catch her again, it'll be much worse."

I heard her take a breath, then she put her hands on her stomach and looked up into the dark.

"It's not over, though, is it?" she said.

"It is for her. And the guy who was partly responsible for me getting my face kicked in is going to be blowing New Orleans in a hurry. I admit that makes me feel good."

"I wish I could share your feeling."

It was quiet in the room, and the moon came out and made shadows in the trees. I felt I was about to lose something, maybe forever. I put my foot over hers and took one of her hands in mine. Her hand was pliant and dry.

"I didn't seek it out," I said. "The trouble came to us. You have to confront problems, Annie. When you don't, they follow you around like pariah dogs."

"You always tell me that one of the main axioms in AA is 'Easy does it.' "

"It doesn't mean you should avoid your responsibilities. It doesn't mean you should accept the role of victim."

"Maybe we should talk about the price we should all be willing to pay for your pride."

"I don't know what to say anymore. You don't understand, and I don't think you're going to."

"What should I feel, Dave? You lie down next to me and tell me you've been with a stripper, that you've run somebody out of New Orleans, that it makes you feel good. I don't know anything about a world like that. I don't think anybody should have to."

"It exists because people pretend it's not there."

"Let other people live in it, then."

She sat up on the side of the bed with her back to me.

"Don't go away from me," I said.

"I'm not going anywhere."

"Lie down and talk."

"It's no good to talk about it anymore."

"We can talk about other things. This is just a temporary thing. I've had a lot worse trouble in my life than this," I said.

She remained seated on the side of the bed, her panties low on her bottom. I put my hand on her shoulder and eased her back down on the pillow.

"Come on, kiddo. Don't lock your old man out," I said.

I kissed her cheeks and her eyes and stroked her hair. I could feel myself grow against her side. But her eyes looked straight ahead, and her hands rested loosely on my shoulders, as though that were the place that obligation required them to be.

I could see the water dripping out of the pecan trees in the moonlight. I didn't care about pride or the feelings that I would have later. I needed her, and I slipped off her panties and pulled off my underwear and held her against me. Her arms rested on my back and she kissed me once lightly on the jaw, but she was dry when I entered her, and her eyes stayed open and unseeing as though she were focused on a thought inside herself.

Out on the bayou I heard the peculiar cry of a bull 'gator calling its mate. I was sweating now, even in the cool wind drawn by the attic fan through the window, and in the mire of thoughts that can occur in such a heart-rushing and self-defeating moment, I tried to justify both my lustful dependency and my willingness to force her to be my accomplice.

I stopped and raised myself off her, my body trembling with its own denial, and worked my underwear back over my thighs. She turned her head on the pillow and looked at me as a patient might from a hospital bed.

"It's been a long day," she said quietly.

"Not for me. I think I'd like to go out and blow the shit out of some tin cans and bottles right now."

I stood up from the bed and put on my shirt and pants.

"Where are you going?" she said.

"I don't know."

"Come back to bed, Dave."

"I'll lock the front door on the way out. I'll try not to wake you when I come back."

I slipped on my loafers and went outside to my truck. The few black clouds in the sky were rimmed with moonlight, and shadows fell through the oaks on the dirt road that led back from New Iberia. The bayou was high from the rain, and I could see the solitary V-shaped ripple of a nutria swimming from the cattails to the opposite shore. I banged and splashed through the muddy pools in the road, and gripped the steering wheel so tightly that my fists were ridged with bone. When I went across the drawbridge, the spare tire in the bed of the pickup bounced three feet in the air.

Main Street in New Iberia was quiet and empty when I parked in front of the poolroom. The oaks along the street stirred in the breeze, and out on the bayou the green and red running lights of a tug moved silently through the opened drawbridge. I could see the bridge tender in his little lighted office. Down the block a man in shirt sleeves, smoking a pipe, was walking his dog past the old brick Episcopalian church that had been used as a hospital by federal soldiers during the War Between the States.

The inside of the poolroom was like a partial return into the New Iberia of my youth, when people spoke French more often than English, when there were slot and race-horse machines in every bar, and the cribs on Railroad Avenue stayed open twenty-four hours a day and the rest of the world was as foreign to us as the Texans who arrived after World War II with their oil rigs and pipeline companies. A mahogany bar with a brass rail and spittoons ran the length of the room; there were four green-felt pool tables in back that the owner sometimes covered with oilcloth and served free gumbo on, and old men played *bourée* and dominoes under the wood-bladed fans that hung from the ceiling. The American and National League scores were written on a big chalkboard against one wall, and the television above the bar always seemed to have a baseball game on it. The room smelled of draft beer and gumbo and talcum, of whiskey and boiled crawfish and Virginia Extra tobacco, of pickled pig's feet and wine and Red Man.

The owner was named Tee Neg. He was an old-time pipeliner and oil-field roughneck who looked like a mulatto and who had three fingers pinched off by a drilling chain. I watched him draw a beer in a frosted schooner, rake the foam off with a ladle, and serve it with a jigger of neat whiskey to a man in denim clothes and a straw hat who stood at the bar and smoked a cigar.

"I hope you're here to play pool, Dave," Tee Neg said.

"Give me a bowl of gumbo."

"The kitchen's closed. You know that."

"Give me some *boudin*."

"They didn't bring me none today. You want a Dr Pepper?"

"I don't want anything."

"Suit yourself."

"Give me a cup of coffee."

"You look tired, you. Go home and sleep."

"Just bring me a cup of coffee, Tee Neg. Bring me a cigar, too."

"You don't smoke, Dave. What you mad at, you?"

"Nothing. I didn't eat tonight. I thought your kitchen was open. You got today's paper?"

"Sure."

"I'm just going to read the paper."

"Anyt'ing you want."

He reached under the bar and handed me a folded copy of the *Daily Iberian*. There were beer rings on the front page.

"Give those old gentlemen in back a round on me," I said.

"You don't have to do that."

"I want to."

"You don't have to do that, Dave." He looked at me steadily in the face.

"So I'm flush tonight."

"Okay, podna. But they buy you one, you go behind the bar and get it yourself. You don't use Tee Neg, no."

I shook open the paper and tried to read the sports page,

but my eyes wouldn't focus on the words. My skin itched, my face burned, my loins felt as though they were filled with concrete. I folded the paper, dropped it on the bar, and walked back outside into the late-spring night.

I drove down to the bay at Cypremort Point and sat on a jetty that extended out into the salt water and watched the tide go out. When the sun came up in the morning the sky was empty and looked as white as bone. Seagulls flew low over the wet, gray sand flats and pecked at the exposed shellfish, and I could smell the odor of dead fish on the wind. My clothes felt stiff and gritty with salt as I walked back to my truck. All the way back to town my visit to the poolroom remained as real and as unrelenting in its detail as a daylong hangover.

Later, Batist and I opened up the bait shop and dock, then I went up to the house and slept until early afternoon. When I woke, it was bright and warm, and the mockingbirds and blue jays were loud in the trees. Annie had left me two wax-paper-wrapped ham and onion sandwiches and a note on the kitchen table.

> *Didn't want to wake you but when I get back from town can you help me find a horny middle-aged guy with a white streak in his head who knows how to put a Kansas girl on rock 'n' roll?*
>
> Love,
> A.

> *P.S. Let's picnic in the park this evening and take Alafair to the baseball game. I'm sorry about last night. You'll always be my special guy, Dave.*

It was a generous and kind note. I should have been content with it. But it disturbed me as much as it reassured me, because I wondered if Annie, like most people who live with alcoholics, was not partly motivated by fear that my unpredictable mood might lead all of us back into the nightmarish world that AA had saved me from.

Regardless, I knew that the problems that had been caused us by the plane crash at Southwest Pass would not go away. And having grown up in a rural Cajun world that was virtually devoid of books, I had learned most of my lessons for dealing with problems from hunting and fishing and competitive sports. No book could have taught me what I had learned from my father in the marsh, and as a boxer in high school I had discovered that it was as important to swallow your blood and hide your injury as it was to hurt your opponent.

But maybe the most important lesson I had learned about addressing complexity was from an elderly Negro janitor who had once pitched for the Kansas City Monarchs in the old Negro leagues. He used to watch our games in the afternoon, and one day when I'd been shotgunned off the mound and was walking off the field toward the shower, he walked along beside me and said, "Sliders and screwballs is cute, and spitters shows 'em you can be nasty. But if you want to make that batter's pecker shrivel up, you throw a forkball at his head."

Maybe it was time to float one by the batter's head, I thought.

Bubba Rocque had bought a ruined antebellum home on the Vermilion River outside of Lafayette and had spent a quarter-million dollars rebuilding it. It was a massive plantation house, white and gleaming in the sun, the three-story Doric columns so thick that two men could not place their arms around them and touch hands. The front gallery was made of Italian marble; the second-story veranda ran completely around the building and was railed with ironwork from Seville and hung with boxes of petunias and geraniums. The brick carriage house had been expanded to a three-car garage; the stone wells were decorated with ornamental brass pulleys and buckets and planted with trumpet and passion vine; the desiccated wood outbuildings had been replaced with a clay tennis court.

The lawn was blue-green and glistening in the water sprinklers, dotted with oak, mimosa, and lime and orange trees, and the long gravel lane that led to the front door was bordered by a white fence entwined with yellow roses. A Cadillac convertible and a new cream-colored Oldsmobile were parked in front, and a fire-engine red collector's MG stuck out of the carriage house. Through the willows on the riverbank I could see a cigarette boat moored bow and stern to the dock, a tarp pulled down snugly on the cockpit.

It was hard to believe that this scene clipped out of *Southern Living* belonged to Bubba Rocque, the kid who used to train for a fight by soaking his hands in diluted muriatic acid and running five miles each morning with army boots on. An elderly Negro servant opened the door but didn't invite me in. Instead, he closed the door partly in my face and walked into the back of the house. Almost five minutes later I heard Bubba lean over the veranda and call down to me, "Go on in, Dave. I'll be right down. Sorry for our crummy manners. I was in the shower."

I let myself in and stood in the middle of the front hall under a huge chandelier and waited for him to come down the winding staircase that curled back into the second floor. The interior of the house was strange. The floors were blond oak, the mantelpiece carved mahogany, the furnishings French antiques. Obviously an expensive interior decorator had tried to recreate the Creole antebellum period. But somebody else had been at work, too. The cedar baseboards and ceiling boards had been painted with ivy vines; garish oil paintings of swampy sunsets, the kind you buy from sidewalk artists in New Orleans's Pirates Alley, hung over the couch and mantel; an aquarium filled with paddle wheels and plastic castles, even a rubber octopus stoppered to one side, sat in one window, green air bubbles popping from a clown's mouth.

Bubba came down the stairs on the balls of his feet. He wore white slacks and a canary-yellow golf shirt, sandals without socks and a gold neck chain, a gold wristwatch with a diamond-and-ruby face, and his spiked butch hair was bleached on the tips by the sun and his skin was tanned almost olive. He was still built like a fighter—his hips narrow, his stomach as flat as boiler plate, the shoulders an ax-handle wide, the arms longer than they should be, the knuckles as pronounced as ball bearings. But it was the wide-set, gray-blue eyes above the gap-toothed mouth that leaped at you more than anything else. They didn't focus, adjust, stray, or blink; they locked on your face and they stayed there. He smiled readily, in fact constantly, but you could only guess at whatever emotion the eyes contained.

"What's happening, Dave?" he said. "I'm glad you caught me when you did. I got to go down to New Orleans this afternoon. Come on out on the patio and have a drink. What do you think of my place?"

"It's impressive."

"It's more place than I need. I got a small house on Lake Pontchartrain and a winter house in Bimini. That's more my style. But the wife likes it here, and you're right, it impresses the hell out of people. You remember when you and me and your brother used to set pins in the bowling alley and the colored kids tried to run us off because we were taking their jobs?"

"My brother and I got fired. But I don't think they could have run you off with a shotgun, Bubba."

"Hey, those were hard times, podna. Come out here, I got to show you something."

He led me through some French doors onto a flagstone patio by a screen-enclosed pool. Overhead the sun shone through the spreading branches of an oak and glinted on the turquoise water. On the far side of the pool was a screened breezeway, with a peaked, shingled roof, that contained a universal gym, dumbbells, and a body and timing bag.

He grinned, went into a prizefighter's crouch, and feinted at me.

"You want to slip on the sixteen-ounce pillows and waltz around a little bit?" he said.

"You almost put out my lights the last time I went up against you."

"The hell I did. I got you in the corner and was knocking the sweat out of your hair all over the timekeeper and I still couldn't put you down. You want a highball? Clarence, bring us some shrimp and *boudin*. Sit down."

"I've got a problem you might be able to help me with."

"Sure. What are you drinking?" He took a pitcher of martinis out of a small icebox behind the wet bar.

"Nothing."

"That's right, I heard you were fighting the hooch for a while. Here, I got some tea. Clarence, bring those goddamn shrimp." He shook his head and poured himself a drink in a chilled martini glass. "He's half senile. Believe it or not, he used to work on the oyster boat with my old man. You remember my old man? He got killed two years ago on the SP tracks. I ain't kidding you. They say he took a nap right on the tracks with a wine bottle on his chest. Well, he always told me he wanted to be a traveling man, poor old bastard."

"A Haitian named Toot and maybe a guy by the name of Eddie Keats came to see me. They left a few stitches in my mouth and head. A bartender in Smiling Jack's on Bourbon told me he sicked them on me by calling one of your clubs."

Bubba sat down across the glass-topped table from me with his drink in his hand. His eyes were looking directly into mine.

"You better explain to me what you're saying."

"I think these guys job out for you. They also hurt a friend of mine," I said. "I'm going to square it, Bubba."

"Is that why you think you're sitting in my house?"

"You tell me."

"No, I'll tell you something else instead. I know Eddie Keats. He's from some toilet up North. He doesn't work for me. From what I hear, he doesn't put stitches in people's heads, he smokes them. The Haitian I never heard of. I'm telling you this because we went to school together. Now we eat some shrimp and *boudin* and we don't talk about this kind of stuff."

He ate a cold shrimp off a toothpick from the tray the Negro had placed on the table, then sipped from his martini and looked directly into my face while he chewed.

"A federal cop told me Eddie Keats jobs out for you," I said.

"Then he ought to do something about it."

"The feds are funny guys. I never figured them out. One day they're bored to death with a guy, the next day they run him through a sausage grinder."

"You're talking about Minos Dautrieve at the DEA, right? You know what his problem is? He's a coonass just like you and me, except he went to college and learned to talk like he didn't grow up down here. I don't like that. I don't like these things you're saying to me, either, Dave."

"You dealt the play, Bubba, when those two guys came out to my house."

He looked away at a sound in the front of the house, then tapped his fingertips on the glass tabletop. His nails were chewed back to the quick, and the fingertips were flat and grained.

"I'm going to explain it to you once because we're friends," he said. "I own a lot of businesses. I got a dozen oyster boats, I got a fish-packing house in New Iberia and one in Morgan City. I own seafood restaurants in Lafayette and Lake Charles, I own three clubs and an escort agency in New Orleans. I don't need guys like Eddie Keats. But I got to deal with all kinds of people in my business—Jews, dagos, broads with their brains between their legs, you name it. There's a labor lawyer in New Orleans I wouldn't spit on, but I pay him a five-thousand-dollar-a-year retainer so I don't get a picket in front of my clubs. So maybe I don't like everybody on my payroll, and maybe I don't always know what they do. That's business. But if you want me to, I'll make some calls and find out if somebody sent Keats and this colored guy after you. What's the name of this motormouth at Smiling Jack's?"

"Forget him. I already had a serious talk with him."

"Yeah?" He looked at me curiously. "Sounds mean."

"He thought so."

"Who's the friend that got hurt?"

"The friend is out of it."

"I think we got a problem with trust here."

"I don't read it that way. We're just establishing an understanding."

"No. I don't have to establish anything. You're my guest. I look at you and it's like yesterday I was watching you leaning over the spit bucket, your back trembling, blood all over your mouth, and all the time I was hoping you wouldn't come out for the third round. You didn't know it, but in the second you hit me so hard in the kidney I thought I was going to wet my jock."

"Did you know I found Johnny Dartez's body in that plane crash out at Southwest Pass, except his body disappeared?"

He laughed, cut a piece of *boudin*, and handed it to me on a cracker.

"I just ate," I said.

"Take it."

"I'm not hungry."

"Take it or you'll offend me. Christ, have you got a one-track mind. Listen, forget all these clowns you seem to be dragging around the countryside. I told you I have a lot of businesses and I hire people to run them I don't even like. You're educated, you're smart, you know how to make money. Manage one of my clubs in New Orleans, and I'll give you sixty thou a year, plus a percentage that can kick it up to seventy-five. You get a car, you cater trips to the Islands, you got your pick of broads."

"Did Immigration ever talk to you?"

"What?"

"After they busted Dartez and Victor Romero. They tried to smuggle in some high-roller Colombians. You must know that. I heard it in the street."

"You're talking about wetbacks or something now?"

"Oh, come on, Bubba."

"You want to talk about the spicks, find somebody else. I can't take them. New Orleans is crawling with them now. The government ought to send massive shipments of rubbers down to wherever they come from."

"The weird thing about this bust is that both these guys were mules. But they didn't go up the road, and they didn't have to finger anybody in front of a grand jury. What's that lead you to believe?"

"Nothing, because I don't care about these guys."

"I believe they went to work for the feds. If they'd been muling for me, I'd be nervous."

"You think I give a fuck about some greasers say they got something on me? You think I got this house, all these businesses because I run scared, because the DEA or Immigration or Minos Dautrieve with his thumb up his pink ass say a lot of bullshit they never prove, that they make up, that they tell to the newspapers or people that's dumb enough to listen to it?"

His eyes were bright, and the skin around his mouth was tight and gray.

"I don't know. I don't know what goes on inside you, Bubba," I said.

"Maybe if a person wants to find out, he's just got to keep fucking in the same direction."

"That's a two-way street, podna."

"Is that right?"

"Put it in the bank. I'll see you around. Thanks for the *boudin.*"

I stood up to leave, and he rose from the table with me. His face was flat, heated, as unknowable as a shark's. Then suddenly he grinned, ducked into a boxer's crouch again, bobbed, and feinted a left at my face.

"Hey, got you!" he said. "No shit, you flinched. Don't deny it."

I stared at him.

"What are you looking at?" he said. "All right, so I was hot. You come on pretty strong. I'm not used to that."

"I've got to go, Bubba."

"Hell, no. Let's slip on the pillows. We'll take it easy on each other. Hey, get this. I went to this full-contact karate club in Lafayette, you know, where they box with their feet like kangaroos or something. I'm in the ring with this guy, and he's grunting and swinging his dirty foot around in the air, and all these guys are yelling because they know he's going to cut my head off, and I stepped inside him real fast and busted him three times before he hit the deck. They had to lead him back to the dressing room like somebody took his brains out with an ice cream scoop."

"I'm over the hill for it, and I still have to work this afternoon, anyway."

"Bullshit. I can see it in your eyes. You'd still like to take me. It's that long reach. It's always a big temptation, isn't it?"

"Maybe."

I was almost disengaged from Bubba and his mercurial personality when his wife walked through the French doors onto the patio. She was at least ten years younger than he. Her black hair was tied with ribbon behind her head; her skin was dark, and she wore a two-piece red and yellow flower-print bathing suit with a matching sarong fastened on one hip. In her hand she carried an open shoe box filled with bottles and emery boards for her nails. She was pretty in the soft, undefined way that Cajun girls often are before they gain weight in their middle years. She smiled at me, sat at the patio table, crossed her legs, arching one sandal off her foot, and put a piece of *boudin* in her mouth.

"Dave, you remember Claudette, from New Iberia?" Bubba said.

"I'm sorry, I'm a little vague on people from home sometimes," I said. "I lived in New Orleans for fourteen years or so."

"I bet you remember her mother, Hattie Fontenot."

"Oh yes, I think I do," I said, my eyes flat.

"I bet you lost your cherry in one of her cribs on Railroad Avenue," Bubba said.

"I'm not always big on boyhood memories," I said.

"You and your brother had a paper route on Railroad Avenue. Are you going to tell me y'all never got paid in trade?"

"I guess I just don't remember."

"She had two colored joints on the corner," he said. "We used to go nigger-knocking down there, then get laid for two dollars."

"Bubba just likes to talk rough sometimes. It doesn't bother me. You don't have to be embarrassed," she said.

"I'm not."

"I'm not ashamed of my mother. She had a lot of good qualities. She didn't use profane language in polite company, unlike some people I know." She had a heavy Cajun accent, and her brown eyes had a strange red cast in them. They were as round as a doll's.

"Bubba, will you make me a gin rickey?" she said.

"Your thermos is in the icebox."

"So? I'd like one in a glass, please."

"She can drink gin rickeys all day and not get loaded," Bubba said. "I think she's got hollow buns."

"I don't think Dave is used to our kind of talk," she said.

"He's married too, isn't he?"

"Bubba . . ."

"What?"

"Would you please get me a drink?"

"All right," he said, taking the thermos and a chilled glass out of the icebox. "I wonder what I pay Clarence for. I damn near have to show him a diagram just to get him to dust."

He poured from the thermos into his wife's glass, then put it in front of her. He continued to look at her with an exasperated expression on his face.

"Look, I don't want to get on your case all the time, but

how about not filing your nails at the table?" he said. "I can do without nail filings in my food."

She wiped the powdered filings off the glass top with a Kleenex, then continued filing her nails over the shoe box.

"Well, I have to go. It was nice meeting you," I said.

"Yeah, I got to pack and get on the road, too. Walk him out to his truck, Claudette. I'm going to make some calls when I get to New Orleans. I find out somebody's been causing you problems, I'll cancel their act. That's a promise. By the way, that bartender better be out of town."

He looked at me a moment, balancing on the balls of his feet, then cocked his fists and jerked his shoulders at an angle as quickly as a rubber band snapping.

"Hey!" he said, grinned and winked, then walked back out the patio toward the circular staircase. His back was triangular, his butt flat, his thighs as thick as telephone posts.

His wife walked with me out to my pickup truck. The wind blew across the lawn and flattened the spray from the sprinklers into a rainbow mist among the trees. Gray clouds were building in the south, and the air was close and hot. Upstairs, Bubba had turned on a 1950s Little Richard record full blast.

"You really don't remember me?" she said.

"No, I'm sorry."

"I dated your brother, Jimmie, in New Orleans about ten years ago. One night we went out to visit you at your fish camp. You were really plastered and you kept saying that the freight train wouldn't let you sleep. So when it went by, you ran outside and shot it with a flare pistol."

I suddenly realized that Bubba's wife wasn't so uncomplicated after all.

"I'm afraid I was ninety-proof a lot of the time back then," I said.

"I thought it was funny."

I tried to be polite, but like most dry alcoholics I didn't want to talk about my drinking days with people who saw humor in them.

"Well, so long. I hope to see you again," I said.

"Do you think Bubba's crazy?"

"I don't know."

"His second wife left him two years ago. He burned all her clothes in the incinerator out back. He's not crazy, though. He just wants people to think he is because it scares them."

"That could be."

"He's not a bad man. I know all the stuff they say about him, but not many people know the hard time he had growing up."

"A lot of us had a hard time, Mrs. Rocque."

"You don't like him, do you?"

"I guess I just don't know your husband well, and I'd better go."

"You get embarrassed too easy."

"Mrs. Rocque, I wish you good luck because I think you're going to need it."

"I heard him offer you a job. You should take it. The people that work for him make a lot of money."

"Yes, they do, and there's a big cost to lots of other people."

"He doesn't make them do anything they don't already want to."

"Your mother ran brothels, but she wasn't a white-slaver and she didn't sell dope. The most polite thing I can say about Bubba is that he's a genuine sonofabitch. I don't even think he'd mind."

"I like you. Come have dinner with us sometime," she said. "I'm home a lot."

*   *   *   *   *

I drove back down the pea-gravel lane and headed toward New Iberia and the picnic in the park with Annie and Alafair. The sun was bright on the tin roofs of the barns set back in the sugarcane fields. The few moss-hung oaks along the road made deep pools of shadow on the road's surface. I had to feel sorry for Bubba's wife. In AA we called it denial. We take the asp to our breast and smile at the alarm we see in the eyes of others.

I had gotten to him when I mentioned Immigration busting two of his mules. Which made me wonder even more what role Immigration played in all of this. They had obviously stonewalled Minos Dautrieve at the DEA, and I believed they were behind the disappearance of Johnny Dartez's body after it was recovered from the plane crash by the Coast Guard. So if I was any kind of cop at all, why hadn't I dealt with Immigration head-on? They probably would have thrown me out of their office, but I also knew how to annoy bureaucrats, call their supervisors in Washington collect, and file freedom-of-information forms on them until their paint started to crack. So why hadn't I done it, I asked myself. And in answering my own question, I began to have a realization about presumption and denial in myself.

chapter
FIVE

ANNIE AND ALAFAIR WERE WRAPPING FRIED CHICKEN IN wax paper and fixing lemonade in a thermos when I got back home. I sat at the kitchen table with a glass of iced tea and mint leaves and looked out the window at the blue jays swooping over the mimosa tree in the backyard. The ducks in my pond were shaking water off their backs and waddling to the bank in the shade created by the cattails.

"I feel foolish about something," I said.

"We'll take care of that tonight," she said, and smiled.

"Something else."

"Oh."

"Years ago when I was a patrolman there was a notorious street character in the Quarter named Dock Stratton. The welfare office would give him a meal-and-lodging ticket at one of their contract hotels, and he'd check into the place, then throw all the furniture out the window—tables, chairs, dresser drawers, lamps, mattresses, everything he could squeeze through the window, it would all come crashing down on the sidewalk. Then he'd run downstairs before anybody could call the heat and haul everything to the secondhand store. But no matter what this guy did, we never busted him. I was new and didn't understand. The other guys told me it was because Dock was a barfer. If he got a finger loose in the back of the car, he'd stick it down his throat and puke all over the seats. He'd do it in a lineup, in a holding cell, in a courtroom. He was always cocked and ready to fire. This guy was so bad a guard at the jail threatened to quit rather than take him on the chain to morning court. So Dock was allowed to drive welfare workers and skid-row hotel managers crazy for years, and when rookies like me asked why, we got treated to a good story.

"Except I discovered there was another reason why Dock stayed on the street. He not only knew every hustler and thief in downtown New Orleans, but he'd been a locksmith before he melted his head with Thunderbird, and he could get into a place faster than a professional house creep. So there were a couple of detectives in robbery and homicide who would use him when things weren't working right in a case. One time they knew a hit man from Miami was in town to take out a labor union agent. They told Dock they were making him a special agent with the New Orleans police department and got him to open up the guy's motel room, steal his gun, his suit-case, all his clothes and traveler's checks, then they picked up the guy on suspicion—it was a Friday, so they could hold him until Monday morning—and kept him in a small cell for two days with three drag queens."

"What's the point?" Annie said. Her voice was flat, and her eyes looked at the sunlight in the trees when she spoke.

"Cops leave certain things and people in place for a reason."

"I know those people you talk about are funny and unusual and interesting and all that, Dave, but why not leave them in the past?"

"You remember that guy from Immigration that came around here? He's never been back to the house, has he? He could make a lot of trouble for us if he wanted to, but he hasn't. I told myself that was because I'd given him reason to avoid us."

"Maybe he has other things to do. I just don't think the government is going to be interested in one little girl." She wore a pair of wash-faded Levi's and a white sun halter, and I could see the brown spray of sun freckles on her back. Her hips creased softly above her belt line while she filled the picnic hamper at the drainboard.

"The government is interested in what they choose to be interested in," I said. "Right now I think they've got us on hold. They sent me a signal, but I didn't see it."

"To tell you honestly, this sounds like something of your own creation."

"That guy from Immigration, Monroe, was asking questions about us at the sheriff's office. He didn't need to do that. He could have cut a warrant, come out here, and done anything he wanted. Instead, he or somebody above him wanted me to know their potential in case I thought I could make problems for them about Johnny Dartez."

"Who cares what they do?" Annie said.

"I don't think you appreciate the nature of bureaucratic machinery once it's set in motion."

"I'm sorry. I'm just not going to invest my life in speculating about what people can do to me."

Alafair was looking back and forth between the two of us, her face clouded with the tone of our voices. Annie had dressed her in pink shorts, a Mickey Mouse T-shirt, and pink tennis shoes with the words LEFT and RIGHT stamped boldly on the rubber tip of each shoe. Annie rubbed her hand over Alafair's head and gave her the plastic draw bag in which we kept the old bread.

"Go feed the ducks," she said. "We'll leave in a minute."

"Feed ducks?"

"Yes."

"Feed ducks now?"

"That's right."

"Dave viene al parque?"

"Sure, he's coming," Annie said.

Alafair grinned at me and went out the back screen to the pond. The sunlight through the trees made patterns on her brown legs.

"I'll tell you one thing, Dave. No matter what those people from Immigration do, they're not going to take her away. She's ours, just as if we had conceived her."

"I didn't tell you the rest of the story about Dock Stratton. After he finished blowing out his wiring with synthetic wine and wasn't any good to anybody, they shipped him off to the asylum at Mandeville."

"So what does this mean? Are you going to become the knight-errant, tilting with the U.S. government?"

"No."

"Do you still want to go to the park?"

"That's the reason I came home, kiddo."

"I wonder, I really do," she said.

"I'd appreciate it if you'd explain that."

"Don't you see it, Dave? It's like you want to taint every moment in our lives with this conspiratorial vision of yours. It's become an obsession. We don't talk about anything else. Either that or you stare into space. How do you think I feel?"

"I'll try to be different."

"I know."

"I really will."

Her eyes were wet. She sat down across the table from me.

"We haven't been able to have our own child. Now one's been given to us," she said. "That should make us the happiest people in the world. Instead, we fight and worry about what hasn't happened yet. Our conversation at home is filled with the names of people who shouldn't have anything to do with our lives. It's like deliberately inviting an obscene presence into your home. Dave, you say at AA they teach you to give it all up to your Higher Power. Can't you try that? Just give it up, cut it out of your life? There's not a problem in the world that time can't help in some way."

"That's like saying a black tumor on your brain will get better if you don't think about it."

The kitchen was silent. I could hear the blue jays in the mimosa tree and the wings of the ducks beating across the pond as Alafair showered bread crumbs down on their heads. Annie turned away, finished wrapping the fried chicken, closed the picnic hamper, and walked out to the pond. The screen door banged on the jamb after her.

That evening there was a big crowd in the park for the baseball game, and the firemen were having a crawfish boil in the open-air pavilion. The twilight sky was streaked with lilac and pink, and the wind was cool out of the south with the promise of rain. We ate our picnic supper on a wooden table under the oak trees and watched the American Legion game and the groups of high school and college kids who drifted back and forth between the bleachers and the tailgates of pickup trucks where they kept beer in washtubs on ice. Out on the bayou the paddle-wheel pleasure boat with its lighted decks slid by against the dark outline of cypress and the antebellum homes on the far bank. The trees were full of barbecue smoke, and you could smell the crawfish from the pavilion and the hot *boudin* that a Negro sold from a handcart. Then I heard a French string band play "Jolie Blonde" in the pavilion, and I felt as though once again I were looking through a hole in the dimension at the south Louisiana in which I had grown up.

> *Jolie blonde, gardez donc c'est t'as fait.*
> *Ta m'as quit-té pour t'en aller,*
> *Pour t'en aller avec un autre que moi.*
> *Jolie blonde, pretty girl,*
> *Flower of my heart,*
> *I'll love you forever*
> *My jolie blonde.*

But seldom did Annie and I speak directly to each other. Instead we talked brightly to Alafair, walked her to the swing sets and seesaws, bought snowcones, and avoided one another's eyes. That night in the almost anonymous darkness of our bedroom we made love. We did it in need, with our eyes closed, without words, with a kiss only at the end. As I lay on my back, arms across my eyes, I felt her fingers leave the top of my hand, felt her turn on her side toward the opposite wall, and I wondered if her heart was as heavy as mine.

I woke up a half hour later. The room was cool from the wind sucked through the window by the attic fan, but my skin was hot as though I had sunburn, the stitches in my scalp itched, my palms were damp on my thighs when I sat on the side of the bed.

Without waking Annie, I washed my face, put on a pair of khakis and an old Hawaiian shirt, and went down to the bait shop. The moon was up, and the willows along the bank of the bayou looked silver in the light. I sat in the darkness at the counter and stared out the window at the water and the outboard boats and pirogues knocking gently against the posts on my dock. Then I got up, opened the beer cooler, and took out a handful of partly melted ice and rubbed it on my face and neck. The amber necks of the beer bottles glinted in the moon's glow. The smooth aluminum caps, the wet and shining labels, the brassy beads inside the bottles were like an illuminated nocturnal still life. I closed the box, turned on the lightbulb over the counter, and called Lafayette information for Minos P. Dautrieve's home number.

A moment later I had him on the phone. I looked at the clock. It was midnight.

"What's happening, Dunkenstein?" I said.

"Oh boy," he said.

"Sorry about the hour."

"What do you want, Robicheaux?"

"Where are these clubs that Eddie Keats owns?"

"You called me up to ask me that?"

I didn't answer, and I heard him take a breath.

"The last time we talked, you hung up the phone in my ear," he said. "I didn't appreciate that. I think you have a problem with manners."

"All right, I apologize. Will you tell me where these clubs are?"

"I'll be frank about something else, too. Are you drinking?"

"No. How about the clubs?"

"I guess things never work fast enough for you, do they? So you're going to cowboy our Brooklyn friend?"

"Give me some credit."

"I try to. Believe me," he said.

"There are a dozen people I can call in Lafayette who'll give me the same information."

"Yeah, which makes me wonder why you had to wake me up."

"You ought to know the answer to that."

"I don't. I'm really at a loss. You're truly a mystery to us. You don't hear what you're told, you make up your own rules, you think your past experience as a police officer allows you to mess around in federal business."

"I'm talking to you because you're the only guy around here with the brains and juice to put these people away," I said.

"I'm not flattered."

"So it's no dice, huh?"

He paused.

"Look, Robicheaux, I think you have a cinder block for a head, but basically you're a decent guy," he said. "That means we don't want you hurt anymore. Stay out of it. Have some faith in us. I don't know why you went out to Bubba Rocque's house this afternoon, but I don't think it was smart. You don't—"

"How'd you know I was out there?"

"We have somebody who writes down license tags for us. You don't flush these guys out by flipping lighted matches at them. If you do, they pick the time and the place and you lose. Anyway, go to bed and forget Eddie Keats, at least for tonight."

"Does he have a family?"

"No, he's a gash-hound."

"Thanks, Minos. I'm sorry I woke you up."

"It's all right. By the way, how'd you like Bubba Rocque's wife?"

"I suspect she's ambitious more than anything else."

"What a romantic. She's a switch-hitter, podna. Five years ago she did a three-spot for shanking another dyke. That Bubba can really pick them, can't he?"

I called an old bartender friend in Lafayette. Minos had given me more information than he thought. The bartender told me Keats owned two bars, one in a hotel off Canal in New

Orleans, the other on the Breaux Bridge highway outside of
Lafayette. If he was at either bar, and if what Minos had said
about him was correct, I knew which one he would probably
be in.

When I was in college, the Breaux Bridge highway contained a string of all-night lowlife bars, oilfield supply yards,
roadhouses, a quarter horse track, gambling joints, and one
Negro brothel. You could find the pimps, hoods, whores, ex-
cons, and white-knuckle crazies of your choice there every Saturday night. Emergency flares burned next to the wrecked
automobiles and shattered glass on the two-lane blacktop, the
dance floors roared with electronic noise and fistfights. You
could get laid, beat up, shanked, and dosed with clap, all in
one night and for less than five dollars.

I parked across the road from the Jungle Room. Eddie Keats
had kept up the tradition. His bar was a flat, wide building
constructed of cinder blocks that were painted purple and then
overprinted with green coconut palms that were illuminated by
the floodlights that were hung in the oak trees in front. But I
could see two house trailers in the back parking lot, which was
kept dark, that were obviously being used by Keats's hot-
pillow action. I waited a half hour and did not see the white
Corvette.

I had no plan, really, and I knew that I should have listened
to Minos's advice. But I still had that same hot flush to my
skin, my breath was quicker than it should have been, my back
teeth ground together without my being aware of it. At 1:30
A.M. I stuck the .45 down in the front of my khakis, pulled my
Hawaiian shirt over the butt, and walked across the road.

The front door, which was painted fingernail-polish red,
was partly open to let out the smoke from inside. Only the bar
area and a pool table in a side room were lighted, and the
dance floor in back that was enclosed by a wooden rail, where

a red-headed girl who had powdered her body heavily to cover her freckles was grinning and taking off her clothes while the rockabilly band in the corner pounded it out. The men at the bar were mostly pipeliners and oilfield roughnecks and roustabouts. The white-collar johns stayed in the darkness at the tables and booths. The waitresses wore black cut-off blouses that exposed the midriff, black high heels, and pink shorts so tight that every anatomical line was etched through the cloth.

A couple of full-time hookers were at the bar, and with a sideways flick of their eyes, in the middle of their conversation with the oilfield workers, they took my inventory as I walked past them to one of the booths. Above the bar a monkey in a small cage sat listlessly on a toy trapeze among a litter of peanut shells and his own droppings.

I knew I was going to have to order a drink. This wasn't a place where I could order a 7-Up without either telling them I was a cop or some other kind of bad news. I just wasn't going to drink it. I wasn't going to drink it. The waitress brought me a Jax that cost three dollars. She was pretty, and she smiled at me and poured from the bottle into my glass.

"There's a two-drink minimum for the floor show," she said. "I'll come back when you're ready for your second."

"Has Toot been in?" I said.

"Who?"

"Eddie's friend, the black guy."

"I'm new. I don't guess I know him," she said, and went away.

A few minutes later three of the oilfield workers went out and left one of the hookers alone at the bar. She finished her drink, picked up her cigarette from the ashtray, and walked toward my booth. She wore white shorts with a dark blue blouse, and her black hair was tied off her neck with a blue bandanna. Her face was round and she was slightly overweight, and when she sat next to me I could smell her hair spray, her perfume, and a nicotine odor that went deep into the lungs. In the glow of light from the bar, her facial hair was stiff with makeup. Her eyes, which never quite focused on my face, were glazed with alcohol, and her lips seemed to constantly suppress a smile that had nothing to do with either of us.

The waitress arrived right behind her. She ordered a champagne cocktail. Her accent was northern. I watched her light a cigarette and blow smoke up into the air as though it were a stylized art.

"Has Toot been around lately?" I said.

"You mean the space-o boon?" she said. Her eyes had a smile in them while she looked abstractly at the bar.

"That sounds like him."

"What are you interested in him for?"

"I just haven't seen him or Eddie for a while."

"You interested in girls?"

"Sometimes."

"I bet you'd like a little piece in your life, wouldn't you?"

"Maybe."

"If you don't get a little piece, it really messes you up inside, doesn't it? It makes everything real hard for you." She put her hand on my thigh and worked her fingers on my knee.

"What time is Eddie going to be in?"

"You're trying to pump me, hon. That's going to give me bad thoughts about you."

"It's just a question."

Her lips made an exaggerated pout, and she raised her hand, touched my cheek, and slid it down my chest.

"I'm going to think maybe you're not interested in girls, that maybe you're here for the wrong reasons," she said.

Then her hand went lower and hit the butt of the .45. Her

eyes looked straight into mine. She started to get up, and I put my hand on top of her arm.

"You're a cop," she said.

"It doesn't matter what I am. Not to you, anyway. You're not in trouble. Do you understand that?"

The alcohol shine had gone from her eyes, and her face had the look of someone caught between fear and an old anger.

"Where's Eddie?" I said.

"He goes to dogfights sometimes in Breaux Bridge, then comes in here and counts the receipts. You want some real trouble, get in his face and see what happens."

"But that doesn't concern you, does it? You've got nothing to gain by concerning yourself with other people's problems, do you? Do you have a car?"

"What?"

"A car." I pressed her arm slightly.

"Yeah, what d'you think?"

"When I take my hand off your arm you're going on your break. You're going out the door for some fresh air, and you're not going to talk to anybody, and you're going to drive your car down the road and have a late supper somewhere, and that phone on the bar is not going to ring, either."

"You're full of shit."

"Make your choice, hon. I think this place is going to be full of cops tonight. You want to be part of it, that's cool." I took my hand away from her arm.

"You sonofabitch."

I looked at the front door. Her eyes went angrily over my face again, then she slid off the vinyl seat and walked to the bar, the backs of her legs creased from sitting in the booth, and asked the bartender for her purse. He handed it to her, then went back to washing glasses, and she went out a side door into the parking lot.

Ten minutes later the phone did ring, but the bartender never looked in my direction while he talked, and after he hung up he fixed himself a scotch and milk and then started emptying ashtrays along the bar. I knew, however, that I didn't have long before her nerves broke. She was afraid of me or of cops in general, but she was also afraid of Eddie Keats, and eventually she would call to see if a bust or a shooting had gone down and try to make the best of her situation.

I had another problem, too. The next floor show was about to start, and the waitress was circling through the tables, making sure everyone had had his two-drink minimum. I turned in the booth and let my elbow knock the beer bottle off the table.

"I'm sorry," I said when she came over. "Let me have another one, will you?"

She picked up the bottle from the floor and started to wipe down the table. The glow from the bar made highlights in her blond hair. Her body had the firm lines of somebody who had done a lot of physical work in her life.

"You didn't want company?" she said.

"Not now."

"Expensive booze for a dry run."

"It's not so bad." I looked at the side of her face as she wiped the rag in front of me.

"It's the wrong place for trouble, sugar," she said quietly.

"Do I look like bad news?"

"A lot of people do. But the guy that owns this place really is. For kicks, he heats up the wires in that monkey's cage with a cigarette lighter."

"Why do you work here?"

"I couldn't get into the convent," she said, and walked away with her drink tray as though a door were closing behind her.

Later a muscular, powerful man came in, sat at the bar, had

the bartender bring him a collins, and began shelling peanuts from a bowl and eating them while he talked to one of the hookers. He wore purple suede cowboy boots, expensive cream-colored slacks, a maroon V-necked terrycloth shirt, and gold chains and medallions around his neck. His long hair was dyed blond and combed straight back like a professional wrestler's. He took his package of Picayune cigarettes from his pants pocket and set it on the bar while he shelled peanuts from the bowl. He couldn't see me because I was sitting far back in the gloom and he had no reason to look in my direction, but I could see his face clearly, and even though I had never seen it before, its details had the familiarity of a forgotten dream.

His head was big, the neck as thick as a stump, the eyes green and full of energy; a piece of cartilage flexed behind the jawbone while he ground peanuts between his back teeth. The tanned skin around his mouth was so taut that it looked as if you could strike a kitchen match on it. His hands were big, too—the fingers like sausages, the wrists corded with veins. The hooker smoked a cigarette and tried to look cool while he talked to her, watching the red tracings of her cigarette in the bar mirror, but whenever she replied to him her voice seemed to come out in a whisper.

However, I had no trouble hearing his voice. It sounded like there was a blockage in the nasal passages; it was a voice that didn't say but told things to people. In this case he was telling the hooker that she had to square her tab, that she was juicing too much, that the Jungle Room wasn't a trough where a broad got free soda straws.

I said earlier I didn't have a plan. That wasn't true. Every drunk always has a plan. The script is written in the unconscious. We recognize it when the moment is convenient.

I slipped sideways out of the vinyl booth. I almost drank from the filled beer glass before I did. In my years as a practicing alcoholic I never left an unemptied glass or bottle on a table, and I always got down the last shot before I made a hard left turn down a one-way street. Old habits die hard.

I took down one of the cues from the wall rack by the entrance to the poolroom. It was tapered and made of smooth-sanded ash and weighted heavily at the butt end. He didn't pay attention to me as I walked toward him. He was talking to the bartender now, snapping peanut shells apart with his thick thumb and popping the nuts into his mouth. Then his green eyes turned on me, focused in the dim light, his glance concentrating as though there were a stitch across the bridge of his nose, then he brushed his hands clean and swiveled the stool casually so that he was facing me directly.

"You're on my turf, butthole," he said. "Start it and you'll lose. Walk on out the door and you're home free."

I kept walking toward him and didn't answer. I saw the expression in his eyes change, the way green water can suddenly cloud with a groundswell. He reached over the bar for a collins bottle, the change rattling in his slacks, one boot twisted inside the brass foot rail. But he knew it was too late, and his left arm was already rising to shield his head.

Most people think of violence as an abstraction. It never is. It's always ugly, it always demeans and dehumanizes, it always shocks and repels and leaves the witnesses to it sick and shaken. It's meant to do all these things.

I held the pool cue by the tapered end with both hands and whipped it sideways through the air as I would a baseball bat, with the same force and energy and snap of the wrists, and broke the weighted end across his left eye and the bridge of his nose. I felt the wood knock into bone, saw the skin split, saw the green eye almost come out of its socket, heard him clatter against the bar and go down on the brass rail with his hands cupped to his nose and the blood roaring between his fingers.

He pulled his knees up to his chin in the litter of cigarette butts and peanut hulls. He couldn't talk and instead trembled all over. The bar was absolutely silent. The bartender, the hookers, the oilfield workers in their hardhats, the waitresses in their pink shorts and cut-off blouses, the rockabilly musicians, the half-undressed mulatto stripper on the dance floor, all stood like statues in the floating layers of cigarette smoke.

I heard someone dial a telephone as I walked out into the night air.

The next morning I drove into New Iberia and picked up a supply of red worms, nightcrawlers, and shiners. It was a clear, warm day with a little wind, and I rented out almost all my boats. While I worked behind the counter in the bait shop and, later, started the fire in the barbecue pit for the lunch customers, I kept looking down the dirt road for a sheriff's car. But none came. At noon I called Minos Dautrieve at the DEA in Lafayette.

"I need to come in and talk to you," I said.

"No, I'll come over there. Stay out of Lafayette."

"Why's that?"

"I don't think the town's ready for Wyatt Earp this morning."

An hour later he came down the dirt road and under the oak trees in a government car, parked by the dock, and walked into the shop. He stooped automatically as he came through the door. He wore a pair of seersucker slacks, shined loafers, a light blue sports shirt, and a red and gray striped tie pulled loose at the collar. His scalp and crewcut blond hair shone in the light. He looked around the shop and nodded with a smile on his face.

"You've got a nice business here," he said.

"Thanks."

"It's too bad you're not content to just run it and stop overextending yourself."

"You want a soft drink or a cup of coffee?"

"Don't be defensive. You're a legend this morning. I came into the office late, because somebody woke me up last night, and everybody was having a big laugh about the floor show at the Jungle Room. I told you we don't get to have that kind of fun. We just fill out forms, advise the slime-o's of their rights, and make sure they have adequate counsel to stay on the street. I heard they had to use a mop to soak up all the blood."

"Are they cutting a warrant?"

"He wouldn't sign the complaint. A sheriff's detective took it to the hospital on a clipboard."

"But he identified me?"

"He didn't have to. One of his hookers got your license number. Eddie Keats doesn't like courtrooms. You're going to walk out of it through no fault of your own. But don't mess with the Lafayette cops anymore. They get provoked when somebody comes into their parish and thinks he can start strumming heads with a pool cue."

"Too bad. They should have rousted him when I got my face kicked in."

"I'm worried about you. You don't hear well."

"I haven't been sleeping a lot lately. Save it for another time, all right?"

"I'm perplexed, too. I know you've been into some heavy-metal shit before, but I didn't figure you for a cowboy. You know, you could have put out that guy's light."

Two fishermen came in and bought a carton of worms and a dozen bottles of beer for their ice chest. I rang up their money on my old brass cash register and watched them walk out into the bright sunlight.

"Let's take a ride," I said.

I left Batist in charge of the shop, and Minos and I rode down the dirt lane in my pickup. The sunlight seemed to click through the thick green leaves overhead.

"I called you up for a specific reason this morning," I said. "If you don't like the way I do things, I'm sorry. You're not in the hotbox, partner. I didn't invite any of this bullshit into my life, but I got it just the same. So I don't think it's too cool when you start making your observations in the middle of my shop, in front of my help and customers."

"Okay. You've got your point."

"I never busted up a guy like that before. I don't feel good about it."

"It's always dumb to play on the wiseguys' terms. But if you needed to scramble somebody's eggs, Keats was a fine selection. I told you about him torching the whore in New Orleans. But believe it or not, we have a couple of things in his file that are even worse. The kid of a federal witness disappeared a year ago. We found him in a—"

"Then why don't you put the fucker away?"

He didn't answer. He turned the wind vane in his face and looked out at the Negro families fishing in the shade of the cypress trees.

"Is he feeding you guys?" I said.

"We don't use hit men as informants."

"Don't jerk me around, Minos. You use whatever works."

"Not hit men. Never. Not in my office." He turned and looked me directly in the face. There was color in his cheeks.

"Then give him a priority and weld the door shut on him."

"You think you're twisting in the wind while we play pocket pool. But maybe we're doing things you don't know about. Look, we never go for just one guy. You know that. We throw a net over a whole bunch of these shitheads at once.

That's the only way we get them to testify against each other. Try learning some patience."

"You want Bubba Rocque. You've got a file on everybody around him. In the meantime his clowns are running loose with baseball bats."

"I think you're unteachable. Why did you call me up, anyway?"

"About Immigration."

"I didn't eat breakfast this morning. Stop up here somewhere."

"You know this guy Monroe that was sniffing around New Iberia?"

"Yeah, I know him. Are you worried about the little girl you have in your house?"

I looked at him.

"You have a way of constantly earning our attention," he said. "Stop there. I'm really hungry. You can pay for it, too. I left my wallet on the dresser this morning."

I stopped at a small wooden lunch stand run by a Negro, set back in a grove of oak trees. We sat at one of the tables in the shade and ordered pork chop sandwiches and dirty rice. The smoke from the stove hung in the sunlit branches of the trees.

"What's this about Immigration?" Minos said.

"I heard they busted both Johnny Dartez and Victor Romero."

"Where'd you get that?" He watched some black children playing pitch-and-catch next to the lunch stand. But I could see that his eyes were troubled.

"From a bartender in New Orleans."

"Sounds like a crummy source."

"No games. You knew that a government agency of some kind had a connection with Dartez or his body wouldn't have disappeared. You just weren't sure about Victor Romero."

"So?"

"I think Immigration was using these guys to infiltrate the sanctuary movement."

He put his hand on his chin and watched the children throwing the baseball.

"What does your bartender friend know about Romero now?" he said.

"Nothing."

"What's this guy's name? We'd like to chat with him."

"So would Bubba Rocque. That means that Jerry—that's his name, and he works at Smiling Jack's on Bourbon—is probably looking for a summer home in Afghanistan."

"You never disappoint me. So you've managed to help scare an informant out of town. Just out of curiosity, how is it that people tell you these things they don't care to share with us?"

"I stuck a cocked .45 up his nose."

"That's right, I forgot. You learned a lot of constitutional procedure from the New Orleans police department."

"I'm correct, though, aren't I? Somehow Immigration got these two characters into the underground railway, or whatever the sanctuary people call it."

"That's what they call it. And no matter what you might have figured out, it's still not your business. Of course, that doesn't make any difference to you. So I'll put it another way. We're nice guys at the DEA. We try to lodge as many lowlifes as we can in our gray-bar hotel chain. And we respect guys like you who are well intended but who have their brains encased in cement. But my advice to you is not to fuck with Immigration, particularly when you have an illegal in your home."

"You don't like them."

"I don't think about them. But you should. I once met a regional INS commissioner, an important man wired right into the White House. He said, 'If you catch 'em, you ought to clean 'em and fry 'em yourself.' I wouldn't want somebody like that on my case."

"It sounds like folksy bullshit to me," I said.

"You're a delight, Robicheaux."

"I don't want to mess up your lunch, but aren't you bothered by the fact that maybe a bomb sent that plane down at Southwest Pass, that somebody murdered a Catholic priest and two women who were fleeing a butcher shop we helped create in El Salvador?"

"Are you an expert on Central American politics?"

"No."

"Have you been down there?"

"No."

"But you give me that impression just the same. Like you've got the franchise on empathy."

"I think you need a whiff of a ville that's been worked over with Zippo-tracks."

"Don't give me that righteous dogshit. I was there, too, podna." The bread in the side of his mouth made an angry lump along his jaw.

"Then don't let those farts at Immigration jerk you around."

He put his sandwich in his plate, drank from his iced tea, and looked away reflectively at the children playing under the trees.

"Have you ever thought that maybe you'd be better off drunk than sober?" he said. "I'm sorry. I really didn't mean that. What I meant to say is I just remembered that I have a check in my shirt pocket. I'll pay for my own lunch today. No, don't argue. It's just been a real pleasure being out with you."

*   *   *   *

The inside of the church was cool and dark and smelled of stone, burning candles, water, and incense. Through the side door I could see the enclosed garden where, as a child, I used to line up with the other children before we made the Stations of the Cross on Good Friday. It was sunny in the garden, and the St. Augustine grass was green and clipped, and the flower beds were full of yellow and purple roses. At the head of the garden, shaded by a rain tree with bloodred blooms on it, was a rock grotto with a waterfall at the bottom and a stone statue of the crucified Christ set back in the recess.

I walked into the confessional and waited for the priest to slide back the small wooden door in the partition. I had known him for twenty-five years, and I trusted his working-class instincts and forgave him his excess of charity and lack of admonition, just as he forgave me for my sins. He slid back the door, and I looked through the wire screen at the round head, the bull neck, the big shoulders in silhouette. He had a small, rubber-bladed fan in the box with him, and his crewcut gray hair moved slightly in the breeze.

I told him about Eddie Keats. Everything. The beating I took, the humiliation, the pool cue shattered across his face, the blood stringing from the fingers cupped over his nose.

The priest was quiet a moment.

"Did you want to kill this man?" he said.

"No."

"Are you sure of that?"

"Yes."

"Do you plan to hurt him again?"

"Not if he leaves me alone."

"Then put it behind you."

I didn't reply. We were both quiet in the gloom of the box.

"Are you still bothered?" he said.

"Yes."

"Dave, you've made your confession. Don't try to judge the right and wrong of what you did. Let it go. Perhaps what you did was wrong, but you acted with provocation. This man threatened your wife. Don't you think the Lord can understand your feelings in a situation like that?"

"That's not why I did it."

"I'm sorry, I don't understand."

"I did it because I want to drink. I burn inside to drink. I want to drink all the time."

"I don't know what to say."

I walked out the side door of the church into the garden. I could hear the waterfall in the grotto, and the odor of the yellow and purple roses and the red flowers on the rain tree was heavy and sweet in the warm, enclosed air. I sat on the stone bench by the grotto and stared at the tops of my shoes.

Later I found Annie weeding the vegetable garden behind our old smokehouse. She was barefoot and wore blue jeans and a denim shirt with no sleeves. She was on her hands and knees in the row, and she pulled the weeds from between the tomato plants and dropped them into a bucket. Her face was hot with her work. I had told her that morning in bed about Eddie Keats. She had said nothing in reply, but had merely gone into the kitchen and started breakfast.

"I think maybe you should go visit your family in Kansas and take Alafair along," I said. I had a glass of iced tea in my hand.

"Why?" She didn't look up.

"That guy Keats."

"You think he's going to come around?"

"I don't know. Sometimes when you bash his kind hard

enough, they stay away from you. But then sometimes you can't tell. There's no point in taking chances."

She dropped a handful of weeds into the bucket and stood up from her work. There was a smear of dirt and perspiration on her forehead. I could smell the hot, dusky odor of the tomato plants in the sunlight.

"Why didn't you think of that earlier?" she said. She looked straight ahead.

"Maybe I made a mistake. I still want you and Alafair to go to Kansas."

"I don't want to sound melodramatic, Dave. But I don't make decisions in my life or my family's because of people like this."

"Annie, this is serious."

"Of course it is. You're trying to be a rogue cop of some kind, and at the same time you have a family. So you'd like to get one part of the problem out of Louisiana."

"At least give it some thought."

"I already did. This morning for about five seconds. Forget it," she said, and walked to the coulee with the weed-filled bucket and shook the weeds down the bank.

When she came back she continued to look at me seriously, then suddenly she laughed.

"Dave, you're just too much," she said. "At least you could offer us Biloxi or Galveston. You remember what you said about Kansas when you visited there? 'This is probably the only place in the United States that would be improved by nuclear war.' And now you'd like to ship me back there?"

"All right, Biloxi."

"No deal, baby love." She walked toward the shade of the backyard, the bucket brushing back and forth against her pants leg.

* * * *

That evening we went to a *fais dodo* in St. Martinville. The main street was blocked off for the dancers, and an Acadian string band and a rock 'n' roll group took turns playing on a wooden platform set back against Bayou Teche. The tops of the trees were green against the lavender and pink light in the sky, and the evening breeze blew through the oaks in the churchyard where Evangeline and her lover were buried. For some reason the rock 'n' roll music in southern Louisiana has never changed since the 1950s. It still sounds like Jimmie Reed, Fats Domino, Clifton Chenier, and Albert Ammons. I sat at a wooden table not far from the bandstand, with a paper plate of rice and red beans and fried *sac-a-lait*, and watched the dancers and listened to the music while Annie took Alafair down the street to find a rest room.

Then rain clouds blackened the western sun temporarily and the wind came up strong and blew leaves, newspapers, beer cups, and paper plates through the streets. But the band kept playing, as though the threat of rain or even an electric storm were no more important a consideration than time and mortality, and for some reason I began to muse on why any of us are what we are, either for good or bad. I didn't choose to be an alcoholic, to have the oral weakness of a child for a bottle, but nevertheless that self-destructive passion, that genetic or environmental wound festered every day at the center of my life. Then I thought about a sergeant in my platoon who was perhaps the finest man I ever knew. If environment was the shaping and determining factor in our lives, his made no sense.

He grew up in a soot-covered foundry town in Illinois, one of those places where the sky is forever seared with smoke and cluttered with the blackened tops of factories and the river so polluted with chemicals and sludge that once it actually caught fire. He lived with his mother in a block of row houses, a world that was bordered on one end by a Saturday-night beer joint and pool hall and on the other by his job as a switchman in the train yard. By all odds he should have been one of those people who live out their lives in a gray and undistinguished way with never a bolder ambition than a joyless marriage and a cost-of-living raise. Instead, he was both brave and compassionate, caring about his men and uncompromising in his loyalties; his intelligence and courage carried both of us through when mine sometimes failed. But even though we served together for seven months, I'll always retain one essential image of him that seemed to define both him and what is best in our country's people.

We had just gotten back to a hot, windblown firebase after two days in Indian country and a firefight in which the Viet Cong were sometimes five feet from us. We had lost four men and we were drained and sick and exhausted the way you are when even in sleep you feel that you're curled inside a wooden box of your own pain and your soul twitches like a rubber band. I had taken my platoon down a trail at night, a stupid and reckless act, had walked into their ambush, lost our point man immediately, and had gotten flanked, and there was only one person to blame for it—me. Although it was now noon and the sun was as hot and bright as a welder's arc overhead, in my mind's eye I still saw the flash of the AK-47s against the black-green of the jungle.

Then I looked at Dale, my sergeant, wringing out his shirt in a metal water drum. His back was brown, ridged with vertebrae, his ribs like sticks against his skin, the points of his black hair shiny with sweat. Then his lean Czechoslovakian face smiled at me, with more tenderness and affection in his eyes than I had yet seen in a woman's.

He was killed eight days later when a Huey tipped the treetops by an LZ and suddenly dipped sideways into the clearing.

But my point about the origins of the personality and the

mysteries of the soul concerns someone else and not my dead friend. A half-dozen stripped-down Harleys, mounted by women in pairs, pulled to the edge of the street barricade, and Claudette Rocque and her friends strolled into the crowd. They wore greasy jeans and black Harley T-shirts without bras, wide studded belts, bandannas around their foreheads like Indians, chains, tattoos, half-topped boots with metal taps. They had six-packs of beer hooked in their fingers, folders of Zig-Zag cigarette papers protruding from their T-shirt pockets. They wore their strange form of sexuality like Visigoth warriors in leather and mail.

But not Bubba's wife. Her breasts hung heavy in a black sun halter that was covered with red hearts, and her jeans were pulled low on her soft, tanned stomach to expose an orange and purple butterfly tattooed by her navel. She saw me through the dancers and walked toward my table, a smile at the edge of her mouth, her hips creasing and undulating with her movement, the top of her blue jeans damp with perspiration against her skin.

She leaned down on the table and smiled into my eyes. There were sun freckles on the tops of her breasts. I could smell beer on her breath and the faint odor of marijuana in her hair. Her eyes were indolent and merry at the same time, and she bit down on her lip as though she had come to a sensuous conclusion for both of us.

"Where's the wifey?" she said.

"Down the street."

"Will she let you dance with me?"

"I'm not a good dancer, Mrs. Rocque."

"I bet you're good at other things, then. Everybody has their special talent." She bit down on her lip again.

"I think maybe I'm one of those people who was born without any. Some of us don't have to seek humility."

She smiled sleepily.

"The sun went behind the clouds," she said. "I wanted to get some more tan. Do you think I'm dark enough?"

I ate from my paper plate and tried to grin good-naturedly.

"Some people say my family has colored and Indian blood in it," she said. "I don't care, though. Like my mother's colored girls used to say, 'The black berry got the sweet juice.' "

Then she touched away a drop of sweat on my forehead with her finger and put it in her mouth. I felt my face redden in the stares from the people on each side of me.

"Last chance to dance," she said, then put her hands behind her head and started to sway her hips to a Jimmy Clanton song the rock 'n' roll band was playing on the stage. She flexed her breasts and rolled her stomach and her eyes looked directly into mine. Her tongue moved around the edges of her mouth as though she were eating an ice cream cone. A family seated next to me got up and moved. She bent her knees so her rear came tight against her jeans, and held her elbows close against the sides of her breasts with her fingers pointed outward, her wet mouth pouting, and went lower and lower toward the ground with the pale tops of her breasts exposed to everyone at the table. I looked away at the bandstand, then saw Annie walk through the crowd with Alafair's hand in hers.

Claudette Rocque and Annie looked at each other with that private knowledge and recognition of intention that women seem to have between one another. But there was no embarrassment in Claudette's face, only that indolent, merry light in her reddish brown eyes. Then she smiled at both of us, put her hand idly on a man's shoulder, and in a moment had moved off with him into the center of the street.

"What was that?" Annie said.

"Bubba Rocque's wife."

"She seems to have enjoyed entertaining you."

"I think she's been hitting on the *muta* this afternoon."

"The what?"

"The reefer."

"I loved the dancing butterfly. She wiggles it around so well."

"She learned it at Juilliard. Come on, Annie, no screws today."

"Butterfly? Butterfly dance?" Alafair said. She wore a Donald Duck cap with a yellow bill that quacked when you squeezed it. I picked her up on my knee and quacked the cap's bill, happy to be distracted from Annie's inquiring eye. Out of the corner of my vision, I saw Claudette Rocque dancing with the man she had found in the crowd, her stomach pressed tightly against his loins.

The next day the doctor snipped the stitches out of my scalp and mouth. When I ran my tongue along the inside of my lip, the skin felt like a rubber bicycle patch with welts in it. Later that afternoon I went to an AA meeting. The air conditioner was broken, and the room was hot and smoky. My mind wandered constantly.

It was almost summer now, and the afternoon seemed to grow hotter as the day wore on. We ate supper on the redwood table in the backyard amid the drone of the cicadas and the dry rumble of distant thunder. I tried to read the newspaper on the porch, but I couldn't concentrate on the words for more than a paragraph. I went down to the dock to see how many boats were still out, then went back up to the house and closed myself in the back room where I kept my weight set and historical jazz collection. I put on an old Bunk Johnson 78, and as the clear, bell-like quality of his horn lifted out of the static and mire of sound around him, I started a series of curls with ninety pounds on the bar, my biceps and chest swelling with blood and tension and power each time I brought the bar from my thighs up to my chin.

In fifteen minutes I was dripping sweat on the wooden floor. I took off my shirt, put on my gym trunks and running shoes, and did three miles on the dirt road along the bayou. The soreness was almost completely gone from my genitals, where I had been kicked by Eddie Keats, and my wind was good and my heartbeat steady all the way down the road. I could have done another two miles. Normally, I would have felt good about all the energy and resilience in my middle-aged body, but I well knew the machinery that was working inside me, and it had nothing to do with health or the breathless twilit evening or the fireflies sparkling in the black-green trees or the bream popping the water's surface along the lily pads. Summer in south Louisiana has always been, to me, part of an eternal song. Tonight I simply saw the fading red spark of sun on the horizon as the end of spring.

It was a strange night. The stars looked hot in the black sky. There was absolutely no wind, and each leaf on the pecan trees looked as though it were etched out of metal. The surface of the bayou was flat and still, the willows and cattails along the banks motionless. When the moon rose, the clouds looked like silver horsetails against the sky.

I showered with cold water and lay in my underwear on top of the sheets in the dark. Annie traced her fingers on my shoulder. Her head lay facing me on the pillow, and I could feel her breath on my skin.

"We can work through it, Dave. Every marriage has a few bad moments," she said. "We don't have to let them dominate us."

"All right."

"Maybe I've been selfish. Maybe I've wanted too much on my terms."

"What do you mean?"

"I've wanted you to be something you're not. I've tried to pretend for both of us that you're finished with police work and all that world back in New Orleans."

"I left it on my own. You didn't have anything to do with it."

"You turned in a resignation, but you didn't leave it, Dave. You never will."

I looked up into the darkness and waited. The moonlight made patterns on our bodies through the turning window fan.

"If you want to go back to it, maybe that's what we should do," she said.

"Nope."

"Because you don't think I can handle it?"

"Because it's a toilet."

"You say that, but I don't think that's the way you feel."

"My first partner was a man I admired a great deal. He had honest-to-God guts and integrity. One time on Canal a little girl was thrown through a windshield and had her arm cut off. He ran into a bar, filled his coat with ice, and wrapped the arm in it, and they sewed it back on. But before that same guy retired he took juice, he—"

"What?"

"He took bribes. He shook down whores for freebies. He blew away a fourteen-year-old black kid on the roof of the welfare project."

"Listen to the anger in your voice. It's like a fire inside you."

"It's not anger. It's a statement of fact. You stay in it and you start to talk and think like a lowlife, and one day you find yourself doing something that you didn't think yourself capa-

ble of, and that's when you know you're really home. It's not a
good moment."

"You were never like that, and you never will be." She put
her arm across my chest and her knee across my thigh.

"Because I got out of it."

"You thought you did, but you didn't." She rubbed her
knee and the inside of her thigh up and down my leg and
moved the flat of her hand down my chest and stomach. "I
know an officer whose physical condition needs some attention."

"Tomorrow I want to talk with the nuns about enrolling
Alafair in kindergarten."

"That's a good idea, skipper."

"Then we'll go to the swimming pool and have lunch in St.
Martinville."

"Whatever you say." She pressed tightly against me, blew
her breath in my hair, and hooked her leg across both my
thighs. "What other plans do you have?"

"There's an American Legion game tomorrow night, too.
Maybe we'll just take the whole day off."

"Can I touch you here? Oh my, and I thought you were so
stoic, couldn't be swayed by a girl's charms. My baby-love is a
big actor, isn't he?"

She kissed my cheek, then my mouth, then got on top of me
in her maternal way, as she always did, and stroked my face
and smiled into my eyes. The moonlight fell on her tan skin
and heavy white breasts, and she raised herself slightly on her
knees, took me in her hand, and pressed me inside her, her
mouth forming a sudden O, her eyes suddenly looking inward
upon herself. I kissed her hair, her ear, the tops of her breasts, I
ran my hands along her back and her shaking, hard thighs,
and finally I felt all the day's anger and heat, which seemed to
live in me like hot sunlight trapped in a bottle of whiskey, dis-

appear in her rhythmic breathing against my cheek and her hands and arms that pressed and caressed me all over as though I could escape from under her love that was as warm, unrelenting, and encompassing as the sea.

My dreams took me many places. Sometimes I would be in a pirogue with my father, deep in the Atchafalaya swamp, the fog thick in the black trees, and just as the sun broke on the earth's rim, I'd troll my Mepps spinner next to the cypress stumps and a largemouth bass would sock into it and burst from the quiet water, rattling with green-gold light. But tonight I dreamed of Hueys flying low over jungle canopy and milky-brown rivers. In the dream they made no sound. They looked like insects against the lavender sky, and as they drew closer I could see the door-gunners firing into the trees. The down-drafts from the helicopter blades churned the treetops into a frenzy, and the machine-gun bullets blew water out of the rivers, raked through empty fishing villages, danced in geometrical lines across dikes and rice paddies. But there was no sound and there were no people down below. I saw a door-gunner's face, and it was stretched tight with fear, whipped with wind, throbbing with the action of the gun. I could see only one of his eyes—squinted, cordite-bitten, liquid with the reflected images of dead water buffalo in the heat, smoking villages, and glassy countryside, where the people had scurried into the earth like mice. His hands were swollen and red, his finger wrapped in a knot around the trigger, the flying brass cartridge casings kaleidoscopic in the light. There were no people to shoot at anymore, but no matter—his charter was clear. He was forever wedded and addicted to this piece of earth that he'd helped make desolate, this land that was his drug and nemesis. The silence in the dream was like a scream.

I woke to the sounds of dry lightning, a car passing on the dirt road by the bayou, the bullfrogs croaking down by the duck pond. I had no analytical interest in the interpretation of dreams. The strange feelings and mechanisms they represented always went away at dawn, and that was all that mattered. I hoped that one day they would go away altogether. I once read that Audie Murphy, the most decorated U.S. soldier of World War II, slept with a .45. I believe he was a brave and good man, but for some the nocturnal landscape is haunted by creatures forged in a devil's furnace. The Greeks called upon Morpheus to abate the Furies. I simply waited on the false dawn, and sometimes with luck I fell asleep again before it arrived.

But this night was alive with too many sounds, too many shards of memory that worked on the edge of the mind like rat's teeth, for me to regain sleep easily. I put on my clack sandals, poured a glass of milk in the kitchen, and walked down to the duck pond in my skivvies. The ducks were bunched in the shadows of the cattails, and the moon and lighted clouds were reflected as perfectly in the still water as though they had been trapped under dark glass. I sat on the bench by the collapsed barn that marked the end of my property, and looked out over my neighbor's pasture and sugarcane field in the moonlight. On the barn wall behind me, whose red paint had long since flaked away, was a tin Hadacol sign from thirty-five years ago. Hadacol had been manufactured by a state senator from Abbeville, and it not only contained enough vitamins and alcohol to make you get up from your deathbed, but the boxtop would allow you admission to the traveling Hadacol show, which one year had featured Jack Dempsey, Rudy Vallee, and an eight-foot Canadian giant. I marveled at the innocence of the era in which I had grown up.

Then I saw the heat lightning flash brightly in the south, and a breeze came up suddenly and broke the moonlight apart in the water and dented the leaves of the pecan trees in my front yard. The cows in the pasture were already bunched, and I could smell rain and sulfur in the air and feel the barometric pressure dropping. I finished the milk in my glass, leaned back against the barn wall with my eyes closed, breathed the wet coolness on the wind, and realized that without even trying I was going to overcome my insomnia that night and go back to bed and sleep by my wife while the rain *tinked* on the window fan.

But when I opened my eyes I saw two dark silhouettes move as quickly and silently as deer out of the pecan trees in the front yard, past my line of vision, onto my front porch. Even as I rose to my feet, widening my eyes in the futile wish that I had seen only shadows, my heart sank with a terrible knowledge that I had experienced only once before, and that was when I had heard the *klatch* of the mine under my foot in Vietnam. Even as I started to run toward the darkened house, even before I heard the crowbar bite into the doorjamb, before the words burst out of my throat, I knew that my nocturnal fears would have their realization tonight and not be dispelled by a false dawn that only fools waited upon. I tripped on my sandals, kicked them from my feet, and ran barefoot over the hard ground, the litter of broken boards and rusty nails from the barn roof, the cattails that grew up the bank from the pond, shouting, "I'm out here! I'm out here!" like a hysterical man lost on a piece of moonscape.

But my words were lost in the thunder, the wind, the splatter of raindrops on the tin roof, the crowbar that splintered the doorjamb, sprung the hinges, snapped the deadbolt, ripped the door open into the living room. Then I heard my own voice again, a sound like an animal's cry breaking out of a wet bubble, and I heard the shotguns roar and saw the flashes leap in the bedroom like heat lightning in the sky. They fired and fired, the pump-actions clacking loudly back into place with each fresh shell, the explosions of flame dissecting the darkness where my wife lay alone under a sheet. Their buckshot blew window glass and curtain material out into the yard, tore divots of wood from the outside wall, rang off the window fan blades. A bolt of lightning struck somewhere behind me, and my own skin looked white and dead in the illumination.

They had stopped shooting. I stood breathless and barefoot in my underwear in the rain and looked through the broken window and ragged curtains at the outline of a man who stared back at me, motionless, his shotgun held at an angle across his chest. Then I heard the pump clack back to feed another shell into the chamber.

I ran to the side of the house, pressed myself against the cypress boards, moved under the windows toward the front, and crouched in the darkness. I heard one of them knock into a wall or door in the dark, trip over the telephone extension, rip the phone from its jack, and throw it down the hall. There was blood on the tops of my feet, a ragged tear in my ankle, but my body had no feeling. My head reeled as though it had been slapped hard with a rolled newspaper, and I could taste the bile rising uncontrollably from my stomach. I had no weapon; my neighbors were away; there was nothing I could do to help Annie. Sweat and rainwater ran out of my hair like insects.

There was nothing else to do but run for the phone in the bait shop. Then I heard the front screen fly back against the wall and both of them come out on the gallery. Their feet were loud on the wood, their steps going in one direction, then another. I pressed against the side of the house and waited. All one of them had to do was jump over the side railing of the gallery, and he would have me at point-blank range. Then their feet stopped, and I realized that their attention was focused on something else. A pickup truck was banging down the dirt road toward the dock, the rain slanting in the beam of a single headlight that bounced off the trees. I knew it must be Batist. He lived a quarter-mile down the road, slept on his screened gallery in the summer, and would have heard and recognized the gunfire, even in the thunder.

"Shit on it. Let's get out of here," one man said.

The other man spoke, but his voice was lost in the rain on the tin roof and a peal of thunder.

"So you come back and do him. It's a lousy hit, anyway. You didn't say nothing about a broad," the first man said. "Sonofabitch, the truck's turning in here. I'm gone. Clean up your own mess next time."

I heard one man jump off the steps and start running. The second man paused, his feet scraped hesitantly on the wood planks, then I heard the step bend under his weight, and a moment later I could see the two of them running at an angle through the trees toward a car parked down by the bayou. With their shotguns at port-arms, they looked like infantry fleeing through a forest at night.

I raced through the front door into the bedroom and hit the light switch, my heart thundering in my chest. Red shotgun shells littered the doorway area; the mahogany foot and head-boards of the bed were gouged and splintered with buckshot and deer slugs; the flowered wallpaper above the bed was covered with holes like black dimes. The sheet, which still lay over her, was drenched with her blood, the torn cloth embedded in wounds that wolves might have chewed. Her curly blond head was turned away from me on the pillow. One immaculate white hand hung over the side of the mattress.

I touched her foot. I touched her blood-flecked ankle. I put my hands around her fingers. I brushed my palm across her curly hair. I knelt like a child by the bed and kissed her eyes. I picked her hand up and put her fingers in my mouth. Then the shaking started, like sinew and bone separating inside me, and I pressed my face tightly into the pillow with my wet hair against her forehead.

I don't know how long I knelt there. I don't remember getting up from my knees. I know that my skin burned as though someone had painted it with acid, that I couldn't draw enough air into my lungs, that the room's yellow light was like a flame to my eyes, that all my joints seemed atrophied with age, that my hands were blocks of wood when I fumbled in the dresser drawer, found the .45, and pushed the heavy clip into the magazine. In my mind's eye I was already running through the yard, across my neighbor's pasture, through the sloping woods of oak and pine on the far side where the dirt road passed before it reached the drawbridge over the bayou. I heard a black kid from my platoon yell, *Charlie don't want to boogie no more. He running for the tunnel. Blow up their shit, Lieutenant.* I saw parts of men dissolve in my fire, and when the breech locked open and I had to reload, my hands shook with anticipation.

But the voice was not a black kid's from my platoon, and I was not the young lieutenant who could make small yellow men in black pajamas hide in their earthen holes. Batist had his big hands on each of my arms, his bare chest like a piece of boilerplate, his brown eyes level and unblinking and staring into mine.

"They gone, Dave. You can't do no good with that gun, you," he said.

"The drawbridge. We can cut across."

"*C'est pas bon. Ils sont pa'tis.*"

"We'll take the truck."

He shook his head to say no, then slipped his huge hand down my arm and took the automatic from my palm. Then he put his arm around my shoulders and walked me into the living room.

"You sit here. You don't got to do nothing, you," he said. The .45 stuck up out of the back pocket of his blue jeans. "Where Alafair at?"

I looked at him dumbly. He breathed through his mouth and wet his lips.

"You stay here. Don't you move, no. *T'comprends*, Dave?"

"Yes."

He walked into Alafair's room. The pecan trees in the yard flickered whitely when lightning jumped across the sky, and the wind swept the rain across the gallery and through my shattered front door. When I closed my eyes I saw light dancing inside a dark window frame like electricity trapped inside a black box.

I rose woodenly from the couch and walked to the doorway of Alafair's room. I paused with one hand on the doorjamb, almost as though I had become a stranger in my preoccupation with my own grief. Batist sat on the side of the bed with Alafair in his lap, his powerful arms wrapped around her. Her face was white and jerking with sobs against his black chest.

"She all right. You gonna be all right, too, Dave. Batist gonna take care of y'all. You'll see," he said. "Lord, Lord, what the world done to this little child."

He shook his head from side to side, an unmasked sadness in his eyes.

chapter SIX

IT RAINED THE DAY OF ANNIE'S FUNERAL. IN FACT, IT rained all that week. The water dripped from the trees, ran in rivulets off the eaves, formed brown pools filled with floating leaves in the yard, covered the fields and canebrakes with a dull, gray-green light. Her parents flew down from Kansas, and I picked them up at the airport in Lafayette and drove them in the rain to a motel in New Iberia. Her father was a big, sandy-haired wheat farmer with square, callused hands and thick wrists, and he looked out the car window silently at the sopping countryside and smoked a cigar and spoke only enough to be polite. Her mother was a thick-bodied Mennonite country woman with sun-bright blond hair, blue eyes, and red cheeks. She tried to compensate for her husband's distance by talking about the flight from Wichita, her first experience in an airplane, but she couldn't concentrate on her words and she swallowed often and her eyes constantly flicked away from my face.

They had had reservations about me when I married Annie. I was a divorced older man with an alcoholic history, and as a homicide detective I had lived in a violent world that was even more foreign to rural Kansas than my Cajun accent and French name. I felt they blamed me for Annie's death. At least her father did, I was sure of that. And I didn't have the strength to argue against that unspoken accusation even with myself.

"The funeral is at four o'clock," I said. "I'll let you all rest up at the motel, then I'll be back for you at three-thirty."

"Where's she at now?" her father said.

"The funeral home."

"I want to go there."

I paused a moment and looked at his big, intent face and his wide-set gray eyes.

"The casket's closed, Mr. Ballard," I said.

"You take us there now," he said.

We buried Annie in my family's plot in the old cemetery by St. Peter's Church in New Iberia. The crypts were made of brick and covered with white plaster, and the oldest ones had cracked and sunk into the earth and had become enwrapped with green vines that rooted into the mortar. The rain fell out of the gray sky and danced on the brick street by the cemetery and drummed on the canvas canopy over our heads. Before the attendants from the funeral home slid Annie's coffin into the crypt and sealed it with an inscribed marble slab, one of them unscrewed the metal crucifix from the top and put it in my hands.

I don't remember walking back to the limousine. I remember the people under the canopy—her parents, Batist and his wife, the sheriff, my friends from town—but I don't remember leaving the cemetery. I saw the rain swirling out of the sky, saw it glisten on the red bricks of the street and the black spiked fence that surrounded the cemetery, felt it run out of my hair and into my eyes, heard a train whistle blow somewhere and freight cars clicking on the tracks that ran through town, and then I was standing in the middle of the manicured lawn of the funeral home, with its hollow wooden columns and false antebellum façade looking the color of cardboard in the dull light, and cars were driving away from me in the rain.

"The truck over here, Dave," Batist was saying. "Come on, we got supper already fixed. You ain't eat all day."

"We've got to take her folks back to the motel."

"They done already gone. Hey, put this coat over your head. You wanta stand out here and be a duck, you?"

He smiled at me, his cannonball head beaded with rain-drops, his big teeth like pieces of carved whalebone. I felt his hand go around my arm, squeeze into the muscle, and lead me to the pickup truck, where his wife stood by the open door in a cotton print dress with an umbrella over her head. I sat quietly between them on the way back to the house. They stopped trying to speak to me, and I stared out the windshield at the muddy pools on the dirt road, the wet sheen on the trunks of the oak trees, the water that rattled down from the limbs over-head, the clouds of mist that hung on the bayou and broke across the truck's hood like the offering of sleep. In the gray light, the row of trees along the road looked like a tunnel that I could safely fall through until I reached a cold, enclosed room beneath the earth where wounds healed themselves, where the flesh did not yield to the worm, where a sealed cas-ket could be opened to reveal a radiant face.

I went back to work at the dock. I rented boats, filled peo-ple's minnow cans with shiners, fixed barbecue lunches, opened bottles of pop and beer with the mechanical smile and motions of a man in a dream. As always, when one unexpect-edly loses someone close, I discovered how kind people could be. But after a while I almost wanted to hide from their well-meaning words of condolence, their handshakes and pats on the back. I learned that grief was a private and consuming emotion, and once it chose you as its vessel it didn't share itself easily with others.

And maybe I didn't want to share it, either. After the scene investigators from the sheriff's department had bagged the bloody sheets from the bed and dug the buckshot out of the bedstead and walls, I closed and locked the door as though I were sealing up a mausoleum filled with pain, which I could resurrect simply by the turn of a key. When I saw Batist's wife heading for the house with scrub brushes and buckets to clean the bloodstains out of the splintered wood, I ran from the bait shop, yelled at her in French with the sharpness of a white man speaking to a Negro woman, and watched her turn back toward her pickup truck, her face hurt and confused.

That night I was awakened by the sound of bare feet on the wooden floor and a door handle turning. I sat up from the couch where I had fallen asleep with the television on, and saw Alafair sitting by the locked bedroom door. She wore her pajama bottoms without a top, and in her hands was the plastic draw bag in which we kept the stale bread. Her eyes were open, but her face was opaque with sleep. I walked toward her in the moonlight that fell through the front windows. Her brown eyes looked at me emptily.

"Feed the ducks with Annie," she said.

"You're having a dream, little guy," I said.

I started to pull the plastic bag gently from her hands. But her eyes and hands were locked inside the dream. I touched her hair and cheek.

"Let's take you back to bed," I said.

"Feed ducks with Annie?"

"We'll feed them in the morning. *En la mañana.*" I tried to smile into her face, then I raised her to her feet. She put one hand on the doorknob and twisted it from side to side.

"*Dònde està?*"

"She's gone away, little guy."

There was nothing for it. I lifted her up on my hip and carried her back into her room. I laid her down on her bed, put the sheet over her feet, sat down beside her, and brushed her soft, downlike hair with my hand. Her bare chest looked small in the moonlight through the window. Then I saw her mouth begin to tremble, as it had in the church, her eyes look into mine with the realization that I could not help, that no one could, that the world into which she had been born was a far more terrible one than any of her nightmares.

"*Los soldados llegaron en la lluvia y le hicieron daño a Annie?*"

The only Spanish words that I understood in her question were "soldiers" and "rain." But even if I had understood it all, I could not have answered her anyway. I was more lost than she, caught forever in the knowledge that when my wife had needed me most, I had left the house to sit by a duck pond in the dark and dwell on the past and my alcoholic neurosis.

I lay down beside Alafair and pulled her against me. I felt the wetness of her eyelash against my face.

Then, one hot, bright afternoon, exactly a week after I had buried Annie, with no dramatic cause at work, with fleecy clouds blowing across the blue sky, I snapped the cap off a bottle of Jax, watched the foam slide over the amber bottle and drip flatly on the wooden floor of the bait shop, and drank it empty in less than a minute.

Two fisherman friends of mine at a table looked briefly at me with dead expressions on their faces, and in the silence of the room I heard Batist drag a kitchen match on wood and light a cigar. When I looked at his face, he flicked the match out the open window and I heard it hiss in the water. He turned away from me and stared out into the sunlight, a curl of smoke rising from his wide-spaced teeth.

I popped open a double-paper bag, put two cartons of Jax inside, poured a small bucket of crushed ice on top of the bottles, and hefted the bag under my arm.

"I'm going to take an outboard down the bayou," I said. "Close it up in a couple of hours and keep Alafair with you till I get back."

He didn't answer and continued to look out at the sunlight on the lily pads and the cane growing along the bank.

"Did you hear me?" I asked.

"Do what you gotta do, you. You ain't got to tell me how to take care of that little girl." He walked up toward the house, where Alafair was coloring a book on the porch, and didn't look back at me.

I opened the throttle on the outboard and watched my yellow-white wake slap against the cypress roots on the bank. Each time I tilted a bottle of Jax to my mouth the sunlight danced like brown fire inside the glass. I had no destination, no place of completion for all the energy that throbbed through my palm, no plan for the day, my life, or even the next five minutes. What was the great value in plans, anyway? I thought. A forest fire didn't have one, or a flood that buried a Kentucky town in mud, or lightning that splintered down into a sodden field and blew a farmer out of his shoes. Those things happened and the world went on. Why did Dave Robicheaux have to impose all this order and form on his life? So you lose control and total out for a while, I thought. The U.S. Army certainly understood that. You declare a difficult geographical and political area a free-fire zone, then you stand up later in the drifting ash and the smell of napalm and define with much more clarity the past nature of the problem.

The gas tank went empty toward evening, and at the bottom of my feet was a melted pile of ice, soggy brown paper, and empty Jax bottles. I rowed the boat to shore, threw the iron anchor weight up on the bank, and walked in the dusk down a dirt road to a Negro juke joint and bought another six-pack of beer and a half-pint of Jim Beam. Then I pushed the boat back out into the center of the bayou and drifted in the current among the trailings of fireflies and the dark tracings of alligator gar just below the water's surface. I sipped from the lip of the whiskey bottle, chased it with the beer, and waited. Sometimes whiskey kicked open a furnace door that could consume me like a piece of cellophane. Other times I could operate for days with a quiet euphoria and kind of control that would pass for sobriety. Then sometimes I looked into memory and saw forgotten moments that I wished I could burn away like film negatives dissolving on a hot coal.

I remembered a duck-hunting trip with my father when I was thirteen years old. We were in a blind on a cold, gray, windswept day, just off Sabine Pass where it dumped into the Gulf, and the mallards and *poules d'eau* had been coming in low all morning since dawn, and we had busted them like dirty smudges all over the sky. Then my father had gotten careless, maybe because he had been drunk the night before, had gotten mud in the barrel of the automatic twelve-gauge, and when three Canadian honkers went over, really too high for a good shot, he stood up quickly, turned with the shotgun at an angle over my head, and blew the barrel into a spray of wadding, cordite, birdshot, and steel needles all over the water's surface. My ears rang with the explosion, and bits of hot powder covered my face like grains of black pepper. I saw the shame in his eyes and smelled the stale beer on his breath as he washed my skin with his wet handkerchief. He tried to make light of it, said that's what he got for not going to Mass yesterday, but there was a troubled realization in his eyes as well as shame, and it was the same look he had whenever he'd been locked up in the parish jail for brawling in a bar.

It was only a quarter-mile back to the camp; it was right across the bay, up a canal that cut back through the sawgrass and cane, a shack built on stilts that looked out on the Gulf. He would be gone only a short time and bring back the sixteen-gauge. I could start shucking out the ducks, which lay in a soft green and blue pile on the flattened yellow grass at the bottom of the blind. Besides, them honker coming back, yeah, he said.

But back in the canal he ran the outboard across a submerged log and snapped off the propeller shaft like a stick.

I waited for him for two hours, my knife bloody from the warm entrails of the ducks. The wind picked up from the south, small waves chucked against the blind, the sky was the color of incinerator smoke. On the Texas side of the shore I heard the dull popping of another hunter's shotgun.

A pirogue was tied to the back of the blind. I broke open my dogleg twenty-gauge, picked up the string of decoys we had set out in a J-formation, filled the canvas game bag with the stiffening, gutted bodies of the ducks, loaded it all in the pirogue's bow, and shoved off toward the canal and the long expanse of sawgrass.

But the wind had shifted and was now blowing hard out of the northeast, and no matter how strongly I rowed on both sides of the pirogue, I drifted toward the mouth of the Pass and the slate-green water of the Gulf of Mexico. I paddled until blisters formed on my hands and broke against the grain of the wood, then I threw the anchor weight overboard, realized when the rope hung straight down that the bottom was too deep to catch, and looked desperately at the Louisiana wetlands sliding farther away from me.

Foam blew off the waves in my face, and I could taste salt

water in my mouth. The pirogue dipped with such force into the troughs that I had to hold on to the gunwales, and my buttocks constricted with fear each time the wooden bottom slammed up into my tailbone. I tried to bail with a tin can, lost the paddle, and watched it float away from me like a yellow stick between the waves. The string of decoys, my shotgun, and the canvas bag of ducks were awash in the bow; uprooted cypress trees and an upside-down wooden shack revolved in the dark current just under the surface beside me. The shack had a small porch, and it broke through the waves into the winter light like a gigantic mouth streaming water.

The state fish-and-game boat with my father on board picked me up that afternoon. They dried me off and gave me warm clothes, and fixed me fried Spam sandwiches and hot Ovaltine in the galley. But I wouldn't talk to my father until the next day, and I talked with him only then because sleep gave me back the familiar relationship that his explanation about the sheared propeller shaft would not.

"It's because you was alone out there," he said. "When somebody make you alone, it don't matter why. You suppose to be mad at them. When your mama run off with a *bourée* man, I didn't care I made her do it, no. I knocked him down on the barroom floor in front of her. When he got up, I knocked him down again. Later I found out he had a pistol in his coat. He could have killed me right there, him. But she didn't let him do it, 'cause she know I gonna get over it. That's why, me, I ain't mad at you, 'cause I know you suppose to be disappoint with me.

"The bad thing is when you make yourself alone. Don't never do that, Dave, 'cause it's like that coon chewing off its own foot when he stick it in the trap."

As I sat in the outboard on the bayou and looked at the red sky and the purple clouds in the west, the breathless air as warm as the whiskey that I raised to my lips, I knew what my father had meant.

A coon can chew through sinew and bone in a few minutes. I had a whole night to work on dismantling myself. I found a good place to do it, too—a Negro bar made of Montgomery Ward brick, set back from a dusty yellow road in a grove of oak trees, a place where they carried barber's razors, mixed bourbon in Thunderbird, and played *zydeco* music so loud it shook the cracked and taped glass windows in front.

Two days later a big-breasted Negro woman in a purple dress picked up my head from a puddle of beer. The sun was low in the east and shining through the window like a white flame.

"Your face ain't no mop, honey," she said, looking down at me with her hand on her hip, a lighted cigarette between her fingers.

Then her other hand went into my back pocket and took out my wallet. I reached for it impotently while she splayed it open.

"I ain't got to steal white men's money," she said. "I just waits for y'all to give it to me. But it's trick, trade, or travel, honey, and it looks like you got to travel."

She put my wallet in my shirt pocket, mashed out her cigarette in the ashtray in front of me, and dialed the phone on the bar while I remained slumped in the chair, the side of my face wet with beer, red balls of light dancing in my brain. Ten minutes later a St. Martin Parish sheriff's car drove me back to the bayou where I had tied my boat and left me standing sick and alone, like a solitary statue, in the wet weeds on the bank.

After I finally got back to the boat dock that afternoon, I asked Batist to keep Alafair until that evening and I slept for three hours on the couch under an electric fan, then got up and shaved and showered and thought I could return a degree of normalcy to my day. Instead, I went into the shakes and the dry heaves and ended up on my knees in front of the wash-basin.

I got back into the shower again, sat under the cold water for fifteen minutes, brushed my teeth, dressed in a pair of clean khakis and a denim shirt, and forced myself to eat a bowl of Grape-Nuts. Even in the breeze from the electric fan, my denim shirt was spotted with sweat.

I picked up Alafair at Batist's house and took her to the home of my cousin, a retired schoolteacher, in New Iberia. I had already deserted Alafair for two days while I was on a drunk, and I felt bad about moving her again to another home, but both Batist and his wife worked and could not watch her full-time, and at that moment I wasn't in sufficient physical or emotional condition to be responsible even for myself, much less anyone else, and also the possibility existed that the killers would come back to my house again.

I asked my cousin to keep Alafair for the next two days, then I drove to the courthouse to find the sheriff. But when I parked my truck I was sweating heavily, my hands left wet prints on the steering wheel, the veins in my brain felt like twisted pieces of cord. I drove to the poolroom on Main Street, sat in the coolness of the bar under the wood-bladed fans, and drank three vodka collinses until I felt the rawness of yesterday's whiskey go out of my chest and the tuning fork stop trembling inside me.

But I was mortgaging today for tomorrow, and tomorrow I would probably postpone the debt again, and the next day and the next, until I would be very far in arrears with a debt that would eventually present itself like an unfed snake given its choice of a wounded rabbit's parts. But at that point I guess I didn't care. Annie was dead because I couldn't leave things alone. I had quit the New Orleans police department, the bourbon-scented knight-errant who said he couldn't abide any longer the political hypocrisy and the addictive, brutal ugliness of metropolitan law enforcement, but the truth was that I enjoyed it, that I got high on my knowledge of man's iniquity, that I disdained the boredom and predictability of the normal world as much as my strange alcoholic metabolism loved the adrenaline rush of danger and my feeling of power over an evil world that in many ways was mirrored in microcosm in my own soul.

I bought a bottle of vodka to take home and didn't touch it again until the next morning.

The four inches I drank for breakfast sat in my stomach like canned heat. I had to keep wiping my face with a towel for a half hour, until I stopped sweating, then I brushed my teeth, showered, put on my cream-colored slacks, charcoal sports shirt, and gray and red striped tie, and an hour later I was sitting in the sheriff's office while he listened indecisively to what I had to say and looked peculiarly at my face.

"Are you hot? You looked flushed," he said.

"Go outside. It must be ninety-five already."

He nodded absently. He scratched the blue and red lines in his soft cheek with a fingernail and pushed a paper clip around on his desk blotter. Through the glass window of the closed office door I could see his deputies doing paperwork at their desks. The building was new and had the cool, neutral, refrigerated smell of a modern office, which was the image it was intended to convey, but the deputies still looked like the rawboned rednecks and coonasses of an earlier time and they still kept cuspidors by their desks.

"How'd you know the department had an opening?" the sheriff said.

"It was in the paper."

"It's detective rank, Dave, but eighteen thousand isn't near what you made in New Orleans. It seems to me you'd be going back to the minor leagues."

"I don't need a lot of money. I've got the boat-and-bait business, and I own my house free and clear."

"There's a couple of deputies out there who want that job. They'd resent you."

"That's their problem."

He opened his desk drawer, dropped the paper clip in it, and looked at me. The soft edges of his face flexed with the thought that had been troubling him since I had told him I wanted the job.

"I'm not going to give a man a badge so he can be an executioner," he said.

"I wouldn't need a badge for that."

"The hell you wouldn't."

"I was a good cop. I never popped a cap unless they dealt the play."

"You don't have to convince me about your past record. We're talking about now. Are you going to tell me you can investigate your own wife's murder with any objectivity?"

I licked my tongue across my lips. I could feel the vodka humming in my blood. Ease up, ease up, ease up, you're almost home, I thought.

"I was never objective in any homicide investigation," I said. "You see the handiwork and you hunt the bastards down. Then, as my old partner used to say, 'You bust 'em or grease 'em.' But I didn't cool them out, Sheriff. I brought them in when I could have left them on the sidewalk and sailed right through Internal Affairs. Look, you've got some deputies out there who probably give you the cold sweats sometimes. It's because they're amateurs. One day they'll own bars or drive trucks or just go on beating up their wives. But they're not really cops."

His eyes blinked.

"They tell you a guy resisted arrest or fell down when they put him in the car," I said. "They're supposed to bring in a hooker, but they can't ever seem to find her. You send them into a Negro neighborhood and you wonder if the town is going to be burning by midnight."

"There's another problem, too. It comes in bottles."

"If I go out of control, fire me."

"Everybody around here likes and respects you, Dave. I don't like to see a man go back to his old ways because he's trying to fly with an overload."

"I'm doing all right, Sheriff." I looked him steadily in the eyes. I didn't like to run a con on a decent man, but most of the cards in my hands were blanks.

"You look like you've been out in the sun too long," he said.

"I'm dealing with it. Sometimes I win, sometimes I lose. If I come in here blowing fumes in your face, pull my plug. That's all I can tell you. Where do you think those killers are now?"

"I don't know."

"They're doing a few lines, getting laid, maybe sipping juleps at the track. They feel power right now that you and I can't even guess at. I've heard them describe it as being like a heroin rush."

"Why are you telling me this?"

"Because I know how they think. I don't believe you do. Those other guys out there don't, either. You know what they did after they murdered Annie? They drove to a bar. Not the first or the second one they saw, but one way down the road where they felt safe, where they could drink Jack Daniel's and smoke cigarettes without speaking to one another, until that moment when their blood slowed and they looked in each other's eyes and started laughing.

"Look at it another way. What evidence do you have in hand?"

"The lead we dug out of the walls, the shotgun shells off the floor, the pry bar they dropped on the porch," he said.

"But not a print."

"No."

"Which means you have almost nothing. Except me. They were out to kill me, not Annie. Every aspect of the investigation will eventually center around that fact. You'll end up interviewing me every other day."

He lit a cigarette and smoked it with his elbow on the desk blotter. He looked through the door glass at the deputies in the outer office. One of them leaned to the side of his desk and spit tobacco juice into a cuspidor.

"I'll have to run it by a couple of other people, but I don't think there'll be any trouble," he said. "But you don't work on just this one case, Dave. You carry a regular load just like the other detectives and you go by the same rules."

"All right."

He puffed on his cigarette and widened his eyes in the smoke, as though dismissing some private concerns from his mind, then he watched my expression closely and said, "Who do you think did it?"

"I don't know."

"You told me that the day after it happened, and I accepted that. But you've had a lot of time to think in the last ten days. I can't believe you haven't come to some conclusion. I wouldn't want to feel you're being less than honest here, and that maybe you're going to try to operate on your own after all."

"Sheriff, I gave motive to any number or combination of people. The bartender at Smiling Jack's is the kind of vicious punk who could blow out your light and drink a beer while he was doing it. I not only ran his head into a window fan and cocked a .45 between his eyes, I turned Bubba Rocque loose on him and made him get out of New Orleans. I messed up Eddie Keats with a pool cue in front of his whores, and I went into Bubba Rocque's house and told him I was going to put my finger in his eye if I found out he sent Keats and the Haitian after me.

"Maybe it was Toot and a guy I don't know. Maybe it was two contract men Bubba or Keats brought in from out of state. Maybe it's somebody out of the past. Once in a while they get out of Angola and keep their promises."

"New Orleans thinks the bartender went to the Islands."

"Maybe, but I doubt it. He's a rat, and a rat goes into a hole. He's more afraid of Bubba than he is of cops. I don't believe he'll be walking around on a beach anywhere. Besides, he's a mama's boy. He probably won't run far from home."

"I'll be truthful with you, Dave. I don't know where to start on this one. We just don't have this kind of crime around here. I sent two deputies to question Keats, and he picked his nose in front of them and told them to bust him or beat feet. His bartender and one of his hookers said he was in the club when Annie was killed."

"Did they question the bartender and the hooker separately?"

He looked away from me. "I don't know," he said.

"That's all right. We can talk to them again."

"I went out to Bubba Rocque's myself. I don't know what to think about a guy like that. You could scratch a match on those eyes and I don't think they'd blink. I remember thirty years ago when he was a kid and he dropped a fly ball in the city park and lost the game for his side. After the game he was eating a snowcone and his daddy slapped it out of his hand and hit him across the ear. His eyes didn't show any more feeling than a couple of zinc pennies."

"What did he tell you?"

"He was home asleep."

"What'd his wife say?"

"She said she was in New Orleans that night. So Bubba doesn't have an alibi."

"He knows he doesn't need one yet. Bubba's a lot smarter than Eddie Keats."

"He said he was sorry about Annie. I think maybe he meant it, Dave."

"Maybe."

"You think he's bad through and through, don't you?"

"Yep."

"I guess I just don't have your mileage."

I started to tell him that any cop who gave the likes of Bubba Rocque an even break would probably not earn much mileage, but fortunately I kept my own counsel and simply asked when I could get a badge.

"Two or three days," he answered. "In the meantime, take it easy. We'll get these guys sooner or later."

As I said, he was a decent man, but the Rotary Club had a larger claim on his soul than the sheriff's department. The fact is that most criminals are not punished for their crimes. In New York City only around two percent of the crimes are punished, and in Miami the figure is about four percent. If you want to meet a group of people who have a profound distrust of, and hostility toward, our legal system, don't waste your time on political radicals; interview a random selection of crime victims, and you'll probably find that they make the former group look like utopian idealists by comparison.

I shook hands with him and walked out into the hazy noonday heat and humidity. In the meadows along the road, cattle were bunched in the hot shade of the oak trees, and white egrets were pecking in the dried cow flop out in the grass. I pulled my tie loose, wiped my forehead on my shirt sleeve, and looked at the long wet streaks on the cloth.

Fifteen minutes later I was in a dark, cool bar south of town, a cold, napkin-wrapped collins glass in my hand. But I couldn't stop perspiring.

Vodka is an old friend to most clandestine drunks. It has neither odor nor color, and it can be mixed with virtually anything without the drinker being detected. But its disadvantage for a whiskey drinker like me was that it went down so smoothly, so innocuously, in glasses filled with crushed ice and fruit slices and syrup and candied cherries, that I could drink almost a fifth of it before I realized that I had gone numb from my hairline to the soles of my feet.

"Didn't you say you had to leave here at four?" the bartender asked.

"Sure."

He glanced up at the illuminated clock on the wall above the bar. I tried to focus my eyes on the hands and numbers. I pressed my palm absently to my shirt pocket.

"I guess I left my glasses in my truck," I said.

"It's five after."

"Call me a cab, will you? You mind if I leave my truck in your lot awhile?"

"How long?" He was washing glasses, and he didn't look at me when he spoke and his voice had the neutral tone that bartenders use to suppress the disdain they feel for some of the people whom they serve.

"I'll probably get it tomorrow."

He didn't bother to answer. He called a cab and went back to washing glasses in the aluminum sink.

Ten minutes later my cab arrived. I finished my drink and set it on the bar.

"I'll send somebody for my truck, podna," I said to the bartender.

I rode back to my house in the cab, packed two changes of clothes in my suitcase, got Batist to drive me to the airport in Lafayette, and by six-thirty I was aboard a commercial flight to Key West, by way of Miami, the late red sun reflecting like pools of fire among the clouds.

I sipped from my second double Beam and soda and looked down at the dark blue and turquoise expanse of water off the western tip of the island, where the Gulf and the Atlantic met, and at the waves sliding across the coral reefs below the surface and breaking against the beaches that were as white as ground diamond. The four-engine plane dipped, made a wide turn out over the water, then flattened out for its approach to the airport, and I could see the narrow strip of highway that ran from Key West to Miami, the coconut palms along the beaches, the lagoons full of sailboats and yachts, the kelp rising in the groundswell, the waves bursting in geysers of foam at the ends of the jetties, and then suddenly the tree-lined and neon-lit streets of Key West in the last red wash of sunset.

It was a town of ficus, sea grape, mahogany and umbrella trees, coconut and royal palms, hanging geraniums, Confederate jasmine, and bougainvillea that bloomed as brightly as blood. The town was built on sand and coral, surrounded by water, the wooden buildings eventually made paintless and gray by salt air. At one time or another it has been home to Indians, Jean Lafitte's pirates, salvagers who deliberately lured commercial ships onto the reefs so they could gut the wrecks, James Audubon, rum runners, Cuban political exiles, painters, homosexuals, dope smugglers, and burnt-out street people who had been pushed so far down in the continent now that they had absolutely no place else to go.

It was a town of clapboard and screened-in beer joints, raw-oyster bars, restaurants that smelled of conch fritters and boiled shrimp and deep-fried red snapper, clearings in the pine trees where fishermen stacked their lobster traps, nineteenth-century brick warehouses and government armories, and shady streets lined with paintless shotgun houses with wooden shutters and sagging galleries. The tourists were gone now because of the summer heat, and the streets were almost empty in the twilight; the town had gone back into itself. The cab-driver had to buy gas on the way to the motel, and I looked out the window at some elderly Negro men sitting on crates in front of a tiny grocery store, at the ficus roots that cracked the sidewalks into concrete peaks, at the dusky purple light on the brick streets and the darkening trees overhead, and for just a moment it was as though I had not left New Iberia, had not taken another step deeper into my problems.

But I had.

I checked into a motel on the southern tip of the island and had a fifth of Beam and a small bucket of ice sent to the room. I had a couple of hits with water, then showered and dressed. Through my window I could see the palm trees thrashing on the deserted beach and the light dying on the horizon. The water had turned as dark as burgundy, and waves were pitch-ing upward against a coral reef that formed a small harbor for a half-dozen sailboats. I opened the glass jalousies wide to let the cool breeze into the room, then I walked downtown to Duval Street and my friend's restaurant where Robin worked as a waitress.

But my metabolism was on empty before I made it to the foot of Duval. I stopped in at Sloppy Joe's and had a drink at the bar and tried to examine all the vague thoughts and strange movements of my day. True, not everything I had done had been impetuous. Robin was still the best connection I had to the collection of brain-fried New Orleans people who served Bubba Rocque, and I had called my friend long distance to make sure she was working at the restaurant, but I could have questioned her on the phone, or at least tried, before deciding I would have to fly to Key West.

Which made me confront, at least temporarily, the real reason I was there: it's lousy to be alone, particularly when you're not handling anything properly. Particularly when you're drunk and starting to fuck up your life again on an enormous scale. And because somebody was playing "Baby Love" on the jukebox.

"Why don't you put some records on the jukebox that aren't twenty years old?" I said to the bartender.

"What?"

"Put some new music on there. It's 1987."

"The jukebox is broken, pal. You better slip your transmission into neutral."

I walked back out onto the street, my face warm with bourbon in the wind blowing off the backside of the island. On the dock by the restaurant I watched the waves slide through pilings, small incandescent fish moving about like smoky green lights below the surface. The restaurant was crowded with customers, and the bar was a well-lighted and orderly place where people had two drinks before dinner. When I walked inside I felt like a diver stepping out of a bathysphere into a hostile and glaring brilliance.

The maître d' looked at me carefully. I had fixed my tie and tried to smooth the wrinkles in my seersucker coat, but I should have put on sunglasses.

"Do you have a reservation, sir?" he said.

"Tell Robin Dave Robicheaux's here. I'll wait in the bar."

"I beg your pardon?"

"Tell her Dave from New Orleans. The last name's hard to pronounce sometimes."

"Sir, I think you'd better see her outside of working hours."

"Say, you're probably a good judge of people. Do I look like I'm going away?"

I ordered a drink at the bar, and five minutes later I saw her come through the door. She wore a short black dress with a white lace apron over it, and her figure and the way she walked, as though she were still on a burlesque runway, made every man at the bar glance sideways at her. She was smiling at me, but there was a perplexed light in her eyes, too.

"Wow, you come a long way to check up on a girl," she said.

"How you doing, kiddo?"

"Not bad. It's turned out to be a pretty good gig. Hey, don't get up."

"How long till you're off?"

"Three hours. Come on and sit in the booth with me. You're listing pretty heavy to port."

"A drunk front came through New Iberia this morning."

"Well, walk over here with mommy and let's order something to eat."

"I ate on the plane."

"Yeah, I can tell," she said.

We sat in a tan leather booth against the back wall of the bar. She blew out little puffs of air with her lips.

"Dave, what are you doing?" she said.

"What?"

"Like, *this*." She flicked her fingernail against my highball glass.

"Sometimes I clean out my head."

"You bust up with your old lady or something?"

"I'm going to get another Beam. You want a cup of coffee or a Coke?"

"Do *I* want coffee? God, that's great, Dave. Look, after the dinner rush I can get off early. Take the key to my apartment and I'll meet you there in about an hour. It's right around the corner."

"You got any hooch?"

"Some beer is all. I've been doing good, Dave. No little white pills, no glug-glug before I go to work. I can't believe how good I feel in the mornings."

"Pick me up at Sloppy Joe's."

"What do you want to go there for? It's full of college dopes who think Ernest Hemingway wrote on the bathroom walls or something."

"See you in an hour, kiddo. You're a sweet girl."

"Yeah, the guys at Smiling Jack's used to tell me that all the time. While they were trying to cop a feel under the table. I think you got hit in the head by lightning this morning."

When she came for me later at Sloppy Joe's, I was by myself at a table in the back, the breeze from a floor fan rising up my trouser leg, fluttering the wet sleeve of my seersucker coat that hung over the side of the table. The big sliding doors on two sides of the building were rolled wide open, and the neon light shone purple on the sidewalk. On the corner, two cops were rousting a drunk. They weren't cutting him any slack, either. He was going to the bag.

"Let's go, Lieutenant," Robin said.

"Wait till the Man leaves. My horizon keeps tilting. Key West is a bad town to have trouble in."

"All I do is flex my boobs and they tip their hats. Such gentlemen. No more booze, honey pie."

"I need to tell you some things. About my wife. Then you have to tell me some more about those people in New Orleans."

"Tomorrow morning. Mommy's going to fix you a steak tonight."

"They killed her."

"What?"

"They blew her to pieces with shotguns. That's what they did, all right."

She stared at me with her mouth parted. I could see the edges of her nostrils discolor.

"You mean Bubba Rocque killed your wife?" she said.

"Maybe it was him. Maybe not. Ole Bubba's a hard guy to second-guess."

"Dave, I'm sorry. Jesus Christ. Did it have something to do with me? God, I don't believe it."

"No."

"It does, though, because you're here."

"I just want to see if you can remember some things. Maybe I just wanted to see you, too."

"I guess that's why you had the hots for me when you were single. Tell me about it when your head's not ninety-proof." She looked around the bar. The floor fan ruffled her short black hair. "This place's a drag. The whole town's a drag. It's full of low-rent dykes and man-eaters that drift down from New York. Why'd you send me over here?"

"You told me you were doing well here."

"Who's doing well when people are out there killing a guy's wife? You messed with them, didn't you, Dave? You wouldn't listen to me."

I didn't answer, but instead picked up my highball glass.

"Forget it. Your milk cow has gone dry for tonight," she said, then took the glass out of my hand and poured it in a pool of whiskey and ice on the table.

She lived on the first floor of an old two-story stucco build-ing with a red tile roof just off Duval Street. A huge banyan tree had cracked one wall, and the tiny yard was overgrown with weeds and untrimmed banana trees. Her apartment had a small kitchen, a bedroom separated by a sliding curtain, and a couch, breakfast table, and chairs that looked like they had come from a Goodwill store.

Robin had a good heart, and she wanted to be kind, but her cooking was truly a challenge, particularly to someone on a bender. She burned the steak black on one side, fried the pota-toes in a half-inch of grease, and filled the apartment with smoke and the smell of burned onions. I tried to eat but couldn't. I'd reached the bottom of my drunk. The cogs on my wheels were sheared smooth, all my wiring was blown, and the skin on my face was thick and dead to the touch. I sud-denly felt that I had aged a century, that someone had slipped a knife along my breastbone and scooped out all my vital organs.

"Are you going to be sick?" she said.

"No, I just need to go to bed."

She looked at me a moment in the light of the unshaded bulb that hung from the ceiling. Her eyes were green, and unlike most of the strippers on Bourbon, she had never needed to wear false eyelashes. She brought two sheets from her dresser in the bedroom and spread them on the couch. I sat down heavily, took off my shoes, and rubbed my hand in my face. I was already starting to dehydrate, and I could smell the alcohol against my palm like an odor climbing out of a dark well. She carried a pillow back to the couch.

"Robin?" I said.

"What are you up to, Lieutenant?" She looked down at me with the light behind her head.

I put my hand on her wrist. She sat down beside me and

looked straight ahead. Her hands were folded, and her knees were close together under her black waitress uniform.

"Are you sure this is what you want?" she said.

"Yes."

"Did you come all the way over here just to get laid? There must be somebody available closer to home."

"You know that's not the way I feel about you."

"No, I don't. I don't know anything of the sort, Dave. But you're a friend, and I wouldn't turn away from you. I just don't want you to lie about it."

She turned off the light and undressed. Her breasts were round and soft against me, her skin tan and smooth in the dark. She hooked one leg in mine, ran her hands over my back, kissed my cheek and breathed in my ear and made love to me as she might to an emotional child. But I didn't care. I was used up, finished, as dead inside as I was the day they slid Annie's casket inside the crypt. The street light made shadows on the banyan and banana trees outside the window. Inside my head was a sound like the roar of the ocean in a conch shell.

The next morning the early light was gray in the streets, then the sun came up red on the eastern horizon, and the banana leaves clicking against the screen window were beaded with humidity. I filled a quart jar with tap water, drank it down, then threw up in the toilet. My hands shook, the backs of my legs quivered, flashes of color popped like lesions behind my eyes. I stood in my underwear in front of the washbasin, cupped water into my face, brushed my teeth with toothpaste and my finger, then threw up again and went into a series of stomach spasms so severe that finally my saliva was pink with blood in the bottom of the basin. My eyes were watering

uncontrollably, my face cold and twitching; there was a pressure band across one side of my head as though I had been
slapped with a thick book, and my breath was sour and trembled in my throat each time I tried to breathe.

I wiped the sweat and water off my face with a towel and
headed for the icebox.

"No help there, hon," Robin said from the stove, where
she was soft-boiling eggs. "I poured the beer out at four this
morning."

"Have you got any ups?"

"I told you mommy's clean." She was barefoot and wearing
a pair of black shorts and a denim shirt that was unbuttoned
over her bra.

"Some of those PMS pills. Come on, Robin. I'm not a
junkie. I've just got a hangover."

"You shouldn't try to run a shuck on another juicer. I took
your wallet, too. You got rolled, Lieutenant."

It was going to be a long morning. And she was right about
trying to con a pro. Normally an alcoholic can jerk just about
anybody around except another drunk. And Robin knew every
ploy that I might use to get another drink.

"Get in the shower, Dave," she said. "I'll have breakfast
ready when you come out. You like bacon with soft-boiled
eggs?"

I turned on the water as hot as I could stand it, pointed my
face with my mouth open into the shower head, washed the
cigarette smoke from the bar out of my hair, scrubbed my skin
until it was red. Then I turned on the cold water full blast,
propped my arms against the tin walls of the stall, and held on
while I counted slowly to sixty.

"The bacon's kind of crisp, I guess," she said after I had
dressed and we were sitting at the table.

The bacon looked like strips torn out of a rubber tire. And

she had hard-boiled the eggs and mashed them up with a spoon.

"You don't have to eat it," she said.

"No, it's really good, Robin."

"Do you feel a lot of remorse this morning? That's what your AA buddies call it, don't they?"

"No, I don't feel remorse." But my eyes went away from her face.

"I was turning tricks when I was seventeen. So you got a free one. Deal me out of your guilt, Dave."

"Don't talk about yourself like that."

"I don't like morning-after bullshit."

"You listen to me, Robin. I came to you last night because I felt more alone than I've ever felt in my life."

She drank from her coffee and set the cup in her saucer.

"You're a sweet guy, but I've got too much experience at it. It's all right."

"Why don't you give yourself some credit? I don't know another person in the world who would have taken me in the way you did last night."

She put the dishes in the sink, then walked up behind me and kissed my hair.

"Just get through your hangover, Streak. Mommy's been fighting her own dragons for a long time," she said.

It wasn't simply a hangover, however. This slip had blown a year of sobriety for me, and in that year of health and sunshine and lifting weights and jogging for miles in the late evening, my system had lost all its tolerance for alcohol. It was similar to pouring a five-pound bag of sugar in an automobile gas tank and opening up the engine full-bore. In a short time your rings and valves are reduced to slag.

"Can I have my wallet?" I said.

"It's under the cushion on the couch."

I found it and put it in my back pocket, then slipped on my loafers.

"You headed for a beer joint?" she said.

"It's a thought."

"You're on your own, then. I'm not going to help you mess yourself up anymore."

"That's because you're the best, Robin."

"Save the baby oil for yourself. I don't need it."

"You've got it wrong, kiddo. I'm going to buy a bathing suit and we're going down to the beach. Then I'm going to take you out to lunch."

"It sounds like a good way to ease yourself back into the bar and keep mommy along."

"No bars. I promise."

Her eyes searched mine, and I saw her face brighten.

"I can fix food for us here. You don't have to spend your money," she said.

I smiled at her.

"I would really like to take you to lunch," I said.

It was a morning of abstinence in which I tried to think in terms of five minutes at a time. I felt like a piece of cracked ceramic. In the clothing store my hands were still trembling, and I saw the salesman step back from my breath. In an open-air food stand on the beach, I drank a glass of iced coffee and ate four aspirins. I squinted upward at the sunlight shining through the branches of the palm tree overhead. I would have swallowed a razor blade for a shuddering rush of Jim Beam through my system.

The snakes were out of their baskets, but I hoped they would have only a light meal and be on their way. I paid a Cuban kid a dollar to borrow his mask and snorkel, then I waded through the warm waves of the lagoon and swam out to open deep water over a coral reef. The water was as clear as green Jell-O, and thirty feet down I could see the fire coral in the reef, schools of clown fish, bluepoint crabs drifting across the sand, a nurse shark as motionless as a log in the reef's shadow, gossamer plants that bent with the current, black sea urchins whose spikes could go all the way through your foot. I held my breath and dove as deep as I could, dropping into a layer of cold water where a barracuda looked directly into my mask with his bony, hooked snout, then zipped past my ear like a silver arrow fired from an archer's bow.

I felt better when I swam back in and walked up on the sand where Robin was lying on a towel among a stand of coconut palms. Also, I had already invested too much of the day in my own misery. It was time to go to work again, although I knew she wasn't going to like it.

"The New Orleans cops think Jerry's in the Islands," I said.

She unsnapped her purse, took out a cigarette and lit it. She pulled her leg up in front of her and brushed sand off her knee.

"Come on, Robin," I said.

"I closed the door on all those dipshits."

"No, I'm going to close the door on them. And like we used to say in the First District, 'weld it shut and burn their birth certificates.' "

"You're a barrel of laughs, Dave."

"Where is he?" I smiled at her and ticked some grains of sand off her knee with my fingernail.

"I don't know. Forget the Islands, though. He used to have a mulatto chick in Bimini. That was the only reason he went over there. Then he got stoned on ganja and dropped her baby on its head. On concrete. He said they've got a coral-rock jail over there that's so black it'd turn a nigger into a white man."

"Where's his mother go when she's not in New Orleans?"

"She's got some relatives in north Louisiana. They used to come in the bar and ask for Styrofoam spit cups."

"Where in north Louisiana?"

"How should I know?"

"I want you to tell me everything Eddie Keats and the Haitian said when they were in your apartment."

Her face darkened, and she looked out toward the surf where some high school kids were sailing a frisbee back and forth over the waves. Out beyond the opening of the lagoon, pelicans were diving into a patch of blue water that was as dark as ink.

"You think my head's a tape deck?" she asked. "Like I should be collecting what these people say while they break my finger in a door? You know what it feels like for a woman to have their hands on her?"

Her face was still turned away from me, but I could see the shiny film on her eyes.

"What do you care what they say, anyway?" she said. "It never makes any sense. They're morons that went to the ninth grade, and they try to act like wiseguys they see on TV. Like Jerry always saying, 'I ain't no swinging dick. I ain't no swinging dick.' Wow, what an understatement. I bet he was in the bridal suite every night at Angola."

I waited for her to continue. She drew on the cigarette and held the smoke down as though she were taking a hit on a reefer.

"The spade wanted to cut my face up," she said. "What's-his-name, Keats, says to him, 'The man don't want us throwing out his pork chops. You just give her a souvenir on her hand or her foot, and I'll bet she'll wear it to church. Under it all, Robin's a righteous girl.' Then the boogie says, 'You always talk with a mouth full of shit, man.'

"What's-his-name thought that was funny. So he laughs and

lights a Picayune and says, 'At least I don't live in a fucking slum so I can be next to a dead witch.'

"How about that for clever conversation? Listening to those guys talk to each other is like drinking out of a spittoon."

"Say that again about the witch."

"The guy lives in a slum around a witch. Or a dead witch or something. Don't try to make sense out of it. These guys buy their brains at a junkyard. Why else would anybody work for Bubba Rocque? They all end up doing time for him. I hear when they get out of Angola he won't give them a job cleaning toilets. What a class guy."

I picked up her hand and squeezed it. It was small and brown in mine. She looked at me in the warm shade, and her mouth parted slightly so I could see her white teeth.

"I have to go back this afternoon."

"Big news flash."

"No cuteness, kiddo. Do you want to go to New Iberia with me?"

"If your conscience bothers you, go to church."

"I have a bait business I could use some help with. I have a little girl living with me, too."

"Life down on the bayou isn't my style, Streak. Come on back here when you're serious."

"You always think I'm running a shuck on you."

"No, you're just a guy that makes impossible rules for himself. That's why you're a mess. Buy a girl lunch, will you?"

Sometimes you leave a person alone. This was one of them.

Out on the ocean a pelican lifted from a green trough and flew by overhead, a bloody fish dripping from its beak.

chapter
SEVEN

THE NEXT MORNING WHEN I AWOKE, BACK IN NEW Iberia, I heard blue jays and mockingbirds in my pecan trees. I put on my gym shorts and tennis shoes and jogged all the way to the drawbridge in the early blue light, drank coffee with the bridge tender, then hit it hard all the way home. I showered and dressed, ate a breakfast of strawberries and Grape-Nuts on the picnic table in the backyard, and watched the breeze ruffle the delicate leaves of the mimosa tree. It had been over thirty hours since I had had a drink. I was still weak, my nerve endings still felt as though they had been touched with lighted matches, but I could feel the tiger starting to let go.

I drove to Lafayette and talked with two priests who had worked with the pilot of the plane that had gone down at Southwest Pass. What they told me was predictable: Father Melancon, the drowned priest, had been a special piece of work. He had been an organizer of migrant farm workers in Texas and Florida, had been busted up with ax handles by company goons outside Florida City, and had served three months' county time in Brownsville for slashing the tires of a sheriff's van that was loaded with arrested strikers. Then he got serious and broke into a General Electric plant and vandalized the nose cone of a nuclear missile. Next stop, the federal pen in Danbury for three years.

I was always fascinated by the government's attempt to control political protest by the clergy in this country. Usually the prosecutor's office would try to portray them as naïve idealists, bumblers who had strayed from their pulpits and convents, and when that didn't work, they were sent up the road with the perverts, geeks, and meltdown cases, which are about the only types that do hard time anymore. However, once they were in the slam, they had a way of spreading their message throughout the convict population.

But the priests in Lafayette didn't recognize the names of Johnny Dartez and Victor Romero. They simply said that Father Melancon had been a trusting man with unusual friends, and that sometimes his unusual friends went with him when he ferried refugees out of villages in El Salvador and Guatemala.

"Romero is a little, dark guy with black curls hanging in his face. He wears a beret," I said.

One of the priests tapped his finger on his cheek.

"You remember him?" I said.

"He didn't wear a beard, but the rest of it was like you say. He was here a month ago with Father Melancon. He said he was from New Orleans but he had relatives in Guatemala."

"Do you know where he is now?"

"No, I'm sorry."

"If he comes around again, call Minos Dautrieve at the Drug Enforcement Administration or call me at this number." I wrote Minos's name and my home number on a piece of paper and gave it to him.

"Is this man in trouble?" the priest said.

"I'm not sure what he is, Father. He used to be a drug courier and street dealer. Now he may be an informer for

Immigration and Naturalization. I'm not sure if he's moving up or down in his moral status."

I drove back to New Iberia through Breaux Bridge so I could stop for lunch at Mulate's. I had deep-fried soft-shell crabs with a shrimp salad and a small bowl of étouffée with French bread and iced tea. Mulate's was a family place now, with only the long mahogany bar and the polished dance floor to remind me of the nightclub and gambling spot it had been when I was in college. The last twenty-five years had changed southern Louisiana a great deal, much of it for the better. The laws of segregation were gone; kids didn't go nigger-knocking on Saturday nights; the Ku Klux Klan didn't burn crosses all over Plaquemines Parish; the demagogues like Judge Leander Perez had slipped into history. But something else was gone, too: the soft pagan ambience that existed right in the middle of a French Catholic culture. Oh, there was still plenty of sleaze around—and narcotics, where there had been none before— but the horse race and slot machines, with their winking lights and rows of cherries and plums and gold bells, had been taken out of the restaurants and replaced with video games; the poolrooms and working-class bars with open bourée games were fewer; the mulatto juke joints, where Negroes and dark- skinned Cajuns had lost their racial identity at the door, were now frequented by white tourists who brought cassette recorders to tape *zydeco* music. The old hot-pillow joints— Margaret's in Opelousas, the Column Hotel in Lafayette, the cribs on Railroad Avenue in New Iberia—were shut down.

I'd like to blame it on the boys at the Rotary and the Kiwa- nis. But that's not fair. We had just become a middle-class peo- ple, that's all.

But one local anachronism had held on to the past success- fully and burgeoned in the present, and that was Bubba Rocque. The kid who would eat a lightbulb for a dollar, set you up with a high-yellow washerwoman for two dollars, throw a cat into the grille of an oncoming car for free, had gone modern. I suspected that he had to piece off a lot of his action to the mob in New Orleans and they probably pulled strings on him sometimes and perhaps eventually they would cannibalize his whole operation, but in the meantime he had taken to drug dealing and big-time pimping like a junkyard dog to lamb chops.

But had he sent the two killers to my house with shotguns? I had a feeling that the net would have to go over a lot of people before I found out. Bubba didn't leave umbilical cords lying around.

That afternoon my detective's appointment with the sheriff's department was approved. I was given a photo identification card and a gold badge, which were contained inside a soft leather wallet; a packet of printed information on departmental policies and employee benefits, which I threw away later without reading; and a Smith & Wesson .38 revolver with worn blueing and two notches filed in the grip. I was to report to work at the sheriff's office at eight the next morning.

I picked up Alafair at my cousin's house in New Iberia, bought ice cream cones for both of us, and played with her on the swing sets in the park. She was a beautiful little girl when the cloud of violent memories and unanswered questions went out of her eyes. Her face was hot and bright with excitement as I swung her on the chains, high up to the edge of the oak limbs, and she was so dark with tan she seemed almost to disappear in the tree's shadows; then she would swish past me in the sunlight, in a roar of squeals, her dusty bare feet just ticking the earth.

We went home and fixed catfish poor-boy sandwiches for

supper, then I drove down the road and hired an elderly mulatto woman, whom I had known since I was a child, as a live-in baby-sitter. That night I packed my suitcase.

I woke early the next morning to the rain falling on the pecan trees and drumming on the gallery. Alafair and the baby-sitter were still asleep. I screwed a hasp and a staple into the door and jamb of Annie's and my bedroom, closed the windows, drew the curtains, and padlocked the door.

Why?

I can't answer. Maybe because it's unholy to wash away the blood of those we love. Maybe because the placement of a tombstone on a grave is a self-serving and atavistic act. (Just as primitive people did, we weight the dead and their memory safely down in the earth.) Maybe because the only fitting monument of those who die violently is the memory of pain they've left behind.

I loaded the .38 revolver with five shells in the cylinder, set the hammer on the empty chamber, and put it in my suitcase. I drank a cup of coffee and hot milk at the kitchen table, took apart my .45 automatic, oiled it, reamed out the barrel with a bore brush, reassembled it, and stuck a full clip back up into the magazine. Then I opened a fresh box of hollow-points and inserted them one at a time with my thumb into a second clip. They were heavy and round in my hand, and they snapped cleanly against the tension of the loading spring. When they flattened out they could blow holes the size of croquet balls in an oak door, destroy the inside of an automobile, leave a key-hole wound in a human being that no physician could heal.

A dark meditation? Yes. Guns kill. That's their function. I had never deliberately kicked a situation into the full-tilt boo-gie. The other side had always taken care of that readily enough. I was sure they would again.

I called the sheriff at his office. He wasn't in. I left a message that I was on my way to New Orleans, that I would see him in one or two days. I looked in on Alafair, who was sleeping with her thumb in her mouth in front of the window fan, then picked up my suitcase, draped my raincoat over my head, and ran through the mud puddles and dripping trees to my truck.

The sun was out but it was still raining when I reached New Orleans at eleven o'clock. I parked my truck on Basin and walked into the old St. Louis Cemetery No. 1, the warm rain hitting on the brim of my hat. There were rows and rows of white-painted brick crypts, the bottom level of tombs often pressed deep into the earth so that you could not read the French on the cracked and worn marble tablets that covered the coffins. Glass jars and rusted tin cans filled with withered flowers littered the ground. Many of the dead had died during one of the city's nineteenth-century epidemics of yellow fever, when the corpses were collected in wagons and stacked like firewood, sprinkled with lime and interred by convicts in chains who were allowed to get drunk before they began their work. Some of the crypts had been gutted by looters, the pieces of bone and moldy cloth and rotted wood raked out onto the ground. On rainy or cold nights, winos crawled inside and slept in fetal positions with bottles of synthetic wine pulled against their chests.

New Orleans's wealthiest and most famous were here: French and Spanish governors, aristocrats killed in duels or in the battle against the British at Chalmette, slave dealers and skippers of clipper ships who ran the Yankee blockade of the city. I even found the grave of Dominique You, the Napoleonic soldier of fortune who became Jean Lafitte's chief gunnery officer. But I was interested in only one grave that day, and even when I found it I couldn't be sure that Marie Laveau was inside it (some people said she was buried in an old oven a couple of blocks away, in St. Louis Cemetery No. 2).

She was known as the voodoo queen of New Orleans during the mid-nineteenth century. She was called a witch, a practitioner of black magic from the Islands, a mulatto opportunist. But regardless, her following had been large, and I suspected that there was still at least one man in this neighborhood who would scoop dirt from her grave and carry it in a red flannel pouch, divine the future by shaking out pigs' bones on the top of her crypt, or one night a month climb into the gutted ruin next to it.

I had no real plan, and it would probably be a matter of luck if I grabbed Toot in that rundown neighborhood around the cemetery. In fact, I was out of my jurisdiction and didn't even have authority to be there. But if I went through official procedure, I would still be in New Iberia and a couple of New Orleans street cops would ask a couple of questions around the neighborhood, provided they had time, and when that didn't work, a night-shift plainclothes with sheaves of outstanding warrants wrapped in rubber bands on his car seat would add Toot's name to the list of wanted suspects in that area and the upshot would be absolutely nothing.

Most criminals are stupid. They creep $500,000 homes in the Garden District, load up two dozen bottles of gin, whiskey, vermouth, and collins mix in a $2,000 Irish linen tablecloth and later drink the booze and throw the tablecloth away.

But I guess my greatest fear was that the locals would scare Toot out of the area, or maybe even nail him and then kick him loose before we could bring him back to New Iberia. It happens. The criminals aren't the only dumb guys in town.

When I was a homicide detective in the First District on Basin we busted a serial killer from Georgia who had murdered people all the way across the South. He was a thirty-five-year-old carnival worker, a blond, rugged-looking man of fearsome physical proportions who wore earrings made out of

gold crucifixes. He had a third-grade education, drew his signature as a child might, and plugged up his toilet with a blanket and flooded the deadlock section of the jail because he
couldn't watch television with the other men in the main holding area; but nevertheless he was able to convince two homicide detectives that he could show them where a young girl
was buried in the levee down in Plaquemines Parish. They put
him in handcuffs rather than leg and waist chains, and drove
him down a board road deep into a swamp.

But he had hidden a paper clip in his mouth. He picked
the lock on his handcuffs, ripped the .357 Magnum out of the
driver's shoulder holster, and blew both detectives all over
the front windshield.

He was never caught again. The bucket of a Ferris wheel fell
on him in Pocatello, Idaho.

I spent the day driving and walking the streets of the neighborhood, from Canal all the way over to Esplanade Avenue. I
talked with blacks, Chicanos, and blue-collar white people in
shoe-shine stands, seven A.M. bars, and corner grocery stores
that smelled of chitlins and smoked carp. Yesterday I had been
a small-town businessman. Today I was a cop, and I got the
reception that cops usually get in a poor neighborhood. They
made me for either a bill collector, a bondsman, a burial insur-
ance man, a process server for a landlord, or Mr. Charlie with
his badge (it's strange how we as white people wonder at
minority attitudes toward us, when we send our worst emissaries among them).

Once I thought I might be close. An ex-boxer who owned a
bar that had a Confederate flag auto tag nailed in the middle
of the front door took the wet end of his cigar out of his
mouth, looked at me with a face that was shapeless with scar
tissue, and said, "Haitian? You're talking about a boon from
the Islands, right?"

"Right."

"There's a bunch of those cannibals over on North Villere. They eat all the dogs in the neighborhood. They even seine the goldfish out of the pond in the park. Don't stay for supper. You might end up in the pot."

The yard of the one-story, wood-frame yellow house he directed me to was overgrown with wet weeds and littered with automobile and washing-machine parts. I drove down the alley and tried to see through the back windows, but the shades were pulled against the late-afternoon sun. I could hear a baby crying. Sacks of garbage that smelled of rotting fish were stacked on the back steps, and the diapers that hung on the clothesline were gray and frayed from hand-washing. I went around front and knocked on the door.

A small, frightened black man with a face like a cooked apple came to within three feet of the screen and looked at me out of the gloom.

"Where's Toot?" I said.

He shook his head as though he didn't understand.

"Toot," I said.

He held his palms outward and shook them back and forth. His eyes were red in the gloom. Two children were coloring in a book on the floor. A wide-hipped woman with an infant on her shoulder watched me from the kitchen door.

"*Vous connaissez un homme qui s'appelle Toot?*" I said.

He answered me in a polyglot of French and English and perhaps African that was incomprehensible. He was also terri-fied.

"I'm not from Immigration," I said. "*Comprenez? Pas Immigration.*"

But he wasn't buying it. I couldn't reach past his fear nor make him understand my words, and then I made matters worse when I asked again about Toot and used the term *ton-*

ton macoute. The man's eyes widened, and he swallowed as though he had a pebble in his throat.

But it was hopeless. Good work, Robicheaux, I thought. Now these poor people will probably stay frightened for days, shuddering every time an automobile slows out front. They would never figure out who I was and would simply assume that I was only a prelude of worse things to come. Then I had another thought. Police officers and Immigration officials didn't give money to illegal immigrants.

I took a five-dollar bill out of my wallet, creased it lengthwise, and slipped it through the jamb of the latched screen.

"This is for your baby," I said. *"Pour vot' enfant."*

He stared at me dumbfounded. When I looked back at the screen from my truck, he and his wife were both staring at me.

I bought a block of cheese, a half-pound of sliced ham, an onion, a loaf of French bread, and a quart of milk in a Negro grocery store, parked by the cemetery, and ate supper while the rain began falling out of the purple twilight. Over on Basin I saw a neon Jax sign light over a barroom.

When you don't nail a guy like Toot in his lair, you look for him in the places that take care of his desires. Most violent men like women. The perverts bust them up; contract hit men use them as both reward for their accomplishment and testimony to their power. I knew almost every black and high-yellow pick-up bar and hot-pillow joint in New Orleans. It was going to be a long night.

I was exhausted when the sun came up in the morning. It had stopped raining about three A.M., and now the pools of water in the street were drying in the hot sunlight, and you could feel the moisture and heat radiate up from the concrete like steam.

I brushed my teeth and shaved in a filling station rest room. My eyes were red around the rims, my face lined with fatigue. I had gone into a dozen lowlife Negro bars during the night, had been propositioned, threatened, and even ignored, but no one knew a Haitian by the name of Toot.

I had coffee and beignets in the Café du Monde, then gave the neighborhood around the cemetery one more try. By now my face had become so familiar up and down Iberville and St. Louis that grocery and drugstore owners and bartenders looked the other way when they saw me coming. The sun was white in the sky; the elephant ears, philodendron, and banana trees that grew along the back alleys were beaded with moisture; the air had the wet, fecund taste of a hothouse. At noon I was ready to give it up.

Then I saw two police cars, with their bubble-gum lights on, parked in front of a stucco house one block up North Villere from the yellow house where the frightened man lived. An ambulance was backed up the driveway to the stairway of the garage apartment. I parked my truck by the curb and opened my badge in my hand and walked up to two patrolmen in the drive. One was writing on a clipboard and trying to ignore the sweat that leaked out of his hatband.

"What have you got?" I said.

"A guy dead in the bathtub," he said.

"What from?"

"Hell if I know. He's been in there two or three days. No air-conditioning either."

"What's his race?"

"I don't know. I haven't been up there. Check it out if you want to. Take your handkerchief with you."

Halfway up the stairs the odor hit me. It was rotten and acrid and sweet at the same time, reeking of salt and decay, fetid and gray as a rat's breath, penetrating and enveloping as the stench of excrement. I gagged and had to press my fist against my mouth.

Two paramedics with rubber gloves on were waiting patiently with a stretcher in the tiny living room while the scene investigator took flash pictures in the bath. Their faces were pinched and they kept clearing their throats. An overweight plainclothes detective with a florid, dilated face stood in the doorway so that I couldn't see the bathtub clearly. His white shirt was so drenched with sweat that you could see his skin through the cloth. He turned and looked at me, puzzled. I thought I might know him from my years in the First District, but I didn't. I turned up my badge in my palm.

"I'm Dave Robicheaux, Iberia Parish sheriff's office," I said. "Who is he?"

"We don't know yet. The landlord's on vacation, there's nothing in the apartment with a name on it," he said. "A meter reader came up the stairs this morning and tossed his cookies over the railing. It's all over the rosebush. It really rounds out the smell. What are you looking for?"

"We've got a warrant on a Haitian."

"Be my guest," he said, and stepped aside.

I walked into the bathroom with my handkerchief pressed over my mouth and nose. The tub was an old iron, rust-streaked one on short metal legs that looked like animal claws. A man's naked black calves and feet stuck up out of the far end of the tub.

"He was either a dumb shit that liked to keep his radio on the washbasin, or somebody threw it in there with him," the detective said. "Any way you cut it, it cooked him."

The water had evaporated out of the tub, and dirty lines of grit were dried around the drain hole. I looked at the powerful hands that were now frozen into talons, the muscles in the big chest that had become flaccid with decomposition, the half-closed eyes that seemed focused on a final private thought, the pink mouth that was still locked wide with a silent scream.

"It must have been a sonofabitch. He actually clawed paint off the sides," the detective said. "There, look at the white stuff under his nails. You know him?"

"His name's Toot. He worked with Eddie Keats. Maybe he worked for Bubba Rocque, too."

"Huh," he said. "Well, it couldn't have happened to a nicer guy, then. What a way to get it. Once over in Algiers I had a case like this. A woman was listening to this faith healer while she was washing dishes. So the faith healer told everybody to put their hands on the radio and get healed, and it blew her right out of her panty hose. What'd y'all have on this guy?"

"Assault and battery, suspicion of murder."

The scene investigator walked past us with his camera. The detective crooked his finger at the two paramedics.

"All right, bag him and get him out of here," he said, and turned to me again. "They'll have to burn the stink out of this place with a flamethrower. You got everything you want?"

"You mind if I look around a minute?"

"Go ahead. I'll wait for you outside."

Propped against the back corner of the closet, behind the racked tropical shirts, the white slacks, the flowered silk vests, I found a twelve-gauge pump shotgun. I opened the breech. It had been cleaned and oiled and the cordite wiped out of the chamber with a rag. Then I unscrewed the mechanism to the pump action itself and saw that the sportsman's plug had been taken out so the magazine could hold five rather than three rounds. On the floor was a half-empty box of red double-ought shotgun shells of the same manufacture as the ones that had littered the floor of Annie's and my bedroom. I rolled one of the shells back and forth in my palm and then put it back in the box.

The detective lit a cigarette as he walked down the stairs into the yard. Afternoon rain clouds had moved across the sun, and he wiped the sweat out of his eyebrows with the flat of his hand and widened his eyes in the breeze that had sprung up from the south.

"I'd like for you to come down to the District and file a report on your man," he said.

"All right."

"Who's this guy supposed to have killed?"

"My wife."

He stopped in the middle of the yard, a dead palm tree rattling over his head, and looked at me with his mouth open. The wind blew his cigarette ashes on his tie.

I decided I had one more stop to make before I headed back to New Iberia. Because of my concern for Alafair, I had given the Immigration and Naturalization Service a wide berth. But as that Negro janitor had told me in high school, you never let the batter know you're afraid of him. When he spreads his feet in the box and gives you that mean squint from under his cap, as though he's sighting on your throat, you spit on the ball and wipe his letters off with it. He'll probably have a change in attitude toward your relationship.

But Mr. Monroe was to surprise me.

I parked the truck in the shade of a spreading oak off Loyola and walked back in the hot sunlight to the INS office. His desk was out on the floor, among several others, and when he looked up from a file folder in his hands and saw me, the skin around his ears actually stretched across the bone. His black hair, which was combed like wires across his pate, gleamed dully in the fluorescent light. I saw his throat swallow under his bow tie.

"I'm here officially," I said, easing my badge out of my side pants pocket. "I'm a detective with the Iberia sheriff's office now. Do you mind if I sit down?"

He didn't answer. He took a cigarette out of a pack on his desk and lit it. His eyes were straight ahead. I sat down in the straight-backed chair next to his desk and looked at the side of his face. By his desk blotter in a silver frame was a picture of him and his wife and three children. A clear vase with two yellow roses in it sat next to the picture.

"What do you want?" he said.

"I'm on a murder investigation."

He held his cigarette to his mouth between two fingers and smoked it without ever really detaching it from his lips. His eyes were focused painfully into space.

"I think you guys have a string on somebody I want," I said.

Finally he looked at me. His face was as tight as paper.

"Mr. Robicheaux, I'm sorry," he said.

"Sorry for what?"

"For . . . about your wife. I'm truly sorry."

"How did you know about my wife?"

"It was in the area section of the *Picayune*."

"Where's Victor Romero?"

"I don't know this man."

"Listen, this is a murder investigation. I'm a police officer. Don't you jerk me around."

He lowered his cigarette toward the desk blotter and let out his breath. People at the other desks were obviously listening now.

"You have to understand something. I do field work with illegal immigrants in the workplace. I check green cards. I make sure people have work permits. I've done that for seven years."

"I don't care what you do. You answer me about Victor Romero."

"I can't tell you anything."

"You think carefully about your words, Mr. Monroe. You're on the edge of obstruction."

His fingers went to his temple. I saw his bottom lip flutter.

"You have to believe this," he said. "I'm very sorry about what's happened to you. There's no way I can express how I feel."

I paused before I spoke again.

"When somebody's dead, apologies have as much value as beating off in a paper bag," I said. "I think you need to learn that, maybe go down to the courthouse and listen to one of the guys on his way up to Angola. Are you following me? Because this is what I believe you guys did: you planted Johnny Dartez and Victor Romero inside the sanctuary movement, and four people ended up dead at Southwest Pass. I think a bomb brought that plane down. I think Romero had something to do with it, too. He's also hooked up with Bubba Rocque, and maybe Bubba had my wife killed. You shield this guy and I'm going to turn the key on you."

I could hear him breathing now. His pate was slick with oil and perspiration under the light. His eyes clicked back and forth.

"I don't care who hears this, and you can make of it what you want," he said. "I'm a career civil servant. I don't make policy or decisions. I try to keep illegals from taking American jobs. That's all I do here."

"They made you a player. You take their money, you take their orders, you take their fall."

"I'm not an articulate man. I've tried to tell you my feelings, but you won't accept that. I don't blame you. I'm just sorry. I don't have anything else to say, Mr. Robicheaux."

"Where's your supervisor?"

"He's gone to Washington."

I looked at the picture of his family on the desk.

"My wife's casket had to be kept closed at the funeral," I said. "You think about that a minute. Also, you tell your supervisor I'm going to run that heroin mule to ground. When I do, I'm going to squeeze him. You better hope none of y'all's names come out of his mouth."

When I walked out the door the only sound in the room was the telex machine clacking.

It was evening when I got home, and Alafair and the baby-sitter had already had their supper. I was hungry and too wired to sleep, so I heated up some dirty rice, shelled crawfish, and cornbread, wrapped it in foil, and packed it in my canvas ruck-sack with my army mess kit and walked down the road in the flaming sunset to a spot on the bayou where my father and little brother and I used to dig for minié balls when I was a boy.

A sugar planter's home had been built there in the 1830s, but the second story had been torched by General Banks's soldiers in 1863 and the roof and the blackened cypress timbers had collapsed inside the brick shell. Over the years the access road had filled with pine seedlings and undergrowth, vandals had prized up the flagstones in the fireplaces, looking for gold coins, and the grave markers had been knocked down in the family burial ground and the graves themselves were recognizable only because of their dark green color and the blanket of mushrooms that grew across them.

Four-o'clocks and wild rosebushes grew along the rim of a small coulee that flowed through the edge of the clearing, past a rotted-out cistern by the side of the house and a blacksmith's forge that was now only a rusty smear in the wet soil. The breeze off the bayou was still strong enough to push the mosquitoes back into the trees, and I sat on a dead cypress stump in the last wash of red sunlight and ate supper from my mess kit. The water was clear, copper-colored, flowing over the rocks in the bottom of the coulee, and I could see small bream hiding under the moss that swung in the current. Along these same banks my father, my brother, and I had dug out a bucket full of minié balls as well as cannister and grapeshot, bits of chain, and chopped-up horseshoes fired by Union cannon into a Confederate rearguard. We used rakes to clear the vines and damp layers of dead leaves from the coulee walls, and the minié balls would drop from the loam like white teeth. They were conical-shaped on one end, with a hollow indentation and three grooved rings on the other, and they always felt heavy and smooth and round in your palm.

In our innocence we didn't think about them as objects that blew muscle away from bone, ripped through linkage and webs of vein, tore the jaw and tongue from a face. I had to become a new colonial and journey across the seas to learn that simple fact. I had to feel a shotgun shell touched by the long black fingers of a man whose mission was to create and capture human misery on Polaroid film.

I put aside my mess kit and tore the petals from a pink rose and watched them drift down onto the water, float along the riffle through the ferns and out into the sunlight. I had more to think about than I wanted to. True, I was sober; the physical pain of my last bender was gone, and the tiger seemed to be in his cage; but I had a lot of tomorrows to face, and in the past that long-distance view of my life had a way of getting me drunk again. Tomorrow at noon I would go to an AA meeting and confess my slip in front of the group, which was not an easy thing to do. I had once again failed not only myself and my Higher Power, but I had betrayed the trust of my friends as well.

I knocked out my mess kit on the cypress stump, and put it away in my rucksack. I thought I heard a car door open and close on the road, but I paid it little attention. The shadows had fallen across the clearing now, and the mosquitoes were lifting in clouds from the trees and undergrowth. I flipped one of the rucksack straps over my shoulder and walked through the pine seedlings toward the sun's last red glare above the main road.

Through the tree trunks I saw the dark outline of a man standing by a maroon Toyota parked on the road. He stood on the far side of the hood, looking at me, his face covered with shadow, motionless, as though he were taking a leak by his tire. For a moment I couldn't see him at all because of a big spreading oak, then the trees thinned and I saw him suddenly swing a bolt-action rifle to his shoulder, the leather sling already wrapped tight around his left forearm, saw the lens of the telescopic sight glint as dark as firelight in a whiskey glass, saw his chest and elbows lean across the low roof of the car with the quick grace of an infantry marksman who never cants his sights and delivers the mail somewhere between your breastbone and throat.

I jumped sideways and rolled through the underbrush just as the rifle roared and a bullet popped leaves off a half-dozen limbs and splintered the side of a pine trunk as though it had been touched lightly with a chainsaw. I heard him work the bolt, even heard the empty shell casing clink off the car metal, but I was running now, zigzagging through the woods, pine branches whipping back across my face and chest, the carpet of dead leaves an explosion of sound under my feet. I had the canvas straps of the rucksack bunched in my left hand, and when his second round went off and tore through the undergrowth and pinged away off the brick of the plantation ruin, I dove on my chest, ripped the sack flap loose from its leather thong, and got my hand around the butt of my .45 automatic.

I think he knew it had turned around on him. I heard him work the bolt, but I also heard the barrel knock against the car roof or windshield and I could hear him shaking the bolt as though he had tried to jam a shell too fast into the chamber. I was up and running again, this time at an angle toward the road so I would exit the woods behind his car. The trees were thickly spaced here, and he fired at my sound rather than shape, and the bullet *thropped* through a briar patch fifteen feet behind me.

I crashed through the undergrowth and came out onto the lighted edge of the woods just as he threw his rifle across the front seat and jumped behind the steering wheel of his car. He was a dark, small man, in jeans and running shoes and a purple T-shirt, with black hair that hung in curls. But I was running so fast and breathlessly that I slipped to my knees on the side of the drainage ditch and almost filled the .45's barrel with dirt. He floored his car, popped the clutch, and spun water out of a muddy pool. I fell forward on my elbows, my arms extended, my left palm cupped under the .45's butt, and began firing.

The roar was deafening. I whanged the first round off his bumper, punched two holes in the trunk, went high once, then blew out the back window with such force that it looked as if it had been gutted by a baseball bat. I rose to my knees and kept firing, the recoil knocking my arm higher with each explosion. His car slid sideways at the bend in the road, smashed against an oak trunk before he righted the front wheels, and I saw my last round blow his taillight into a tangle of wires and broken red plastic. But I didn't hit his gas tank or a tire, or punch through his firewall into the engine block, and I heard him winding up his gearbox until it almost screamed as he disappeared beyond a flooded canebreak on the side of the road.

chapter
EIGHT

AFTER I HAD CALLED IN A DESCRIPTION OF THE shooter and his Toyota at the boat dock, I went back out on the road with a flashlight and hunted for the shells he had ejected from his rifle. Two fully loaded gravel trucks had passed on the road and crushed one of the .30-06 shells flat in the dirt and half buried the other in a muddy depression, but I prized each of them out with the awl of my Swiss army knife and dropped them in a plastic bag. They were wet and muddy and scoured from being ground under the truck's tires, but a spent cartridge thrown from a bolt-action rifle is always a good one to recover a print from, because usually the shooter presses each load down with his thumb and leaves a nice spread across the brass surface.

The next morning I listened quietly while the sheriff shared his feelings about my going to New Orleans for two days without authorization. His face was flushed, his tie pulled loose, and he talked with his hands folded on his desk in order to conceal his anger. I couldn't blame him for the way he felt, and the fact that I didn't answer him only made him more frustrated. Finally he stopped, shifted his weight in the chair, and looked at me as though he had just abandoned everything he had said.

"Forget that bullshit about procedure. What bothers me is the feeling I've been used," he said.

"I called before I left. You weren't in," I said.

"That's not enough."

Again I didn't answer him. The bagged rifle shells were on his desk.

"Tell me the truth. What would you have done if you'd found the Haitian alive?" he asked.

"Busted him."

"I want to believe that."

I looked out the window at a bright green magnolia tree in the morning haze.

"I'm sorry about what I did. It won't happen again," I said.

"If it does, you won't have to resign. I'll take your badge myself."

I looked at the magnolia tree a moment and watched a hummingbird hang over one of the white flowers.

"If we get a print off those shells, I want to send it to New Orleans," I said.

"Why?"

"The scene investigator dusted the radio that was in the bathtub with the Haitian. Maybe there's a connection with our shooter."

"How?"

"Who knows? I want New Orleans to give us a copy of Victor Romero's sheet and prints, too."

"You think he was the shooter?"

"Maybe."

"What's the motive?"

"Hell if I know."

"Dave, do you think maybe you're trying to tie too many things together here? I mean, you want your wife's killers. But you've only got one set of suspects that you can reach out and touch, so maybe you've decided to see some threads that aren't there. Like you said, you put a lot of people in Angola."

"The ex-con who snuffs you wants you to see his face and enjoy a couple of memories with him. The guy who shot at me last night did it for money. I don't know him."

"Well, maybe the guy's car will show up. I don't know how he got it out of the parish with all those holes in it."

"He boosted it, and it's in the bayou or a garage somewhere. We won't find it. At least not for a while."

"You're really an optimist, aren't you?"

I spent the day doing the routine investigative work of a sheriff's detective in a rural parish. I didn't enjoy it. For some reason, probably because he was afraid I'd run off again, the sheriff assigned me a uniformed deputy named Cecil Aguillard, an enormous, slow-witted redbone. He was a mixture of Cajun, Negro, and Chitimacha Indian; his skin was the color of burnt brick, and he had tiny, turquoise-green eyes and a pie-plate face you could break a barrel slat across without his changing expression. He drove seventy miles an hour with one hand, spit Red Man out the window, and pressed on the pedals with such weight and force that he had worn the rubber off the metal.

We investigated a stabbing in a Negro bar, the molestation of a retarded girl by her uncle, an arson case in which a man set fire to his own fish camp because his drunken guests wouldn't leave his party by the next morning, and finally, late that afternoon, the armed robbery of a grocery store out on the Abbeville road. The owner was a black man, a cousin of Cecil Aguillard, and the robber had taken ninety-five dollars from him, walked him back to the freezer, hit him across the eye with his pistol barrel, and locked him inside. When we questioned him he was still shaking from the cold, and his eye was swollen into a purple knot. He could only tell us that the robber was white, that he had driven up in a small brown car with an out-of-state license plate, had walked inside with a hat on, then suddenly had rolled down a nylon stocking over his face, mashing his features into a blur of skin and hair.

"Somet'ing else. He took a bottle of apricot brandy and a bunch of them Tootsie Roll," the Negro said. "I tell him 'Big man with a gun, sucking on Tootsie Roll.' So he bust me in the face, him. I need that money for my daughter's col'ech in Lafayette. It ain't cheap, no. You gonna get it back?"

I wrote on my clipboard and didn't reply.

"You gonna get it back, you?"

"It's hard to tell sometimes."

I knew better, of course. In fact, I figured our man was in Lake Charles or Baton Rouge by now. But time and chance happeneth to us all, even to the lowlifes.

On our radio we heard a deputy in a patrol car run a check on a 1981 tan Chevette with a Florida tag. He had stopped the Chevette out on the Jeanerette road because the driver had thrown a liquor bottle at a road sign. I called the dispatcher and asked her to tell the deputy to hold the driver until we got there.

Cecil drove the ten-mile distance in less than eight minutes. The Chevette was pulled over on the oyster-shell parking lot of a ramshackle clapboard dance hall built back from the road. It was five P.M., the sun was orange over the rain clouds piled in the west, and Haliburton and cement and pickup trucks were parked around the entrance to the bar. A deeply tanned man in blue jeans, with no shirt on, leaned with one arm hooked over the open door of his Chevette, spitting disgustedly between his legs. His back was tattooed with a blue spider caught in a web. The web extended over both of his shoulder blades.

"What have you got on him?" I said to the deputy who had held him for us.

"Nothing. Littering. He says he works seven-and-seven off-shore."

"Where'd he break the bottle?"

"Back there. Against that railroad sign."

"We'll take it from here. Thanks for your help," I said.

The deputy nodded and drove off in his car.

"Shake this guy down, Cecil. I'll be back in a minute," I said.

I walked back to the railroad crossing, where an old LOUISIANA LAW—STOP sign was postholed by the side of the gravel bedding. The wooden boards were stained with a dark, wet smear. I picked up pieces of glass out of the gravel and soot-blackened weeds until I found two amber-colored pieces that were hinged together by an apricot brandy label.

I started back toward the parking lot with the pieces of wet glass in my shirt pocket. Cecil had the tattooed man spread on the front fender of the Chevette and was ripping his pockets inside out. The tattooed man turned his head backwards, said something, and started to stand erect, when Cecil simultaneously picked him up in the air by his belt and slammed his head down on the hood. The man's face went white with concussion. Some oilfield roughnecks in tin hats, their denims spattered with drilling mud, stopped in the bar entrance and walked toward us.

"We're not supposed to bruise the freight, Cecil," I said.

"You want to know what he said to me?"

"Ease up. Our man here isn't going to give us any more trouble. He's already standing in the pig flop up to his kneecaps."

I turned to the oilfield workers, who obviously didn't like the idea of a redbone knocking around a white man.

"Private party, gentlemen," I said. "Read about it in the paper tomorrow. Just don't try to get your name in the story today. You got my drift?"

They made a pretense of staring me sullenly in the face, but a cold beer was much more interesting to them than a night in the parish jail.

The tattooed man was leaning on his arms against the front fender again. There were grains of dirt on the side of his face where it had hit the hood, and a pinched, angry light in his eyes. His blond hair was uncut and as thick and dry as old straw. Two Tootsie Roll wrappers lay on the floor of his car.

I looked under the seats. Nothing was there.

"You want to open the hatchback for us?" I said.

"Open it yourself," he said.

"I asked you if you wanted to do that. You don't have to. It beats going to jail, though. Of course, that doesn't mean you're necessarily going to jail. I just thought you might want to be a regular guy and help us out."

"Because you got no cause."

"That's right. It's called 'probable cause.' Were you in Raiford? I like the artwork on your back," I said.

"You want to look in my fucking car? I don't give a shit. Help yourself," he said, pulled the keys from the ignition, popped up the hatchback, and pulled open the tire well. There was nothing inside it except the spare and a jack.

"Cuff him and put him behind the screen," I told Cecil.

Cecil pulled the man's hands behind his back, snapped the handcuffs tightly onto his wrists, and walked him back to our car as though he were a wounded bird. He locked him behind the wire mesh that separated the back and front seats, and waited for me to get into the passenger's seat. When I didn't, he walked back to where I stood by the Chevette.

"What's the deal? He's the one, ain't he?" he said.

"Yep."

"Let's take him in."

"We've got a problem, Cecil. There's no gun, no hat, no

nylon stocking. Your cousin's not going to be able to identify him in a lineup, either."

"I seen you pick up them brandy glass. I seen you look at them Tootsie Roll paper."

"That's right. But the prosecutor's office will tell us to kick him loose. We don't have enough evidence, podna."

"My fucking ass. You get a beer, you. Come see in ten minutes. He give you that stocking, you better believe, yeah."

"How much money was in his wallet?"

"A hunnerd, maybe."

"I think there's another way to do it, Cecil. Stay here a minute."

I walked back to our car. It was hot inside, and the handcuffed man was sweating heavily. He was trying to blow a mosquito away from his face with his breath.

"My partner wants to bust you," I said.

"So?"

"There's a catch. I don't like you. That means I don't like protecting you."

"What are you talking about, man?"

"I went off duty at five o'clock. I'm going to get me a shrimp sandwich and a Dr Pepper and let him take you in. Are you starting to see the big picture now?"

He shook back his damp hair from his eyes and tried to look indifferent, but he didn't hide fear well.

"I have a feeling that somewhere between here and the jail you're going to remember where you left that gun and stocking," I said. "But anyway it's between you and him now. And I don't take stock in rumors."

"What? What the fuck you talking about rumors, man?"

"That he took a suspect into the woods and put out his eye with a bicycle spoke. I don't believe it."

I saw him swallow. The sweat ran out of his hair.

"Hey, did you see *The Treasure of the Sierra Madre?*" I asked. "There's a great scene in there when this Mexican bandit says to Humphrey Bogart, 'I like your watch. I think you give me your watch.' Maybe you saw it on the late show at Raiford."

"I ain't playing this bullshit, man."

"Come on, you can do it. You pretend you're Humphrey Bogart. You drive your car back to that convenience store and you give the owner your hundred dollars and that Gucci watch you're wearing. It's going to brighten up your day. I guarantee it."

The mosquito sat on the end of his nose.

"Here comes Cecil now. Let him know what you've decided," I said.

The light was soft through the trees as I drove along the bayou road toward my house that evening. Sometimes during the summer the sky in southern Louisiana actually turns lavender, with strips of pink cloud in the west like flamingo wings painted above the horizon, and this evening the air was sweet with the smell of watermelons and strawberries in somebody's truck patch and the hydrangeas and night-blooming jasmine that completely covered my neighbor's wooden fence. Out on the bayou the bream were dimpling the water like raindrops.

Before I turned into my lane I passed a fire-engine-red MG convertible with a flat tire by the side of the road, then I saw Bubba Rocque's wife sitting on my front step with a silver thermos next to her thigh and a plastic cup in her fingers. She wore straw Mexican sandals, beige shorts, and a low-cut white blouse with blue and brown tropical birds on it, and she had pinned a yellow hibiscus in her dark hair. She smiled at me as I walked toward her with my coat over my shoulder. Once again I noticed that strange red cast in her brown eyes.

"I had a flat tire. Can you give me a ride back to my aunt's on West Main?" she asked.

"Sure. Or I can change it for you."

"There's no air in the spare, either." She drank from the cup. Her mouth was red and wet, and she smiled at me again.

"What are you doing down this way, Mrs. Rocque?"

"It's Claudette, Dave. My cousin lives down at the end of the road. I come over to New Iberia about once a month to see all my relatives."

"I see."

"Am I putting you out?"

"No. I'll be just a minute."

I didn't ask her in. I went inside to check on Alafair and told the baby-sitter to go ahead and serve supper, that I would be back shortly.

"Help a lady up. I'm a little twisted this evening," Claudette Rocque said, and reached her hand out to mine. She felt heavy when I pulled her erect. I could smell gin and cigarettes on her breath.

"I'm sorry about your wife," she said.

"Thank you."

"It's a terrible thing."

I held the truck door open for her and didn't answer.

She sat with her back at an angle to the far door, her legs slightly apart, and moved her eyes over my face.

Oh boy, I thought. I drove out of the shadows of the pecan trees, back onto the bayou road.

"You look uncomfortable," she said.

"Long day."

"Are you afraid of Bubba?"

"I don't think about him," I lied.

"I don't think you're afraid of very much."

"I respect your husband's potential. I apologize for not asking you in. The house is a mess."

"You don't get backed into a corner easily, do you?"

"Like I said, it's been a long day, Mrs. Rocque."

She made an exaggerated pout with her mouth.

"And you're not going to call a married lady by her first name. What a proper law officer you are. Do you want a gin rickey?"

"No, thanks."

"You're going to hurt my feelings. Has someone told you bad things about me?"

I watched a sparrow hawk glide on extended wings down the length of the bayou.

"Did someone tell you I was in St. Gabriel?" she said. Then she smiled and reached out and ticked the skin above my collar with her nail. "Or maybe they told you I wasn't all girl."

I could feel her eyes moving on the side of my face.

"I've made the officer uncomfortable. I think I even made him blush," she said.

"How about a little slack, Mrs. Rocque?"

"Will you have a drink with me, then?"

"What do you think the odds are of your having a flat tire by my front lane?"

Her round doll's eyes were bright as she looked at me over her raised drinking cup.

"He's such a detective," she said. "He's thinking so hard now, wondering what the bad lady is up to." She rubbed her back against the door and flattened her thighs against the truck seat. "Maybe the lady is interested in you. Are you interested in me?"

"I wouldn't go jerking Bubba around, Mrs. Rocque."

"Oh my, how direct."

"You live with him. You know the kind of man he is. If I was in your situation, I'd give some thought to what I was doing."

"You're being rude, Mr. Robicheaux."

"Read it like you want. Your husband has black lightning in his brain. Mess around with his pride, embarrass him socially, and I think you'll get to see that same kid who wheeled his crippled cousin into the coulee."

"I have some news for you, sir," she said. Her voice wasn't coy anymore, and the red tint in her brown eyes seemed to take on a brighter cast. "I did three years in a place where the bull dykes tell you not to come into the shower at night unless you want to lose your cherry. Bubba never did time. I don't think he could. I think he'd last about three days until they had to lock him in a box and put handles on it and carry it out in the middle of an empty field."

I drove onto the drawbridge. The tires thumped on the metal grid. I saw the bridge tender look at Claudette Rocque and me with a quizzical expression on his face.

"Another thought for you, sir," she said. "Bubba has a couple of sluts he keeps on tap in New Orleans. I'm not supposed to mention them. I'm just his cutie-pie Cajun girl that's supposed to clean his house and wash his sweat suits. I've got a big flash for you boys. Your jockstrap stinks."

In the cooling dusk I passed a row of weathered Negro shacks with sagging galleries, a bar and barbecue joint under a spreading oak, an old brick grocery store with a lighted Dixie beer sign in the window.

"I'm going to drop you at the cab stand," I said. "Do you have money for cabfare?"

"Bubba and I own cabs. I don't ride in them."

"Then it's a good night for a walk."

"You're a shit," she said.

"You dealt it."

"Yeah, you got a point. I thought I could do something for you. Big mistake. You're one of those full-time good losers. You know what it takes to be a good loser? Practice." On East Main she pointed ahead in the dusk. "Drop me at that bar."

Then she finished the last of her thermos and casually dropped it out the truck window into the street. It sprang end over end on the concrete. A group of men smoking cigars and drinking canned beer in front of the bar turned and stared in our direction.

"I was going to offer you a hundred-thousand-dollar-a-year deal to run Bubba's fish-packing house in Morgan City," she said. "Think about that on your way back to your worm sales."

I slowed the truck in front of the bar. The neon beer signs made the inside of the cab red. The men outside the bar entrance had stopped talking and were looking at us.

"Also, I don't want you to drive out of here thinking you've been in control of things tonight," she said, and got up on her knees, put her arms around my neck, and kissed me wetly on the cheek. "You just missed the best lay you'll ever have, pumpkin. Why don't you try some pocket pool at your AA meetings? It really goes with your personality."

But I was too tired to care whether she had won the day or not. It was a night of black clouds roiling over the Gulf, of white electricity jumping across the vast, dark dome of sky above me, of the tiger starting to walk around his cage. I could almost hear his thick, leathery paws scudding against the wire mesh, see his hot orange eyes in the darkness, smell his dung and the fetid odor of rotted meat on his breath.

I never had an explanation for these moments that would

come upon me. A psychologist would probably call it depression. A nihilist might call it philosophical insight. But regardless, it seemed there was nothing for it except the acceptance of another sleepless night. Batist, Alafair, and I took the pickup truck to the drive-in movie in Lafayette, set out deck chairs on the oyster shells, and ate hot dogs and drank lemonade and watched a Walt Disney double feature, but I couldn't rid myself of the dark well I felt my soul descending into.

In the glow of the movie screen I looked at Alafair's upraised and innocent face and wondered about the victims of greed and violence and political insanity all over the world. I have never believed that their suffering is accidental or a necessary part of the human condition. I believe it is the direct consequence of corporate avarice, the self-serving manipulations of politicians who wage wars but never serve in them themselves, and, perhaps worse, the indifference of those of us who know better.

I've seen many of those victims myself, seen them carried out of the village we mortared, washed down with canteens after they were burned with napalm, exhumed from graves on a riverbank where they were buried alive.

But as bad as my Indochinese memories were, one image from a photograph I had seen as a child seemed to encapsulate the dark reverie I had fallen into. It had been taken by a Nazi photographer at Bergen-Belsen, and it showed a Jewish mother carrying her baby down a concrete ramp toward the gas chamber, while she led a little boy with her other hand and a girl of about nine walked behind her. The girl wore a short cloth coat like the ones children wore at my elementary school. The lighting in the picture was bad, the faces of the family shadowy and indistinct, but for some reason the little girl's white sock, which had worked down over her heel, stood out in the gloom as though it had been struck with a shaft of gray light. The image of her sock pushed down over her heel in that cold corridor had always stayed with me. I can't tell you why. But I feel the same way when I relive Annie's death, or remember Alafair's story about her Indian village, or review that tired old film strip from Vietnam. I commit myself once again to that black box that I cannot think myself out of.

Instead, I sometimes recall a passage from the Book of Psalms. I have no theological insight, my religious ethos is a battered one; but those lines seem to suggest an answer that my reason cannot, namely, that the innocent who suffer for the rest of us become anointed and loved by God in a special way; the votive candle of their lives had made them heaven's prisoners.

It rained during the night, and in the morning the sun came up soft and pink in the mist that rose from the trees across the bayou. I walked out to the road and got the newspaper from the mailbox and read it on the front porch with a cup of coffee.

The phone rang. I went inside and answered it.

"What are you doing driving around with the dyke?"

"Dunkenstein?" I said.

"That's right. What are you doing with the dyke?"

"None of your business."

"Everything she and Bubba do is our business."

"How'd you know I was with Claudette Rocque?"

"We have our ways."

"There wasn't a tail."

"Maybe you didn't see him."

"There wasn't a tail."

"So?"

"Have you got their phone tapped?"

He was silent.

"What are you trying to tell me, Dunkenstein?" I asked.

"That I think you're crazy."

"She used the phone to tell somebody I gave her a ride into New Iberia?"

"She told her husband. She called him from a bar. Some people might think you're a dumb shit, Robicheaux."

I looked at the mist hanging in the pecan trees. The leaves were dark and wet with dew.

"A few minutes ago I was enjoying a cup of coffee and the morning paper," I said. "I think I'm going to finish the paper now and forget this conversation."

"I'm calling from the little grocery store by the drawbridge. I'll be down to your place in about ten minutes."

"I think I'll make a point of being on my way to work by then."

"No, you won't. I already called your office and told them you'd be late. Hang loose."

A few minutes later I watched him drive his U.S. government motor pool car up my front lane. He closed his car door and stepped around the mud puddles in the yard. His loafers were shined, his seersucker slacks ironed with knife-edge creases, his handsome blond face gleaming with the closeness of his shave. He wore his polished brown belt high up on his waist, which made him look even taller than he was.

"Have you got another cup of coffee?" he said.

"What is it you want, Minos?" I held the screen open for him, but I imagine my face and tone were not hospitable.

He stepped inside and looked at Alafair's coloring book on the floor.

"Maybe I don't want anything. Maybe I want to help you," he said. "Why don't you try not to be so sensitive all the time? Every time I talk with you, you're bent out of joint about something."

"You're in my house. You're running on my meter. You haven't given me any help, either. Cut the bullshit."

"All right, you've got a legitimate beef. I told you we'd handle the action. We didn't. That's the way it goes sometimes. You know that. You want me to catch air?"

"Come on in the kitchen. I'm going to fix some Grape-Nuts and strawberries. You want some?"

"That sounds nice."

I poured him a cup of coffee and hot milk at the kitchen table. The light was blue in the backyard.

"I didn't talk to you at the funeral. I'm not good at condolences. But I wanted to tell you I was sorry," he said.

"I didn't see you there."

"I didn't go to the cemetery. I figure that's for family. I think you're a stand-up guy."

I filled two bowls with Grape-Nuts, strawberries, and sliced bananas, and set them on the table. He put a big spoonful in his mouth, the milk dripping from his lips. The overhead light reflected off his crewcut scalp.

"That's righteous, brother," he said.

"Why am I late to work this morning?" I sat down at the table with him.

"One of those shells you picked up had a beautiful thumbprint on it. Guess who New Orleans P.D. matched it with?"

"You tell me, Minos."

"Victor Romero is shooting at you, podna. I'm surprised he didn't get you, too. He was a sniper in Vietnam. I hear you shot the shit out of his car."

"How do you know New Orleans matched his print? I haven't even heard that."

"We had a claim on him a long time before you did. The city coordinates with us anytime his name pops up."

"I want you to tell me something, with no bullshit. Do you think the government can be involved in this?"

"Be serious."

"You want me to say it again?"

"You're a good cop. Don't fall for those conspiracy fantasies. They're out of style," he said.

"I went down to Immigration in New Orleans. That fellow Monroe is having some problems with personal guilt."

"What did he tell you?" His eyes were looking at me with new interest.

"He's one of those guys who wants to feel better. I didn't let him."

"You mean you actually think somebody in the government, the INS, wants you hit?"

"I don't know. But no matter how you cut it, right now they're got shit on their noses."

"Look, the government doesn't knock off its own citizens. You're sidetracking into a lot of claptrap that's not going to lead you anywhere."

"Yeah? Try this. What kind of Americans do you think the government uses down in Central America? Boy Scouts? Guys like yourself?"

"That's not here."

"Victor Romero sure is."

He let out his breath.

"All right, maybe we can stick it to them," he said.

"When's the last time you heard of the feds dropping the dime on each other? You're a laugh a minute, Minos. Finish your cereal."

"Always the PR man," he said.

That afternoon the street was filled with hot sunshine when Cecil Aguillard and I parked our car in front of the poolroom on Main in New Iberia. Some college boys from Lafayette had pried the rubber machine off the wall of the men's room and had taken it out the back door.

"They ain't got rubbers in Lafayette? Why they got to steal mine?" said Tee Neg, the owner. He stood behind the bar, pointing his hand with the three missing fingers at me. The wood-bladed fans turned overhead, and I could smell *boudin* and gumbo in the kitchen. Several elderly men were drinking draft beer and playing *bourée* at the felt tables in back. "They teach them that in col'ech? What I'm gonna do a man come in here for his rubber?"

"Tell them to take up celibacy," I said.

Tee Neg's mouth was round with surprise and insult.

"*Mais* I don't talk like that, me. What's the matter you say something like that to Tee Neg? I think you gone crazy, Dave."

I walked out of the coolness of the poolroom into the hot sunlight to find Cecil, who had gone next door to get a description of the college boys' car. Just then a cream-colored Oldsmobile with tinted windows pulled out of the traffic. The driver didn't try to park; he simply stopped the car at an angle to the curb, dropped the transmission into neutral, flung open the door, and stepped onto the street with the engine still running. His hair was brushed with butch wax, his skin tanned as dark as a quadroon's. He wore expensive gray slacks, loafers with tassels, a pink polo shirt; but his narrow hips, wide shoulders, and boilerplate stomach made his clothes look like an unnecessary accident on his body. The wide-set, gray-blue eyes were round and staring and showed no expression, but the skin of his face was stretched so tight there were nests of fine white lines below his temples.

"What's happening, Bubba?" I said.

His fist shot out from his side, caught me squarely on the chin, and knocked me back through the open door of the pool-room. My clipboard clattered to the floor, I tried to catch myself against the wall, and then I saw him come flailing toward me out of the bright square of sunlight. I took two off the side of the head, ducked into a crouch, and smelled his cologne and sweat and heard his breath go out between his teeth as he missed with a roundhouse. I had forgotten how hard Bubba could hit. He rose on the balls of his feet with each punch, his muscular thighs and buttocks flexing like iron against his slacks. He never de-fended; he always attacked, swinging at the eyes and nose with such a vicious energy that you knew that once you were hurt he wouldn't stop until he had chopped your face into raw pork.

But I still had the reach on him, and I jabbed him in the eye with my left, saw his head come erect with the shock of the blow, and then I caught him flat on the jaw with a right cross. He reeled backwards and knocked over a brass cuspidor that rolled wetly across the floor. There was a red circle around his right eye, and I could see my knuckle marks on his cheek. He spit on the floor and hitched his slacks up on his navel with his thumb.

"If that's your best shot, your ass is glue," he said.

Suddenly Cecil burst through the doorway, his jaw filled with Red Man, his baton and handcuffs clattering on his pistol belt, and picked up Bubba from behind, pinning his arms to his sides, and threw him headlong into a *bourée* table and cir-cle of chairs.

Bubba got to his feet, his slacks stained with tobacco juice, and I saw Cecil slip his baton out of its plastic ring and grip it tightly around the handle.

"You turning candy-ass on me, Dave?" Bubba said.

"How you like I break your face?" Cecil said.

"You were messing with Claudette. Don't lie about it, either, you sonofabitch. Keep Bruno on his chain, and I'll put out your lamp."

"You're a dumb guy, Bubba."

"So I didn't get to go to college like you. You want to finish it or not?"

"You're busted. Turn around and put your hands on the table."

"Fuck you. I'll put that deputy's badge up your butt."

Cecil started toward him, but I motioned him back. I grabbed Bubba's arm, which was as hard as a cedar post in my hand, and spun him toward the table.

Vanity, vanity.

His torso turned back toward me as though it were powered by an overstressed spring, his fist lifting into my face like a balloon. His eyes were almost crossed with the force he put into his blow. But he was off balance, and I bobbed sideways, felt his knuckles rake across the top of my ear, then drove my right fist as hard as I could into his mouth. Spittle flew from his lips, his eyes snapped open wide, his nostrils flared white with pain and shock. I caught him again with my left, above the eye, then swung under his guard into his ribcage, right below the heart. He doubled over and fell back against the bar and had to hold on to the mahogany trim to keep from going down.

I was breathless, and my face felt numb and thick where he had hit me. I pulled my handcuffs loose from the back of my belt. I snapped one cuff over Bubba's wrist, then pulled his other arm behind him and locked on the second cuff. I sat him down in a chair while he hung his head forward and spit a string of bloody saliva between his knees.

"You want to go to the hospital?" I asked.

He was grinning, with a crazy light in his eyes. There was a red smear, like lipstick, on his teeth.

"*Brasse ma chu*, Dave," he said.

"You going to cuss me because you lost a fight?" I said.

"You've got more class than that, Bubba. Do you want to go to the hospital or not?"

"Hey, Tee Neg," he said to the owner. "Give everybody a round. Put it on my tab."

"You ain't got a tab," Tee Neg said. "You ain't getting one, either."

Cecil walked Bubba out to the car and locked him in behind the wire screen. Green flecks of sawdust from the poolroom floor were stuck to the butch wax in his hair. Through the car window he looked like a caged animal. Cecil started the engine.

"Drive over into the park for a minute," I said.

"What for?" Cecil asked.

"We're in no hurry. It's a nice day. Let's have a spearmint snowcone."

We crossed the drawbridge over Bayou Teche. The water was brown and high, and dragonflies flicked over the lily pads in the sunlight. Close along the banks I could see the armored backs of gars turning in the shade of the cypress trees. We drove through the oak-lined streets into the park, passed the swimming pool, and stopped behind the baseball bleachers. I gave Cecil two one-dollar bills.

"How about getting us three cones?" I said.

"Dave, that man belong in jail, not eating snowcones in the park, no," he said.

"It's something personal between me and Bubba, Cecil. I'm going to ask you to respect that."

"He's a pimp. He don't deserve no slack."

"Maybe not, partner. But it's my collar." I winked at him and grinned.

He didn't like it, but he walked away through the trees toward the concession stand by the swimming pool. I could see kids springing off the diving board into the sunlit blue water.

"Do you really think I was messing around with your wife?" I asked Bubba through the wire-mesh screen.

"What the fuck do *you* call it?"

"Clean the shit out of your mouth and answer me straight."

"She knows how to get a guy on the bone."

"You're talking about your wife."

"So? She's human."

"Don't you know when you're being jerked around? You're supposed to be a smart man."

"You thought about it when she was in your truck, though, didn't you?" he said, and smiled. His teeth were still pink with his blood. His arms were pulled behind him by the handcuffs, and his chest looked as round and hard as a small barrel. "She just like to flash her bread around sometimes. They all do. That doesn't mean you get to unzip your pants.

"Hey, tell me the truth, I really shook your peaches with that first shot, didn't I?"

"I'm going to tell you something, Bubba. I don't want you to take it the wrong way, either. Go to a psychiatrist. You're a rich man, you can afford it. You'll understand people better, you'll learn about yourself."

"I bet I pay my gardener more than you make. Does that say something?"

"You're not a good listener. You never were. That's why one day you're going to take a big fall."

I got out of the car and opened the door.

"What are you doing?" he said.

"Step out."

I put one hand under his arm and helped him off the seat.

"Turn around," I said.

"What's the game?"

"No game. I'm cutting you loose."

I unlocked the cuffs. He rubbed his wrists with his hands. In the shade, the pupils of his gray-blue eyes stared at me like burnt cinders.

"I figure what happened at Tee Neg's was personal. So this time you walk. If you come at me again, you're going up the road."

"Sounds like a Dick Tracy routine to me."

"I don't know why, but I have a strong feeling you're a man without a future."

"Yeah?"

"They're going to eat your lunch."

"Who's this 'they' you're talking about?"

"The feds, us, your own kind. It'll happen one day when you never expect it. Just like when Eddie Keats set one of your hookers on fire. She was probably thinking about a vacation in the Islands when he knocked on her door with a smile on his face."

"I've had cops give me that shuck before. It always comes from the same kind of guys. They got no case, no evidence, no witness, so they make a lot of noise that's supposed to scare everybody. But you know what their real problem is? They wear J. C. Higgins suits, they drive shit machines, they live in little boxes out by an airport. Then they see a guy that's got all the things they want and can't have because most of them are so dumb they'd fuck up a wet dream, so they get a big hard-on for this guy and talk a lot of trash about somebody cooling out his action. So I'll tell you what I tell these other guys. I'll be around to drink a beer and piss it on your grave."

He took a stick of gum out of his pocket, peeled off the foil, dropped it on the ground, and fed the gum into his mouth while he looked me in the eyes.

"You through with me?" he asked.

"Yep."

"By the way, I got drunk last night, so don't buy yourself any boxing trophies yet."

"I gave up keeping score a long time ago. It comes with maturity."

"Yeah? Tell yourself that the next time you look at your bank account. I owe you one for cutting me loose. Buy yourself something nice and send me the bill. I'll see you around."

"Don't misunderstand the gesture. If I find out you're connected to my wife's death, God help you, Bubba."

He chewed his gum, looked off at the swimming pool as though he were preparing to answer, but instead walked away through the oak trees, the soles of his loafers loud on the crisp, dead leaves. Then he stopped and turned around.

"Hey, Dave, when I straighten out a problem, the person gets to see this face. You give that some thought."

He walked on farther, then turned again, his spiked hair and tan face mottled with sun and shadow.

"Hey, you remember when we used to play ball here and yell at each other, 'I got your Dreamsicle hanging'?" he said, grinning, and grabbed his phallus through his slacks. "Those were the days, podna."

I bought a small bag of crushed ice, took it back to the office with me, and let it melt in a clean plastic bucket. Every fifteen minutes I soaked a towel in the cold water and kept it pressed to my face while I counted to sixty. It wasn't the most pleasant way to spend the afternoon, but it beat waking up the next day with a face that looked like a lopsided plum.

Then, just before quitting time, I sat at my desk in my small office, while the late sun beat down on the sugarcane fields across the road, and looked once again at the file the New Orleans police department had sent us on Victor Romero. In his front and side mug shots his black curls hung down on his forehead and ears. As in all police station photography, the black-and-white contrast was severe. His hair glistened as though it were oiled; his skin was the color of bone; his unshaved cheeks and chin looked touched with soot.

His criminal career wasn't a distinguished one. He had four misdemeanor arrests, including one for contributing to prostitution; he had done one hundred eighty days in the parish jail for possession of burglar tools; he had an outstanding bench warrant for failing to appear on a DWI charge. But contrary to popular belief, a rap sheet often tells little about a suspect. It records only the crimes he was charged with, not the hundreds he may have committed. It also offers no explanation of what goes on in the mind of a man like Victor Romero.

His eyes had no expression in the photographs. He could have been waiting for a bus when the camera lens clicked. Was this the man who had murdered Annie with a shotgun, who had fired point-blank at her with buckshot while she screamed and tried to hide her face behind her arms? Was he made up of the same corpuscle, sinew, and marrow as I? Or was his brain taken hot from a furnace, his parts hammered together in a shower of sparks on a devil's anvil?

Next morning the call came in from the St. Martin Parish's sheriff's office. A black man, fishing in his pirogue by the Henderson levee, had looked down into the water and seen a submerged automobile. A police diver had just gone down on it. The automobile was a maroon Toyota and the driver was still in it. The parish coroner and a tow truck were on their way from St. Martinville.

I called Minos at the DEA in Lafayette and told him to meet me there.

"This impresses me," he said. "It's professional, it's cooperative. Who said you guys were rural bumblers?"

"Put the cork in it, Minos."

Twenty minutes later, Cecil and I were at the levee on the edge of the Atchafalaya swamp. It was already hot, the sun shimmered on the vast expanse of water, and the islands of willow trees looked still and green in the heat. Late-morning fishermen were trying for bluegill and goggle-eye in the pilings of the oil platforms that dotted the bays or in the shade of the long concrete causeway that spanned the entire marsh. Turkey buzzards floated high on the updrafts against the white sky. I could smell dead fish in the lily pads and cattails that grew along the shore. Farther out from the bank, the black heads of water moccasins stuck out of the water like motionless twigs.

The ground had been wet when the car went off the crown of the levee. The tire tracks ran down at an angle through the grass and buttercups, cut deeply through a slough, and disappeared in the silt beyond a deep-water dropoff. The tow-truck driver, a sweating, barrel-chested man in Levi's with no shirt, fed the hook and cable off the truck to the police diver, who stood in the shallows in a bright yellow bikini with a mask and snorkel strapped to his face. Under the rippling sunlight on the water, I could see the dim outline of the Toyota.

Minos parked his car and walked down the levee just as the tow-truck driver engaged his winch and the cable clanged taut against the Toyota's frame.

"What do you figure happened?" Minos said.

"You got me."

"You think you parked one in him, after all?"

"Who knows? Even if I did, why would he drive out here?"

"Maybe he went away to die. Even a piece of shit like this guy probably knows that's one thing you got to do by yourself."

He saw me look at the side of his face. He bit off a hangnail, spit it off the end of his tongue, and looked at the wrecker cable quivering against the surface of the water.

"Sorry," he said.

A cloud of yellow sand mushroomed under the water, and suddenly the rear end of the Toyota burst through a tangle of lily pads and uprooted cattails into the sunlight. The tow-truck driver dragged the car clear of the water's edge and bounced it on the bank, the broken back window gaping like a ragged mouth. Two St. Martin Parish sheriff's deputies opened the side doors, and a flood of water, silt, moss, yellowed vegetation, and fish-eels cascaded out on the ground. The eels were long and fat, with bright silver scales and red gills, and they writhed and snapped among the buttercups like tangles of snakes. The man in the front seat had fallen sideways so that his head hung out the passenger's door. His head was strung with dead vines and covered with mud and leeches. Minos tried to see over my shoulder as I looked down at the dead man.

"Jesus Christ, half his face is eaten off," he said.

"Yep."

"Well, maybe Victor wanted to be part of the bayou country."

"It's not Victor Romero," I said. "It's Eddie Keats."

chapter
NINE

A DEPUTY STARTED TO PULL HIM BY HIS WRISTS ONTO the grass, then wiped his palms on his pants and found a piece of newspaper in the weeds. He wrapped it around Keats's arm and jerked him out on the ground. The water sloshed out of Keats's suede cowboy boots, and his shirt was unbuttoned and pulled up on his chest. There was a black, puffed hole the size of my thumb in his right ribcage, with a seared area around the skin flap, and an exit wound under the left armpit. The deputy nudged Keats's arm with his shoe to expose the wound better.

"It looks like somebody scooped it out with a tablespoon, don't it?" he said.

The coroner motioned to two paramedics who stood by the back of an ambulance parked at the top of the levee. They pulled the gurney out of the ambulance and started down the slope with it. A black body bag was folded under one of the canvas straps.

"How long has he been in the water?" I asked the coroner.

"Two or three days," he said. He was a big, fat, bald man, with a shirt pocket full of cigars. His buttocks looked like watermelons. He squinted in the brightness of the sun's reflection off the water. "They turn white and ripen pretty fast in this weather. He hasn't gotten mushy yet, but he was working on it. Y'all know him?"

"He was a low-level button man," I said.

"A what?"

"A contract killer. The bargain-basement variety," Minos said.

"Well, somebody sure stirred his hash for him," the coroner said.

"What kind of gun are we talking about?" Minos said.

"It's going to be guesswork because there's no bullet. Maybe some fragments, but they won't help much. Offhand, I'd rule out a rifle. The muzzle flash burned his skin, so it was pressed right up against him. But the angle was upward, which would mean the shooter would have to hold the rifle low and depress the stock before he fired, which wouldn't make much sense. So I'd say he was killed with a pistol, a big one, maybe a .44 Magnum or a .45 loaded with soft-nosed shells or hollow-points. He must have thought somebody stuffed a hand grenade down his throat. Y'all look perplexed."

"You might say that," Minos said.

"What's the problem?" the coroner said.

"The wrong guy's in the car," I said.

"He sounds like the right guy to me. Count your blessings," the coroner said. "You want to look through his pockets before we bag him up?"

"I'll be over to St. Martinville later," I said. "I'd like a copy of the autopsy report, too."

"Hell, come on over and watch. I'll have him apart in ten minutes." His eyes were bright, and a smile worked around the corners of his mouth. "Relax. I just like to have a little fun with you guys sometimes. I'll have a copy ready for you by tonight."

The paramedics unzipped the body bag and lifted Eddie

Keats into it. A fish-eel fell out of his pants leg and flipped in the weeds as though its back were broken.

A few minutes later, Minos and I watched the ambulance, the coroner's car, and the two St. Martin Parish sheriff's cars disappear down the levee. The tow-truck driver was having trouble with his winch, and he and Cecil were trying to fix it. A hot wind blew across the marsh and ruffled the water and flattened the buttercups around our feet. I could smell the schools of bluegill that were feeding on the mosquitoes in the shade of the willow islands.

Minos walked down to the Toyota and rubbed his thumb over one of my .45 holes in the trunk. The hole was smooth and silver around the edges, as though it had been cut by a machinist's punch.

"Are you sure Keats wasn't in the car when Romero shot at you?" he said.

"Not unless he was hiding on the floor."

"Then how did he get into the Toyota, and what did some-body have to gain by blowing up his shit and then dumping him with a car we were bound to find?"

"I don't know."

"Give me your speculations."

"I told you, I don't know."

"Come on, how many people had reason to snuff him?"

"About half the earth."

"Around here, how many people?"

"What are you getting at?"

"I'm not sure. I just know I want Bubba Rocque, and the people who could help me put him away keep showing up dead. That pisses me off."

"It probably pissed Keats off a lot worse."

"I don't think that's clever."

"I've got a revelation for you, Minos. Homicide isn't like

narcotics. Your clientele breaks the law for one reason—money. But people kill each other for all kinds of reasons, and sometimes the reasons aren't logical ones. Particularly when you're talking about Keats and his crowd."

"You know, you always give me the feeling you tell other people only what you think they should know. Why is it that I always have that feeling about you?"

"Search me."

"I also have the feeling that you don't care how these guys get scratched, as long as they're off the board."

I walked down to the Toyota's open passenger door, rested my arm on top, and looked inside again. There wasn't much of significance to see: shards of glass on the floorboards, two exit holes in the cloth of the passenger's seat, pieces of splintered lead embedded in the dashboard, a long furrow in the head-liner. A warm, wet odor rose from the upholstery.

"I think Romero drove the Toyota out here to dump it," I said. "I think Keats was supposed to meet him with another car. Then for some reason Romero blew him away. Maybe it was just an argument between the two of them. Maybe Keats was supposed to whack him and it didn't go right."

"Why would Keats want to whack Romero?"

"How the hell should I know? Look, we shouldn't even be talking about Romero. He should have been sent up the road when he first got busted. Why don't you turn the screws on your colleagues?"

"Maybe I have. Maybe they're not happy with the situation, either. Sometimes these assholes get off their leashes. One time we put a street dealer in the protected-witness program and he paid us back by shooting a liquor store clerk. It works out like that sometimes."

"I'm not sympathetic. Come on, Cecil. See you around, Minos."

Cecil and I headed down the levee past boat rentals, the bait shops and beer joints, the fish camps set up on stilts. Out in the water, the strips of moss on the dead cypress trees lifted and fell in the wind. I bought Cecil a catfish plate in a Negro café in Breaux Bridge, then he drove back to New Iberia while the heat danced on the road in front of us.

I spent the next two hours doing paperwork at the office, but I couldn't concentrate on the forms and folders that were spread around my desktop. I was never good at administration or clerical tasks, primarily because I always felt they had little to do with the job at hand and were created for people who made careers of running in place. And like most middle-aged people who hear the clock ticking in their lives, I had come to resent a waste or theft of my time that was far greater than any theft of my goods or money.

I fixed a cup of coffee and stared out the window at the trees in the sunlight. I called home to check on Alafair, then called Batist at the dock. I went to the rest room when I really didn't have to go. Then once again I looked at my uncompleted mileage report, my time and activity report, my arrest reports on local characters who had already bonded out and would probably be cut loose altogether before court appearance. I opened the largest drawer in my desk and dropped all my paperwork into it, eased the drawer shut with my shoe, signed out of the office, and went home just in time to see a taxicab leave Robin Gaddis with her suitcase on my front porch.

She wore patent leather spiked heels with Levi's, and a loose blouse that looked as if it was touched with pink and gray shades by a watercolor brush. I turned off the truck's engine and walked toward her across the dead pecan leaves in the yard. She smiled and lighted a cigarette, blowing the smoke up into the air, and tried to look relaxed and pleasant, but her eyes were bright and her face tight with anxiety.

"Wow, this is really out among the pelicans and the alligators," she said. "You got snakes and nutrias and all that stuff crawling around under your house?"

"How you doing, Robin?"

"Ask me after I'm sure I'm back on earth. I flew on one of those greaseball airlines where the pilot's got a three-day beard and blows garlic and Boone's Farm all over the place. We were dropping through the air pockets so fast you couldn't hear the engines, and all the time they're playing mambo music on the loudspeakers and I'm smelling reefer out of the front of the plane."

I took her hand, then felt as awkward as she. I put my arms lightly around her shoulders and kissed her cheek. Her hair was warm and there were fine drops of perspiration behind her neck. Her stomach brushed against me, and I felt my loins quiver and the muscles in my back stiffen.

"I guess it's not your day for Cro-Magnon bear hugs," she said. "That's cool, Streak. Don't worry about it. I'm copacetic. Don't worry about what you might have to tell me, either. Mommy's been taking care of herself a long time. I just got this urge to get on a thirty-nine-dollar flight with Kamikaze Airlines and couldn't resist."

"What happened in Key West?"

"I made a change that didn't work out."

"Like what?"

Her eyes went away from me and looked out into the hot shade of the pecan trees.

"I couldn't take serving corn fritters to the Howdy Doody crowd from Des Moines any longer. I met this guy who owns a disco on the other side of the island. It's supposed to be a high-class joint, full of big tippers. Except guess what? I find out it's full of queers, and the guy and his head bartender are running a clever late-hour scam on these guys. A tourist comes in, some guy who's not out of the closet yet, who's probably got a wife and kiddies in Meridian, and when he's good and shitfaced and trying to cop some kid's bread, they use his MasterCard to run off a half-dozen charges for thirty-dollar magnum bottles of champagne and trace his signature on them later. When he gets the bill a month later in Meridian, he's not going to holler about it because he either doesn't remember what he did or he doesn't want anybody to know he was hanging around with Maneaters Incorporated.

"So one night just after closing I told the owner and his bartender I thought they were a couple of pricks. The owner sits on the stool next to me, with a kindly smile on his face like I just walked off the cattle truck, and slides his hand up my leg. All the time he's looking me in the eyes because he knows that mommy doesn't have any money, that mommy doesn't have another job, that mommy doesn't have any friends. Except I'm drinking a cup of coffee that's hot enough to take the paint off a battleship, and I pour it right on his oysters.

"I heard the next day he was walking around like he had a mousetrap hanging off his equipment. But"—she clicked her tongue and tossed back her hair—"I've got a hundred and twelve bucks, Streak, and no compo because the guy and his bartender told the state employment office I was fired for not ringing up drinks and pocketing the money."

I rubbed the back of her neck with my hand and picked up her suitcase.

"We have a big house. It gets hot during the day sometimes, but it's cool at night. I think you'll like it," I said, and opened the screen for her. "I need somebody to help me at the dock, too."

And I thought, *Oh Lord.*

"You mean sell worms and that stuff?" she said.

"Sure."

"Wow. Worms. Out of sight, Streak."

"I have a little girl and a baby-sitter who live with me, too. But we have a room in back we don't use. I'll put a foldout bed in it and a fan in the window."

"Oh."

"I sleep out here on the couch, Robin."

"Yeah, I see."

"Insomnia and all that bullshit. I watch the late show every night until I fall asleep."

I saw her eyes stray to the lock and hasp on my bedroom door.

"It looks like a great place. Did you grow up here?" she said.

"Yes."

She sat down on the couch and I saw the fatigue come into her face. She put out her cigarette in the empty candy dish on my coffee table.

"You don't smoke, do you? I'm probably polluting your house," she said.

"Don't worry about it."

"Dave, I know I'm making complications for you. I don't mean to. A girl just gets up against the wall sometimes. You know, it was either hit on you or go back to the T-and-A circuit. I just can't cut that anymore."

I sat down next to her and put my arm around her shoulder. I felt her resist at first, then she laid her head under my chin. I touched her cheek and her mouth with my fingers and kissed her forehead. I tried to tell myself that I would be only a friend to her and not her ex-lover whose heart could be so easily activated by a woman's quiet and regular breathing against his chest.

But my life's history was one of failed promises and resolutions. Alafair, the baby-sitter, Robin, and I ate red beans, rice, and sausage on the kitchen table while it thundered outside and the wind shook the trees against the house and the rain clattered on the roof in sheets and poured off the eaves. Then the skies cleared, and the moon came up over the wet fields and the breeze smelled of earth and flowers and sugarcane. She came into the living room after midnight. The moonlight fell in ivory squares on the floor, and the outline of her long legs and bare shoulders and arms seemed to glow with a cool light. She sat on the couch, leaned over me, and kissed me on the mouth. I could smell her perfume and the baby powder on her neck. She put her fingers on my face, slipped them through my hair, brushed the white patch above my ear as though she were discovering a curiosity in me for the first time. She wore a short negligee, and her breasts were stiff against the nylon, and when I moved my hands up her sides and along her back, her skin was as hot to the touch as if she had been in the sun all day. I pulled her lengthwise against me, felt her thighs open, felt her hand take me inside her. Then I was lost inside her woman's heat, the sound her mouth made against my ear, the pressure of her calves inside mine, and finally my own confession of need and dependency and my inability to impose order on my life. Once I thought I heard a car on the road, and I felt myself jerk inside, as though I were being pulled violently from sleep, but she propped herself up on her elbows over me, looked quietly into my face with her dark eyes, and kissed me on the mouth while her hand pressed me inside her again, as though her love were enough to dispel shadows from the corners of my nocturnal heart.

The telephone woke me at four A.M. I answered it in the kitchen and closed the door to the hall so as not to wake the rest of the house. The moon was still up, and a soft ivory light fell on the mimosa tree and redwood picnic table in the backyard.

"I found a bar with an honest-to-God *zydeco* band," Minos said. "You remember Clifton Chenier? These guys play just like Clifton Chenier used to."

I could hear a jukebox, then the record stopped and I could hear bottles clinking.

"Where are you?"

"I told you. In a bar in Opelousas."

"It's pretty late for *zydeco*, Minos."

"I've got a story for you. Hell, I've got a bunch of them. Did you know I was in army intelligence in Vietnam?"

"No."

"Well, it's no big deal. But sometimes we had problems that fell outside the rulebook. There was this French civilian who gave us a lot of trouble."

"Do you have your car?"

"Sure."

"Leave it in the parking lot. Take a cab to a motel. Don't drive back to Lafayette. You understand?"

"Listen, this French civilian was hooked in with the VC in Saigon. He had whores and some people on our bases reporting to him, and maybe he helped torture one of our agents to death. But we couldn't prove it, and because he had a frog passport, he was a touchy item to deal with."

"I'm not interested in talking with you about Vietnam."

"In the meantime the major is looking like a dumb shit that can't handle the action. So we call in a sergeant who did little jobs for us from time to time, like crawl into a ville at night and slit somebody's throat from ear to ear with a barber's razor. He was going to get the frog with a night scope, nail him from fifty yards out and be back at the NCO club for beers before they could blot the guy's brains off the wallpaper.

But guess what? He got the wrong fucking house. A Dutch businessman was eating snails with his chopsticks, and our good sergeant blew his face all over his wife's blouse."

"I've got some advice for you, Minos. Fuck Vietnam. Get it the hell out of your life."

"I'm not talking about Vietnam. I'm talking about you and me, podna. It's like something F. Scott Fitzgerald wrote. We serve a vast, vulgar, meretricious enterprise."

"Look, get something to eat and I'll come up there."

"There's some government people who want to cut a deal with Romero."

"What?"

"He's got a lot of shit on a lot of people. He's valuable to us. Or at least to somebody."

I felt my hand clench on the telephone receiver. The wooden chair I sat on felt hard against my bare thighs and back.

"Is this straight?" I said. "Your people are talking with Romero? They know where he is?"

"Don't say 'my people.' He got word to some other federal agents in New Orleans. They don't know where he is, but he says he'll come in for the right deal. You know what I told them?"

I could hear my breath against the holes in the telephone.

"I told them, 'Cut all the fucking deals you want. Robicheaux ain't going to play,' " he said. "I have to say that made me feel kind of good."

"Which bar are you in?"

"Forget about me. I was right, though, wasn't I? You're not going to bargain?"

"I want to talk with you tomorrow."

"Hell, no. What you hear now is all you get. Now I want you to tell me something fair and square. You don't have to admit anything. Just tell me I'm wrong. You found the Toyota, you rounded up Keats, you took him out to the levee and put that .45 of yours between his ribs and blew his lungs out his mouth. Right?"

"Wrong."

"Come on, Robicheaux. You showed up at the Haitian's in New Orleans right after the cops did. What are the odds of you just blundering into a situation like that? Then another guy you truly hate, somebody whose nose you crushed into marmalade with a pool cue, shows up dead by the Henderson levee. Keats was from Brooklyn. He didn't know anything about that area. Neither does Romero. But you've been fishing that swamp all your life. If anybody else but a bunch of coonass cops were handling this case, you'd be in jail."

"Take two vitamin B's and four aspirin before you go to bed," I said. "You won't run the four-minute mile tomorrow, but at least the snakes won't be crawling."

"I'm all wet, huh?"

"You've got it. I'm going to sign off now. I hope they don't put you through the wringer. For a government man, you're a pretty good guy, Dunkenstein."

He was still talking when I eased the phone receiver back into the cradle. Outside, I could hear night birds calling each other in the fields.

After work that day, I took Robin and Alafair down to Cypremort Point for dinner. We ate boiled shrimp and blue-point crabs in a ramshackle, screened-in restaurant by the bay, and in the mauve twilight the water looked flat and gray, rippled in places by a slight breeze, like wrinkles in a skim of paint, and in the west the distant islands of sawgrass were edged with the sun's last red glow on the horizon. Behind us I could see the long, two-lane road that led down through the

Point, the dead cypress trees that were covered with shadows now, the fishing shacks built up on stilts above the flooded woods, the pirogues tied to the cabin pilings, the carpet of blooming lily pads on the canals, the herons that lifted on extended wings into the lavender sky like a whispered poem.

The big electric fans in the restaurant vibrated with their own energy; the wood tables were littered with crab shells; bugs beat against the screen as the light went out of the sky; and somebody played "La Jolie Blonde" on the jukebox. Robin's dark hair moved in the breeze, and her eyes were bright and happy, and there was a smear of *sauce piquante* on the corner of her mouth. With all her hard mileage, she was a good girl inside and she took hold of my affections in a funny way. You fall in love with women for different reasons, I guess. Sometimes they are simply beautiful and you have no more control over your desire for them than you do in choosing your nocturnal dreams. Then there are others who earn their way into your soul, who are kind and loyal and loving in the way that your mother was or should have been. Then there's that strange girl who walks unexpectedly off a side street into the middle of your life, the one who is nothing like the indistinct and warm presence who has lived with you for so long on the soft edge of sleep. Instead, her clothes are all wrong, her lipstick mismatched, her handbag clutched like a shield, her eyes wide and bright, as though the Greek Furies were calling to her from the stage wings.

Robin and I made an agreement. I would discharge the baby-sitter, and she would help me take care of Alafair and work at the bait shop. She promised me she was off the booze and dope, and I believed her, although I didn't know how long her resolution would last. I don't understand alcoholism, and I cannot tell you for sure what an alcoholic is. I've known some people who quit on their own, then became white-knucklers who boiled with a metabolic and psychological misery that finally caused them to blow out their doors and come into AA on their kneecaps. I've known others who simply stopped drinking one day and lived out their lives in a gray, neutral area like people who had clipped all the sharp edges off their souls until they seemed to be operating on the spiritual energies of a moth. The only absolute conclusion I ever made about alcoholics was that I was one of them. What others did with booze had no application to my life, as long as they didn't press it on Dave Robicheaux, who was altogether too willing a victim.

We drove back through the long corridor of dead cypress trees, the fireflies lighting in the dark, and rented a VCR and a Walt Disney movie at the video store in New Iberia. Later, Batist came by the house with some fresh *boudin*, and we heated it in the oven and made lemonade with cracked ice and mint leaves in the glasses and watched the movie in the living room under the wood-bladed fan. When I got up to fill the lemonade pitcher again, I looked at the flicker of the screen on Robin's and Alafair's and Batist's faces and felt a strange sense of family belonging that I hadn't felt since Annie's death.

I went home for lunch the next day and was eating a ham-and-onion sandwich at the kitchen table when the phone rang. It was a beautiful, sunny day, the sky a clear blue above the trees, and through the back window I could see Alafair playing with one of my calico cats in the backyard. She wore her LEFT and RIGHT pink tennis shoes, a pair of denim pedal pushers, and the yellow Donald Duck T-shirt that Annie had bought for her, and she swung a piece of kite twine back and forth in front of the cat's churning paws. I chewed on the ham and bread in my mouth and placed the telephone receiver idly against my ear. I could hear the dull whirring of a long-distance connection, like wind blowing in a conch shell.

"Is this Robicheaux?"

"Yes. Who's this?"

"The cop, right?" His voice sounded as if it were strained through wet sand.

"That's right. You want to tell me who this is?"

"It's Victor Romero. I got a lot of people on my case, and I'm hearing a lot of stuff I don't like to hear. Most of it's got your name in it."

The piece of sandwich felt stiff and dead in my jaw. I pushed my plate away and felt myself sit up straight in my chair.

"You still there?" he said. I heard a peculiar thump, then a hissing sound in the background.

"Yes."

"Everybody wants to cut a slice out of my ass, like I'm responsible for every crime in Louisiana. They got the word on the street that maybe I'm going away for thirty years. They're talking that maybe I killed some people in a plane, that maybe they'll turn me over to the locals and get me fried in Angola. So everybody in New Orleans hears the feds got a big hard-on for me, that don't nobody touch me because I'm like the stink on shit and they better not get it on their hands, either. You listening to me?"

"Yes."

"So I told them I'd deal. They want these big fuckers, and I get some slack. I tell them I'll come in for three. No more than three, that's it. Except what do I hear? This cat Robicheaux is a hardtail and he don't play. So you're fucking me, man."

I could feel my heart beating, feel the blood in the back of my neck and in my temples.

"Do you want to meet somewhere and talk?" I said.

"You must be out of your goddamn mind."

Then I heard the thump again, followed by the hissing sound.

"I want to talk to those cocksuckers at the DEA," he said. "I want you to tell them no charges because you thought somebody shot at you. You get the fuck off my back. I get that message from the right guy, and maybe I deliver something you want."

"I don't think you've got anything to bargain with, Romero. I think you're a nickel-and-dime mule that everybody's tired of. Why don't you write all this bullshit on a postcard and I'll read it when I don't have anything else to do."

"Yeah?"

I didn't answer. He was quiet a moment, then he spoke again.

"You want to know who set up the whack on your wife?"

I was breathing deeply now, and wires were trembling inside my chest. I swallowed and kept my voice as flat as possible.

"All I hear from you is noise. You got something to trade, get it out of your mouth or stop bothering me," I said.

"You think I'm talking noise, huh? Try this, motherfucker. You had a fan in your bedroom window. You had a telephone in your hall, except somebody tore it out of the wall for you. And while they did your old lady, you were hiding outside in the dark."

I felt my hand slide up and down my flexed thigh. I had to wet my lips before I could speak again. I should have been silent, said nothing, but the control was now gone.

"I'll find you," I said hoarsely.

"Find me and you find nothing. I got all this from the boon. You want the rest of the story, you come up with a deal that don't leave me in the barrel. You got a guilty conscience, man, and I ain't taking your fall."

"Listen—"

"No, I talk, you listen. You get together with that bunch of farts at the Federal Building and decide what you want to do. You come up with the right numbers—and I'm talking three years max, in a minimum-security joint—then you run an ad in the *Times-Picayune* that says, 'Victor, your situation is approved.' I see that ad, maybe a lawyer's gonna call up the DEA and see about a meet."

"Eddie Keats tried to dust you. They're going to take you out just like they did the Haitian. You're running out of rat-holes."

"Kiss my ass. I ate bugs and lizards for thirty-eight days and came back with eleven gook ears on a stick. I'm buying the paper Sunday morning. After that, forget it. Clean up your own shit."

Before he hung up I thought I heard a streetcar bell clang.

The rest of the afternoon I tried to recreate his voice in my mind. Had I heard it once before, in a rumble of thunder, on my front porch? I couldn't be sure. But the thought that I had held a conversation about plea-bargaining with one of Annie's murderers worked and twisted in my brain like an obscene finger.

Sometime after midnight, I woke with a thick, numb feeling in my head, the kind you have after you've been out in a cold wind a long time by yourself. I sat quietly on the edge of the couch, my bare feet resting in a square of moonlight on the floor, and opened and closed my hands as though I were seeing them for the first time. Then I unlocked Annie's and my bedroom and sat on the edge of the mattress in the dark.

The bloody sheets and bedspread had been carried off in a vinyl evidence bag, but the mattress and the wooden bedstead were filled with holes that I could fit my fingers into as though

I were probing the wounds in Our Lord's hands. The brown patterns all over the bedstead and the flowered wallpaper could have been slung there by a paintbrush. I rubbed my hand across the wall and felt the stiff, torn edges of the paper where the buckshot and deer slugs had torn through the wood. The moon shone through the pecan tree outside and made an oval of light in my lap. I felt as solitary as if I had been sitting in the bottom of a dry, cool well, with strips of silver cloud floating by against a dark sky.

I thought about my father and wished he were there with me. He couldn't read or write and never once traveled outside the state of Louisiana, but his heart possessed an intuitive understanding about our lives, our Cajun vision of the world, that no philosophy book could convey. He drank too much and he'd fistfight two or three men in a bar at the same time, with the enthusiasm of a boy hitting baseballs; but inside he had a gentle heart, a strong sense of right and wrong, and a tragic sense about the cruelty and violence that the world sometimes imposes upon the innocent.

He told me a story once about a killing that he'd seen as a young man. In my father's mind, the victim's death was emblematic of all the unjust and brutal behavior that people are capable of in groups, although in reality the victim was not an innocent man. It was the winter of 1935, and a criminal who had robbed banks with John Dillinger and Homer Van Meter had been flushed out of Margaret's whorehouse in Opelousas, a brothel that had been operating since the War Between the States. Cops chased him all the way to Iberia Parish, and when his car slid into a ditch, he struck out across a frozen field of sugarcane stubble. My father and a Negro were pulling stumps with a mule and trace chains and burning them in big heaps when the robber ran past them toward the old barn by our windmill. My father said he wore a white shirt with cufflinks and a bow tie, with no coat, and he gripped a straw boater in his hands as though it were his last possession on earth.

A cop fired a rifle from the road, and one of the robber's legs collapsed and he went down in the middle of the stubble. The cops all wore suits and fedoras, and they walked in a line across the field as though they were flushing quail. They formed a half-circle around the wounded man, while he sat with his legs straight out before him and begged for his life. My father said that when they started shooting with their revolvers and automatic pistols, the man's shirt exploded with crimson flowers.

With crimson flowers that turned brown, that can be bruised into a grain of wood, that flake and shale away under the touch of my fingers. Because they impaled her upon this bedstead and this wall, drove her screams and her fear and her agony deep into this wood, translated these cypress boards, hewn by my father, into her crucifix.

I felt a hand on my shoulder. I stared up at Robin, whose face and body looked strangely pale in the moonlight that fell through the pecan tree into the room. She slipped her hand under my arm and pulled me up gently from the edge of the bed.

"It's no good for you in here, Streak," she said quietly. "I'll fix us warm milk in the kitchen."

"Sure. Is the phone still ringing?"

"What?"

"The phone. I heard it ringing."

"No, it didn't ri— Dave, come on out of here."

"It didn't ring, huh? When I used to have the DTs, dead people would call me up on the phone. It was a crazy way to be back then."

*   *   *   *

That morning I drove back to New Orleans to look for Victor Romero. As I said before, his sheet wasn't much help, and I knew that undoubtedly he was a more intelligent and far more dangerous man than it indicated. However, it was also obvious from his record that he had the same vices and sordid preoccupations and worm's-eye view of the world as did most of his kind. I talked with street people in the Quarter, bartenders, some strippers who hooked on the side, late-hour cabdrivers who pimped for the strippers, a couple of black Murphy artists, door spielers on Bourbon, a fence in Algiers, a terminal junkie who was down to shooting into his wasted thighs with an eyedropper insulated with the white edge of a one-dollar bill. If they admitted having known Romero, they said they thought he was dead, out of the country, or in federal custody. In each instance, I might as well have held a conversation with a vacant lot.

But sometimes what you don't hear is a statement in itself. I was convinced he was still in New Orleans—I had heard the streetcar bell in the background when he called—and if he was in town, somebody was probably hiding or supporting him, because he wasn't pimping or dealing. I went down to First District headquarters on the edge of the Quarter and talked to two detectives in vice. They said they had already tried to find Romero through his relatives, and there weren't any. His father had been a fruit picker who disappeared in Florida in the 1960s, and the mother had died in the state mental hospital at Mandeville. There were no brothers or sisters.

"How about girlfriends?" I said.

"Outside of whores, you're talking about his fist," one of the detectives said.

I drove back to New Iberia in a late-afternoon shower. The sun was shining while it rained, and the yellow surface of the Atchafalaya marsh danced with light.

I turned off at Breaux Bridge and parked my truck on the Henderson levee and stood among the buttercups and blue-bonnets and watched the light rain fall on the bays and the flooded cypress trees. The levee was thick with enormous black and yellow grasshoppers that sprang out of the grass, their lacquered backs shining in the wet light. When I was a boy, my brother and I would trap them with our straw hats, bait our trotline with them at sunset and string it between two abandoned oil platforms, and in the morning the line would be so taut and heavy with mudcat that it would take both of us to lift it clear of the water.

I was becoming tired of being a policeman again. Hold your soul against an emery wheel long enough, and one day you'll have only air between your hands. And with that thought in mind, I left Alafair with Batist that night and took Robin to the races at Evangeline Downs in Lafayette. We ate shrimp and steak in the clubhouse, then went back out to the open-air seats and sat in a box by the finish line. It was a balmy night, and heat lightning flickered all over the southern horizon; the sod, still damp from the afternoon shower, had been freshly raked, and halos of moisture glowed in the arc lamps overhead. Robin wore a white cotton sundress with purple and green tiger lilies printed on it, and her tanned neck and shoulders looked smooth and cool in the shadowy light. She had never been to a horse race before, and I let her pick the horses in the first three races. She chose one horse because of the white stockings on its feet, a second because of the jockey's purple silks, a third because she said the jockey's face was shaped like a toy heart. All three placed or showed, and she was hooked. Each time the horses thundered around the last turn and then spread out from the rail as they went into the home stretch, the jockeys whipping the quirts into their flanks, the torn sod flying in the air, she would be on her feet, her arms locked in mine, her breast pressed hard against me, her whole body jiggling and bouncing with excitement. We cashed $178 worth of tickets at the pay window that night, and on the way home we stopped at a late-hour market and bought Batist and his wife a fruit-and-cheese basket with a bottle of Cold Duck in it. When I turned the truck off on the dirt road that led along the bayou south of New Iberia, she was asleep with her head on my shoulder, her hand limp inside my shirt, her lips parted in the moonlight as though she were going to whisper a little girl's secret to me.

I hadn't been able to find the living, so I thought I might have better luck investigating the dead. The next afternoon Cecil and I drove to the Jungle Room on the Breaux Bridge road to see what we could learn, if anything, about Eddie Keats's connection to Victor Romero. In the blazing sunlight, the white shale parking lot and the purple cinder-block front wall with its painted coconut trees and fingernail-polish-red front door were like a slap across the eyes. But the inside was as dark as a cave, except for the soft lights behind the bar, and it smelled of the insecticide that an Orkin man was spraying with a tank in the corners of the building. Two weary and hung-over-looking women were smoking cigarettes and drinking Bloody Marys at the bar. The bartender was putting long-necked beer bottles in the cooler, his wide back ridging with muscle each time he bent over. He had platinum hair and bronze arms and he wore no shirt and a flowered silver vest that shone like dull tin. High up on the wall was the wire cage where the monkey sat among his peanut hulls and soiled newspapers.

I showed my badge to the two women and asked them when was the last time they had seen Eddie. Their eyes looked at nothing; they blew smoke up in the air, flipped their ashes into ashtrays, and were as unknowledgeable and lifeless as cardboard cutouts.

Had they seen Victor Romero lately?

Their eyes were vague and empty, and their cigarettes moved back into their mouths in slow motion and then back out into the exhaled smoke.

"I understand the funeral was this morning. Did Eddie get a nice service?" I said.

"They cremated him and put him in a vase or something. I got up too late to go," one of the women said. Her hair was dyed red and tied back tight against her head like wire. Her skin was white and shiny, tight as a lampshade over the bone, and there was a knot of blue veins in her temple.

"I bet he was a great guy to work for," I said.

She turned on the barstool and looked me full in the face. Her brown eyes were liquid and malevolent.

"I'm supposed to talk to people that buy me a drink," she said. "Then I'll put my hand in your lap and we'll talk about your rising expectations. You want somebody to help you with your rising expectations, officer?"

I put my office card in front of her.

"If you ever get tired of comic-book routines, call this number," I said.

The bartender put the last beer bottle in the cooler and walked toward me on the duckboards behind the bar, pressing a stick of Num-Zit against his tooth and gum.

"I'm Eddie's brother. You want something?" he said. His tan was almost gold, the kind that comes from applying chemicals to the skin in the sun, and the exposed hair sticking out from under his arms was bleached on the tips. He had the same thick, veined neck, powerful shoulders, and adenoidal Brooklyn accent that his brother had had. I asked him when he had seen Eddie Keats last.

"Two years ago, when he come up to visit in Canarsie," he said.

"You know Victor Romero?"

"No."

"How about Bubba Rocque?"

"I don't think I know the name."

"Did you know a Haitian named Toot?"

"I don't know none of these people. I just come down to take care of Eddie's business affairs. It's a big tragedy."

"I think you're violating the law, Mr. Keats."

"What?"

"I think you're contributing to prostitution."

His green eyes looked at me carefully. He took a Lucky Strike from a pack on the liquor counter behind him and lit it. He removed a piece of tobacco from his tongue with his finger-nails. He blew the smoke out the side of his mouth.

"What's the game?" he said.

"No game. I'm just going to see if I can get you closed up."

"You had some kind of deal with Eddie?"

"No, I didn't like Eddie. I'm the guy who busted a pool cue across his face. What do you think of that?"

He looked away and took another puff off his cigarette. Then he focused again on my face, a wrinkled wedge of concern between his eyes.

"Look, you didn't like my brother, that's your problem. But I ain't Eddie. You got no reason to be down on me, man. I'm a cooperative guy. If I got to piece off a little action, that's cool. I ran a nigger bar in Bedford-Stuyvesant. I got along with every-body. That ain't easy to do in Bed-Stuy. I want to get along here, too."

"No. I don't have the problem. You do. You're a pimp and you're cruel to animals. Cecil, come over here," I said.

Cecil was leaning against the wall by the cue rack, with his arms folded in front of him, a dark light in his face. Like many people of color, he didn't like the class of white people that Keats's brother and the two prostitutes represented to him. He walked toward us with his massive weight, his mouth a tight line, a lump of Red Man as taut as a golf ball inside his jaw. He opened and closed his hands at his sides.

The bartender stepped backwards.

"Now wait a minute," he said.

"Mr. Keats wants us to take down that monkey cage," I said.

"I was t'inking that same t'ing myself," Cecil said, and used the barstool to climb up on the bar. Then he stepped with one foot over onto the liquor counter and shook the monkey cage loose from a hook screwed into the ceiling. His huge shoe knocked over a half-dozen bottles of whiskey that rolled off the counter and crashed on the duckboards. The monkey's eyes were wide with fright, his leathery paws enmeshed in the wire screen. Cecil held the cage out stiffly with one arm and dropped to the floor again.

"The lady has my office card. You can file a complaint if you don't like it. Welcome to south Louisiana, podjo," I said.

Cecil and I went outside into the white glare of sunlight on the shale parking lot. Then he walked into the shady grove of live oaks behind the bar and set the cage down in the grass. I unfastened the wire on the door and pulled it open. The monkey sat in his wet tangle of newspaper, too frightened to move, his tail pressed up one side of the cage. Then I tilted the cage forward and he toppled out on the grass, chattered and squeaked once, and climbed high into the fork of an oak, where he looked back at us with his wide eyes. The wind blew the moss in the trees.

"I like working wit' you, Dave," Cecil said.

*   *   *   *

But sometimes when an investigation seems to go nowhere, when the street people stonewall you and a lowlife like Victor Romero seems to have Vaseline all over him, a door quietly drifts open on the edge of your vision. It was Saturday, the day after Cecil and I had gone to Keats's bar, and I was reading the *Times-Picayne* under the canvas umbrella on the dock. Even in the shade, the light was bright on the newsprint and hurt my eyes. Then the sun went behind clouds and the day was suddenly gray and the breeze came up and ruffled the water and bent the cattails and reeds along the bank. I pinched my eyes with my fingers, and glanced again at the state wrap-up column in the second section. At the bottom of the column was a five-line wire service story about the arrest in northeastern Louisiana of a man who was suspected of robbing apartment mailboxes in a welfare project and assaulting elderly people for their social security checks. His name was Jerry Falgout.

I went inside the bait shop and called the sheriff's office there. The sheriff wasn't in, and the deputy I spoke to, who sounded black, wasn't cooperative.

"Is this guy a bartender in New Orleans?" I said.

"I don't know."

"What did you get on him from Baton Rouge?"

"You gotta ask the sheriff that."

"Come on, he's in your custody. You must know something about him. Has he been in Angola?"

"I don't know. He don't say."

"What's his bond?"

"A hundred thousand."

"Why so high?"

"He pushed an old woman down the stairs at the project. She's got a fractured skull."

I was about to give up talking to the deputy and call the sheriff at his home. I tried one more question.

"What *does* he tell you?"

"He don't like it here and he ain't no swinging dick."

Fifteen minutes later I was in the pickup truck on the road to Lafayette, headed toward the northbound four-lane, while the arching limbs of oak trees swept by overhead.

The country began to change as I drove north of the Red River. The sugarcane and rice fields were behind me now. The black earth and flooded cypress and oak trees were replaced by pastureland and piney woods, lumber mills and cotton acreage, sandy red roads that cut through limitless pecan orchards, Negro towns of paintless shacks and clapboard beer joints and old brick warehouses built along railroad spurs. The French and Spanish names were gone from the mailboxes and the fronts of general stores, too. I was back into the Anglo-Saxon South, where the streets were empty on Sunday and the Baptist churches were full and Negroes baptized in the river bottoms. It was peckerwood country, where Klansmen still burned crosses on rural roads at night and rednecks had coon-on-a-log contests in which a raccoon was chained by his foot to a log in a pond while people sicked their hunting dogs on him.

But history had had its joke with some of those northern parishes. Since the 1960s, Louisiana Negroes had become registered voters in large numbers, and in those parishes and towns where whites were a minority, the mayors' offices and the sheriffs' departments and the police juries had become filled with black people. Or at least that was what had happened in the town upriver from Natchez where Jerry Falgout was being held in the old brick jail behind a courthouse that Yankee soldiers had tried to burn during the Civil War.

It was a poor town, with brick streets and wooden colonnades built over the dilapidated storefronts. On the town square were a bail-bond office, a café, a dime store, and a barber college with a Confederate flag, now flaked and peeling, painted above the door. The elevated sidewalks were cracked and sagging, and the iron tethering rings set in the concrete bled rusty streaks into the gutters. The courthouse building and lawn and the Confederate cannon and the World War I monument were covered in deep shadow by the oak trees that towered above the second story. I walked up the courthouse sidewalk past the scrolled-iron benches where groups of elderly Negro men, in overalls or seersucker slacks, sat and stared out of the shade at the shimmering blaze of light on the street.

A black deputy walked me out the back door of the courthouse into the visiting room of the jail. The bars on the windows and the grid of iron strips on the main door were layered with both white and yellow paint. The room wasn't air-conditioned, and it was hot and close inside and smelled of the oil on the wood floors and tobacco juice that someone had been spitting in a box of sawdust in one corner. A white trusty in jail denims brought Jerry Falgout down a spiral metal stairs at the back of the dark hall and walked him into the visiting area.

His bottom lip was purple and swollen, and there was a crust of blood in one of his nostrils. He kept widening his nostril and sniffing as though he were trying to open a blocked nasal passage. At the corner of one eye was a long, red, scraped area, like a smear of dirty rouge. The trusty went back upstairs, and the deputy locked us in. Jerry sat across from me, his hands limp on top of the wooden table, his eyes sullen and pained as they looked into mine. I could smell the sour reek of his dried sweat.

"What's going on up there?" I said.

"It's a nigger jail. What do you think?"

"Were these black people you've been robbing?"

"I didn't rob nobody, man. I was up here visiting my relatives."

"Cut the dogshit, Jerry."

"Come on, man. You think I'm gonna rob somebody, I'm gonna rob niggers in a welfare project? Some old lady got thrown down a stairs or something. She was already senile, now she's got a fractured skull, and she says I done it. The night screw is her nephew. So guess what he tells all the boons upstairs?"

"Sounds like a bad situation, all right."

"Yeah, you're all heart."

I looked at him a moment before I spoke again.

"You haven't hit the shower in a while, Jerry."

He turned his face away from me, and a small circle of color formed in one cheek.

"They got you made for stuff, partner?" I said.

"Look, man, I tried to get along. It didn't matter to me if they were colored or not. I tried to make a stinger, you know, a hot plate for these guys so we could warm up the macaroni in the evening. Then this big black bastard walks dripping wet out of the shower and picks up the pot, with his bare feet on the concrete floor. It popped him so hard he looked like somebody shoved a cattle prod up his butt. So he blames me for it. First, he starts throwing shit at me—macaroni and plates and tin cups. Then he starts grinning and tells me his cock is all charged up now. He says he's gonna take a white boy's cherry the next time I come into the shower. And then the other boons are gonna get seconds."

His face was flushed now, his eyes narrow and glistening.

I walked over to a rust-streaked sink against one wall and filled a paper cup from the tap. I set the water in front of him and sat back down.

"Is your mother going to go bond?" I said.

"She's gotta put up ten grand for the bondsman. She ain't got that kind of gelt, man."

"How about a property bond?"

"She ain't got it. I told you." His eyes avoided mine.

"I see."

"Look, man, I did five years in Angola. I did it with guys that'd cut your face up with a razor for twenty dollars. I seen a snitch burned up in his cell with a Molotov cocktail. I seen a kid drowned in a toilet because he wouldn't suck some guy off. I'm not gonna get broke by a nigger jail in some back-water shithole."

"You want out of here?"

"Yeah. You got connections with Jesse Jackson?"

"Save the hard-guy routine for another day, Jerry. Do you want out of here?"

"What do you think?"

"You robbed the mails, which is a federal offense. They'll file against you eventually, but I know somebody who can probably hurry it up. We'll get you into federal custody, and you can forget this place."

"When?"

"Maybe this week. In the meantime I'll call the FBI in Shreveport and tell them there's a serious civil rights violation going on here. That ought to get you into isolation until you're transferred to federal custody."

"What do you want?"

"Victor Romero."

"I told you everything I know about the guy. You got a fucking obsession, man."

"I need a name, Jerry. Somebody who can turn him."

"I ain't got any. I'm telling you the truth. I got no reason to cover for this cat."

"I believe that. But you're plugged into a lot of people.

You're a knowledgeable man. You sell information. If you remember, you sold me and Robin for a hundred dollars."

His eyes looked out the barred window at the shade trees on the lawn. He brushed at the dried blood in his nostril with one knuckle.

"I'm floating around on an ice cube that's melting in a toilet," he said. "What can I tell you? I got nothing to deal with. You wasted your drive up here. Why don't you get those vice cops to help you? They think they know everything."

"They have the same problem I do. A guy with no family and no girlfriend is hard to find."

"Wait a minute. What do you mean no family?"

"That's the information at the First District."

I saw a confident, mean light come back into his eyes.

"That's why they don't never catch anybody. He's got a first cousin. I don't know the cat's name, but Romero brought him into the bar six or seven years ago. The guy pulled a scam that everybody in the Quarter was laughing about. Some guys robbed Maison Blanche of about ten thousand dollars in Botany 500 suits. Of course, there's a big write-up about it in the *Picayune*. So Romero's cousin gets ahold of a bunch of these Hong Kong specials, you know, these twenty-buck suits that turn into lint and threads the first time you dry-clean them. He stops business guys up and down Canal and says, 'I got a nice suit for you. A hundred bucks. No labels. Know what I mean?' I heard he made two or three grand off these stupid shits. After they found out they got burned, they couldn't do anything about it, either."

"Where is he now?"

"I don't know. I only saw him once or twice. He's the kind of guy that only makes a move once in a while. I think he ran a laundry or something."

"A laundry? Where?"

"In New Orleans."

"Come on, where in New Orleans?"

"I don't know, man. What the fuck I care about a laundry?"

"And you're sure you don't know this guy's name?"

"Hell, no. I told you, it was a long time ago. I been straight with you. You gonna deliver or not?"

"Okay, Jerry. I'll make some phone calls. In the meantime, you try to remember this laundry man's name."

"Yeah, yeah. Y'all always got to go one inch deeper in a guy's hole, don't you?"

I walked to the iron door and rattled it against the jamb for the deputy to let me out.

"Hey, Robicheaux, I don't have any cigarettes. How about a deck of Luckies?" Jerry said.

"All right."

"Put a piece of paper with how many packs are in the carton, too. That trusty helps himself."

"You got it, partner."

The deputy let me out, and I walked back into the breezy area between the jail and the courthouse. I could smell the pines on the lawn, the hydrangeas blooming against a sunny patch of wall, hot dogs that a Negro kid was selling out of a cart on the streetcorner. I looked back through the jail window at Jerry, who sat alone at the wooden table, waiting for the trusty to take him back upstairs, his face now empty and dull and as lifeless as tallow.

chapter
TEN

I WAITED UNTIL MONDAY, WHEN BUSINESSES WOULD BE open, and drove to New Orleans in the pink light of dawn and began looking up and down the St. Charles Avenue streetcar line for laundries and dry cleaners. At one time New Orleans was covered with streetcar tracks, but now only the St. Charles streetcar remains in service. It runs a short distance down Canal, the full length of St. Charles through the Garden District, past Loyola and Tulane and Audubon Park, then goes up South Carrollton and turns around on Claiborne. This particular line has been left in service because it travels along what is probably one of the most beautiful streets in the world. St. Charles and the esplanade in its center are covered by a canopy of enormous oak trees and lined on each side by old, iron-scrolled brick homes and antebellum mansions with columned porches and pike-fenced yards filled with hibiscus, blooming myrtle and oleander, bamboo, and giant philodendron. So most of the area along the streetcar line is residential, and I had to look only in a few commercially zoned neighborhoods for a laundry or dry cleaner's that might be operated by Victor Romero's cousin.

I found only four. One was run by black people, another by Vietnamese. The third one was run by a white couple on Carrollton, but I believed it was set too far back from the street for me to have heard the streetcar bell over the telephone. However, the fourth one, a few blocks southwest of Lee Circle, was only a short distance from the tracks, and its front doors were open to let out the heat from inside, and through the big glass window I could see a telephone on the service counter and behind it a white man thumping down a clothes press in a hiss of steam.

The laundry was on the corner, with an alley behind it, and by the garbage cans a wooden stairway led up to a living area on the second floor. I parked my pickup across the street under an oak tree in the parking lot of a small take-out café that sold fried shrimp and dirty rice. It was a hot, languid day, and the grass on the esplanade was still wet with dew in the shade, the bark on the palm trees was stained darkly with the water that had leaked from the palm fronds during the night, and the streetcar tracks looked burnished and hot in the sunlight. I went inside the café, called the city clerk's office, and found out the laundry was operated by a man named Martinez. So there was no help by way of connection with family names, except for the fact that the laundry operator was obviously Latin. It was going to be a long wait.

I opened both doors of the truck to let in the breeze and spent the morning watching the front door and back entrance and stairway of the laundry. At noon I bought a paper-plate lunch of shrimp and rice from the café and ate it in the truck while a sudden shower beat down on the street and the oak tree above my head.

I was never good at surveillance, in part because I didn't have the patience for it. But more important was the fact that my own mind always became my worst enemy during any period of passivity or inactivity in life, no matter how short the duration. Old grievances, fears, and unrelieved feelings of guilt and black depression would surface from the unconscious without cause and nibble on the soul's edges like iron teeth. If I didn't *do* something, if I didn't take my focus outside myself, those emotions would control me as quickly and completely as whiskey did when it raced through my blood and into my heart like a dark electrical current.

I watched the rain drip out of the oak branches and hit on the windshield and hood of my truck. The sky was still dark, and low black clouds floated out of the south like cannon smoke. Annie's death haunted me. No matter who had fired the shotguns in our bedroom, no matter who had ordered and paid for it, the inalterable fact remained that her life had been made forfeit because of my pride.

Now I had to wonder what it was I really planned if I caught Victor Romero and learned that he had killed Annie. In my mind I saw myself spread-eagling him against a wall, kicking his feet apart, ripping a pistol loose from under his shirt, cuffing him so tightly that the skin around his wrists bunched like putty, and forcing him down into the back seat of a New Orleans police car.

I saw those images because they were what I knew I should see. But they did not represent what I felt. They did not represent what I felt at all.

It stopped raining around three, and then, with the sun still shining, it showered again around five and the trees along the avenue were dark green in the soft yellow light. I went inside the café and ate supper, then went back out to the truck and watched the traffic thin, the laundry close, the shadows lengthen on the street, the washed-out sky become pink and lavender and then streaked with bands of crimson in the west. The neon signs came on along the avenue and reflected off the pools of water in the gutters and on the esplanade. A Negro who ran a shoeshine stand in front of a package store had turned on a radio in a window, and I could hear a ball game being broadcast from Fenway Park. The heat had gone out of the day, lifting gradually out of the baked brick and concrete streets, and now a breeze was blowing through the open doors of my truck. The big olive-green streetcar, its windows now lighted, rattled down the tracks under the trees. Then, just as the twilight faded, an electric light went on in the apartment above the laundry.

Five minutes later, Victor Romero came down the wooden back stairs. He wore a pair of Marine Corps utilities, an over-sized Hawaiian print shirt with purple flowers on it, a beret on his black curls. He stepped quickly over the puddles in the brick alley and entered the side door of a small grocery store. I took my .45 from the glove box, stuck it inside my belt, pulled my shirt over the butt, and got out of the truck.

I had three ways I could go, I thought. I could take him inside the store, but if he was armed (and he probably was, because his shirt was pulled outside his utilities) an innocent person could be hurt or be taken hostage. I could wait for him at the side entrance to the store and nail him in the alley, but that way I would lose sight of the front door, and if he didn't go directly back to the apartment and instead left by the front, I could lose him altogether. The third alternative was to wait in the shadows by my truck, the angular lines of the .45 hard against my stomach, my pulse racing in my neck.

I opened and closed my hands, wiped them on my trousers, breathed deeply and slowly through my mouth. Then the screen door opened into the alley, and Romero stepped out into the neon light with a sack of groceries in his arm and looked blankly toward the street. His black curls hung down from under his beret, and his skin looked purple in the neon reflection off the bricks. He hitched his belt up with his thumb, looked down toward the other end of the alley, and jumped across the puddle. When he did, he pressed his hand against the small of his back. I watched him climb the stairs, go inside the apartment, close the screen, and walk in broken silhouette past a window fan.

I crossed the street, paused at the bottom of the stairs, pulled back the receiver on the .45, and slid a hollow-point round into the chamber. The pistol felt heavy and warm in my hand. Upstairs I could hear Romero pulling groceries out of his sack, pouring tap water in a pan, clattering pans on a stove. I held on to the bannister for balance and eased up the stairs two at a time while the streetcar rattled down the tracks out on St. Charles. I ducked under the window at the top of the stairs and then flattened myself against the wall between the screen door and the window. Romero's shadow moved back and forth against the screen. Swallows glided above the trees across the street in the sun's last red light.

I heard him set something heavy and metal on a tabletop, then walk past the screen again and into another room. I took a deep breath, tore open the door, and went in after him. In the hard electric light, he and I both seemed caught as though in the sudden flash of a photographer's camera. I saw the stiff spaghetti noodles protruding from a pot of steaming water on the stove, a loaf of French bread and a block of cheese and a dark bottle of Chianti on the drainboard, an army .45 like mine, except chrome-plated, where he had placed it on a breakfast table. I saw the animal fear and anger in his face as he stood motionless in the bedroom doorway, the tight mouth, the white quiver around his pinched nostrils, his hot black eyes that stared both at me and at the pistol that he had left beyond his grasp.

"You're busted, sonofabitch! Down on your face!" I yelled.

But I should have known (and perhaps I already did) that a man who had lived on snakes and insects and crawled alone through elephant grass with an '03 Springfield to the edge of a Vietcong village would not allow himself to be taken by a small-town cop who was foolish enough to extend the game after one side had just lost badly.

One of his hands rested on the edge of the bedroom door. His eyes stared into mine, his face twisted with some brief thought, then his arm shot forward and slammed the door in my face. I grabbed the knob, turned it, pushed and threw my weight against the wood, but the spring lock was set solidly in the jamb.

Then I heard him jerk a drawer out on the floor and a second later I heard the clack of metal sliding back on metal. I leaped aside and tumbled over a chair just as the shotgun exploded a hole the size of a pie plate through the door. The buckshot blew splinters of wood all over the kitchen, raked the breakfast table clean of groceries, whanged off the stove and pot heating on the burner. I was off balance, on my knees, pressed against the wall by the jamb, when he let off two more rounds at a different angle. I suspected the barrel was sawed off, because the pattern spread out like cannister, ripped through the wood as though it had been touched with a chain saw, and blew dishes into the air, water out of the pot, a half-gallon bottle of ketchup all over the far wall.

But when he ejected the spent casing and fired again, I gave him something to think about, too. I remained flat against the wall, bent my wrist backward around the doorjamb, and let off two rounds flush against the wood. The recoil almost knocked the pistol from my hand, but a .45 hollow-point fired through one surface at a target farther beyond makes an awe-inspiring impression on the person who happens to be the target.

"You've had it, Romero. Throw it down. Cops'll be all over the street in three minutes," I said.

The room was hot and still. The air smelled heavily of cordite and an empty pot burning on the stove. I heard him snick two shells into the shotgun's magazine and then heard his feet thundering up a wooden stairway. I stood quickly in front of the door, the .45 extended in both arms, and fired the whole clip at an upward angle into the bedroom. I chopped holes out of the wood that looked like a jack-o'-lantern's mouth, and even among the explosions of smoke and flame and splintered lead and flying pieces of door I could hear and even glimpse the damage taking place inside the room: a mirror crashing to the floor, a wall lamp whipped into the air against its cord, a water pipe bursting inside a wall, a window erupting into the street.

The breech locked open, and I ripped the empty clip out of the handle, shoved in another one, slid the top round into the chamber, and kicked the shattered door loose from the jamb. By the side wall, safe from my angle of fire, was a stairway that pulled out of the ceiling by a rope. I pointed my .45 at the attic's dark opening, my blood roaring in my ears.

The room was quiet. There was no movement upstairs. Particles of dust and threads of fiberboard floated in the light from the broken ceramic lamp that swung back and forth on its cord against the wall. Down the street I heard sirens.

I had every reason to believe that he was trapped—even though Victor Romero had survived Vietnam, thrived as a street dealer and pimp, gotten out from under federal custody after he probably killed the four people in the plane at Southwest Pass, escaped unhurt in the Toyota when I punched it full of holes with the .45, and managed in all probability to blow away Eddie Keats. It wasn't a record to ignore.

For the first time I glanced through a side window and saw a flat, tarpapered roof outside. There were air vents on it from the laundry, a lighted neon sign, two peaked enclosures with small doors that probably housed ventilator fans, the rusted top of an iron ladder that dropped down to ground level.

Then I saw the boards at the edge of the attic entrance bend with his weight as he moved quietly toward the wall and a probable window that overlooked the roof. I raised the .45 and waited until one board eased back into place and the edges of the next one moved slightly out of the flat, geometric pattern that formed the ceiling, then I aimed just ahead of the spread between his two feet and began firing. I pulled the trigger five times, deliberately and with calculation, saving three shells in the clip, and let the recoil bring each round farther back from the point of his leading foot and the attic entrance.

I think he screamed at one point. But I can't be sure. I didn't really care, either. I've heard that scream before; it represents the failure of everything, particularly of hope and humanity. You hear it in your dreams; it replays itself even when they die silently.

He fell back through the attic opening and crashed on the floor by the foot of the ladder. He lay on his back, one leg bent under him, his eyes filled with black light, his mouth working for air. A round had cut off three fingers of his right hand. The hand trembled with shock on the floor, the knuckles rattling on the wood. There was a deep sucking wound in his chest, and the wet cloth of his shirt fluttered in the wound each time he tried to breathe. Outside, the street was filled with sirens and the revolving blue and red lights of emergency vehicles.

He was trying to speak. His mouth opened, his voice clicked in the back of his throat, and blood and saliva ran down his cheek into his black curls. I knelt by him, as a priest might, and turned my ear toward his face. I could smell his dried sweat, the oil in his hair.

". . . did her," he rasped.

"I can't understand."

He tried again, but he choked on the saliva in his throat. I turned his face to the side with my fingers so his mouth would drain.

His lips were bright red, and they formed a wet smile like a clown's. Then the voice came out in a long whisper, smelling of bile and nicotine: "I did your wife, motherfucker."

He was dead two minutes later when three uniformed cops came through the apartment door. A flattened round had caught him in the lower back, tunneled upward through his trunk, and torn a hole in his lung. The coroner told me that the spine had probably been severed and that he was paralyzed when he crashed down the ladder. After the paramedics had lifted him on a stretcher and taken him away, his blood left a pattern like horsetails on the wooden floor.

I spent the next half hour in the apartment answering questions asked by a young homicide lieutenant named Magelli. He was tired and his clothes were wilted with perspiration, but he was thorough and he didn't cut corners. His brown eyes seemed sleepy and expressionless, but when he asked a question, they remained engaged with mine until the last word of my answer was out of my mouth, and only then did he write on his clipboard.

Finally he put a Lucky Strike in his mouth and looked around again at the litter in the kitchen and the buckshot holes in the walls. A drop of perspiration fell out of his hair and spotted the cigarette paper.

"You say this guy worked for Bubba Rocque?" he said.

"He did at one time."

"I wish he'd made enough to buy an air conditioner."

"Bubba has a way of dumping people after their function is over."

"Well, you might have a little trouble about jurisdiction and not calling us when you made the guy, but I don't think it'll be serious. Nobody's going to mourn his passing. Come down to the district and make a formal statement, then you're free to go. Does any of his stuff help you out?"

In the other room the bed was covered with bagged articles of evidence and clothing and personal items taken by the scene investigator from the attic, kitchen, bedroom floor, dressers, and closets: Romero's polyester suits, loud shirts and colored silk handkerchiefs; the chrome-plated .45 that he had probably used to kill Eddie Keats; a twelve-gauge Remington sawed off at the pump, with a walnut stock that had been cut down, tapered, and sanded until it was almost the size of a pistol grip; the spent shell casings; a whole brick of high-grade reefer; a glass straw with traces of cocaine in it; an Italian stiletto that could cut paper as easily as a razor blade; a cigar box full of pornographic photographs; a bolt-action, scoped .30-06 rifle; a snapshot of him in uniform and two other marines with three Vietnamese bar girls in a nightclub; and finally a plastic bag of human ears, now withered and black, laced together on a GI dogtag chain.

His life had been used to till a garden of dark and poisonous flowers. But in all his memorabilia of cruelty and death, there wasn't one piece of paper or article of evidence that would connect him with anyone outside his apartment.

"It looks like a dead end," I said. "I should have called you all."

"It might have come out the same way, Robicheaux. Except maybe with some of our people hurt. Look, if he'd gotten out on that roof, he'd be in Mississippi by now. You did the right thing."

"When are you going to pick up his cousin?"

"Probably in the morning."

"Are you going to charge him with harboring?"

"I'll tell him that, but I don't think we can make it stick. Take it easy. You did enough for one night. All this shit eventually gets ironed out one way or another. How do you feel?"

"All right."

"I don't believe you, but that's all right," he said, and put his unlit, sweat-spotted cigarette back in his shirt pocket. "Can I buy you a drink later?"

"No, thanks."

"Well, all right, then. We'll seal this place, and you can follow us on down to the district." His sleepy brown eyes smiled at me. "What are you looking at?"

The breakfast table was an old round one with a hard rubber top. Among the streaks of canned food that had been blown off the table by Romero's shotgun blast was a pattern of dried rings that looked as if they had been left there by the wet impressions of glasses or cups. Except one set of rings was larger than the other, and they were both on the same side of the table. The rings were gray and felt crusty under my fingertips.

"What's the deal?" he said.

I wet my fingertip, wiped up part of the residue, and touched it to my tongue.

"What's it taste like to you?" I said.

"Are you kidding? A guy who collected human ears. I wouldn't drink out of his water tap."

"Come on, it's important."

I wet my finger and did it again. He raised his eyebrows, touched a finger to one of the gray rings, then licked it. He made a face.

"Lemon or lime juice or something," he said. "Is this how you guys do it out in the parishes? We use the lab for this sort of stuff. Remind me to buy some Listerine on the way home."

He waited. When I didn't speak, the attention sharpened in his face.

"What's it mean?" he said.

"Probably nothing."

"Oh no, we don't play it that way here, my friend. The game is show-and-tell."

"It doesn't mean anything. I messed up tonight."

He took the cigarette back out of his pocket and lit it. He blew the smoke out and tapped his finger in the air at me.

"You're giving me a bad feeling, Robicheaux. Who'd you say he confessed to killing before he died?"

"A girl in New Iberia."

"You knew her?"

"It's a small town."

"You knew her personally?"

"Yes."

He chewed on the corner of his lip and looked at me with veiled eyes.

"Don't make me revise my estimation of you," he said. "I think you need to go back to New Iberia tonight. And maybe stay there, unless we call you. New Orleans is a lousy place in the summer, anyway. We're clear about this, aren't we?"

"Sure."

"That's good. I aim for simplicity in my work. Clarity of line, you might call it."

He was quiet, his eyes studying me in the kitchen light. His face softened.

"Forget what I said. You look a hundred years old," he said. "Stay over in a motel tonight and give us your statement in the morning."

"That's all right. I'd better be on my way. Thank you for your courtesy," I said, and walked out into the darkness and the wind that blew over the tops of the oak trees. The night sky was full of heat lightning, like the flicker of artillery beyond a distant horizon.

Three hours later I was halfway across the Atchafalaya basin. My eyes burned with fatigue, and the center line on the highway seemed to drift back and forth under my left front tire. When I thumped across the metal bridge spanning the Atchafalaya River, the truck felt airborne under me.

My system craved a drink: four inches of Jim Beam straight up, with a sweating Jax draft on the side, an amber-gold rush that could light my soul for hours and even let me pretend that the serpentarium was closed forever. On both sides of the road were canals and bayous and wind-dimpled bays and islands of willows and gray cypresses that were almost luminous in the moonlight. In the wind and the hum of the truck's engine and tires, I thought I could hear John Fogarty singing:

> *Don't come 'round tonight*
> *It's bound to take your life,*
> *A bad moon's on the rise.*
> *I hear hurricanes a-blowing,*
> *I know the end is coming soon.*
> *I feel the river overflowing*
> *I can hear the voice of rage and ruin.*

I pulled into a truck stop and bought two hamburgers and a pint of coffee to go. But as I continued down the road, the bread and meat were as dry and tasteless in my mouth as confetti, and I folded the hamburgers in the grease-stained sack and drank the coffee with the nervous energy of a man swallowing whiskey out of a cup with the morning's first light.

Romero was evil. I had no doubt about that. But I had

killed people before, in war and as a member of the New Orleans police department, and I know what it does to you. Like the hunter, you feel an adrenaline surge of pleasure at having usurped the province of God. The person who says otherwise is lying. But the emotional attitude you form later varies greatly among individuals. Some will keep their remorse alive and feed it as they would a living gargoyle, to assure themselves of their own humanity; others will justify it in the name of a hundred causes, and they'll reach back in moments of their own inadequacy and failure and touch again those flaming shapes that somehow made their impoverished lives historically significant.

But I always feared a worse consequence for myself. One day a curious light dies in the eyes. The unblemished place where God once grasped our souls becomes permanently stained. A bird lifts its span of wings and flies forever out of the heart.

Then I did a self-serving thing that impersonated a charitable act. I pulled off the causeway into a rest area to use the men's room, and saw an elderly Negro man under one of the picnic shelters. Even though it was a summer night, he wore an old suitcoat and a felt hat. By his foot was a desiccated cardboard suitcase tied shut with a rope, the words *The Great Speckled Bird* painted on one side. For some reason he had lighted a fire of twigs under the empty barbecue grill and was staring out at the light rain that had begun to fall on the bay.

"Did you eat tonight, partner?" I asked.

"No, suh," he said. His face was covered with thin brown lines, like a tobacco leaf.

"I think I've got just the thing for us, then," I said, and took my half-eaten hamburger and the untouched one from the truck and heated them on the edge of the grill. I also found two cans of warm Dr Pepper in my toolbox.

The rain slanted in the firelight. The old man ate without speaking. Occasionally his eyes looked at me.

"Where are you going?" I said.

"Lafayette. Or Lake Charles. I might go to Beaumont, too." His few teeth were long and purple with rot.

"I can take you to the Salvation Army in Lafayette."

"I don't like it there."

"It might storm tonight. You don't want to be out here in an electrical storm, do you?"

"What chu doing this for?" His eyes were red, the lines of his face as intricate as cobwebs.

"I can't leave you out here at night. It's not good for you. Sometimes bad people are out at night."

He made a sound as though a great philosophical weariness were escaping from his lungs.

"I don't want no truck with them kind. No, suh," he said, and allowed me to pick up his suitcase and walk him to the pickup.

It started raining outside of Lafayette. The sugarcane fields were green and thrashing in the wind, and the oak trees along the road trembled whitely in the explosions of lightning on the horizon. The old man fell asleep against the far door, and I was left alone in the drumming of the rain against the cab, in the sulfurous smell of the air through the wind vane, in the sulfurous smell that was as acrid as cordite.

When I awoke in the morning, the house was cool from the window fans, and the sunlight looked like smoke in the pecan trees outside the window. I walked barefoot in my undershorts to the bathroom, then started toward the kitchen to make coffee. Robin opened her door in her pajamas and motioned me inside with her fingers. I still slept on the couch and she in the back room, in part because of Alafair and in part, perhaps, because of a basic dishonesty in myself about the nature of our relationship. She bit down quietly on her lip with a conspiratorial smile.

I sat on the edge of the bed with her and looked out the window into the backyard. It was covered in blue shadow and dripping with dew. She put her hands on my neck and face, rubbed them down my back and chest.

"You came in late," she said.

"I had to take an old man to the Sally in Lafayette."

She kissed my shoulder and traced her hand down my chest. Her body was still warm from sleep.

"It sounds like somebody didn't sleep too well," she said.

"I guess not."

"I know a good way to wake up in the morning," she said, and touched me with her hand.

She felt me jerk involuntarily.

"You got your chastity belt on this morning?" she said. "Scruples about mommy again?"

"I blew away Victor Romero last night."

I felt her go quiet and stiff next to me. Then she said in a hushed voice, "You killed Victor Romero?"

"He dealt it."

Then she was quiet again. She might have been a tough girl raised in a welfare project, but she was no different from anyone else in her reaction to being in proximity to someone who has recently killed another human being.

"It comes with the fucking territory, Robin."

"I know that. I wasn't judging you." She placed her hand on my back.

I stared out the window at the yard, my hands on my knees. The redwood picnic table was dark with moisture.

"You want me to fix breakfast for you?" she said finally.

"Not now."

"I'll make toast in a pan, the way you like it."

"I don't want anything to eat right now."

She put her arms around me and squeezed me. I could feel her cheek and her hair on my shoulder.

"Do you love me, Dave?" she said.

I didn't answer.

"Come on, Streak. Fair and square. Do you love me?"

"Yes."

"No, you don't. You love things about me. There's a difference. It's a big one."

"I'm not up to this today, Robin."

"What I'm telling you is I understand and I got no complaint. You were decent to me when nobody else was. You know what it meant to me when you took me to midnight Mass at the Cathedral? I never had a man treat me with that kind of respect before. Mommy thought she had Cinderella's glass slippers on."

She picked up my hand in hers and kissed it on the back. Then, almost in a whisper, she said, "I'll always be your friend. Anytime, anywhere, for anything."

I slipped my hand up her back, under her pajama top, and kissed the corner of her eye. Then I drew her against me, felt her breath on my chest, felt her fingers on my thighs and stomach, and I lay down next to her and looked at her eyes, the tanned smoothness of her skin, the way her lips parted when I touched her; then she pressed hard against me for a brief moment, got up from the bed and slid the bolt on the door and took off her pajamas. She sat beside me, leaned over my face and kissed me, her mouth smiling as though she were looking at a little boy. I pulled off my undershorts, and she sat on top of me, her eyes closing, her mouth opening silently, as she took me inside her. She put her hands in my hair, kissed my ear, then stretched herself out against my body and tucked her feet inside my calves.

A moment later she felt me tense and try to hold back before I gave in to that old male desire that simply wants to complete that bursting moment of fulfillment, whether the other person gets to participate or not. But she raised herself on her arms and knees and smiled at me and never stopped her motion, and when I went weak inside and felt sweat break out on my forehead and felt my loins heat like a flame burning in a circle through paper, she leaned down on my chest again and kissed my mouth and neck and forced her hands under my back as though some part of me might elude her in that final, heart-twisting moment.

Later we lay on top of the sheets under the fan while the sunlight grew brighter in the tree limbs outside. She turned on her side, looking at my profile, and took my fingers in hers.

"Dave, I don't think you should be troubled like this," she said. "You tried to arrest him, and he tried to kill you for it."

I looked at the shadows of the wood-bladed fan turning on the ceiling.

"Look, I know New Orleans cops who would have just killed the guy and never given him a chance. Then they'd plant a gun on him. They've got a name for it. What do they call it?"

"A 'drop' or a 'throwaway.' "

"You're not that kind of cop. You're a good man. Why do you want to carry this guilt around?"

"You don't understand, Robin. I think maybe I'm going to do it again."

Later I called the office and told them I wouldn't be in that day, then I put on my running shorts and shoes, lifted weights under the mimosa tree in the backyard, and ran three miles along the bayou road. Wisps of fog still hung around the flooded roots of the cypress trees. I went inside the paintless wood frame general store at the four-corners, drank a carton of orange juice and talked French with the elderly owner of the store, then jogged back along the road while the sun climbed higher into the sky and dragonflies dipped and hovered over the cattails.

When I came through the front screens, hot and running with sweat, I saw the door of Annie's and my bedroom wide open, the lock and hasp pried loose from the jamb, the torn wood like a ragged dental incision. Sunlight streamed through the windows into the room, and Robin was on her hands and knees, in a white sun halter and a pair of cut-off blue jean shorts, dipping a scrub brush into a bucket of soapy water and scouring the grain in the cypress floor. The buckshot-pocked walls and the headboard of the bed were wet and gleaming, and by a bottle of Clorox on the floor was another bucket filled with soaking rags, and the rags and the water were the color of rust.

"What are you doing?" I said.

She glanced at me, then continued to scrub the grain without replying. The stiff bristles of the brush sounded like sandpaper against the wood. The muscles of her tan back rippled with her motion.

"Damn you, Robin. Who gave you the fucking right to go into my bedroom?"

"I couldn't find your keys, so I pried the lock off with a screwdriver. I'm sorry about the damage."

"You get the fuck out of this room."

She paused and sat back on her heels. There were white indentations on her knees. She brushed the perspiration out of her hairline with the back of her wrist.

"Is this your church where you go every day to suffer?" she said.

"It's none of your business what it is. It's not a part of your life."

"Then tell me to get out of your life. Say it and I'll do it."

"I'm asking you to leave this room."

"I have a hard time buying your attitude, Streak. You wear guilt like a big net over your head. You ever know guys who are always getting the clap? They're not happy unless some broad has dosed them from their toenails to their eyes. Is that the kind of gig you want for yourself?"

The sweat was dripping off my hands onto the floor. I breathed slowly and pushed my wet hair back over my head.

"I'm sorry for being profane at you. I truly am. But come outside now," I said.

She dipped the brush in the bucket again and began to enlarge the scrubbed circle on the floor.

"Robin?" I said.

She concentrated her eyes on the strokes of the brush across the wood.

"This is my house, Robin."

I stepped toward her.

"I'm talking to you, kiddo. No more free pass," I said.

She sat back on her heels again and dropped the brush in the water.

"I'm finished," she said. "You want to stand here and mourn or help me carry these buckets outside?"

"You didn't have the right to do this. You mean well, but you didn't have the right."

"Why don't you show some respect for your wife and stop using her? If you want to get drunk, go do it. If you want to kill somebody, do it. But at least have the courage to do it on your own, without all this remorse bullshit. It's a drag, Dave."

She picked up one of the buckets with both hands to avoid spilling it, and walked out the door past me. Her bare feet left damp imprints on the cypress floor. I continued to stand alone in the room, the dust spinning in the shafts of light through the windows, then I saw her cross the backyard with the bucket and walk toward the duck pond.

"Wait!" I called through the window.

I gathered up the soiled rags from the floor, put them in the other bucket, and followed her outside. I stopped by the aluminum shed where I kept my lawn mower and tools, took out a shovel, and walked down to the small flower garden that Batist's wife had planted next to a shallow coulee that ran through my property. The soil in the garden was loamy and damp from the overflow of the coulee and partly shaded by banana trees so the geraniums and impatiens didn't burn up in the summer; but the outer edge was in full sun and it ran riot with daisies and periwinkles.

They weren't the cornflowers and bluebonnets that a Kansas girl should have, but I knew that she would understand. I pushed the shovel into the damp earth and scooped out a deep hole among the daisy roots, poured the two buckets of soap and water and chemicals into the dirt, put the brush and rags into the hole, then put the buckets on top and crushed them flat with my foot, and covered the hole back up with a wet mound of dirt and tangle of severed daisy and periwinkle roots. I uncoiled the garden hose from the side of the house and watered the mound until it was as slick and smooth as the ground around it and the chemicals had washed far below the root system of the flower bed.

It was the kind of behavior that you don't care to think about or explain to yourself later. I cleaned the shovel under the hose, replaced it in the shed, and walked back into the kitchen without speaking to Robin. Then I took a shower and put on a fresh pair of khakis and a denim shirt and read the newspaper at the redwood table under the mimosa tree. I could hear Robin

making lunch in the kitchen and Alafair talking to her in a mixture of Spanish and English. Then Robin brought a ham-and-
onion sandwich and a glass of iced tea to me on a tray. I didn't
look up from the table when she set it on the table. She
remained standing next to me, her bare thigh only an inch from
my arm, then I felt her hand touch me lightly on the shoulder
and finger my damp collar and tease the hair along my neck.

"I'll always be your biggest fan, Robicheaux," she said.

I put my arm around her soft bottom and squeezed her
against me, my eyes shut.

Late that afternoon Minos Dautrieve was at my front door,
dressed in blue jeans, tennis shoes without socks, and a paint-
flecked gold shirt. A fishing rod stuck out the passenger's window of his parked Toyota jeep.

"I hear you know where all the big bass are," he said.

"Sometimes."

"I've got some fried chicken and Dixie beer and soda in the
cooler. Let's get it on down the road."

"We were thinking of going to the track tonight."

"I'll have you back early. Get your butt moving, boy."

"You've really got the touch, Minos."

We hitched my trailer and one of my boats to his jeep and
drove twenty-five miles to the levee that fronts the southwestern
edge of the Atchafalaya swamp. The wind was down, the water
quiet, the insects just beginning to rise from the reeds and lily
pads in the shadows of the willow islands. I took us across a
long bay dotted with dead cypresses and oil platforms, then up a
bayou, deep into the swamp, before I cut the engine and let the
boat drift quietly up the entrance of a small bay with a narrow
channel at the far end. I still didn't know what Minos was up to.

"On a hot day like this, they get deep in the holes on the

shady side of the islands," I said. "Then just before dusk they move up to the edge of the channel and feed where the water curves around the bank."

"No kidding?" he said.

"You have a Rapala?"

"I might have one of those."

He popped open his tackle box, which had three layers of compartments in it, all of them filled with rubber worms, spinners, doll flies, surface plugs, and popping bugs.

"What's it look like?" he said.

"Guess what, Minos? I gave up being a straight man for government agents when I resigned from the New Orleans department."

He clipped a Devil Horse on his swivel and flipped it neatly across the channel into open water with a quick spring of his wrist. Then he retrieved it through the channel back into the bay and cast again. On the third cast I saw the quiet surface of the water balloon under the lily pads, then the dorsal fin of a bigmouth bass roll like a serpent right in front of the lure, the scales hammered with green and gold light, and then the water exploded when he locked down on the lure and Minos socked the treble hook hard into his jaw. The bass went deep and pulled for a hole among the reeds, clouding the water with mud, but Minos kept the tip of the rod up, the drag tight, and turned him back into the middle of the bay. Then the bass broke through the surface into the air, rattling the lure and swivel against his head, and splashed sideways like a wood plank whipped against the surface, before he went deep again and tried for the channel and open water.

"Get him up again," I said.

"He'll tear it out of his mouth."

I started to speak again, but I saw the line stop and quiver against the current, tiny beads of water glistening on the stretched monofilament. When Minos tried to turn the handle of the spinning reel, the rod dipped over the side. I put the hand net, which I had been holding, back under the seat of the boat. Suddenly the rod flipped up straight and lifeless in Minos's palm, the broken line floating in a curlicue on top of the water.

"Sonofabitch," he said.

"I forgot to tell you there are a bunch of cypress stumps under this bay. Don't feel bad, though. That same bass has a whole collection of my lures."

He didn't speak for almost five minutes. He drank a bottle of Dixie beer, put the empty back in the cooler, then opened another one and lit a cigar.

"You want some chicken?" he said.

"Sure. But it's getting late, Minos. I still want to go to the track tonight."

"I'm keeping you?"

I joined the sections of my Fenwick fly rod and tied a black popping bug with a yellow feather and red eyes to the tapered leader. I stuck the hook into the cork handle and handed him the rod.

"This is a surefire killer for goggle-eye," I said. "We'll go out into the open water and throw back into the bank, then I've got to hit the road, partner."

I pulled the foot-long piece of train rail that I used as an anchor, left the outboard engine tilted up on the stern, and paddled us through the channel into the larger bay. The air was purple, swallows covered the sky, and a wind had come up and was blowing the insects back into the flooded trees so that the bream and sunfish and goggle-eye perch were feeding deep in the shadows. The western sky was a burnt orange, and cranes and blue herons stood in the shallows on the tips of the sandbars and islands of cattails. Minos dropped his cigar hissing into the water, false-cast in a figure eight over his head, and laid the popping bug right on the edge of the lily pads.

"How do you feel about wasting Romero?" he said.

"I don't feel anything."

"I don't believe you."

"So what?"

"I don't believe you, that's all."

"Is that why we're out here?"

"I had a phone conversation with that homicide lieutenant, Magelli, this morning. You didn't tell him it was your wife Romero killed."

"He didn't ask."

"Oh yeah, he did."

"I don't feel like talking about this, Minos."

"Maybe you ought to learn who your friends are."

"Listen, if you're saying I was out to pop Romero, you're wrong. That's just the way it worked out. He thought he might have another season to run. He lost. It's that simple. And I think day-after analysis is for douchebags."

"I don't give a damn about Romero. He should have been a bar of soap a long time ago." He missed a strike among the lily pads and ripped the popping bug angrily back through a leaf.

"Then what's all this stuff about?"

"Magelli said you figured out something in Romero's apartment. Something you weren't telling him about."

I drew the paddle through the water and didn't answer.

"It had to do with lime juice or something," he said.

"The only thing that counts is the score at the end of the game. I made a big mistake in not using the New Orleans cops to bust Romero. I don't know how to correct it. Let it go at that, Minos."

He sat down in the boat and stuck the hook of the popping bug into the cork handle of the rod.

"Let me tell you a quick story," he said. "In Vietnam I worked for a major who was both a nasty and stupid man. In free-fire zones he liked to go dink-pinking in his helicopter— farmers in a field, women, water buffalo, whatever was around. Then his stupidity and incompetence compromised a couple of our agents and got them killed. I won't go into detail, but the VC could be imaginative when they created object lessons. One of those agents was a Eurasian school-teacher I had something of a relationship with.

"I thought a lot about our major. I spent many nights think-ing long and hard about him. Then one day an opportunity presented itself. Out in Indian country where you could paint the trees with a fat, incompetent fellow and then smoke a little dope and just let a bad day float away in the wind. But I didn't do it. I wasn't willing to trade the rest of my life—my con-science, if you will—for one asshole. So he's probably still out there, fucking people up, getting them killed, telling stories about all the dinks he left floating in the rice fields. But I'm not crazy today, Robicheaux. I don't have to live with a shitpile of guilt. I don't have to worry about the wrong people showing up at my house one day."

"Save your concern. I've got nothing of any value to go on. I blew it."

"I'd like to believe you're that humble and resigned."

"Maybe I am."

"No, I know guys like you. You're out of sync with the rest of the world, and you don't trust other people. That's why you're always thinking."

"Is that right?"

"You just haven't figured out how to pull it off yet," he said. His face was covered with the sun's last red light. "Even-tually you'll try to hang them up in a meat market."

chapter
ELEVEN

HE WAS WRONG. I HAD ALREADY QUIT TRYING TO figure out how to pull it off. Instead, I had spent the entire day brooding on an essential mistake I had made in the investigation, a failure to act upon a foregone conclusion about how Bubba and his wife operated—namely, that they used people. They used them in a cynical and ruthless fashion and then threw them away like soiled Kleenex. Johny Dartez muled for Bubba and drowned in the plane at Southwest Pass; Eddie Keats kept Bubba's whores in line and Toot trimmed ears for him, and now one had been dumped in a swamp and the other had been cooked in his own bathtub; and finally in my pride and single-mindedness I had stumbled into the role of Victor Romero's executioner.

The board was swept clean. I had always thought of myself as a fairly smart cop, an outsider within the department, a one-eyed existentialist in the country of the blind, but I could not help comparing my situation with the way cops everywhere treat major crimes. We unconsciously target the most available and inept in that myriad army of metropolitan lowlifes: addicts, street dealers, petty thieves, hookers and a few of their johns, storefront fences, and the obviously deranged and violent. With the exception of the hookers, most of these people are stupid and ugly and easy to convict. Check out the residents in any city or county jail. In the meantime the people who would market the Grand Canyon as a gravel pit or sell the Constitution at an Arab rug bazaar remain as socially sound as a silver dollar dropped into a church basket.

But you don't surrender the ballpark to the other team, even when your best pitch is a letter-high floater that they drill into your breastbone. Also, there are certain advantages in situations in which you have nothing to lose: you become justified in throwing a bucketful of monkey shit through the ventilator fan. It might not alter the outcome of things, but it certainly gives the other side pause.

I found Bubba the next morning at his fish-packing house south of Avery Island, a marsh and salt-dome area that eventually bleeds into Vermilion Bay and the Gulf. The packing house was made of tin and built up on pilings over the bayou, and the docks were painted silver so that the whole structure looked as bright and glittering as tinfoil in a sea of sawgrass, dead cypress, and meandering canals. His oyster and shrimp boats were out, but a waxed yellow cigarette boat floated in the gasoline-stained water by the dock.

I parked my truck in the oyster-shell lot and walked up a ramp onto the dock. The sun was hot, reflecting off the water, and the air smelled of dead shrimp, oil, tar, and the salt breeze off the Gulf. Bubba was filling an ice chest with bottles of Dixie beer. He was bare-chested and sweating, and his denims hung low on his narrow hips so that the elastic of his undershorts showed. There wasn't a half-inch of fat on his hips or flat stomach. His shoulders were covered with fine brown hair, and across his deeply tanned back were chains of tiny scars.

Behind him, two pale men with oiled dark hair, who wore print shirts, slacks, tassel loafers, and sunglasses, were leaning over the dock rail and shooting pigeons and egrets with a pellet rifle. The dead egrets looked like melting snow below the water's surface. I thought I recognized one of the men as an ex-driver for a notorious, now-deceased New Orleans gangster by the name of Didoni Giacano.

Bubba smiled up at me from where he squatted by the ice chest. There were drops of sweat in his eyebrows and his spiked hair.

"Take a ride with us," he said. "That baby there can eat a trench all the way across the lake."

"What are you doing with the spaghetti-and-meatball crowd?"

One of the pale-skinned, dark-haired men looked over his shoulder at me. The sun clicked on his dark glasses.

"Friends from New Orleans," Bubba said. "You want a beer?"

"They're shooting protected birds."

"I'm tired of pigeons shitting on my shrimp. But I don't argue. Tell them." He smiled at me again.

The other man at the rail looked at me now, too. Then he leaned the pellet rifle against the rail, unwrapped a candy bar, and dropped the paper into the water.

"How big is the mob into you, Bubba?"

"Come on, man. That's movie stuff."

"You pay big dues with that crowd."

"No, you got it wrong. People pay *me* dues. I win, they lose. That's why I got these businesses. That's why I'm offering you a beer. That's why I'm inviting you out on my boat. I don't bear grudges. I don't have to."

"You remember Jimmy Hoffa? There was none tougher. Then he thought he could make deals with the Mob. I bet they licked their teeth when they saw him coming."

"Listen to this guy," he said, and laughed. He opened a

bottle on the side of the ice chest, and the foam boiled over the top and dripped flatly on the dock.

"Here," he said, and offered me the bottle, the beer glistening on the back of his brown hand.

"No, thanks," I said.

"Suit yourself," he said, and raised the bottle to his mouth and drank. Then he blew air out through his nose and looked at his cigarette boat. The scars on his back were like broken necklaces spread across his skin. He shifted his weight on his feet.

"Well, it's a beautiful day, and I'm about to go," he said. "You got something you want to tell me, 'cause I want to get out before it rains."

"I just had a couple of speculations. About who's making decisions for you these days."

"Oh yeah?" he said. He drank from the beer with one hand on his hip and looked away at the marsh, where some blue herons were lifting into the sky.

"Maybe I'm all wet."

"Maybe you got a brain disease, too."

"Don't misunderstand me. I'm not taking away from your accomplishment. I just have a feeling that Claudette has turned out to be an ambitious girl. She's been hard to keep in the kitchen, hasn't she?"

"You're starting to piss me off, Dave. I don't like that. I got guests here, I got a morning planned. You want to come along, that's cool. Don't be messing with me no more, podna."

"This is the way I figure it. Tell me if I'm wrong. Johnny Dartez wasn't a stand-up guy, was he? He was a dumb lowlife, a street dip not to be trusted. You knew that one day he'd trade your butt to the feds, so either you or Claudette told Victor Romero to take him out. Except he killed everybody in that plane, including a priest.

"Then I stumbled into the middle of things and complicated matters even more. You should have left me alone, Bubba. I wasn't any threat to you. I'd already disengaged when your monkeys started coming around my house."

"What's all this shit about?" one of the Italians said.

"Stay out of it," Bubba said. Then he looked back at me. His thick hand was tight around the beer bottle. "I'll tell you something, and I'll tell you only once, and you can accept it or stick it sideways up your ass. I'm *one* guy. I'm not a crime wave. You're supposed to be a smart college guy, but you always talk like you don't understand anything. When you mess with the action out of New Orleans, you fuck with hundreds of people. You wouldn't leave it alone, they slammed the door on your nose. Stop laying your shit off on me."

"Claudette was in Romero's apartment."

"What are you talking about?"

"You heard me."

"She don't go anyplace I don't know about."

"She had her thermos of gin rickeys with her. She left wet prints all over his kitchen table."

His gray-blue eyes stared at me as though they had no lids. His face was frozen, his jaw hooked sideways like a barracuda's.

"You really didn't know, did you?" I said.

"Say all that again."

"No, it's your problem. You work it out, Bubba. I'd watch my ass, though. If she doesn't eat up your operation, these guys will. I don't think you're in control of things anymore."

"You want to find out how much I'm in control? You want that nose busted all over your face right here? Come on, is that what you want?"

"Grow up."

"No, you grow up. You come out to my home, you come

out to my business, you talk trash about my family in front of my friends, but you don't do nothing about it. It's like you're always leaking gas under people's noses."

"You should have seen a psychiatrist a long time ago. You're fucking pathetic, Bubba."

He swirled the beer in his bottle.

"That's your best shot?" he said.

"You couldn't understand. You don't have the tools to."

"All right, you had your say. How about getting out of here now?"

"You don't have your father around anymore to slap your face in front of other people or beat you with a dog chain, so you married a woman like Claudette. You're pussy-whipped by a dyke. She's pulling apart your whole operation, and you don't even know it."

The skin around his eyes stretched tight. His eyes looked like marbles.

"I'll see you around," I said. "Rat-hole some money in Grand Cayman. I think you'll need it when Claudette and these guys get finished with you."

I started down the wooden ramp toward the parking lot and my truck. His beer bottle clattered to the dock and rolled across the boards, twisting a spiral of foam out of the neck.

"Hey! You don't walk off! You hear me? You don't walk off!" he said, jabbing his finger at my face.

I continued toward the truck. The oyster-shell parking lot was white and hot in the sunlight. He was walking along beside me now, his face as tight as the skin of an overinflated balloon. He pushed at my arm with his stiffened hand.

"Hey, you got wax?" he said. "You don't talk to me like this! You don't get in my face in front of my friends and walk away!"

I opened my truck door. He grabbed my shoulder and

turned me back toward him. His sweating chest was criss-crossed with veins.

"Swing on me and you're busted. No more high school bull-shit," I said.

I slammed the truck door and drove slowly out of the lot over the oyster shells. His dilated face, slipping past the window, wore the expression of a man whose furious energies had suddenly been transformed into a set of knives turning inside him.

That afternoon I left work early and enrolled Alafair in kindergarten at the Catholic school in New Iberia for the fall semester, then I took her with Batist and me to seine for shrimp in the jug boat out on the salt. But I had another reason to be out on the Gulf that day: it was the twenty-first anniversary of my father's death. He had been a derrick man on a drilling rig, working high up on the monkey board, when the crew hit an oil sand earlier than they had expected. There was no blowout preventer on the wellhead, and as soon as the drill bit tapped into that gas dome far below the Gulf's floor, the rig began to tremble and suddenly salt water, sand, and oil exploded from the hole under thousands of pounds of pressure, and then the casing jettisoned, too. Metal spars, tongs, coils of chain, huge sections of pipe clattered and rang through the rigging, a spark jumped off a steel surface, and the wellhead ignited. The survivors said the roar of flames looked like someone had kicked open hell's front door.

My father clipped his safety belt onto the guy wire that ran from the monkey board to the roof of the quarter-boat and jumped. But the rig caved with him, crashed across the top of the quarter-boat, and took my father and nineteen other roughnecks down to the bottom of the Gulf with it.

His body was never found, and sometimes in my dreams I would see him far below the waves, still wearing his hardhat and overalls and steel-toed boots, grinning at me, his big hand raised to tell me that everything was all right.

That was my old man. Sheriff's deputies could jail him, saloon bouncers could bust chairs across his back, a *bourée* dealer could steal his wife, but the next morning he would pretend to be full of fun and brush yesterday's bad fortune aside as something not even worth mentioning.

I let Alafair sit behind the wheel in the pilot's cab, an Astros baseball cap sideways on her head, while Batist and I took in the nets and filled the ice bins with shrimp. Then I made a half-mile circle, cut the engine, and let the boat drift back over the spot where my father's rig had gone down in a torrent of cascading iron and geysers of steam twenty-one years ago.

It was twilight now, and the water was black-green and covered with froth that slipped down in the troughs between the waves. The sun was already down, and the red and black clouds on the western horizon looked as though they had risen from a planet burning under the water's surface. I opened the scuba gear box, took out the bunch of yellow and purple roses I had snipped earlier, and threw them out on the flat side of a wave. The petals and clustered stems broke apart in the next wave and floated away from each other, then dimmed and sank below the surface.

"He like that, him," Batist said. "Your old man like flowers. Flowers and women. Whiskey, too. Hey, Dave, you don't be sad. Your old man wasn't never sad."

"Let's boil some shrimp and head for home," I said.

But I was troubled all the way in. The twilight died in the west and left only a green glow on the horizon, and as the moon rose, the water turned the color of lead. Was it the memory of my father's death that bothered me, or my constant propensity for depression?

No, something else had been stirring in my unconscious all day, like a rat working its whiskers through a black hole. A good cop puts people away; he doesn't kill them. So far I had made a mess of things and hadn't turned the key on anyone. To compensate, I had wrapped barbed wire around the head of a mental cripple like Bubba Rocque. I didn't feel good about it.

Minos called me at the office the next morning.

"Did you hear from the Lafayette sheriff's department about Bubba?" he said.

"No."

"I thought they kept you informed."

"What is it, Minos?"

"He beat the shit out of his wife last night. Thoroughly. In a bar out on Pinhook Road. You want to hear it?"

"Go ahead."

"Yesterday afternoon they started fighting with each other in their car outside the Winn Dixie, then three hours later she's slopping down the juice in the bar on Pinhook with a couple of New Orleans greaseballs when Mad Man Muntz skids his Caddy to a stop in the parking lot, crashes through the front door, and slaps her with the flat of his hand into next week. He knocked her down on the floor, kicked her in the ass, then picked her up and threw her through the men's room door. One of the greasers tried to stop it, and Bubba splattered his mouth all over a wall. That's no shit. The bartender said Bubba hit the guy so hard his head almost twisted off his neck."

"You're enjoying this, Minos."

"It beats watching these fuckers park their twenty-grand cars at the racetrack."

"Where is he now?"

"Back home, I guess. She had to go to Lourdes for stitches, but she and the greaseball aren't filing charges. They don't seem to like participating in the legal process, for some reason. Do you have any idea what triggered Bubba's toggle switch?"

"I went out to his fish business by Avery Island yesterday."

"So?"

"I poured some iodine on a couple of severed nerve endings."

"Ah."

"Let's get it all out here, Minos. I think Claudette Rocque was behind my wife's death. Bubba's a sonofabitch, but I'm convinced he would have come after me head-on. He's prideful, and he's wanted to put out my light since we were kids. He'd never admit to himself that he had to hire somebody to do it. I think Claudette sent Romero and the Haitian to kill me, and when they murdered Annie instead and then Romero missed me again, she came around the house with a poontang act and a hundred-thou-a-year job. When that didn't work, she got Bubba jealous and turned him loose on me. Anyway, I'm sure she was in Romero's apartment. She left stains on the table from that thermos of gin rickeys she always carries around."

"So that's what that lime juice business was about?"

"Yes."

"And of course it's worthless as evidence."

"Yes."

"So you decided to stick a fork in Bubba's nuts about his old lady?"

"That's about it."

"You want absolution now?"

"All right on that stuff, Minos."

"Quit worrying about it. They're both human toilets. My advice to you now is to stay away from them."

"Why?"

"Let things run their course."

I was silent.

"He's psychotic. She collects *cojones*," he said. "You spit in the soup. Now let them drink it. It might prove interesting. Just stay the fuck away from it, though."

"No one will ever accuse you of euphemism."

"You know what your problem is? You're two people in the same envelope. You want to be a moral man in an amoral business. At the same time you want to blow up their shit just like the rest of us. Each time I talk to you, I never know who's coming out of the jack-in-the-box."

"I'll see you. Stay in touch."

"Yeah. Don't bother thanking me for the call. We do this for all rural flatfeet."

He hung up. I tried to call him back, but his line was busy. I drove home and ate lunch with Batist out on the dock under the canvas awning. It was hot and still and the sun was white in the sky.

I couldn't sleep that night. The air was breathless and dry, and the window and ceiling fans seemed unable to remove the heat that had built up in the wood of the house all day long. The stars looked hot in the sky, and out in the moonlight I could see my neighbor's horses lying down in a muddy slough. I went into the kitchen in my underwear and ate a bowl of ice cream and strawberries, and a moment later Robin stood in the doorway in her lingerie top and panties, her eyes adjusting sleepily to the light.

"It's just the heat. Go back to sleep, kiddo," I said.

She smiled and felt her way back down the hall without answering.

But it wasn't the heat. I turned off the light and sat outside on the steps in the dark. I wanted to put Claudette and Bubba Rocque away more than anything else in the world; no, I wanted worse for them. They epitomized greed and selfishness; they injected misery and death into the lives of others so they could live in wealth and comfort. And while they had dined on blackened redfish in New Orleans or slept in a restored antebellum home that overlooked carriage house and flower garden and river and trees, their emissaries had torn my front door open and watched my wife wake terrified and alone in front of their shotgun barrels.

But I couldn't take them down by provoking a sociopath into assaulting his wife. This may sound noble; it's not. The alcoholic recovery program I practiced did not allow me to lie, manipulate, or impose design or control over other people, particularly when its intention was obviously a destructive one. If I did, I would regress, I would start to screw up my own life and the lives of those closest to me, and eventually I would become the same drunk I had been years ago.

I fixed coffee and drank it out on the front porch and watched the first pale band of light touch the eastern sky. It was still hot, and the sun broke red over the earth's rim and turned the low strips of cloud on the horizon to flame; it was a sailor's warning, all right, but this morning was going to be one of endings and beginnings for me. I would no longer flay myself daily because I couldn't extract the vengeance my anger demanded; I wouldn't try to control everything that swam into my ken; and I would humbly try to accept my Higher Power's plan for my life.

And finally I would refuse to be a factor in the squalor and violence of Bubba and Claudette Rocque's lives.

As always when I surrendered a problem or a self-serving mechanism inside myself to my Higher Power, I felt as though an albatross had been cut from my neck. I watched the sun's red glow rise higher into the pewter sky, saw the black border of trees on the far side of the bayou become gray and gradually green and distinct, heard my neighbor turn on his sprinkler hose in a hiss of water. There was no wind, and because it hadn't rained in two days there was dust from the road on the leaves of my pecan trees, and the shafts of spinning light between the branches looked like spun glass.

But I had learned long ago that resolution by itself is not enough; we are what we do, not what we think and feel. In my case that meant I didn't want any more damage to Claudette Rocque on my conscience; it meant no more rat-fucking, no more insertion of fishhooks in Bubba's head; the game was simply going into extra innings. It meant telling both of them all that.

I shaved and showered, put on my loafers and seersucker slacks, clipped on my badge and belt holster, drank another cup of coffee in the kitchen, then drove down the dirt road toward New Iberia and the old highway to Lafayette. The weather had started to change abruptly. A long, heavy bank of gray clouds that stretched from horizon to horizon was moving out of the south, and as the first shadows passed across the sun, a breeze lifted above the marsh, stirred the moss on the cypresses, and flickered the dusty leaves of the oaks along the road.

I could feel the barometric pressure dropping. The bream and goggle-eye had already started hitting along the edge of the lily pads, as they always did before a change in the weather, and the sparrow hawks and cranes that had been gliding on the hot updrafts from the marsh were now circling lower and lower out of the darkening sky. Main Street in New Iberia was full of dust, the green bamboo along the banks of Bayou Teche bending in the wind. At the city limits the Negro owner of a fruit stand, which had been there since I was a boy, was carrying his lugs of strawberries from the shade tree by the highway back inside the stand.

Twenty minutes later I was approaching the Vermilion River and the antebellum home of Bubba and Claudette Rocque. The air was cool now, the clouds overhead blue-black, the sugarcane green and rippling in the fields. I could smell rain in the south, smell the wet earth on the wind. Up ahead I could see the pea-gravel entrance to Bubba's home, the white fences entwined with yellow roses, the water sprinklers twirling among the oak, mimosa, lime, and orange trees on his lawn. Then I saw his maroon Cadillac convertible, the immaculate white top buttoned down on the tinted windows, turn out of the drive in a scorch of gravel and roar down the highway toward me. Its weight and speed actually buffeted my truck as it sucked past me like an arrow off an archer's bow. I watched it grow smaller in the rearview mirror, then saw its brake lights come on by a filling station and restaurant. I turned into his drive.

Even though it was cool, the curtains were drawn on the windows and the fans for the central air-conditioning hummed on the side of the house and a couple of window units upstairs were turned on full blast and dripping with moisture. I walked up on the wide marble porch and twisted the brass bell handle, waited and twisted again, then knocked loudly with my fist. I could hear no sound inside the house. I walked around the side, past a flower bed of wilted geraniums that was sopping from a soak hose, and tapped on the glass of the kitchen door. There was still no answer, but the MG and the Oldsmobile were parked in the carriage house and I thought I could smell fried bacon. The light in the sky had changed, and the air was moist and looked green through the trees, and dead oak leaves clicked and tumbled across the grass like bits of dried parchment.

I put my hands on my hips and looked in a circle at Bubba's clay tennis court and gazebos and myrtle hedges on the river and stone wells hung with ornamental chains and brass buckets and was about to give it up and mark it off when I saw the wind blow smoke and powdered ash and red embers from behind an aluminum lawn shed in back.

I walked across the grass and around the shed and looked down upon an old ash and garbage heap, on top of which were the collapsed and blackened remains of a mattress. The cover had almost all burned away, and the stuffing was smoldering and rising in the wind in black threads. But one side of the mattress had not burned entirely, and on it was a dirty red stain that was steaming from the heat. I opened my Puma knife, knelt, and cut the stained material away. It felt stiff and warm between my fingers as I folded it and placed it in my pocket. Then I found a garden hose in the shed, connected it to a spigot by a flower bed, and sprinkled the mattress until all the embers were dead. A rancid odor rose in the steam.

I walked back across the lawn, pried a brick up from the border of the geranium bed, and knocked out a pane in the back door. I turned the inside handle and stepped into a Colonial-style kitchen of brass pots and pans hung on hooks above a brick hearth. The smell of bacon came from a skillet on the stove and from a single grease-streaked plate on the breakfast table. The air-conditioning was turned so high that my skin felt instantly cold and dead, as though the house had been refrigerated with dry ice. I walked through a pine-paneled television den with empty bookshelves and two black bearskins nailed at angles on the wall, into a chandeliered dining room whose walnut cabinets were filled with shining crystal ware, and finally into the marble-floored entrance area by the spiral staircase.

I walked slowly upstairs with my hand on the bannister.

The furnishings and colors and woodwork of the second story had the same peculiar, mismatched quality as the downstairs, like an impaired camera lens that wouldn't focus properly. The bathroom door gaped open at the top of the stairs, exposing a pink shag rug, gold fixtures on the washbasin and bathtub, and pink wallpaper with a silver erotic design on it. The plastic rings on the shower bar hung empty, except for one of them that still held a torn eyelet and a small piece of vinyl from the curtain.

I found the master bedroom farther down the hall. Through the French doors that gave onto the gallery I could see the tops of the oak trees beating in the wind. I turned on the light and looked at the canopied bed that was centered against one wall. The sheets, bedspread, pillows, and mattress were gone. Only the box spring remained in the wooden frame. I walked in a circle around the bed and felt the rug. It was still damp in two places and smelled of dry-cleaning fluid or spot remover.

I knew it was time to call the Lafayette Parish sheriff's office. I was overextended legally, in the home on questionable grounds, and perhaps even in danger of tainting evidence in a homicide. But legality is often a matter that is decided after the fact, and I believed sincerely that someone owed me ten more minutes.

I went out a side door onto the flagstone patio, past the screened-in pool and the breezeway where Bubba kept his dumbbells, universal gym, and punching bags, and found a garden rake leaned against the carriage house. The wind was blowing stronger now, the first raindrops clicking against the upstairs windows.

Even though the flower bed by the side of the house was flooded from the soak hose, the leaves of the geraniums still looked like wilted green paper. I began to rake the dirt and the plants out of the bed. The soil was rich and black and had been built up with compost, and as I scooped it out on the gravel, milky puddles formed in the hollows. A foot down, the rake's head struck something solid. I worked the dirt and torn plants and root systems back over the brick border and created a long, shallow depression through the center of the garden, the rake's teeth again touching something thick and resistant. Then I saw the edge of a vinyl shower curtain rise on one of the teeth and a pajama-clad knee protrude through the soil. I scraped around the edges of the body, watched the feet and shoulders and brow take shape, as though I were its creator and sculpting it from the earth.

I set the rake on the gravel and cut the soak hose in half with my knife to release a strong jet of water. Then I washed the soft dirt, which looked like black coffee grounds, from Bubba's face. He rested on top of the shower curtain, his gray-blue eyes open, his face and hands and feet absolutely blood-less. The handle and the metal back of the cane knife she had used stuck out of the dirt by his head. The cut across the side of his neck went all the way to the bone.

I turned off the soak hose and went back through the kitchen door and called the Lafayette Parish sheriff's office and Minos Dautrieve, then I started toward my truck. Dead leaves swirled all over the yard in the wind, the sky was black, and the few raindrops that struck my face were as hard as BBs.

Behind me I heard the phone ring. I went back inside and picked up the receiver.

"Hello," I said.

"Bubba? This is Kelly. What's the deal on this dago linen service?" a man's voice said over the hum of long-distance wires. "Claudette says I'm supposed to hire these guys. What the fuck's going on over there?"

"Bubba's dead, partner."

"What? Who is this?"

"I'm a police officer. What's your name?"

He hung up the phone.

I drove back down the gravel lane toward the highway while the thick limbs of the oak trees beat against one another overhead. The black thunderheads on the southern horizon were veined with lightning. The air was almost cold now, and the young sugarcane was bent to the ground in the wind. I rolled up my windows, turned on the windshield wipers, and felt the steering wheel shake in my hand. Pieces of newspaper and cardboard were flying in the air across the highway, and the telephone wires flopped and bounced like rubber bands between the poles.

I passed a cement plant and a sidetracked Southern Pacific freight, and then I saw the maroon convertible parked in front of a truck stop that had a small lounge attached to it. It began raining hard just as I walked inside.

Because the Negro janitor was mopping the floor and wiping down the tables, the curtains were open and the overhead lights were turned on. In the light you could see the cigarette burns on the floor, the mending tape on the booths, and the stacked beer cases in the back corner. An overweight barmaid was drinking coffee and talking with two oilfield roughnecks at the bar. The roughnecks wore tin hats and steel-toed boots and had drilling mud splattered on their clothes. One of them rolled a matchstick in his mouth and said something to me about the weather. When I didn't answer, he and his friend and the woman continued to look at me and the pistol and badge on my belt.

Claudette Rocque was at a table by the back door. The door was open and mist was blowing through the screen. Out on the railway tracks I could see the rust-colored SP freight cars shining in the rain. She sipped her gin rickey and looked at me across the top of the glass. Her face was bruised and fatigued, and her brown eyes, which had that strange red cast to them, were glazed and sleepy with alcohol. There was an outline of adhesive tape around the stitches on her chin, and the skin was puckered on the tip of the bone. But her yellow sundress and the orange bandanna in her hair were fresh and clean and even looked attractive on her, and I guessed that she had showered and changed after she had dragged Bubba downstairs on the shower curtain, dug up the garden, buried him, replanted the geraniums, and burned the mattress and pillows and sheets. She inhaled from her filter-tipped cigarette and blew smoke out toward me.

"You had a hard night," I said.

"I've had worse."

"You should have taken him somewhere else. You might have gotten away with it."

"What *are* you talking about?"

"I dug him up. The cane knife, too."

She drank from her glass and puffed on the cigarette again. Her eyes looked vaguely amused.

"Drink it up, Claudette. You're going on a big dry."

"Oh, I wouldn't count on that, pumpkin. You ought to watch more television. Battered wives are in fashion these days."

I slipped the handcuffs off the back of my belt, took the cigarette out of her mouth and dropped it on the floor, and cuffed her wrists through the back of the chair.

"Oh, our law officer is so uncorruptible, so noble in his AA sobriety. I bet you might like a slightly bruised fuck, though. It's your last chance, sugarplum, because I'll be out on bond tomorrow morning. You should give it some thought."

I turned a chair around backwards and sat across from her.

"You did three years and you think you're con-wise, but you're still a fish," I said. "Let me give you the script. You won't do time because you cut Bubba's throat. Nobody cares when somebody like Bubba gets killed, except maybe the people he owes money to. Instead, a jury of unemployed roughnecks, fundamentalist morons, and welfare blacks who don't like rich people will send you up the road because you're an ex-con and a lesbian.

"Of course, you'll think that's unfair. And you'll be right, it is. But the greatest irony is that the people who'll send you back to St. Gabriel will never hear the name of the innocent girl you had murdered. Some people might call it comedy. It'll make a good story in the zoo."

Her reddish-brown eyes were narrow and mean. The bruise over the lid of one eye looked like a small blue mouse. I walked to the pay phone on the wall by the bar and called the sheriff's office. Just as I was about to hang up, I heard Claudette scrape the chair across the floor and smash it with her weight against the wall. She snapped the back loose from the seat, and then with the broken wood supports hanging from her manacled wrists, she went out the screen door into the rain.

I followed her across the field toward the railroad tracks. The bottom of her yellow dress was flecked with mud, and her bandanna fell off her head and her hair stuck wetly to her face. The rain was driving harder now, and the drops were big and flat and cold as hail. I grabbed her by the arm and tried to turn her back toward the truck stop, but she sat down in a puddle of gray water. Her arms, twisted behind her by the handcuffs, were ridged with muscle.

I leaned over and tried to lift her to her feet. She sat in the water with her legs apart, her shoulders stooped, her head down. I pulled her by the arms, her dead weight and wet skin slipping out of my hands. She fell sideways in the water, then she got to her knees and I thought she was going to stand up. I bent down beside her and lifted under one arm. She looked up at me in the rain, as though she was seeing me for the first time, and spit in my face.

I stepped back from her, used my handkerchief, and threw it away. She stared fixedly across the fields at the green line of trees on the horizon. Water ran rivulets out of her soaked hair and down over her face. I walked to an empty freight car on the siding and pulled an old piece of canvas off the floor. It was stiff and crusted with dirt but it was dry. I spread it over her so that she looked like she was staring out of a small, peaked house.

"It's the Mennonite way of doing things," I said.

But she wasn't interested in vague nuances. She was looking at the sheriff's deputies and Minos Dautrieve stepping out of their cars in the truck-stop parking lot. I stood beside her and watched them make their way across the drenched field toward us. Through the open doors of the freight car I could see chaff spinning in the wind, and in the distance the gray buildings of the cement plant looked like grain elevators in the rain. Minos was calling to me in the echo of thunder across the land, and I thought of drowned voices out on the salt and wheat fields in the rain. I thought of white-capping troughs out on the Gulf and sunflowers and wheat fields in the rain.

EPILOGUE

I WORKED TWO MORE WEEKS WITH THE sheriff's department and then hung it up. In August the sun came up white every morning and the air was hazy with humidity and even your lightest clothes stuck to your body like wet paper. I rented a clapboard bungalow by the Texas coast, and Robin and Alafair and I spent two weeks fishing for gafftop and white and speckled trout. At dawn, when the tide was drawn out over the flats, the gulls squeaked and circled in the sky and dipped their beaks into the pools of trapped shellfish, then the long, flat expanses of wet sand became rose-tinted and purple, and the palm tree in our side yard would stand like a black metal etching against the sun.

It was always cool when we took the boat out in the morning, and the wind would come up out of the southeast and we could smell the schools of trout feeding under the slicks they made on the water. We took the boat across a half-moon bay that was bordered on each side by sand spits, sawgrass, and dead cypress, and just as we crossed over the last sandbar into deep water and entered the Gulf, we would see those large floating slicks, like oil that had escaped from a sunken freighter, and we'd bait our hooks with live shrimp, cast on the edge of the slick, and pop our wood floats loudly against the surface. Occasionally we'd hook gafftop, and we always knew it was a catfish by the way he'd pull straight down for the bottom and not break the surface until we had socked the treble hook all the way through his head and forced him to the top. But a speckled trout would run and strip line off the drag, turn across your bow or stern and go under your boat if he could, and even when you got the net under him he'd still try to break your rod across the gunnel.

We'd put cold drinks and sausage, cheese, and onion sandwiches in the ice chest, and by noon, when we had eaten our lunch and the sun was straight up in the sky and the salt was crusty on the hot bow of the boat, the ice would be covered with rows of silver trout, their gills open and red, their teeth hooked wide, their eyes like black glass.

It was late August when we went back to New Iberia, and then one morning Robin was gone. I read the letter at the breakfast table in my underwear while the backyard turned from blue to gray in the early light. She had left coffee for me on the stove and a bowl of Grape-Nuts and strawberries on the table.

> *I had the cab stop up on the road so I wouldn't wake you. Goodbyes and apologys are for the Rotary and the dipshits, right? I love you, babe. Its important you understand and believe that. You turned me around and cared about me when nobody else did. And I mean nobody. Your not like any guy I new before. You hurt for other people and for some reason you feel guilty about them. But thats not love, Dave. Its something else and I dont understand it really. I think maybe you still love Annie. I guess thats the way its suppose to be. But I think youve got to find that out for yourself and you dont need me in the way.*

Hey, this is no big deal. Im going to work as a cashier at your brothers resterant on Dauphine, so if you ever want to hit on a hot broad you know where to go. Im off the juice and pills too thanks to a good hearted roach I know. Thats not a bad thing to put on your score card.

My love to Alafair
Take it easy,
Streak Robin

I did strange things during that last week in August. On a twilight evening I walked across the deserted campus of USL in Lafayette, where I attended college in the 1950s. The quadrangle was filled with shadows, the warm breeze blew through the brick walkways, and the dark green oaks were filled with the sounds of birds in the gathering dusk. I sat in a late-hour café by the SP yard and listened over and over to a 1957 Jimmy Clanton record on the jukebox while redbone gandy walkers, glistening with sweat, tore up the track outside in the glare of burning flares, and long strips of freights clattered by in the darkness. I played dominoes with the old men in the back of Tee Neg's pool hall, chipped minié balls out of the coulee's dirt wall by the ruined sugar planter's house on the bayou, and drove my truck down the levee deep into the marsh, where an abandoned community of shacks on stilts still stood, rotting and gray, against the willows and cypress. Forty years ago my father and I had come here for a *fais dodo* on July Fourth, and the people had cooked a pig in the ground and drunk wine out of Mason jars and danced to an accordion band on a houseboat until the sun was a red flare on the horizon and the mosquitoes were black on our skin.

As I stared out the truck window at the gray tops of the trees, the shacks hanging in pieces on the stilts, the water black and still in the dying light, I heard a solitary bullfrog croak, then the flooded woods ached with sound. Three blue herons sailed low against the late sun, and with a sinking of the heart I knew that the world in which I had grown up was almost gone and it would not come aborning again.

And maybe Bubba Rocque and I had been more alike than I cared to admit. Maybe we both belonged to the past, back there in those green summers of bush-league baseball and crab boils and the smoke of neighborhood fish fries drifting in the trees. Every morning came to you like a strawberry bursting on the tongue. We ran crab traps and trotlines in the bay with our fathers, baited crawfish nets with bloody chunks of nutria meat, cleaned boxes of mudcat with knife and pliers, and never thought of it as work. In the heat of the afternoon we sat on the tailgate of the ice wagon at the depot, watching the troop trains roll through town, then fought imaginary wars with stalks of sugarcane, unaware that our little piece of Cajun geography was being consumed on the edges like an old photograph held to a flame. The fiery rifts in evening skies marked only the end of a day, not the season or an era.

But perhaps age has taught me that the earth is still new, molten at the core and still forming, that black leaves in the winter forest will crawl with life in the spring, that our story is ongoing and it is indeed a crime to allow the heart's energies to dissipate with the fading of light on the horizon. I can't be sure. I brood upon it and sleep little. I wait like a denied lover for the blue glow of dawn.